P9-CDE-731

Fiona Range

Fiona Range

Mary McGarry Morris

VIKING

VIKING
Published by the Penguin Group
Penguin Putnam Inc., 375 Hudson Street,
New York, New York 10014, U.S.A.
Penguin Books Ltd, 27 Wrights Lane,
London W8 5TZ, England
Penguin Books Australia Ltd, Ringwood,
Victoria, Australia
Penguin Books Canada Ltd, 10 Alcorn Avenue,
Toronto, Ontario, Canada M4V 3B2
Penguin Books (N.A.) Ltd, 182–190 Wairau Road,
Auckland 10, New Zealand

Penguin Books Ltd, Registered Offices:
Harmondsworth, Middlesex, England

First published in 2000 by Viking Penguin,
a member of Penguin Putnam Inc.

1   3   5   7   9   10   8   6   4   2

PUBLISHER'S NOTE
This is a work of fiction. Names, characters, places, and incidents either are
the product of the author's imagination or are used fictitiously, and any
resemblance to actual persons, living or dead, business establishments,
events, or locales is entirely coincidental.

LIBRARY OF CONGRESS CATALOGING-IN-PUBLICATION DATA
Morris, Mary McGarry.
Fiona Range / Mary McGarry Morris.
p.   cm.
ISBN 0-670-89156-8
I. Title.
PS3563.0874454 F56   2000
813'.54—dc21   99-087724

This book is printed on acid-free paper.

(∞)

Printed in the United States of America
Set in Janson
Designed by Kathryn Parise

To my children,

Mary Margaret
Sarah
Melissa
Michael
Amy

With love, admiration,
and gratitude.

Fiona Range

Chapter 1

I t was dark, so dark, yet somewhere far away, deep in the night a bird was chirping. Fiona Range's eyes fluttered and closed, then shot open into blackness. She couldn't breathe. Every nerve throbbed with the blind acuity of fear. Hot at her neck was the foul, ragged snore of a naked man. She gasped, stiffening as he stirred. The musky reek of sweating loins rose up from the sheets. He grunted, then rolled onto his belly, his hairy arm falling like a club across her bare chest. She struggled to sit up, but his arm shifted, pinning her shoulders. His snore grew sluggish. All she could see was the back of his head. "Hey! Hey, wake up!" she whispered, chin rigid against his arm. Her mind raced with blurred images.

She remembered leaving the party, then cold hands stuffing her legs into a car so he could close the door. It must have been him, this name-less, faceless man in her bed. He had helped her up to her apartment, because she kept stumbling on the stairs. She hadn't been able to find her key so he had dumped out her purse on the hallway floor, but then he kept trying to unlock the wrong door, and all she could do was laugh. And then—oh, God—her prissy neighbor, Mr. Clinch, peered out and pointed across the hall. "That door," he hissed. "That's where she belongs." In there. Here—on this bed where he took off her clothes, and begged her to please, please stop laughing while they made love, then afterwards, when it was over and she wanted to hold him he buried his face in the pillow and sobbed.

1

What in God's name had she done? Only her eyes moved. The darkness began to take shape now with the faint glow of dawn swelling behind the window shade. The room was the same shambles of boxes and magazines, books for her course, her uniform, a Coke can on the windowsill, clothes piled everywhere, scarves on the doorknob, bras on the floor. Shoes, boots, socks. Scattered price tags. She'd buy things, makeup, sweaters, CDs, wear them, play them, let the bags drift to the floor. What the hell did it matter? Her life was a mess, out of control. There was a stranger in her bed.

"Hey! Hey, you!" She was going to be sick. "C'mon, wake up! Wake up!" She jostled his arm until he curled onto his side. On her feet now she reeled dizzily, then groped her way to the bathroom. She sat on the toilet and groaned, her throbbing head heavy in her hands.

It had been a birthday party for her friend Terry's husband, Tim; a double celebration because the previous day, Brad and Krissy Glidden's first baby had been born after years of trying. Brad Glidden and Tim had been best buddies since high school. It had been Fiona's first night out in months. All she'd wanted was to feel a little happy for a little while, but oh God, what had she done? She had danced with everyone, even with poor, brain-damaged Larry Belleau, who kept slobbering her with kisses, then the next thing she knew they were both in the pool. God, she'd even danced with Goldie, the stinking collie, until Tim said she was disgusting and told her to leave. Brad Glidden insisted she have coffee first, so she was drinking coffee and eating stuffed grape leaves on Terry's kitchen stool. Then the dog jumped up on his hind legs, his fur prickly against her chest while she fed him grape leaves. She shuddered remembering the feel of Goldie's slimy yellow teeth as she kissed his mouth. She had no idea who was curled up in her bed.

She took deep breaths, trying to calm her stomach enough so she could stand up. She had to brush her teeth, had to scrub away this disgusting taste: dog breath and him, whoever the hell that was out there. She scrubbed until her gums bled. His smell was still on her.

Larry Belleau. She froze with her hand on the doorknob, suddenly afraid it was him. Larry had never been right since his diving accident at the quarry years ago. Most people avoided him, because he was such

a nuisance, but she had always gone out of her way to be nice to him.
My God, she hadn't gone that far out of her way, had she? No, the guy
in her bed was thin, and Larry was huge. And besides, Larry didn't
drive. Maybe it was someone she didn't even know, a total stranger,
someone she'd met on the way into the building last night.

When she came out of the bathroom, he was gone. The blanket lay
heaped on the floor. The front door was ajar. Across the hallway Mr.
Clinch's door opened as he reached out for his newspaper. Their eyes
met, and he looked away. She darted back inside and yanked up the
shade to see her lover running barefoot down the walk to his car. His
shirt was unbuttoned, and he carried his shoes. He glanced up as he
fumbled his key into the door lock. She saw the panic on his face, the
terror, the same revulsion she was feeling. It was Brad Glidden. Krissy
and their new baby were coming home from the hospital in the morning. This morning. Today—in that car, the car she had left the party in,
the very same white Volvo station wagon that was squealing out of the
parking lot now.

"Bastard, no-good bastard," she muttered as she turned on the
lights, wincing in the glare. What had she been thinking, sleeping with
Brad Glidden? But as usual, she hadn't been thinking, hadn't cared or
been careful. And now this mess. "Nothing but messes, nothing but
goddamn messes, messes, messes," she groaned as she kicked the scattered clothes into a heap. She staggered and had to catch herself on the
table edge. She hated her life, hated her new apartment in this decrepit
building. After six weeks she was still living out of boxes. It was too
small and dark and more expensive than her old place where she'd still
be if she hadn't taken pity on Todd Prescott last summer. Because of
him, she'd been evicted and her family had washed their hands of her.
And to top it all off she'd just slept with Krissy's husband. "Jesus
Christ! What's wrong with me?" she moaned, pressing her fingers into
her throbbing temples.

Too drained by the shower steam to even wash, she held on to the
soap bar and let hot water run down her back. When she stepped out
she barely had enough energy to towel herself off, much less dry her
hair. She combed the dark waves straight and dripping wet against her
neck, then put on her pink uniform, shuddering as the cool nylon

clung to her damp skin. Her eyes stung so much she could barely keep them open as she tugged the sheets off the bed and threw them onto the pile of clothes, but she had to leave all the lights on and the radio playing and the window wide open to keep herself awake she thought as she curled up on the bare mattress for just a minute while the brisk September breeze rasped the crooked shade back and forth against the window frame.

She woke up at six forty-five. The coffee shop opened at six-thirty. Wincing, she lifted her head slowly from the pillow, then made her way to the door. She had been late often enough, but had never missed a day of work in any job.

Fiona Range's teeth had been filled without novocaine, her wounds stitched without anesthesia, her heart broken too many times to count. Once as a child she fell from a tree and broke her arm but didn't tell her aunt until hours later when her favorite show had ended. When she was fifteen her appendix burst before she realized the severity of her daylong belly pain. Hearing that the same thing had happened to her mother as a girl had pleased her, because it was another brush-stroke in the hazy portrait of Natalie Range, the wild young woman who drove off weeping one rainy afternoon, never to return. In the ensuing thirty years her mother had not once called or written or cared. And Fiona was only the tougher for it.

She still bristled whenever anyone in the family referred to her high threshold for pain. It seemed to reduce her strength to a blankness, a numbness, a dead nerve, a deficit, one more congenital flaw bequeathed by an errant mother and rumored father, Patrick Grady, the town eccentric, who ignored her existence.

Two months ago when she'd been evicted, her cousins declared her an emotional burden, a bigger drain on their parents than any familial responsibility warranted. And so, like her mother, Fiona had also walked away without guilt or regret. They said they were tired of all her mishaps, tired of caring for someone who only cared about herself. But it had been precisely that, the caring, that always caused her so much trouble. The only reason she'd let Todd Prescott stay in her apartment over the Fourth of July weekend was because he had been so sick and depressed.

But didn't she know Todd was still using drugs? her uncle Charles had asked. What had she been thinking? My God, a drug raid in his own niece's apartment. Taken in and raised with his own children, she had been given every advantage, the same care and attention as her cousins, and yet there were always these messes, these fiascoes, these—

"Crimes!" her cousin Jack had sputtered, too incensed to notice or heed his father's cold stare. The judge was not used to being interrupted, certainly not in his own home, and never by his son. "Yes! Crimes!" Jack declared with the same disdain and relish with which he had always regarded her transgressions.

Well, call them what you will, her cousin Ginny had said; it was time to draw the line.

They could at least listen to her side of it, Fiona had demanded. Of course she'd known Todd was using drugs; that's why she'd finally broken up with him a year ago, but she had no idea he was selling coke. She had been out of the apartment working or partying most of that long, hot weekend. And when she was there it hadn't occurred to her that his visitors were all buying from him.

"Well with such classic judgment we can only thank God the undercover cop knew who you both were," Jack said.

"What he knew was that I didn't have a goddamn thing to do with any of it!"

"What he knew was that you were Judge Hollis's niece, and that this would probably destroy him if it got out," Jack had said through clenched teeth with both sisters nodding; even Elizabeth, who had always been her staunchest defender.

"You don't believe me, do you?"

"No!" cried Jack and Ginny, and Elizabeth had closed her eyes, sighing.

"Well then, I guess I'm out of here," she'd said, slamming the door behind her. She was tired of their disapproval, the silent censure, their eagerness always to assume the worst. If they wanted her back they knew where she was.

It must have been the same for her mother all those years ago when Patrick Grady came home from Vietnam, one side of his handsome face bunched up in rippling scars from napalm burns. He denied Fiona was his child and refused to marry Natalie, who had then just slammed the door and left her misery behind. In steely tribute to her mother, Fiona still passed Grady on the street without blinking an eye or slowing her pace.

Most people in town tolerated Grady, attributing his strangeness to a war no one would admit to having supported, but she had never felt any pity for the man and certainly no sense of obligation. He was an outsider because he wanted to be, and she was an outsider because he hadn't wanted the responsibility of fatherhood.

Fiona Range had learned long ago to take what life dealt and make the best of it. She might be hurt, but no one would see her bleed. She would be in control, in complete control, and right now as she drove to work the trick was to think it all through. As long as she got everything straight in her own head, then it didn't matter what anyone else thought. Brad Glidden wasn't about to tell anyone, and neither was she. She had brought this on herself and she would plow through it. Pain was just another level of consciousness, and working against it now seemed as desirable an ache as grinding sore teeth. That's just the way things went in a place like Dearborn. You could find a ghost on every street corner if you looked hard enough. But she never had to look because the past was with her every day and everywhere. Even her job was a daily reminder now that Chester had recently married Maxine, who used to go out with Patrick Grady. Fiona might be able to change what she became, but nothing could change what she came from. And to tell the truth, most days she didn't give a damn. But then, most days didn't start off the way this one had.

She pulled down the narrow alley and parked behind Chester's Coffee Shop. In the kitchen Chester Adenio was frying eggs and turning bacon on the grill. The smell of sputtering grease turned her stomach. She had to open the back door again and take a deep breath of fresh air.

"Hurry up and get out front!" Chester called. Sandy Rudman, the other waitress, wasn't there yet. "Come on! Come on! Maxine's having a bird out there," Chester said.

By his own admission, Maxine had been the worst waitress he ever had. After two months of tearful breakdowns every time sh

dropped a tray or made a mistake on an order, Chester had put her on
the register. The coffee shop certainly didn't need a full time cashier-
hostess, but Chester had fallen in love. Counting back correct change
and seating parties during rush hours soon proved as stressful as waitressing, but with Chester's encouragement and increasing devotion,
Maxine persevered.

He and Maxine had been married only a few months. Chester
would have preferred that she stay home, but the coffee shop had en-
dowed Maxine with a status she'd never had living in the town housing
project. This drab, worn little place had become her dream, her show-
case.

Fiona tied her apron, then opened the door into the dimly lit dining room. Maxine's bright red suit and orangey hair darted like flames
through the hunched shadows as she poured coffee and passed out
menus. Fiona groaned. George Grimshaw was sitting right there in
the booth by the door. He was the last person on earth she felt like
talking to right now. Looking up from his open paper, he nodded po-
litely at Maxine's mindless prattle. His dark blue van was parked out
front. "GRIMSHAW AND SON, PLUMBING CO." said the gold-leafed letters
on the door, though his father had died recently, leaving George alone
in both the business and their little bungalow on Elm Street.

George had been only eight when his mother died. It was then that
Fiona's cousin Elizabeth began to look out for him. He and Elizabeth
had been a couple from third grade all the way through high school,
before drifting apart in the last few years. He still asked about her, and
last Christmas when Elizabeth was home they'd gone out for coffee a
few times. Fiona had known George all her life, but little more than
small talk ever passed between them. He had never been able to hide
his disapproval of Elizabeth's wild cousin.

Chester's bell rang and Fiona wheeled gratefully around back into
the kitchen. With the whoosh of the closing door the bright row of
funnels, ladles, and spoons swayed over the workbench, and she felt
dizzy. She watched Chester place a sprig of curly parsley between the
shimmering yolks, then rip the completed order slip from the nail.
Fresh parsley and lemon slices, like Maxine's growing wardrobe, proof
that he and his wife ran a first-class operation here.

"For your funeral, I'm going to send a wreath of fresh parsley. I promise," she said as he dabbed grease from the plate rim with a towel. "Maybe even spell out Chester with lemon wedges." Her hoarse laughter exploded into a coughing spasm that made her sore eyes water and nose run. She leaned on the counter. Her chest ached. She only smoked when she drank. Last night must have been a two-packer.

"You look like shit warmed over," Chester said through a grin of sharp little teeth as he picked up the plate.

"Aren't you the sweet guy."

"Jesus, your hands're shaking." He peered out at her. "Don't tell me you're back with Prescott, that loser, again, that asshole."

"Chester, how many times do I have to tell you? I am footloose and fancy-free. I do what I want; go where I want." She tried to laugh, but the boozy rasp clotted in her throat. She turned quickly to cough it away.

"It's not so funny anymore," he called as she headed into the dining room with the plate of eggs. "You'll see. One of these mornings you're going to wake up and wonder what the hell happened. Where did it all go? Your good looks, your friends, your whole life!"

She stopped dead, then turned around and kicked open the door so hard it banged back on the wall. "Look, Adenio," she growled, advancing on him. "I don't go around giving my unwanted opinion about you watering down the milk and the soup and the juice and even the goddamn ketchup bottles every night, do I?"

"Well I hate seeing such a beautiful woman as you just giving it away to every—"

"What? What'd you just say?" She dropped the plate wobbling onto the counter.

He stared back. "You heard what I said."

"Look, just keep it to yourself, okay?"

The door flew open. "Shh, shh, shh!" Maxine pleaded, finger at her mouth as she wiggled into the kitchen on spiked heels, her snug skirt binding her knees in a geisha-like gait. "There's customers out there!" She pointed back at the still swinging doors. "Customers!" she gasped.

"Well maybe you don't want to hear it," Chester continued, his whiskery chin out over the shelf, "but you work for me so I'm gonna say it. You're no cute little party girl anymore. It's way past that now, so who the hell do you think you are, dragging in here like that? You look like crap, you stink like booze and whatever the hell else you do!" He threw down his greasy towel.

"Chester!" Maxine ran around the bench and grabbed his arm. "Please, please stop! The customers!"

"So? What? Am I fired? You want me to quit?" Fiona demanded, her raw voice confirming every accusation. Her head trembled as she reached back and untied her apron. "Fine! I've got no problem with that!"

"No!" Maxine gasped from behind as she tried to retie the apron strings. "He just wants you to settle down a little bit. Tell her!" she implored her husband.

He reached into the large tin egg bowl, taking two eggs in one hand which he cracked neatly on the stove edge then opened onto the sizzling grill.

"Tell her!" Maxine demanded.

"She knows," Chester said. He scraped the unserved cold eggs from the plate into the trash, but saved the bacon.

"Chester!" Maxine warned in a rising teary whisper. "Don't you do this to me, Chester! Don't!"

"It's okay," Fiona said, watching him reheat the bacon. If he said one more word Maxine would storm out again in tears and she'd be all alone out front. "Chester means well. He's just not used to a woman having as good a time as a guy, that's all."

"It's not the same thing, and it never will be!" Chester growled as he garnished the new plate with parsley before passing it to her. "A man doesn't get a reputation like a woman does!"

"Chester, I was born with a reputation. You know that!" she called back.

"No, not a reputation! With that big, fat chip on your shoulder! That's your trouble!" he shouted after her.

Heads turned when she entered the dining room. Her regulars smiled, relieved she was back. Maxine's fussing could jangle early-morning nerves.

"Fiona!" George Grimshaw said as she served him. It was obvious he had heard the raised voices, as had her party of grinning landscapers in the next booth. His earnest face mirrored every emotion, and right now it was red. "You're looking good. As usual," he added with a stiff smile.

"Thanks, and the same to you too, George."

Muscular in his dark blue shirt and work pants, he looked better than good with his buzz cut and his clear bright eyes, his square solid body and flat healthy stomach this Saturday morning. Probably lifted weights at night when everyone else was out having a good time. Probably hadn't had a good— She caught herself with a bawdy chuckle that seemed to make him squirm. She glanced back at the landscapers and flipped the page on her order pad. One man was drumming his fingers on the table. "We've been waiting for you, beautiful," he said with a wink.

"Guess who I just ran into," George said as she started toward them. "Brad Glidden!" He grinned.

"Yah. So?" Her heart began to race.

"He told me about the baby. That's so great. I know they've been trying a long time."

"Yah, they have." Her mouth was dry.

"He looked terrible. Course I didn't tell him that. I think he was probably on his way home from the hospital or something."

"Probably." She stepped back.

"Oh, and I saw your uncle the other day at the courthouse," he said before she could leave.

"The courthouse! Don't tell me you're in trouble, George!" She tapped the pad on his shoulder and turned.

"No!" he said with an urgency that made her look back. "Actually, I was working near there so I thought I'd stop in and say hello." He stared up intently at her. "I think your uncle Charles was surprised to see me."

"Well, no more than me, George. But, hey, you better start eating. I'll catch you later."

"But wait!" he said as she turned away again. "What do you think about Elizabeth's big news?" he asked with a faltering smile.

"I don't know, George, what do you think?" She tried to laugh. She

hadn't heard a word from anyone in the family since their July banishment of her. But he probably knew that too.

"I was really surprised."

"Yah, me too."

"But you must be glad to finally have her back now, huh?" He tugged at his open collar.

"Of course." She took a deep breath.

"So I guess she's home for good now," he said almost as if it were a question, and, not knowing what else to do, she nodded. There was an odd pleading cast to his eyes as he continued to stare.

"Hey, you better eat your eggs while they're still hot." The thought of having her cousin back made her smile even though she'd had to hear it from George Grimshaw. Elizabeth taught in a boarding school in New York. In these last few years she'd seldom come home for any length of time.

"Well, will you give her my best then when you see her?" George said as she headed toward the next booth.

"Yah, sure," she said, surprised he wouldn't just call himself. Through the years Elizabeth wouldn't be home an hour before the phone would start to ring with George's dogged invitations for coffee, a drink, a movie, a ride, a walk, whatever Elizabeth wanted, though she had seemed uneasy with his company her last few times home. In the park there was a huge copper beech tree and into the bark of its elephantine trunk had years ago been carved "Geo + Liz 4ever." Pathetic, she thought, as she took the men's orders. Elizabeth had gone away and made a new life and here sat poor George hunched over greasy coffee shop eggs, still hoping, still yearning for his childhood love.

"And don't forget, beautiful, extra homefries for Eddie, tell Chester," called the oldest man in the crew as she started for the kitchen with their order.

"Yah, yah, yah," she muttered, wondering suddenly if Elizabeth's eating problem had returned, though last summer she'd looked great. She'd even put on enough weight so that they were almost the same size again, an observation that had sent Ginny into a paroxysm of raised eyebrows and mimed warnings; as if Elizabeth had gotten so fragile over the years she couldn't take a little kidding. But then Ginny had always been jealous of the bond between her younger sister and her cousin. Inseparable as children, Fiona and Elizabeth were only four months apart in age, though poles apart in temperament. They'd grown up sharing secrets, the same bedroom, and a deep affection for one another. Their paths diverged eleven years ago when they went off to college; Elizabeth to Smith and Fiona, with Uncle Charles's pull, to Dearborn Community. As expected Elizabeth had graduated with honors, gone on for her master's, and had been teaching ever since. To no one's surprise Fiona had flunked out freshman year.

She pushed open the kitchen door to find Chester slumped over the counter, brow in hand.

"Jesus, not again," she groaned. Maxine had stormed out.

"Don't." His heavy eyes lifted. "Don't even start."

"Even if I wanted to, I couldn't." She sighed, passing the order slip. "Eddie said extra homefries." She leaned her brow against the cool metal shelf. Her head hurt.

"Eddie! Who the hell's Eddie?" He flung the slip at her. "Eddie who?"

"I don't know. Eddie. What's it matter?" She threw it back.

"The way you said it, like, Eddie: like it's some friend, Eddie, I'm supposed to know from God knows where. Jesus Christ! They're all the same, these people; they come in here, they think they're entitled, like I'm just some bum, some scag. Like I got nothing better to do than this!"

"Huh?" She shook her head in dull exasperation. "Look, it's just some guy named Eddie. One of the landscapers. From Greenbow, alright?"

"Yah, and what the fuck does he want from me?" he bellowed, pounding the counter with a force that sent all the funnels, ladles, and spoons clanging into one another.

"A few fucking extra homefries!" She glared at him.

An hour later Maxine returned freshly made up, her lips painted a glossy plum, her tear-stung eyes gleaming with black liner. She was still upset with Chester, but determined to make things right. Chester continued to be a ball of nerves, but if he said anything she'd be gone. Self-control was a painful new discipline. For twenty years he'd ranted and raved and no one had ever given a damn until Maxine.

At noon Sandy Rudman still hadn't shown up. Every table was taken, and the wave-crashing fury in Fiona's head had subsided to a dull ache. Maxine was trying to help, but she had just dropped a tray of Cokes which Fiona was wiping up. For fifteen minutes a man and a woman had been sitting at the front table. They stared glumly over closed menus. Chester's pickup bell kept ringing. Fiona hurried into the kitchen for the order. When she came out the couple were on their way to the door.

"I'm so sorry," Maxine chirped after them. "Believe me, this doesn't usually happen, but—" The door closed in her face, and when she turned tears welled in her eyes, and her blunt, pitted jaw trembled.

"Hey," Fiona said, squeezing her hand. "It's okay. It's all right." She tried to make Maxine laugh. "What's the worse that can happen? We got another thirty minutes of hell here, and then it'll be over."

"I feel like I'm falling apart," Maxine said in a small voice. She turned abruptly toward the window so no one could see, though all eyes were on her.

"Well could you maybe just hang in there for a couple more minutes?" Fiona whispered at her ear.

"I'm just not any good at this," Maxine gasped. "I'm just no good, and that's why Chester wants to sell this place."

"No, he doesn't," Fiona scoffed in a low voice.

"Yes!" Maxine looked up. "He told me! That's why I went home!"

Now Chester's bell rang with a frantic tempo.

"Look, go do the register. I'll get the order."

"Do you think it would help if I said anything?" Maxine asked.

"He'll get over it," Fiona said, racing off.

"That's not what I meant," Maxine said as the kitchen door swung shut.

The turkey clubs were up along with two tuna plates. Spatula in each hand, Chester worked the covered grill like a xylophonist, flipping shaved steaks, hamburgers, a grilled cheese, patting down fish cakes.

"One more minute on the steak and cheese, two on the burgs!" he called over his sweaty shoulder. "How's it going?"

"Fine, but you forgot the fries," Fiona said, checking the slip.

He slid down to the fry basket, gave it a shake, then dumped the sizzling french fries into a dish. "How's she doing out there?" he asked, bending to read the next order.

"Great!" she called as she backed through the door into the hushed dining room, where Maxine was addressing her customers.

"And so I just wanted you to know that's what's happening and to tell you how much we really, really appreciate your patience. We really do. Really. You're all very nice people, and we want to thank you. So thank you. Thank you very much. Believe me, it means an awful lot to Chester and I."

The silence swelled as Maxine serenely mounted her stool at the register. Those who knew Chester either bit their lips or covered their mouths. No one dared laugh under the quick sweep of Fiona's warning eyes.

The coffee shop was empty when Sandy finally showed up at two-thirty. Mandy, her three-year-old, had been up all night with croup and hadn't slept until this morning. Sandy had made the mistake of lying down too for a quick nap that lasted until two o'clock.

"You gotta get your phone back on," Sandy said, following Fiona around. "My car wouldn't start, and I needed somebody to stay with Brandy. I ended up having to call a freaking cab. Five bucks he charged me, plus I had to drag them both down to the emergency room at four in the morning!" Sandy's greatest skill was making everyone else feel responsible for her troubles.

"That's too bad," Fiona said; one reason to be grateful her phone had been shut off. At least it had cut down on the number of mercy missions to Sandy's. And yet she felt bad for Sandy, having to raise two children alone when she was just a kid herself. Her parents had thrown her out with her second pregnancy. Her pretty face made her sweetness a liability.

"Yah, but one good thing," Sandy was saying. "I met that friend of yours there, that Todd Prescott. And he even gave us a ride home. He was so nice!"

"Oh yah, I'm sure. And what was he doing in the emergency room at four in the morning? An overdose maybe?"

"No, his friend was sick." Sandy frowned and bit her lip. A minute later she said, "I was wondering, do you still, I mean, do you still have, like, you know, feelings for him?"

"Yah, I do," Fiona said. "Strong feelings of hate and disgust."

"Oh, that's good." Sandy grinned. "Because he asked me out for coffee sometime, but like I told him, you know, I just wouldn't do that, I mean, I couldn't if you were, well you know, still having feelings, like, if you still liked him. In that way, I mean."

She put her hands on Sandy's shoulders. "Sandy, if I ever hear that you went out with that dirtball Todd Prescott I will never, ever speak to you or have anything to do with you ever again. Do you understand?"

"But we can't even speak now," Sandy said, pouting. "How come you won't get your phone turned back on?"

"First, I have six months' worth of bills to pay."

"Jeez, six months!" Sandy said. "How'd you do that?"

"Well, let's see. I had to get new shocks on my car and new tires so it'd pass inspection. And because of that asshole Prescott I got thrown out of my apartment so I had to go get a new one which meant I had to come up with a security deposit and first and last month's rent." She looked back at Sandy. "Plus I have a few people who owe me money."

Sandy winced. "I know, I know, I know." "What's it up to now?"

"A hundred and twenty." It was probably twice that. Sandy was always broke, and how could Fiona refuse when it was for milk or baby food.

"I've almost got it, honest to God," Sandy said.

"Yah, okay." Her eyes felt so heavy now she could barely keep them open. Thank God she didn't have a class tonight.

She was in her car the minute her shift ended. A horn tooted behind her. George Grimshaw was getting out of his van at the mouth of the alley. She rolled down her window.

"Maxine said you just left. I was hoping I'd catch you." He leaned on the door. He smelled of dampness and oil. There was a smudge of grease on his chin she kept wanting to rub off, more out of irritation than any fondness for him.

"Yah, I'm beat. I got this brutal headache."

"You look tired."

"Lunch was crazy. We were out straight, and Sandy never showed up. It was insane."

"You must be beat."

She bit her lip. Hadn't she just said that?

"I tried to call you last night, but your phone's not in service—or at least that's what the operator said."

"Yah, I got sick of all the telemarketing calls, so I had it shut off," she said with a straight face.

"You could let your machine screen the calls. That's what I do."

"But then you're still being harassed."

"Yes, but at least you'd have a phone."

"A phone perhaps, George Grimshaw, but what about principles?" she said, then shuddered with a deep yawn.

"You better get home and rest." He patted her door and stood up.

"Yah, I better." She shifted into reverse then looked back quickly. "So why were you trying to call me? What'd you want?"

"Nothing really. I just thought I'd call, see how things're going." He shrugged. "You know, just uh—"

"Just uh, to talk about Elizabeth maybe?" she interrupted, then felt guilty seeing him wince. Poor George. He had no idea how near he stood right now to a deadly viper.

"No," he said quickly, then leaned down to the window again. "I was just going to ask if you wanted to, well, that is, if you might consider going out sometime. With me, that is," he added, pointing to his chest.

"Are you serious?" She couldn't help laughing. For one so volatile, so unpredictable herself, she was never prepared when steadier souls veered off course.

"Yes," he said with an emphatic nod. "I'm dead serious. I mean, you've known me a long time. You know I don't say things I don't mean."

"Well no; I mean, yes, I guess you don't."

"So what do you think? Will you consider it?" He grinned.

"Yah! Sure, I'll consider it." She burst out laughing again. "Oh

George," she groaned, as he stepped back from the car. "I'm so sorry. I'm just a mess, I'm so out of it. Of course I'll go out with you. You name it. Tell me when, time and place, and I'll be ready!"

"Tonight! Seven o'clock!" he said, grinning. "We'll grab a bite somewhere, then maybe catch a movie," he called, then ran back to move his van, before she could say she hadn't meant tonight.

She had slept for a couple of hours before George arrived in a cloud of cologne that made her eyes water and her nose run. He was all dressed up in a sport jacket and tie. He'd been lucky enough to get reservations at the Orchard House, he said with an uneasy glance at her jeans.

"Well when you said a bite to eat, I just figured . . ."

"Oh no! I know, I just thought the Orchard House would be nice. I haven't been there in so long. My fault, I should have called and told you."

"But I don't have a phone, right?"

"Right. But still, I should have let you know."

"You just did." She laughed. "So I'll change. I don't mind."

She ran into her bedroom and put on a skirt. When she came out he was still standing by the door, glancing through the coffee-swollen pages of an old *Time* magazine. There was no place to sit because the chair and sofa were piled with clothes and boxes. "I'm still unpacking," she said as she locked the door. His quick smile brought back Elizabeth's patient bewilderment with chaotic Fiona. She was already dreading the evening. Across the way her neighbor's door opened a crack. "Hey, Mr. Clinch," she called, tapping on his door as she passed. Little creep, she thought with an uneasy shiver. What if he knew Brad or Krissy? Her head hurt. George's cologne was making her feel queasy again. She didn't want to do this, didn't want to be with him, but he was lonely, and in some fuzzy, unconnected logic—the pulsebeat from her sound, moral upbringing—it seemed a way to make up for last night. Penance: her hair shirt, George.

"I've never moved," he said, following her down the stairs. "Must be kind of exciting though. Having everything clean and new and freshly painted."

About as exciting as going out with you, she was thinking.

It was cold inside the plumbing van. The loud rumble and rattle of pipes and tools with every bump and turn was painful to hear and made the ride to the Orchard House seem even longer. Tiny white lights outlined the branches of the gnarled apple trees surrounding the old farmhouse that for years had been the best restaurant in Dearborn.

Fiona couldn't remember the last time she'd been here. The waiting area was a small front parlor furnished with upholstered chairs and on one wall a long black church pew. She settled into a red wingback chair while George waited in the hallway for the hostess to return. She watched, amused to see him so nervous. He kept leaning over and peering out the window by the front door. He checked his watch for the third time, then glanced around before removing the reservations book from its stand. He turned a page, then quickly put it back just as the hostess arrived. She wondered if he had lied about having a reservation. But now the hostess was saying their table was ready.

As soon as they were seated George ordered whiskey, straight up. Fiona was surprised to see him reach for it the minute it came. He drank half. Never much of a drinker, he was obviously nervous, his store of small talk already depleted on the ride here. He kept looking at his watch. The dull throb in her head was gaining momentum. Let him start the conversation for a change, she thought, slipping two aspirin from her pocket. She gulped them down with her soda water and immediately felt guilty. Poor George, it wasn't his fault. He was just too damn nice, never wanting to offend anyone or, God forbid, cause a stir, but his uneasiness was really getting to her. Why did he keep looking around at all the other tables like that? It made him seem furtive, as if he didn't belong here, as if he were an intruder in so fine a place as this, as if he were a little boy again, the plumber's son in the middle of the night on the cellar stairs. He smiled at her and nodded, then turned again to look back over his shoulder. An older couple had just entered the dining room. The hostess seated them at the round, candlelit table behind George. He checked his watch. "It's filling up fast. Just one more left," he said of the empty table by the door. He took a long breath, then glanced back at the door again and sighed deeply.

"Do you think it's too crowded?" she asked. He was a nervous wreck. "We don't have to stay here. We can go someplace else."

"Oh no! This is great! It's so beautiful here." He drummed his fingers on the padded tabletop and looked around again. "It's always been your aunt and uncle's favorite place. They celebrate all their important occasions here," he said, his voice thinning with alarm. He cleared his throat and didn't seem to know what to say next.

She stared at him. And here's another bulletin, she wanted to say: your father's favorite place was Foster's Pond. He caught a lot of fish there. "Really?" she said, her tongue in mortal combat with her heart as she took up the menu. What in God's name had she let herself in for?

He looked around again. Two women, both in black dresses, were being seated at the table by the door. He checked his watch. "Well! Here we go," he said, opening his menu with an anxious grin. "The grilled mushrooms! That's your aunt Arlene's favorite. And your uncle Charles, he always orders the crab cakes," he said so reverently she felt like screaming.

"And what about Elizabeth, George, what does she like?" she asked, straining to at least be civil.

"It used to be the snails." He glanced up and shrugged. "But who knows now."

"Um, that's true." She pretended to study the menu. "She has been away a long time."

"Yes. And people change. Some people."

"But not you, right?" she said too quickly.

He lowered the menu, his mouth opening then closing again before he spoke. "I didn't mean that the way it sounds. I'd never say anything bad about . . . about anyone in your family. I hold every single one of them in only the highest, the utmost regard." He squirmed under her bemused gaze.

"Feel better now that you've gotten that out?" She began to wonder if the message he was struggling to deliver came from Elizabeth.

"It's just that I don't want anything taken the wrong way. By anyone!" he said. "Well, what I mean is, Elizabeth has her life now, and I have mine, but of course there's always going to be the family, even though they're separate. I mean apart. Well, in certain situations, that is. What I mean is, from you and me. Like right now." Pausing, he peered at the menu as if for his place in the text. "The thing is, the Hollis family, well, they're all such wonderful people." Seeming only more frustrated, he took a deep breath.

"Can I tell you a little secret, George? Something you may not know." She leaned forward and lowered her voice. She had just recognized the couple at the table behind him. They were the Goldbergs, old friends of her aunt and uncle. She hadn't seen them in years. "The Hollises, they fart and they burp just like everybody else. Just like you and me."

"But they all try really hard, you know, like your uncle," George said. "I mean, he's probably the finest man, the most principled man I've ever known. He's always trying to help people."

"Huh!" she scoffed with a little thud of her fist on the table. "Always trying to help people! I'll tell you the kind of help. It's all for show, for credit. To get their picture in the paper or their name on another goddamn plaque somewhere, that's all they care about! Believe me!"

They both looked up sheepishly with the waitress's arrival.

The minute she left with their order, Fiona told him about this summer's banishment. The Goldbergs had grown silent. She spoke softly, but felt herself getting upset again. "I mean, there I was with no place to go, and my family, well if I can even call them that now." She rolled her eyes. "The Hollises, I should say. Yah, the Hollises with all their family unity and loyalty talk. And then when I was never more in need of unity and loyalty not one of them would help me or even believe me."

"Not even Elizabeth?"

"No! She wouldn't even look at me. I asked if I could move back home for a while, and Uncle Charles said, 'No, Fiona. We finally have to say *no* to you.' At first I didn't really get it. I figured they thought I wanted to move back home for good or something. No, no, just a week, I tried to tell them, two weeks. A month at the most, just till I find another place. 'No, Fiona!' Uncle Charles says like I'm in his courtroom or something. 'It isn't even that you stepped over the line once too often, but that you've stepped over it too far this time.'

"'What? What line?' I asked him. 'Selling drugs!' he says, looking at me, you know, like I'm some trashy defendant he can't stand the sight of anymore, and then he just walks out of the room!

"'But it wasn't me!' I start yelling. 'You know it wasn't me! You know it was Todd Prescott. Jesus, I mean, selling drugs! How can you even think that of me?'

"'I'm sorry,' Aunt Arlene says. 'But you're thirty years old now and you know we've always done our best and given you everything that was in our power to give.' And the whole time she's talking she can barely even look at me too. 'So now, Fiona,' she says, 'I'm afraid we have to let you suffer the full consequences of your actions.'" Fiona's voice quavered and she had to take a deep breath. "And so with that she started sobbing so hard she couldn't talk, which of course only made everyone even more upset with me."

She sat back, relieved by the waitress's arrival with their salads. She had never seen her aunt so distraught. Her hands had trembled out to Fiona in such helpless anguish that Jack had to call his father to help get her upstairs.

"What about Todd?" George asked the minute the waitress left.

"That prick!" she blurted, and the Goldbergs turned with cold stares. "I'm sorry," she said quickly, then buried her face in her hands. "Oh God," she whispered. "They know my aunt and uncle."

"They couldn't hear," he said softly, staring at his salad. His face was red. "Not with all this hubbub," he added, and they both laughed. They began to eat. It was George who finally broke the silence. "What I meant was, wouldn't he tell them the truth if you asked him? I should think he at least owes you that."

"Well, that's because you think like a decent, responsible man, and all Todd cares about is himself. But you know what kills me, what's so ironic here? No matter what he does his family gets him out of one mess after another, and me, I don't even do anything, and my family— excuse me, the Hollises—they just want me out of their lives. I don't know, maybe they always did." She gave a bitter laugh. "And I was just too dense to notice."

"But what about Elizabeth? I mean, she knows what Prescott's like, and she knows you better than anyone!"

"I don't know. I think she's been away so long she just listens to them now." Elizabeth's rejection was still the deepest wound. She shrugged with a forced smile. "But then again, who knows, maybe she's waiting for me to call her." She paused. This was his cue. "Or maybe not," she said.

"Yah. She's changed, so she thinks everyone else has too," George said slowly, as if interpreting a foreign language.

"Something like that." She sighed. So maybe this *was* just a night out with lonely George.

The waitress served their dinners. As they began to eat he seemed determined to talk only about food: what they were eating now; his self-description as a die-hard meat and potatoes man, declared with the staunch pride of a political affiliation.

No wonder Elizabeth had stayed in New York all this time, Fiona thought, blinking the glaze from her eyes as he asked if she did much cooking.

"I try not to," she said.

He not only loved to cook, but was determined to share the details of every single meal he had prepared in the last week. "So then, what I did last night was make this kind of hash thing with the last two slices of meatloaf."

"Here, try some of this." She held a forkful of her veal to his mouth.

Surprised, he kept looking at her, cheeks reddening as he chewed. "Thank you. Would you like to try some of mine?"

"Sure," she said, and his hand shook as he raised a forkful of tenderloin to her mouth. "Delicious!" She nodded. "And really tender too." She returned to her dinner. When she looked back up he was still watching her. "Aren't you going to finish?" She gestured at his plate.

"Yah, I was just . . . thinking," he said quickly, then winced as if with regret.

"Um," she said, taking a big bite of her roll. "Dangerous habit to get into." She finished the roll, then started on another as if chewing and nodding might facilitate the somber pronouncement he clearly needed to make.

"You see, Elizabeth and I . . . well, that's beside the point." He swallowed hard. "The thing is, I'm really enjoying this. I am! Are you?"

"Yes. This has been great," she added weakly, then apologized for all her complaining about the Hollises, but until tonight she had been too hurt to tell anyone.

"At least you get things out." He looked at her. "Elizabeth never does. I mean, everything always has to be so cheery and upbeat. But I think that's part of what happened."

"What do you mean?"

"I don't know how to put this," he began slowly, "but in some ways I used to think Elizabeth was almost perfect, that she was almost too good."

"Oh God, I used to tell her that all the time, and then I'd feel so guilty!" She laughed, but could see this wasn't at all what he had been trying to say.

"I mean, I know we were just kids when we were going together, but now I think it was more that Elizabeth felt responsible for me than she ever really . . . well . . . well, you know what I mean." He cleared his throat, looking so miserable that she put her hand over his and assured him her cousin had loved him. In fact, she had told Fiona countless times growing up that she knew she would never love anyone the way she loved George Grimshaw.

Poor George, she thought, embarrassed by his wan smile. Poor George, Elizabeth used to say when they were children. You know what people call him, the plumber's son, she would fume, typically finding injustice in what was a fact of life. His father often had to take him along on emergency calls. George had spent many nights on strangers' cellar steps doing homework under a dim bulb or dozing in the truck while his father plunged and reamed his metal snake through clogged waste pipes. Fiona remembered the time Elizabeth finally pre-vailed upon her father to call Mr. Grimshaw and tell him to drop George off whenever he needed to. In his terse, polite way Mr. Grim-shaw let the Judge know he and his boy were managing just fine, thank you.

"Good night, Mr. and Mrs. Goldberg," Fiona said as she pushed in her chair.

"Oh!" Mindy Goldberg said. "Fiona! I didn't know that was you."

"Yah, right," she said under her breath as George followed her to the door.

She said it was too late for the movies so they were rattling and clanging their way home. A bundle of copper piping kept rolling from one side of the van to the other. George had been quiet for the last few miles. Just as they turned onto Route 28 he suggested a nightcap at Pacer's. He'd installed their plumbing, but he'd never gone in as a customer, he said all in a rush.

"I'm really tired. Plus I can feel that headache coming back," she said, touching both temples.

"Maybe some other time," he said quickly. "I'm just curious more than anything. It's weird, you know it's the same with a lot of the new houses I do; you lay out all the lines, then after, you drive by and you can't help wondering who the people are and what the family's like." He looked over and laughed. "I know! You're thinking, oh my God, George Grimshaw's just as weird as he ever was."

"No, I wasn't. As a matter of fact, I never thought you were weird. Far from it."

"Yes you did. Admit it." He laughed again.

"No, I always thought you were a really nice guy. All right, maybe a little too nice," she added, laughing.

"Dull."

"No! Steady. Dependable."

"And that spells double dull." He laughed. "You want to know what I thought of you?"

She winced. "No."

"I thought you were the most exciting girl I knew. I remember once I told Elizabeth how sometimes I'd get short of breath just being around you, and she said she did too."

"Oh Jesus!"

"No, that's a compliment! And I meant it that way then too. I never knew what you were going to say or do. I mean, you weren't afraid of anything or anyone."

She was silent for a moment. "Yes I was. I still am."

"Of who? Of what?" he scoffed. "Name one thing you're afraid of."

"I don't know, but I do, I get afraid." She looked over, amazed to be having such a conversation with him. "I don't like being by myself, but then when I'm with people I get, like, irritated and I just want them to leave me alone. Now that's really strange, isn't it?"

"No, I know what you mean."

Looking out at the lit windows they were passing, she was aware of a rigidity so dull and cold, yet as central to her being that it felt as if a steel rod ran from her skull to her heels. Fatigue and her hangover might make her easy prey, but it was usually in these raw moments when she saw most clearly that the Hollises had never really had a place for her. They'd done their duty and that was all. She'd never felt as loved as their own children. But then, that was the luck of the draw. No one's fault. It wasn't, as Uncle Charles was fond of saying, that everyone was born flawed. No, some were just born more blessed than others.

"You know what else I always thought?" George asked, as he slowed at the intersection. "I always thought we were an awful lot alike in some ways. I mean, we both didn't have mothers."

"But we had Elizabeth!" she said quickly.

"That we did," he sighed, starting to turn.

"I changed my mind! Let's go check out your pipes."

Pacer's was noisy and dark. A layer of smoke hung overhead like a sagging tent top. Racing silks, riding whips, and jockey caps covered the barn board walls.

"Hey, George! Georgie!" came a chorus of voices, mostly male, as they made their way to an empty booth in back. She'd forgotten how popular George had always been. George and Elizabeth both.

"Fiona Range!" said their waitress, a tall redhead in a jockey cap. Fiona only dimly recognized her. "I met you last night at the party!"

"Kahlua and ice," Fiona said. Oh God, yes. The party.

"That was great, you and Larry Belleau dancing. I never saw him have such a good time," the waitress told George now. "After, he kept saying, 'I love Fiona. I love her so much!' Poor Larry."

"Larry Belleau?" George looked confused.

"Yah," the waitress said. "Larry Belleau. It was so funny! Then the dog started barking so she starts dancing with the dog and then Larry's standing there watching and he starts like this howling, so then—"

"Look, we're in kind of a hurry, if you don't mind," Fiona interrupted.

"I know, but I just thought it was so—"

"I don't care what you thought!" Fiona stared at her. "Like I said, we're in a hurry.

Shrugging, the waitress rolled her eyes at George, who quickly ordered the same as Fiona. "Do I know her?" he asked when the waitress left.

"Now how the hell would I know that?" she snapped.

"What I meant was, did we go school with her?" He drew himself up stiffly on the bench.

"I'm sorry. Some people just bring out the evil in me." Seeing his mouth drop open, she tried to explain. "I mean her, the waitress." She had to lean across the table to be heard. Beyond the swinging stable doors to her left there were pool tables, and for a moment the only sound was the crash of balls hitting one another. "You didn't think I meant you, did you?"

"Tell you the truth, I wasn't sure." He looked weary now, his eyes heavy and dark.

The waitress returned with their drinks and gave them a check. Instead of running a tab, since they were in such a big rush, she added, with a cold look at Fiona before leaving.

"Did you really dance with Larry Belleau and the dog?" George asked, trying not to smile.

"No! Not together anyway. I mean, they each had their turn!" Just last night and she could barely remember past a blur of laughter and loud music. And suddenly now, Brad Glidden helping her onto the toilet. Oh God.

George laughed and said he'd considered going to the party, but when he got home from work he was too tired. "Sounds like a good time. I should've gone!"

"Yah! You should've." She held her breath and tried to smile back.

Suddenly a man's voice rose angrily in the back room. Other voices followed in sharp rebuke. "Alright, alright! C'mon, just rack 'em up," someone called. Once again the balls clicked against one another.

It was quiet for a moment. George leaned forward. "So do you know this guy, Elizabeth's fiancé?"

She stared, then shook her head in bewilderment. Her cheeks stung with the invisible slap. "I didn't even know she was engaged." Tears blurred her eyes at this ultimate and undeniable proof of her estrangement. She may have been raised by the Hollises, but they were a family, and as a family had closed ranks against her. Even Elizabeth. Her dear, dearest Elizabeth.

"Fiona!" George tried to take her hand, but she pulled away and sat rigidly, hands in her lap, head erect. "I'm sorry. I thought you knew."

She shook her head and took a deep breath. Why was she so stunned? They'd made themselves perfectly clear. They'd done their duty, fed her and clothed her, put a roof over her head, and now did not owe her a thing more. "Well!" She managed a bright, brief smile.

"Fiona, can I have your hand, please?"

She hesitated, then put her hand on the table.

"There. Now you've got it," he said, squeezing it.

"Got what?"

"Anything. Whatever you need, ally, friend, buddy." He laughed. "Plumber!"

"Anything else?" she teased with a low, wicked chuckle as she tickled his palm.

"I don't know. What else do you need?"

"Let's see, right now, I could use a good . . ." She enjoyed the rising color in his cheeks as she paused to drain the last of her drink. "A good decent man in my life," she continued.

"Then consider the job taken!" His raw-voiced, boyish exuberance made her skin crawl. Under the table her feet tapped a furious beat, and she was already despising the next man in hobbling barefoot flight across her parking lot. Last night had been a mistake, disgusting and inexcusable, and she saw with stunning clarity not just how easy but how ruinous this next one might be. Still grinning, George suggested another drink, but she was tired. She wanted to leave. She needed to get out of here, away from the garbled voices, the sly games and pretense. No one was honest, and she was the biggest liar of all—not in pretending to need someone, but in pretending to care, because that was the worst, the most unforgivable lie. She picked up her purse and said she'd better get home. He peered at the check in the dim candlelight and fumbled in his pocket for money.

"I heard that! C'mere! C'mere, you little son of a bitch!" a man roared in the back room. There was a crash, then a jolt as something banged into the wall behind them. "C'mon, say it again. Say it to my face," the man demanded.

"Aw, c'mon, Patrick. He didn't say nothin'."

"Leave him. He's just an asshole kid." There was nervous laughter. "He doesn't know who the hell he's talking to."

"Yah, you don't know who you're talking to, creep."

"I'm talking to a fucking asshole, that's who I'm talking to," a younger voice panted. "Him, fucking scarface there."

"Son of a bitch!" a man bellowed, and then there was sudden scuffling and grunting. The wall thudded.

"You're talking to a war hero, you little asshole. He's got a Silver Star. What the hell you got besides your big mouth?" a gray-haired man in a baseball cap said as he shoved a skinny younger man in black through the swinging door. As the two men came by the table, George's arm shot out like a post to keep Fiona from harm. Just then the door swung open again and through it lunged Patrick Grady. Pushing the man in the cap aside, he hooked his arm around the younger man's throat and with a blow to his side dropped him to his knees, then kicked him in the back.

Four men rushed out from the back room. George stood up, but was blocked by the scuffle. The man in the cap cinched his arms around Grady's waist. His face flattened against Grady's back as he tried to keep him from kicking the slumped-over young man, who grunted with each sharp blow.

"Stop it!" She was on her feet and halfway out of the booth before George could stop her. "Stop it! Don't to that!" she cried, hitting Grady's arm.

He turned, looking as startled as she was. His gleaming eyes burned into hers. "What're you doing? What do you want?" he growled.

"I'm Fiona." Her heart was pounding. "Fiona Range. You know who I am." Every hair on her body rose, every nerve ending pulsated. Her breath came in shallow gasps.

"C'mon, Patrick, it's okay," the man in the baseball cap said as Patrick's eyes shot back to the young man crawling toward the door.

"Yah, let him go," one of the men said.

"He won't come mouthing off in here again," another assured Grady.

She watched him return to the back room surrounded by men whose uneasy pity had kept him safe but at bay all these years. "My God. What kind of animal is he?"

"Fiona, I'm sorry you had to—"

"He's so mean, so vicious. If they hadn't stopped him, my God, he would have killed that kid."

"It's Vietnam. It's that whole combat thing. He—"

"The way he looked at me. His eyes, they were filled with so much hate."

"No, he was in such a rage he didn't know what was going on."

"He knew. He knew who I was," she said, bewildered by the pressure in her chest as she headed for the door.

"Oh, that. Yah, well sure. I didn't mean that," George said, following her outside.

"He didn't even say anything." She took a deep breath of the pure night air. The black sky glittered with yellow stars. Her heart was still pounding.

"Yah, but don't forget, I mean, think of it, after all this time what can he say?" He was just like Elizabeth, always trying to speak for the misunderstood, and in the process only seeming as dense himself. He opened the van door for her.

"Hello," she answered coldly. "That's all he ever had to say. Just a goddamn, simple hello."

"Oh, Fiona. C'mere," he said, reaching out as she climbed in, but she slid to the edge of the seat before he could touch her.

Chapter 2

In the middle of Monday's breakfast rush, George Grimshaw slid into a booth then kept looking around nervously.

"So these are plumber's hours?" Fiona said when she got to his table.

"Actually, I was halfway here and then I remembered my propane tanks back in the shop, so I had to turn around and go—"

"I'm sorry about the other night," she interrupted. It had bothered her all weekend. After leaving Pacer's and not saying one word all the way back, she had jumped out of the van and hurried into her building. "I was such a bitch."

"No, you weren't! You were upset."

"So? I shouldn't have taken it out on you. I didn't even thank you for dinner."

"Fiona, I wasn't expecting anything. You don't have to thank me. Really," he added, his meaningful gaze filling her with anxiety.

"Well—anyway, I just did." She flipped over a new order slip, then tapped her pen against the pad while he studied the menu.

Let's see, he mused, what did she think? Which should he have, English muffins or toast, scrambled eggs or fried, grapefruit juice or orange? "I know," he said, returning the menu. "Surprise me!"

"No. You tell me what you want." She stared down at him.

"I'm sorry. I didn't mean to be a bother." He shook his head. "I'm sorry."

"No, it's just we're so busy." She gestured at the line by the register.

"I know. I wasn't even thinking of that."

"The thing is, people say that, then they won't eat what I bring."

"Well I wouldn't have done that, but that's beside the point, really." His forced smile made her feel terrible. "I'll have coffee and a bran muffin, grilled, please."

Each time she passed his table she could feel him watching her over his newspaper. When she brought the muffin, he asked if she'd like to see a movie tonight.

"No!" Seeing him stiffen, she explained that her class was tonight. Tomorrow night then, or any night, he added. Whatever was best for her. She had a paper to write, and before she could even start she had a ton of reading to do, she said, backing off toward the kitchen with the frantic ring of Chester's bell.

When she came out, George asked when the paper was due. Soon, she said. Well if she needed a break some night, maybe they could grab a quick bite somewhere, he suggested. She said she'd probably be at the library every night this week. The paper hadn't even been assigned yet, but the last thing she needed right now was a man in her life, and especially not Elizabeth's ex-boyfriend. With any other guy she'd have no problem getting the message across. But George's earnest, hopeful smile was as troubling as it was confusing.

Her next trip out of the kitchen found Larry Belleau squeezed into the booth next to George. Larry's old faded blue-and-gold Dearborn High jacket was so tight now that the sleeves hiked up on his beefy arms. He wore his Red Sox cap backwards, the plastic tab compressing his brow into a fleshy protrusion. Thirty years old, he still dressed like the teenager he'd been when the diving accident at the quarry shattered his skull, leaving him frozen in emotional adolescence. He hunched forward on both elbows, his animated conversation driven by his need to say as much as he could before his listener escaped. Without pausing for breath or thought, he gulped one frantic sentence into the next, the connected syllables almost sounding like another language. His booming voice filled the dining room. George smiled patiently. Praying Larry wouldn't say anything about the party or Brad Glidden, she gave him a glass of water and a menu.

"Good morning!" she said with a quick smile.

"Hi Fiona." He grinned and kept nodding. "You're pretty you're so pretty I—"

"Thanks, but what'll it be, Larry? Juice? Coffee? Can I get you some coffee, Larry?"

"No no gotta go to work already had my breakfast just wanted to come in to come in see you say hi I had a really good time—"

"Whoops, Chester's bell!" She glanced toward the kitchen. "My order's up."

"Wait!" Larry seized her wrist. "Just wait wait please just wait!"

"Larry," George cautioned in a low voice. "Let go. Don't hold on to her like that."

"Oh!" Larry said, pulling back. He sat on his hands. "It's just my father's really mad I'm not supposed to drink he said I act stupid and nobody wants me around because he said he said I offend people." He grabbed her hand again. "Did I offend you did I did I offend you at the party did I Fiona?"

"No, of course not, Larry." She held her breath and slipped her hand away.

Larry grinned. "It was fun it was so much fun huh?" He nodded eagerly.

"Yah, it was."

"Yah will you go out with me Fiona yah will you will you please please please?" His voice grew louder. "We can go to McDonald's we can go tonight I have money a lot of money see," he said, stiffening back on the seat as he dug deeply into his pockets and tossed crumpled bills onto the table.

"I can't, Larry. I can't, I'm just so busy."

"Please Fiona please please please!" he begged, hands clasped at his chin.

Heads were turning. Maxine watched from the register.

"Hey, come on, Larry, get up. It's time to go," George said.

Larry got up and stood by the table. The minute George was out of the booth Larry slid back in. Easily given to tearful outbursts, his frustration was most always with himself. Though he couldn't recall the actual dive, he remembered what he had been, what he had wanted to be, and in moments like this, despised the child he was.

"Now, come on, Larry, come on, get up. I'll give you a ride to work," George said.

"But I want to go out with Fiona I want to I do!" Larry insisted, hitting the table with his fist.

"Well you can't, so come on, let's go," George said with a firm grip on Larry's arm.

"Why why can't I?" Larry cried, leaning back and trying to pull away. "Tell me why why because I changed because I'm different because you think I'm stupid now that's why isn't it?"

"Because, she can't, that's all," George said, bending close.

"But you like me you do you do don't you Fiona?" Larry called over George's shoulder.

She nodded. "Yes, I do."

Larry grinned. "I know you kissed me and I kissed you I kissed you back didn't I?" His point made, Larry grinned at George. "See see I told you I did I kissed Fiona so why can't we why can't we go on a date?"

"Because she goes with me, that's why. So come on, let's go!" George ordered in a quiet voice.

Larry's mouth dropped open. "Oh oh oh I'm sorry I'm sorry George I am I really am I really really am," he said, almost tipping the table in his haste to stand. "I didn't know that I would've never asked her swear to God George never I never would've," he insisted, following George to the door.

She fled into the bright, noisy sanctuary of the kitchen. She watched Chester ladle pancake batter onto the grill. It wasn't fair, she thought, torn between anger and pity for Larry. At one time or another, most everyone had sneaked through the woods to party and swim in the ice-cold quarry with its sheer granite ledges. Because the quarry was on Patrick Grady's land, it was the one risk Fiona had never taken. After Larry's accident she had been glad when his family sued Grady. She leaned on the counter now and asked Chester what the outcome had been.

"They settled with Patrick's insurance company," Chester called over his shoulder. He was flipping frozen sausage patties onto the grill, dealing them out like cards. "They did all right, but they didn't get what they really wanted."

"What was that?" she shouted over the drone of the exhaust fan.

"To prove he'd been negligent. They wanted the quarry drained so it wouldn't happen to any other kid."

"What do you mean, negligent?"

"Kids'd go up there and do drugs with him."

She had never believed that. She remembered a few guys, Todd especially, selling pot to Grady. But that was all. Grady had been as mean and unfriendly then as now.

"So I guess the Belleaus figured he made his property accessible to their kid too," Chester was saying. "But the thing is, he always had that land posted. Always. For years, with 'No Trespassing' signs, which I guess is what saved him. Otherwise he would have lost everything. That land's all he's got. Aside from disability checks."

"I wonder why he doesn't sell it then?" she said.

"Ask your uncle," Chester said, turning the pancakes. He glanced back. "He'd know."

"Uncle Charles?"

"Yah, the Judge," he said with a startling rancor.

"I thought you liked my uncle."

"I do. It's him helping Grady, that's what I don't get."

She pointed at herself. "Moi perhaps?"

"All the more reason to let him sink in his own shit if you ask me. No-good son of a bitch belongs in jail, that's where he belongs."

"Jail! Why? You mean Larry's accident?" she asked as the door swung open. Maxine rushed in, looking for her.

"Yah, that's what I mean."

"But didn't you and Grady used to be friends once?" From the corner of her eye she saw Maxine by the door staring at her husband.

"I tolerated him, and that's a hell of a lot more than scum like him deserves," Chester said.

"Chester!" Maxine gasped.

"She asked, didn't she?" He flung down the spatula with a clang.

The door opened again and Maxine slipped into the dining room.

▪

The next time George came into the coffee shop Fiona thanked him for getting Larry out without a scene.

"I hope that didn't make you feel, well, uncomfortable or anything. Me saying we're dating," George said with a shrug.

"Like I said, I appreciated it," she answered, ignoring the hopeful inflection.

"So how's the paper going?"

"Great." Seeing his eager smile, she added that with all the reading she'd really only just started writing the paper.

"Well, you know what they say." He gave a smart nod. "Begun is half done."

"Is that what they say?" She burst out laughing.

"Something like that," he muttered, then picked up his check. He peered at it then slid to the end of the booth.

"George." She put her hand on his shoulder before he could stand. "I wasn't laughing at you."

"That's okay." He smiled up at her. "Really."

And that seemed even more confusing, that for George it probably was okay.

A few days passed before she saw him again. She gave him a menu, then snatched it away, saying she would order for him. The rush was over and there were only a few people left.

"Here you go," she said, arriving with Chester's special, a Mexican omelet that smelled good, however vomitous its consistency with all the chopped red, yellow, and green peppers swimming in runny cheeses. "Try it," she urged when he hesitated. "And if you don't like it I'll get something else."

"I will, but first I was wondering if you'd like to go out to dinner this weekend." Either night, whichever was better for her.

She was busy both nights, she lied. Actually she had no plans at all. What about Sunday then, he asked. They could drive up to Rye, walk the beach, go to Portsmouth for a few hours, then stop for dinner at the Exeter Inn on the way back. That sounded like a great day, she said, but she was going to need the whole weekend to work on her paper.

"But thanks, George." She could see he didn't believe her.

"Thanks for what?"

"For asking. And for always being so damn nice."

"Which may be my biggest problem here," he said softly.

"No! God, no! In fact, just the opposite."

"The opposite! Oh, so I'm not such a nice guy." His forced laughter fell between them like slow gray rain.

"What I mean, George, is that I can be a raving, flaming bitch, and that's not what you're looking for."

"Looking? Who says I'm looking?"

"You know what I mean."

"What if I told you I wasn't the least bit interested in you?"

She laughed. "Then I'd be insulted as hell!"

"What if I said I just need someone to talk to sometimes, to go places with."

"So in other words you'd be using me!"

"No! No, we'd be like friends. You know, if you want to talk or you just feel like going for a ride or something, we could do that."

"So we'd be using each other!"

"Well I wouldn't be thinking of it that way."

"But those things never work, George. They just don't," she said, then felt terrible when she saw how red his face had gotten.

Her American history course was at Dearborn Community College. She was tired and the fluorescently bright classroom was too warm. Lee Felderson had already kept everyone an extra forty-five minutes to review for the first quarterly exam, though most of the time had been devoted to test-taking skills.

"Read the question thoroughly, break it down into parts," Lee Felderson was saying.

With a loud sigh Fiona got up and opened a window. She couldn't believe they were actually writing this all down.

"Organize your ideas." Lee Felderson sat back against her desk. Once a plain, sensible, too-earnest girl in her teens, she had lightened her hair and shed probably half her body weight, Fiona guessed. She

only wore short, tight skirts and dresses now. Four years older than
Fiona, Lee and Fiona's cousin Ginny had been best friends in high
school. What Fiona remembered most about those years was Ginny's
door bursting open and Lee lumbering down the stairs in tears.
Ginny's insensitivity was legendary, though in the family it was considered "frankness," while Fiona's own frankness had always been assailed
as thoughtlessness. Ginny was like her father, Aunt Arlene had always
said of her older daughter: too honest for her own good.

"Don't be afraid to jot down ideas, make notes and even outlines
right here in the margins." Lee Felderson held up a blue book and
turned to the last page. "Some people prefer making notes here, and
that's fine. I'll certainly know that's what you're doing. And if you don't
want to leave anything to chance, just write 'notes' in big, bold letters
at the top of the page."

Fiona groaned as the nineteen-year-old boy beside her printed
"NOTES" at the top of his notes. Idiots. She couldn't bear to sit here
much longer.

The class finally ended with Lee Felderson's announcement of
another review session next week if anyone was interested. Fiona
raised her hand to ask if it would be a review of the actual material "or
just more stuff like tonight," she said, stifling a yawn. The room was
silent.

"I try to meet the needs of the group, Ms. Range, and because there
are a fair number of older students here like yourself, students who
may not have taken a test in a number of years, I think it's as important
to teach the techniques of test-taking as it is the material itself."

"Oh sure. No problem," Fiona said with a flip of her hand.

"I would hope not." Lee Felderson's gaze was as cold as her voice.

Fiona was getting into her car when Kendra Jones raced up and
asked if she and her friend Ann could have a ride home. Just out of high
school, they were always bumming rides from someone.

Fiona asked where they lived, adding that she was tired and was
heading straight home, which was right in downtown Dearborn. Oh
well then, Kendra said, starting to back away, they did live a lot further
out than that, way out past the quarry.

"All right, hop in," Fiona said.

"Are you sure? Do you know where that is?" both girls asked, climbing in.

"Yah, I know where the quarry is."

She hunched over the wheel as she drove. There were no lights or houses along this section of road that ran through the most remote part of town. If it weren't for patches of moonlight through the gathering clouds, all would be black. The girls hadn't stopped talking since they'd pulled out of the parking lot.

She hadn't been out here in years, she realized as she came around the curve just past the town woods with its tall, spindly pines. She slowed down. Ahead was a small white cottage with a wide brick chimney in the middle of the roof. Patrick Grady's house. A variety of No Trespassing signs—tin, wood, cardboard, new and old—were nailed to the trees, fences, and porch. She peered out, but could see no car in the driveway that ran behind the house. The only light came from a tiny dormer window over the front door, and she wondered if it was his bedroom. She wondered if he lived alone, if he had a dog or a cat, or if he ever sat in the weathered Adirondack chair that seemed to be sinking into the side yard. She knew he'd always lived there, that next to his house there used to be a road leading into the quarry. But years ago a barbed wire fence had been put up to close off access through his property. To get to the quarry now you had to drive into the Industrial Park, then hike in through the town woods that bordered his property.

"Do you know who lives there?" She gestured back at the house. "Well, yah! Patrick Grady, the guy with the scar," Ann said.

"Do you know him? Fiona asked.

"Oh God, no. He's like, weird, you know, like some kind of hermit or something."

"What do you mean?"

"If you even go near there he, like, freaks," Kendra added.

"What do you mean, freaks?"

"Well, like this one time he caught my brother and his buddies there up at the quarry and he actually chased them through the woods. He was like screaming and throwing things at them like rocks and branches and things. My brother said he was so scared he almost wet his pants."

"That is weird."

"Yah, my father said he was like this really cool guy once," Ann said. "I guess he got all screwed up in Vietnam or something like that."

"Really?" She was enjoying talking about him with people who knew nothing of their connection. "Do you know what happened? I mean, how he got so screwed up?"

"The war, I guess, I don't know. He's wicked scary-looking though," Kendra said with a shiver.

"My father said he got wounded by an American plane or something. Can you imagine? I mean, like, how unfair is that?" Ann said as they pulled into her driveway.

After she dropped them off she came back past Grady's house, driving as slowly as she could without actually stopping. Behind the house there was a crooked shed, and beyond that a small, dark pond, then the woods.

She was back in town, driving down Main Street when she saw Todd Prescott come out of the drugstore. He wore jeans and a red jacket, and as always, even after two months in rehab, was deeply tanned with pale streaks in his blond hair. He was one of those handsome men whose boyishness becomes only more pronounced and pathetic with age. As she passed she stared straight ahead. "I've wasted half my life on that loser," she whispered to remind herself. It wasn't until the corner that she dared glance in the mirror. His hand was still up, waving, trying to catch her eye. He probably needed a ride. She'd heard he was working for his father at the furniture store. Her throat was dry. Something ached low in her belly. The old longing had shrunk to this alien place in her being, a conquered dominion, still more his than her own.

Two years older than her, he had been spoiled, lazy, always in trouble, and her first real boyfriend. He cheated on her constantly. They were forever fighting, breaking up, making up. He got her pregnant when she was sixteen. His wealthy family had owned Prescott's Fine Furniture all of its staid ninety-seven years, and Todd was their only child. Mr. Prescott provided the money for the abortion because she didn't dare tell her aunt and uncle. On the morning of the appointment Todd didn't show up. When Fiona called, Mrs. Prescott said he was sick and couldn't come to the phone. Elizabeth and George drove her to the clinic in Boston and stayed until it was over. She and Todd were back together the very next day.

Fiona drove past her street. It was ten o'clock, and she was tired, but she dreaded going home to that cramped, messy apartment. She thought about calling George Grimshaw. In fact, why even call? She was only a block away. She turned onto Elm Street and drove past his house, relieved to see his lights out. She took a left onto Maple Avenue and stopped in front of the big old house Terry and Tim had bought last winter. She hadn't seen Terry since the party. She got out of the car and looked toward the back of the house. The kitchen light was on. Terry was standing over the sink.

She hurried down the walk and tapped lightly on the side door so she wouldn't wake up their little boys. She glanced up at the darkened windows. If she was really lucky Tim would be asleep too. She cringed as the dog began to bark.

"Fiona!" Terry said, opening the door, the collie beside her. "Are you okay? Is everything all right?" she whispered, looking out toward the street.

"Yah, what do you think, I'm being followed?" She laughed and stepped inside.

"Well I don't know! I don't hear from you, and now suddenly here you are out of the blue!" Terry said.

"I was going by and I saw your light so I thought I'd stop in and say hi."

It wasn't until they were sitting at the kitchen table that she realized Terry was in her bathrobe and slippers. The dog wagged his tail and she reached down to pat him.

"He wants to dance," Terry said.

"Sorry, Goldie." She laughed. "I can only stay a minute," she said, a little hurt when Terry didn't object.

There were circles under Terry's eyes, and her face was puffy. Her pregnancy was beginning to show. Her dark hair was streaked with white paint.

"The kitchen looks great," Fiona said, looking around at the new oak cupboards and yellow walls. "Did you just paint in here?"

"Yah, this summer. You saw it! The night of the party," Terry added, making it almost seem like a question.

"Where's Tim?" Fiona glanced toward the unlit dining room.

"In bed." Terry said he'd spent the night putting a new ceiling in the den.

The den. Upstairs the little boys asleep, and Tim in bed waiting for his wife. Terry and Tim had been married right after high school. They had both worked for a couple of years before having children, Terry as a secretary and Tim as a painter. In those ten years they had saved every penny, and now they had the house, the babies, and Tim's video store in the mall. And what did she have to show for the same ten years?

Terry was staring at her.

"I'm keeping you up. Why don't we get together some night this week?" She started to get up.

"Wait! Don't leave. Stay a little while longer, please," Terry whispered, her hand on Fiona's arm. "My life is so dull. I can't stand it! Tell me what you've been doing. Please! I need something exciting to think about."

"All right, but you can't laugh," Fiona said.

"I won't! I promise! Tell me! Come on, tell me!" Terry squeezed her arm.

"I'm a coed, believe it or not!" she said, grinning. "I'm taking American history at Dearborn Community, and I love it. It's only three credits, but if I do well, then I'll take two more courses next semester. And then I thought—"

"Come on, Fiona! You're going out with someone, aren't you?"

She said no, but Terry persisted. "Yes you are. You're seeing someone. I know you are. You are, aren't you?"

"Why do you keep saying that?"

"Because I know you," Terry said with a forced lilt in her voice. "And I can always tell when you're lying. Come on, tell me. I won't tell anyone. I promise. Not a soul. You know you can trust me."

She could tell by the look on Terry's face that she already knew. George must have run into Tim and told him.

"It was just one date. No big deal," she said, and Terry's eyes widened.

"Where'd you go?" Terry asked, watching carefully.

"The Orchard House."

"You did? When? What night?" Terry asked, mouth agape, hand at her breast.

"Last week. Actually it was the night after your party. Saturday. George wanted to go to a movie after, but it was late, so we stopped at Pacer's."

"George? Who's George?" Terry asked, shaking her head.

"George Grimshaw. Who'd you think I was talking about?"

"I don't know. I didn't know." Terry looked confused. "George Grimshaw! God, what'd you do, talk about Elizabeth all night?"

They both looked up. A child was crying. Terry said Frankie had gone to bed with a temperature.

"Aren't you going to go up?" Fiona said.

"No, he's all right." Terry listened a moment. "Sounds like he's going back to sleep."

The crying stopped, but Fiona stood up. She really had to go, she said, heading for the door.

"Fiona, wait! You heard about Brad and Krissy's baby, right?"

"Yah, I knew the night of the party. The baby was born the day before, remember?"

"I mean about the baby's heart," Terry said. "There's a problem with one of the valves. The poor little thing's in Children's."

No, she hadn't heard anything at all, she said.

"Brad and Krissy just about live there." Surgery was a possibility, Terry explained, but first the baby had to get stronger. "It breaks your heart to see him, tiny little thing all wired up to machines and monitors. Brad's taking it worse than Krissy. She told Tim she's really worried about him."

Fiona felt sick to her stomach.

There was creaking on the darkened stairs, then Tim came around the corner into the kitchen, squinting, with Frankie on his ship. The little blond boy was sucking his thumb, his plump cheeks shiny red.

"Didn't you hear him?" Tim said, passing him into Terry's arms. "He's been crying for the last ten minutes."

"I thought he stopped," Terry said, cheek on her son's brow. "Poor, sweet Frankie doesn't feel good, does he?" she crooned at his ear.

"He's burning up," Tim said, still not acknowledging Fiona.

"I'll take care of him." Terry jiggled the whimpering child on her hip. "You go back to bed now." She tried giving him a cup of water, but he pushed it away.

"I can't believe you let him cry like that," Tim said.

"I told you, I thought he stopped." Terry glared at him as she wet a dishtowel under the faucet then dabbed Frankie's temples and brow with it.

"Well he didn't," Tim said through clenched teeth.

"It's my fault, Tim. I'm sorry. I didn't know it was so late," Fiona said.

He opened the refrigerator and took out a carton of milk.

"Tim!" Terry said as he got a glass from the dishwasher. "Tim!" she said again, but he continued to ignore Fiona.

"Hey, it's okay. You know me, I see a light and I figure maybe there's a party going on," Fiona said, opening the door.

He turned then. He drank the milk slowly, eyes riddled with loathing as he watched her leave.

The minute the door closed she heard Terry say, "How could you do that?"

"Easy. It was real easy," Tim said.

"Well, I don't care, she's my friend and—"

"She's a screwup and every time she comes around you turn into one too!"

"You don't know her. She's a good person."

"Face it, she's a pig, Terry!

Fiona tiptoed down the steps and slid into her car, cringing as she turned the key, feeling even more exposed and shabby with the old engine's roar. She squinted as she drove. She didn't want to see anyone or anything familiar, not a car, house, or street sign.

For the next week she got up at five and jogged three miles before work. She unpacked every box in the apartment, cleaned the three tiny rooms, and hung curtains in the bathroom. After her Monday night class she stayed for the extra help and even tutored Kendra and Ann one night at the library. She ate only fish, vegetables, grains, and fruit. Vowing that caffeine and alcohol would never again pass her lips, she drank eight glasses of water a day. Her good health showed. Whatever she was doing she should keep it up, Chester said. Bestowing her highest compliment, Maxine said she looked like a model.

A few nights later, instead of going straight through the intersection, she turned abruptly onto Elm Street. There was a light on in George's house. Before she could change her mind, she hurried onto his front porch and rang the bell.

"Is it too late for company?" she asked when he opened the door.

"Oh no, I was just watching the game. Come in! I'm so glad you're here." He grinned. He was in his pajamas and bathrobe. His hair was wet and he looked freshly shaved.

"I'll just stay a few minutes," she said. "I have to get up so early, and I know you do too."

"That's okay. We can both be a little tired in the morning." He picked up the remote and turned off the television. "Here, sit down." He gestured to one end of the sofa. "Actually I was just thinking about you." He sat at the other end. "Then the doorbell rings and here you are."

She'd been on her way home from class, she said, when all of a sudden her car veered sharply then came to a dead stop in front of his house.

"What do you think happened?" he asked, smiling.

"I think I've been so damned self-disciplined lately my funky old car can't stand me anymore."

"That's great. Especially if it brings you here," he said, laughing.

"Yah, except I don't know how long I can stand me either." She began telling him about her constant struggle between thinking she was the smartest person in the class, then suddenly worrying that maybe things weren't as simple as they seemed, that maybe the complexities were apparent to everyone else but her.

"Like tonight I was in the middle of an answer and it got real quiet in the room and the teacher's looking at me and all of a sudden I thought, they don't know what the hell I'm talking about! So maybe this is some kind of manic high I'm on and nobody wants to tell me."

He chuckled. "You underestimate yourself," he said, half turning as he put his arm over the back of the sofa.

She laughed. "It's kind of like the opposite. People have always underestimated me, so to compensate I tend to overestimate my abilities." She laughed. "And then I end up with this huge gap, like some kind of weird void I flounder around in."

"You never seem like you're floundering to me." He was touching the ends of her hair.

"Well, you're not in my history class," she said as the hair brushed the nape of her neck.

"No, but I've known you a long time."

"Long enough to know better," she said with a deep shiver.

"To know what better?"

"To know better than fool with my hair like that."

"I'm sorry!" Red-faced, he pulled away quickly then sat very still with his arms folded.

"George, I was kidding. I was only kidding." She groaned and held up her hands. "See! Look at me! I'm floundering, now, right here before your very eyes. George," she coaxed, sliding closer. She put his hand back on her hair. "I like that. It feels good."

"Are you sure?" he said so uneasily that she leaned closer, just a breath of a kiss passing between them. He sighed, and she kissed him again, gently, for a long time. When she started to ease away, he pulled her against him. He slid his hands under her sweater and she shivered as his rough fingers stroked her back. He smelled of soap and shaving lotion. She could taste peppermint on his tongue. She put her hand on his hard flat stomach and could feel his deep moan.

"I should go now," she said against his open mouth.

"Why?"

"I don't know. I think I have to study." Even her eyelids ached.

"But you already know it all," he said in a hoarse whisper.

"Yah, that's right." She nibbled his lower lip.

The telephone rang. He reached so quickly behind her that she fell against the sofa arm with a little laugh.

"Hello?" His face reddened as he turned away to listen. "Nothing, just . . . Oh! . . . Well . . . Well, that's good . . . But you didn't have to call. I would've . . . No, I know . . . I know."

She knew by his expression that the voice in his ear was a woman's.

"You will . . . You know you will . . . Well, anyway, I better go. I'm . . . No! No, I didn't. When?" A stricken look came over him now as he listened, nodding. "Oh God. That's awful. That's just so awful . . . I know . . . Especially after waiting so long . . . Well, okay then, let me know . . . Maybe I'll see you there then . . . Maybe . . . I don't know . . . No, nothing!" His voice dropped. "No, just me . . . I do? I don't know, I'm just tired, maybe that's it . . ."

"And who pray tell was that?" she teased when he hung up. She put both arms around his neck. She liked the bristly feel of his cropped hair against her cheek.

"Elizabeth," he said with a hard swallow.

"Elizabeth?" She sat back. "What did she want?"

"She was telling me about the fiancé." He looked at her. "She doesn't think he likes it here."

"Huh?" She shook her head in disbelief. "And what are you supposed to do about it?"

"She just wanted to talk, I guess, that's all," he said, so regretfully that she jumped up.

"So call her back, George. For godsakes, don't let me interfere."

"No, I didn't mean it that way. Please, Fiona, come here." He took her in his arms. "We're just friends, that's all. That's all we are."

"Who do you mean, me or Elizabeth?" she said, stiffening. She wanted to go.

"I don't mean you," he said sadly.

She pulled away before he could kiss her. "She asked if someone was here, didn't she?"

He nodded.

"So why didn't you tell her?"

"I didn't think you'd want me to."

They stared at each other.

"George! You should see the look on your face. Devastation! Utter devastation, that's the look. And that's okay. I can understand that." She put on her jacket. "So let's not make things any more complicated than they already are."

He shook his head. "No! No, it's what she just told me about Brad and Krissy Glidden's baby."

"What?

"He died. A little while ago."

She gasped and covered her face with her hands.

"I'm sorry, Fiona. I forgot. You and Krissy are friends," he said, trying to put his arm around her again, but she moved back.

"I better go now. I'm tired. I'm really tired."

As she came down the walk every step felt leaden and clumsy. She had no memory of the drive home, but here she stood now in her vestibule staring at the envelope taped to her mailbox.

Her name was written in Aunt Arlene's careful script, the small, precisely shaped letters, without flourish, boldness, or precarious slant of angle to mark her as anything but the sensible woman she was.

My dear Fiona,

I am writing this note because I have tried many times to call you. Apparently your phone has been shut off, and you still don't have it connected.

"Which obviously means you fucked up again," Fiona muttered as she read.

As I'm sure you know by now, Elizabeth is engaged to Rudy Larkin, a wonderful young man from New York. We are all getting together for dinner Monday night so that he can meet everyone, and we want you to be with us.

I know there have been some difficult moments lately, but we are a family and in the end that is the bond to which we must adhere. Please make every effort to come for dinner. It will mean a great deal to Elizabeth. We all look forward to seeing you. I've missed you very much.

                    Love,
                    Aunt Arlene and Uncle Charles

She threw the crumpled note into the trash. The hell with them. They didn't really want her to come. Elizabeth must have insisted. Uncle Charles had refused to sign his name so Aunt Arlene had done it. Yes, Rudy, you fine young man, there is someone missing, our dear screwup, Fiona. Every family has one, and she's ours.

All that night she dreamed of Brad Glidden's corpse on top of her in this room, in this bed. No matter how she struggles she cannot push him away. She cannot speak or breathe, but the window is open, and somewhere a baby is crying to the ceaseless pulse of Uncle Charles's voice rising and falling through the years and the long moonless night: Uncle Charles would say, Uncle Charles always said, Uncle Charles said, Uncle Charles is saying, the trouble with you, Fiona, is you don't think before you speak. The trouble with you, Fiona, is you don't think before you act. The trouble with you, Fiona, is you don't think. The trouble with you, Fiona, is you. The trouble with Fiona is you. The trouble. Fiona is the trouble.

Chapter 3

■

The coffee shop had just closed. Late-afternoon rain had been pre- dicted, and the sky through the plate glass window was heavy and gray. With the lowering darkness came even more dread.

"Sandy'll finish that," Maxine called from the register.

"Yah, what're you waiting for?" Sandy seemed as eager as Maxine for her to leave.

"I'm almost done," Fiona said. She tore open another package of paper napkins.

"Your aunt and uncle'll think I made you late. So go, just go!" Max- ine cried. Her rouged cheeks blazed with excitement.

Fiona had brought a change of clothes to work for Elizabeth's din- ner tonight, but now she wasn't sure if she should go. She wasn't ready to be with them. All she could think about was the baby's death. She knew she couldn't change what had happened. And even if she could, if she were given back that one night and did not sleep with Brad Glid- den, would his baby's heart be healthy? Would he be alive? No, no, of course not. It had been like this throughout the day, with each bout of logic spiraling her more tightly inward until she felt not only removed, but oddly stranded. She did not even look up now as Sandy dumped out the flatware bins. The usually agitating crash of knives, forks, and spoons onto the metal tray seemed as extraneous a commotion as the distant storm.

For the first time in her life she felt deeply afraid and insecure. Her brash self-confidence, with all its old defenses and excuses, was being undermined the way a deep current erodes an embankment. So invisible was the weakening that every step, each shift in weight felt treacherous. The baby's death wasn't her fault. She knew it wasn't. Of course it wasn't. The pitiful excuses kept flashing through her thoughts like surreal images through the window glass of a speeding train: the baby's weak heart, the baby's weak and stupid father, holding her as she stumbled up the steps because she had been drunk, and weak, and stupid, and because, because, because of her recklessness, because of her sin a price had been demanded, a terrible punishment exacted, and now anything could happen, anything at all, and she needed to do something—something that would change it all back and put everything into place. But what? She looked around the empty coffee shop. She needed to be with her family. She needed to go home. She would be safe there. There were only a few more napkin dispensers to fill and then she would leave.

"I wonder if she's having her cheese pinwheels. The paper had her recipe. I think it was last Christmas, you know that holiday food thing? On the Social Set page," Maxine was telling Sandy, whose blank gaze only seemed to encourage her. "Well, anyway, when I saw it was Arlene Hollis's recipe I just had to make them. I wasn't even having a party, but they were so good I ate every one myself. Fiona, you be sure and tell your aunt how much I love her cheese pinwheels. They were so gourmet! And I'll bet the dinner'll be like that too tonight—really, really gourmet! In fact, I just thought! I saw your aunt Arlene in the supermarket the other day! Well, she doesn't know me, so of course I didn't say anything, but anyway it was the poultry section, and she was near those little what-do-you-call-them, you know, gaming hens. Corn . . . Corn something . . ."

"Corn Ware!" Sandy called.

"Yah, those Corn Ware gaming hens, and I bet that's what the engagement dinner'll be tonight."

"Cornish game hens, you mean," Fiona said stiffly, adding that big family dinners were usually turkey.

"Turkey," Maxine repeated with a look of wonder. Well if that didn't just prove what down-to-earth, real people the Hollis family was, she continued, her proprietary chatter about the family making Fiona feel even more exposed and vulnerable. The Hollises were such wonderful people, upstanding and so generous whenever their help was needed. Why just last Christmas when the Dodsons' house burned, Judge Hollis put the entire family up in one of his properties rent-free until they could rebuild. Maxine knew from personal experience what a kind, fair man he was, she said with a sharp nod, as if expecting Fiona to disagree. "And believe me, there's a lot more I could tell. But that's the way that man is. All Judge Hollis wants is to help people and he doesn't need the whole world knowing about it."

Fiona had heard this cryptic comment from Maxine before, but she refused to be baited. She was used to people feeling obliged to point out her ingratitude to the Hollises.

Maxine was telling Sandy what a nice person the Judge's wife, Arlene, was. "She was always that way. You never would've known the Ranges had money. They were just the nicest girls, Arlene and Natalie."

Fiona looked up, startled. Natalie. Natalie. Yes. Natalie, she thought, smiling, and without knowing why felt a wholeness taking shape in the unfamiliar sound and cadence of her mother's spoken name.

"Now what about your cousin, Jack?" Maxine called from her wobbling stool at the register. She grabbed the counter edge to steady her rickety perch. "He's in computers, right?"

"No, he's a court officer," Fiona said. After his layoff Jack had been unemployed for almost a year before his father got him a job in one of the district courts in Boston.

"Oh, so he's following in his father's footsteps," Maxine said with an approving smile.

"He's not a lawyer," she said. And had never wanted to be one, though Uncle Charles had urged him in that direction. Jack had wanted to make a name in his own field, but had been forced into his father's.

"Now, he's married to Susan Daley, right? She is so pretty!" Maxine called to Sandy. "Do they have any children?"

"No, Susan works for ZyCo," Fiona said.

"That's right. She's got some really important job. She travels all over the country, right? And she's got the most beautiful blond hair. So light it's like silver," Maxine told Sandy.

The Ice Princess, Fiona thought with a surge of old jealousy. The family's eager acceptance of the accomplished Susan had made Fiona even more of an outsider. It had been the same with Ginny's handsome husband, Bob Fay; and now she would be further displaced by Elizabeth's fiancé. And yet just thinking about them all made her feel calmer, more centered.

"Now how about Ginny, does she still work at the nursery school, the big one down on South Main Street?" Maxine asked.

"Actually, she runs it." She expected the next question to be about Ginny and Bob Fay's separation last June. Ginny had discovered that Bob was having an affair. For someone who took such pride in her ability to see through bullshit, Ginny had certainly been wearing blinders when she met Bob Fay. Ginny had been devastated by her husband's betrayal with his pretty young secretary. Ginny's personality was her most attractive feature. The prediction that tall, square-jawed Ginny would come into her own as her mother had, with time mellowing the awkward angularities into a unique, almost masculine beauty, had yet to be fulfilled.

"Where's your cousin's fiancé from?" Sandy called from below the counter where she squatted scrubbing the stainless steel bins.

"New York," Fiona called back. A logical assumption.

"What's his name again?" Maxine asked.

She paused to remember what the note said. "Uh, Rudy Larkin."

"What's he do?" Maxine asked.

"He's a teacher." A guess.

"Oh, so they'll probably live in New York then," Maxine said.

"Not necessarily. That's the good thing about teaching. You can always get a job no matter what." She glanced at the clock, suddenly dreading all their polite scrutiny, the weary patience, the disapproval chilling every hug and cry of "Oh Fiona!"

"My girlfriend's sister's a teacher," Sandy called up. "Only she says it's not like it used to be. She says they've been churning out so many teachers now the marks are glutted."

"What the hell're you talking about?" Fiona snapped.

Sandy tilted back on her heels and frowned. "You've heard that expression," she said uneasily.

"Do you mean the marks are glutted or do you mean the markets are glutted?" Fiona asked, as ashamed of her venom as energized by it. Articulation was a hallmark of the Hollises, who considered it a duty to point out one another's grammatical errors. Better a loving nudge than the sting of a stranger's criticism, Uncle Charles would always say.

"Whatever!" Sandy rolled her eyes and sank back down behind the counter.

"I suppose it'll be a big wedding like the older one, Ginny, had," Maxine said in a dreamy voice.

"They haven't decided," Fiona said, remembering the stress of Ginny's elaborate wedding. Elizabeth had been her older sister's maid of honor. The medication it took to quell Elizabeth's anxiety attacks had by the day of the ceremony reduced her cousin to a placid wraith, whose limp hand kept seeking Fiona's. She hoped they weren't trying to pressure Elizabeth into a big wedding.

She hurried into the bathroom and changed into a long yellow skirt and loose white sweater. She preferred short skirts and sexy tops that showed off her body, but these were the kind of simple, flowing clothes all the Hollis women wore. Leaning close to the mirror, she brushed her eyelashes with mascara until they glistened thickly black. She stepped back, pleased, her dark eyes even darker, her skin whiter, her red lips wider and fuller. She always felt too made up and brassy around them. She came out of the bathroom feeling excited. Suddenly all that mattered was seeing everyone again, especially Elizabeth. She hoped this Rudy was good enough for her sweet cousin, whose dearest virtue was usually her undoing: putting everyone else ahead of herself.

"What about you, Fiona?" Maxine called. "It'll be your turn next. Aren't you and Elizabeth the same age?"

"We're four months apart." As little girls they had enjoyed pretending to be twins, though they didn't look anything alike. Fiona was the dark-haired, sensual image of her mother, and Elizabeth was blond with the delicate, patrician features of her father.

"So you'll probably be the next one married," Maxine said.

"Yah, especially since George Grimshaw can't keep his eyes off you." Sandy giggled, then the flatware fell with an unnerving clatter as she dumped it all back into the gleaming bins.

There was a close rumble of thunder, then a streak of lightning through the hard, gray sky as Fiona ran out to her car. She couldn't wait to tell them she was taking a night course. She was unlocking her door when a white Saab convertible pulled into the alley.

"Hello, beautiful. I was hoping I'd see you," Todd Prescott called, grinning.

"Yah, well I'm in a hurry, Todd, so move out of my way, will you?" she called back.

"I will, but first I have to tell you something."

"No, you don't!"

"But there's something—"

"Jesus, you don't get it, do you?"

"Come here, come sit in the car with me, please? Just for a minute. I promise, that's all it'll take."

"No, I have to go somewhere, and I don't want to be late, so will you please move?"

"I just wanted to tell you how sorry I am about what happened last—"

"Uh-uh, Todd, don't want to hear it," she said, then got inside her car. She turned the key. The engine gave one faint groan, then died and wouldn't start again.

"So where'd you steal it from?" she said, running her hand across the soft red leather dashboard. Todd had promised to drive her straight home and nowhere else.

"What do you mean steal? It's mine!" he said, laughing.

"I take it then your father got all the charges dropped."

"The cops were such screwups there weren't any," he said with a scornful chuckle.

"Oh really?" She shook her head. Once again Mr. Prescott had managed to save Todd's hide. "So what's this a reward for then?" Probably for staying away from her. His family had always blamed the trashy Fiona for their son's troubles. Mr. Prescott had told Todd once that she was "nothing but bad baggage like her mother, Natalie, and her father, Patrick Grady."

"No reward. As a matter of fact, I'm doing what you always said I should. I'm working my hump off loading trucks at the warehouse. My father says I gotta learn the business the same way he did, from the bottom up."

"Well, that's good. I hope you do then, Todd."

"Do what?" he asked, grinning at her again.

"Make something of yourself. It's about time, isn't it?"

He laughed, and his hand fell from the wheel to her thigh. "God, I've missed you, Fee. You have no idea," he said, his touch and raspy voice sending the old current through her bones. She pushed his hand away. She had been fourteen when they first made love.

"You've missed me too, come on, I can tell."

"Oh really?" she said, relieved to see the rambling old farmhouse ahead.

"Nobody makes me feel the way you do. And I mean that in every way," he said, returning his hand to her leg. "Every possible way."

"Toddie!" She sat forward as he drove past the pale gray house with the big red barn in back. The driveway was filled with cars. They were all there.

"We'll go up to the beach house. No one's there," he said.

"No! Don't be ridiculous! Jesus, Todd!" she cried as he pulled off the road into a clearing. "My family, they're waiting! I have to go to dinner!"

"I'll take you to dinner! Where do you want to go?" he said, laughing as he tried to pull her to him.

"No, don't!" She struggled and batted away his hands. "Stop it! God damn it, Todd, leave me alone. Just stop it!" She shoved him back against his door. It was starting to rain, and they were getting wet.

He stared at her with pink-rimmed, glassy eyes. His pupils were dilated. He was high, and she hadn't even known it. "I heard something. I heard something funny about you." She knew by his sly laugh he meant Brad Glidden.

"Please, Todd, will you just bring me back?"

"Something about you and George Grimshaw. Tell me it's not true, babe. Tell me you're not that desperate."

"Todd, will you please bring me home? Please? I'm begging you."

He looked up as if he had just realized it was raining. "Is it true?" he asked, starting the car. "Just tell me that." He pushed a button and the convertible top closed over them.

"No. Of course it's not true," she said, remembering his need whenever they broke up to know not only the names of anyone she'd dated, but every lurid detail.

"Because you're still my dirty girl, aren't you, little Fee-fee?" He reached for her again. She kept trying to push him away, but his fingers dug into her arms. He looked up as headlights bounced over the foggy rise ahead.

"Shit!" he said as a police cruiser drove slowly past them. As soon as it was gone he pulled onto the road. A minute later the same cruiser bore down on them from behind, siren blaring, lights flashing.

"Pull over!" she yelled. He hadn't even been speeding. The cruiser just needed room to pass. Todd hunched over the slick wheel, gripping it with both hands. The narrow road ahead was a roller-coaster of curves and turns. "Toddie!" she warned, her hand on the door. "If you don't pull over I'm jumping out." There was a field on their right, and he turned into it. The cruiser followed. With every hummock and rut the Saab jolted in to the air. The cruiser loomed on their tail. As they bounced along, Todd's swearing convulsed into sobs. She pleaded with him to stop. This made no sense, and now he was just making the whole thing worse. At the edge of the field, he jerked the wheel, turning the car so suddenly that the front wheels caught in a deep gully. They lurched to a sudden stop. His head whiplashed back then hit the wheel as hers met the dashboard. Blood trickled down the side of his face. She touched her throbbing cheekbone, relieved to find no cut.

"All right, Prescott, out of the car," Officer Jim Luty ordered as Fiona looked up into a gun barrel.

"You get that gun away from me!" she yelled, shrinking back against the seat.

"Come on, Prescott, open the door and get out!" Luty opened Todd's door and tried to pull him out, but Todd slumped dazed and moaning, his face in his hands.

"Leave him alone, he's hurt!" she said.

Luty leaned closer. "Prescott, can you hear me?"

"Why'd you do that?" she demanded of the young patrolman, who'd been a few years behind them in school.

"He should've stopped!" Luty's voice rose. "All he had to do was stop!"

"He wasn't doing anything wrong. He wasn't even speeding. You were just harassing him!"

"Harassing him! He's driving a stolen car!"

"What?" She scrambled to get out. "What do you mean, stolen?" She kept touching her tender cheekbone.

The report had come in a little while ago, the tall, slope-shouldered policeman explained as the light rain blistered his shiny visor. The Saab had been stolen from Dexter Carey's driveway. Hearing his next-door neighbor's name, Todd looked up with a feeble grin.

"That's it!" she cried, throwing up her hands in disgust.

"Hey! Fiona!" Luty shouted as she stormed off through the tall, wet grass. "Where do you think you're going?"

She headed toward the road. "Home!" she called back. Her family was all there and she'd be damned if she'd let a loser like Todd Prescott foul this up too. "Loser," she panted as she marched along.

"Get back here, Fiona! You get back here right now!" Luty demanded.

"Nothing but a loser," she panted.

"You're staying right here!" Luty's big hand clamped down on her shoulder.

"No I'm not!" She jerked free and hurried on ahead.

"Yes you are!" he insisted, hurrying alongside.

"Oh no I'm not!"

"Oh yes you are!" There was a hard cold click as the metal cuff snapped around one wrist then her other.

"You bastard!" she hissed.

"I'm sorry," he said, steering her back to the Saab where Todd sat with his head back on the seat now. "But you can't just stomp off like that in the middle of an arrest."

"You can't arrest me! I was just getting a ride home!"

"Yah, in a stolen car!"

"How was I supposed to know it was stolen?"

"You could've asked!"

"Oh, yah, okay, what? Every time somebody gives me a ride I gotta ask to see the registration?"

"With Prescott you'd better," Luty said, and hearing his name Todd's head rose. He looked around.

"No," she shouted, advancing on him with Luty at her heels. "Because Todd Prescott is a screwup and I will never ever as long as I live even speak to the asshole. Do you hear me, Prescott, you loser, you stupid, stupid loser," she said as he regarded her with a weak smile.

Above them on the road a gray Volvo had slowed to a stop. A tall, skinny man in a yellow shirt and navy blazer jumped out and, leaving his door open, ran toward them. "Officer," he hollered, identifying himself as a doctor. "Is anyone hurt? Does anyone need help?" He glanced at Fiona, who stood cuffed against the cruiser. "Are you all right?"

"Oh yah, I'm just fine. Can't you tell?" she said, rolling her eyes.

"Just him." Luty gestured to Todd. The doctor leaned into the car to look at Todd. He asked a few questions, then ran back to his car and returned with a black leather case which he opened on the hood of the Saab. He wiped blood from Todd's forehead, then peeled open an H-shaped bandage and stretched it over the gash. A second cruiser arrived. Groaning, Fiona turned and closed her eyes. She knew this cop too, Gil Liota. He bent over Todd, who seemed alert and talkative now. His serene responses to Liota's questions rose in surreal snatches. ". . . forced off the road . . . a terrible misunderstanding . . ."

Someone touched her shoulder. "You sure you're okay now?" the doctor asked, and she could only nod. He left, then moments later Todd's father sped up with his neighbor Dexter Carey, who was nervously trying to explain that it had all been a big mix-up. Carey said he had totally forgotten that Todd would be coming by this morning to pick up the Saab.

"Yah, right," she muttered.

Mr. Prescott glanced between the officers, nodding as if to validate each of Carey's points. Just completely slipped his mind, Carey said. And so when he looked out and saw the car gone his first thought was to immediately call the police and report it stolen. Which had obviously been a terrible blunder. Mr. Prescott assured him it was a mistake anyone might make. Especially in this day and age.

"Why was Mr. Prescott picking up the Saab?" Luty asked.

"No, no, not Mr. Prescott. Todd," Carey said, and Mr. Prescott smiled patiently.

"Yes, that's who I meant," Luty said, and Carey and Mr. Prescott looked at each other.

"Well, to have the . . ." Carey started to answer.

"To bring it to the . . ." Mr. Prescott said simultaneously.

"To the car wash," Todd said, and now both men echoed, "That's right, to bring it to the car wash. The car wash, yes, that's exactly right."

A few minutes later Dexter Carey drove off in his muddy Saab, its tailpipe jiggling inches from the ground. Mr. Prescott assured the grim-faced officers there would be no accusations made, no blame assigned in the matter of Todd's injuries. As far as he was concerned it was a misunderstanding most likely colored by the taint of past unfortunate events. And the presence of certain people, he might as well have added with his foul look at Fiona. He said he'd better hurry up and get his son to the family physician. No, Todd was protesting as they drove off, he had to pick Sandy up. He'd promised to give her a ride home from work.

Jim Luty waved now as he drove past Fiona. He had dropped her off at the corner so no one in the house would see her getting out of the cruiser. She hurried up the back steps and slipped into the big warm kitchen. They were all in the dining room. Forks clinked, and she could hear Uncle Charles's deep voice telling a story that made Elizabeth and Ginny both cry out at once in laughing protest.

"No, Dad's right. He's right. I remember," Jack insisted over his sisters' howls.

"See! Jack knows. He remembers," Uncle Charles said, and now the women at the table were protesting that Jack didn't know. He couldn't. He hadn't even been there. He always did this, Ginny cried, taking his father's side against the girls.

"Girls?" Uncle Charles said. "Now if I'd said that you'd be accusing me of God knows what kind of loathsome chauvinism."

Fiona smiled. The stripped turkey carcass was on the counter. Gravy simmered on the stove. She turned it down, then put a scrap of dark meat in her mouth and tiptoed toward the little bathroom under the back stairs. She wanted to at least comb her hair.

"Fiona!" Aunt Arlene said from the doorway. "I thought I heard someone in here." Halfway across the room she stopped, her wide, toothy smile fading. "What in God's name happened to your face?"

"I don't know. What?" She held her breath as her aunt came toward her.

"Your cheek," Aunt Arlene said, peering closely as she touched Fiona's face. "It's so red. And your hair. You should see your hair!" She looked down. "And you've got burrs all over your skirt!"

"I had a little car trouble," she said, wincing. "That's why I'm so late. I'm sorry."

"Well anyway, you're here," her aunt said, hugging her so tightly that Fiona bit her lip and closed her eyes with almost dizzying relief. "And that's the most important thing now, isn't it?" she whispered at Fiona's ear, then drew back to look at her again. "I've missed you, little girl," she said with a tremulous smile as she kept trying to smooth down Fiona's mussed hair. "I've missed you an awful, awful lot!"

"I've missed you too," Fiona said with a hard swallow.

"Arlene?" Uncle Charles called from the dining room.

There was a pause. "Coming!" Aunt Arlene answered, her strained excitement bringing a squeal from the hushed room as a chair scraped back from the table. The door burst open.

"Fiona! Oh, I'm so happy you're here!" Elizabeth cried, throwing her arms around her. Her fine blond hair whisked across Fiona's face. She smelled the way she always did, like a delicate, lemony flower.

Behind her through the still swinging door they all looked toward the kitchen. The only light in the long, narrow dining room came from candles burning overhead in the ornate crystal-and-silver chandelier. The flickering reflection was caught in the pale silk threads of the mauve wallpaper. Watching from the head of the table was the stern, high-boned face she had grown up fearing. She would look up from a book or the television, suddenly and unaccountably distressed, only to find her uncle's bright blue eyes trained on her. "I'm a mess," she protested as Elizabeth led her into the dining room, saying she was the only one Rudy hadn't met yet.

"He's in the bathroom," Ginny said, staring up at Fiona with a look of alarm.

"I know. I look awful," she tried to explain as Jack stood up and hugged her.

"Just a bit mussed," said his wife, Susan, reaching to pat her arm. "It's all this rain, so much moisture in the air."

"I was in such a hurry, I bumped myself getting out of the car." Her voice faltered with the deft incision of her uncle's laser-sharp stare: The Judge had heard all the stories, every lame excuse for crime and mishap. "I'm sorry I'm so late. It was my car, you see—"

"Oh here we go," Ginny said with her throaty laugh. "Fiona's cars. Remember the little VW, the white one?"

"Yes I do, and I thought that was a darn good car," Bob Fay said to no one in particular, and Fiona was surprised to see him here.

"Fiona!" Ginny gasped, pointing as Fiona came closer. "Your face, it's bruised."

"That's what I was saying. I had an accident. I bumped my head."

"An accident?" Aunt Arlene said, her face white. "And what was Rudy just—"

"Well not like a colliding type accident," she hastened to explain.

"You mean collision," Jack said with a quick look at his father.

"Yah, not like that. What happened was, my car wouldn't start. The rain, I guess, so I was getting a ride over, and we hit a pothole or a bump or something."

"Who was driving?" Ginny asked.

"This girl I work with," she said. "Sandy. But she's okay." Again she touched her cheek. It was starting to swell. The burdock on her skirt hem scratched her legs as she walked to the end of the table and bent to kiss Uncle Charles's smooth pink cheek. Though no part of him moved, he seemed to recoil with her touch, his smile waning into forced melancholy as if he dared not risk appearing happy for fear she would do something to shatter it.

"It's good to see you again, but are you sure you're all right?" he asked, lifting his napkin.

"I'm fine! Really!" she said, her own smile fading as he patted the cheek she'd just kissed. "I didn't get anything on you, did I?" she asked, then pulled out her chair next to Elizabeth where she always sat.

"That's Rudy's place!" Elizabeth said quickly, her entreating glance meant to remind her father of some pledge they'd probably extracted in the event Fiona came. Feet shuffled with an uneasy burst of dry coughing and throat-clearing.

"Over here!" Aunt Arlene said, arranging a napkin, plate, and silverware onto the table across from Elizabeth.

So they hadn't expected her. Aunt Arlene's invitation had been deliberately late with the hope she wouldn't come. Well she had, and now everyone was tense.

Out in the hallway the bathroom door opened. "Here he is!" Elizabeth announced, smiling at the lanky man in the yellow shirt and navy blazer entering the room. "Rudy, come meet my favorite cousin, Fiona," she said, arms around them both. "Fiona, this is my fiancé, Rudy Larkin." Burrs studded the cuffs of his wrinkled chinos.

"Doctor Larkin," Ginny added.

"Hello, Fiona," he said, smiling, his eyes scanning her hot face. "Well we finally get to meet, but I have to admit I feel as if I've known you for quite a while now."

"Really?" she snapped with such a warning stare that he looked away.

"I've told him all about you, Fiona." Elizabeth's arm tightened on her waist.

"Well not everything, I hope." She laughed nervously and eased from her cousin's embrace down into the chair.

"All the good things," Elizabeth said as she and Rudy sat down.

Urging Fiona to fill her plate, Arlene kept passing mashed potatoes, squash, turkey.

"Fiona was just staying how she was in some kind of accident on her way here," Elizabeth told Rudy, then to Fiona said, "And talk about a coincidence, Rudy stopped to help some guy whose car went into the field off Bradley Road. He said the police were there, and they had some frazzled-looking woman in handcuffs."

"The driver's forehead was cut," Rudy added, slicing his turkey. "He just needed a butterfly on it."

"I wonder why they were in handcuffs," Ginny said.

The fiancé leaned over and said something at Elizabeth's ear. Fiona stared at her plate, fully expecting him to explain that only the frazzled woman had been handcuffed. Elizabeth passed him the gravy.

"Probably went through a stop sign or something," Jack said. "It doesn't take much in Dearborn."

"Probably some drug thing," Bob Fay proclaimed, looking toward the Judge with raised eyebrows, his ingenuous reminder of who the greater sinner was at this table.

Or adultery, Fiona thought, glaring at him. The simplest thing would be to leave right now; just say, nice to meet you, Dr. Larkin, and I hope you all have a good life without me. She shouldn't have come. They were a family. There was little room for her now in the expanding complexities of their relationships. It must have seemed this same way to her mother, who had probably gotten up from this very table and walked out that door, and in all the years since had never looked back. "Thank you," she said, taking the gravy boat from her aunt, whose hand shook. An emotional barometer, Aunt Arlene couldn't stand discord, rancor of any kind. The lines in her strong, square face were faint, but her tightly bunned hair was completely gray. Fiona wondered if her mother's hair was that gray yet. Natalie was six years younger than Arlene.

"Actually," Rudy said, "I was thinking of bank robbery or homicide, the cop seemed so upset."

"Police officer," Jack corrected. Susan stared at her husband.

"Sorry. Didn't mean to offend anyone," Rudy said. He looked amused.

Fiona held her breath as she set down the gravy boat. Aunt Arlene continued to pass more bowls, cranberry sauce, stuffing.

Ginny leaned forward. "Fiona, you must have gone right by it."

"Yah," she said. "But with the rain I couldn't see much."

"So it's not such a dull town, is it?" Elizabeth asked her fiancé.

"You're the one who keeps saying dull," he corrected, leaning close and grinning as he wagged his finger at her. "I think the word I used was 'quiet.'" He winked and looked around the table. "Elizabeth thinks she's lured me into the furthest reaches of boredom."

Face coloring, Elizabeth looked at him. "Except I didn't lure you," she said softly, and Rudy continued to smile as if he didn't know quite what to say.

"That's right. You didn't," he said with a self-conscious swallow.

"No, she just said, 'That's it, big boy, we're outta here.' Right, Lizzie?" Fiona said in her huskiest Mae West growl, but Elizabeth didn't look up or answer and now Fiona thought Elizabeth was upset with her for coming late and looking like such a mess. Or maybe just for showing up at all.

"Well, the most excitement way out here is one of Lucretia Kendale's yard sales," Jack said into the pause, and everyone laughed too quickly as they glanced at Elizabeth.

Ginny explained to Rudy that Lucretia Kendale was the wealthy old woman down the road who advertised yard sales just so she could visit with people who came.

"It's usually just junk she puts out," Susan said.

"Except the last couple of weekends she put up a sign that said House for Sale," Jack said.

"Poor thing just wants a little company, that's all," Aunt Arlene said.

"Well, we've got our share of crime here, don't let anyone tell you otherwise," Bob Fay said to Rudy. "Most of it's runoff from Collerton, our poor little city next door. Mucho Hispanics," he said, shaking his head, either not noticing or not caring that everyone had fallen silent. "And mucho drugs." He sighed. "There's just no keeping it out, I'm afraid."

"More turkey, Bob?" asked Aunt Arlene.

Fiona touched her tender cheek.

Rudy smiled at her. "You probably should get some ice on that," he said.

She assured him it was fine, which was Elizabeth's cue to bridge the

gap between herself and her fiancé with the old tales of Fiona's courage, the teeth filled without anesthesia, all the tearless injuries.

"You must have an unusually high threshold for pain," Rudy said,
watching her.

She could feel her eyes smoldering again. "Just naturally numb,"
she said with an uneasy smile, not sure where this was headed.

"She's always been like that," Uncle Charles said from the end of
the table.

"A stoic," added Aunt Arlene.

"So who was the man they arrested?" Ginny asked Rudy. "Did you
get his name?"

"I didn't ask," he said.

"But I'll bet you got his Blue Shield number, right?" Bob Fay chor-
tled, and only Rudy laughed. Ginny might have forgiven him, but no
one else had.

"What about the woman? Did anyone say who she was?" Ginny
asked.

"No, no one said." Rudy turned and asked Susan to pass the rolls.
"And the butter, please," he added as Ginny leaned forward again.
This was his second helping and his plate was heaped with food.

"What did she look like?" Ginny persisted.

"Tell you the truth, I didn't get that close a look. Rolls?" he asked
Elizabeth, who shook her head. "How about you, Fiona?" he said, offering the basket.

"Thank you." She took one, her face burning with shame and gratitude. For a few moments there was only eating, and no one spoke
until Aunt Arlene pronounced the white meat a little dry. Oh no. Absolutely not. It was very moist. Perfect. It was quite tender, everyone
rushed to assure her.

"Oh! I almost forgot. I'm taking a course. American history at
Dearborn. And Ginny, guess who my teacher is! Lee Felderson!"
Fiona said. She grinned as they all began to talk at once, congratulating her for taking a course, wishing her luck, and warning her about
how serious Lee Felderson had always been. They laughed as Fiona
described the ridiculous review sessions.

"Well, just make sure you don't take advantage of her friendship with Ginny, Fiona," Uncle Charles said.

"Dad!" Elizabeth and Jack both said, as Ginny sputtered, "Friendship! For God's sake, Dad, I haven't seen her in ages."

"I wouldn't do that. Of course, I wouldn't," Fiona shot back, provoking a wave of nervous chatter that rose and fell around the table. Her uncle stared at his plate. He could seem so alone at times, so isolated, eating in silence, his attention occasionally snagged by laughter or a stray comment, or a curious phrase that would have to be repeated, the entire story retold so he'd understand. It was the nature of his work, the pathetic stories, the desperate excuses, the constant lies some days just draining him, Aunt Arlene would explain, always trying to compensate for his distance. His breathing had grown deep and labored now with the uneasiness he had caused.

"I like that sweater, Uncle Charles," Fiona said of his black crew neck. "It's a big improvement over your ratty old cardigan." His gray cardigan with the suede elbow patches had always been a joke between them. Suddenly, she wanted to be the one to reel him back in. She wanted to make him smile the way she'd been able to as a little girl.

"You think so?" he said stiffly. And with his quick glance away from her bruised face, she seethed with an old resentment at always being the outsider here, a pariah among the cherished, his sister-in-law's bastard, the obligation that continued to embarrass him.

"I gave that to Daddy for his birthday," Ginny told her. "And I made him promise he'd wear it tonight."

"Daddy was fifty-nine last week," Elizabeth told Rudy.

"And next year's the big Six O," Bob Fay added.

Fiona squirmed. Without Aunt Arlene's call to remind her, she had forgotten her uncle's birthday.

"And don't forget Susan's is in two weeks," Aunt Arlene said quickly.

Glancing up, Fiona caught Rudy studying her, as if she were some strange new disease he'd just encountered.

Susan laughed and said that since she was going to be thirty-five she'd appreciate everyone just skipping over hers and moving on to whoever's birthday was next.

"That would be my mother's then. December six," Fiona said, her voice strangely, unaccountably raised. She's going to be what, forty-nine, Aunt Arlene?"

"Yes," said Aunt Arlene. "Forty-nine, that's right."

"Fiona's mother was younger than my mother," Elizabeth explained to Rudy.

It angered Fiona to see Aunt Arlene sip her wine and turn back to her movie discussion with Ginny. She was trying so hard here, but they didn't care. And why should they? She was just another of the many acts of kindness and generosity they'd performed over the years. Susan was asking Elizabeth if she and Rudy had considered the Tabor Club for their reception. Ginny was telling her mother that *Terms of Endearment* was probably on every emotional level the best woman's movie ever made. Bob Fay checked his watch. He was beginning to look miserable. Other than Rudy, no one had spoken to him. Elizabeth held up her hand and frowned as Rudy tried to pass her the mashed potatoes. She had hardly eaten anything on her plate. Uncle Charles was buttering a roll and Jack was just getting up to go to the bathroom when Fiona announced, "She said to say hello to everyone for her."

"Who?" Ginny asked. "Who said?"

"My mother."

"Natalie, your mother?"

"Yes," she said with as offhanded a shrug as could be managed with everyone staring at her. She cut a piece of turkey and put it in her mouth.

"When? When was this?" Ginny asked in a low, breathless voice. Growing up, Ginny had always been suggesting ways to track down Fiona's mother—personal ads, a private detective—only to be reminded by Aunt Arlene that those things cost a great deal of money. It had been Ginny's idea to try and make enough money then with a lemonade stand.

"A while ago. Well, not too long ago, a couple of weeks, I guess."

"Fiona! I can't believe it," Elizabeth cried. "You mean you've talked to her? To Natalie? Your mother? My aunt?"

She nodded. Her hands writhed in her lap and her foot tapped.

"Oh! Fiona!" Elizabeth ran around the table to hug her. "Oh, that's so wonderful. I can't believe it! After all this time! Oh, I'm so happy for you!"

Her cousins and their companions smiled and expressed their pleasure. She had Uncle Charles's full attention now. Still silent, Aunt Arlene sat very still, her hand covering her mouth.

Elizabeth sighed. "Imagine, after all these years."

"What exactly did she say?" Ginny asked.

"Not a whole lot, really. Just that she wondered how I was doing."

"And what did you say?"

"Well, that I was fine." She shrugged. "I was so surprised. I was shocked."

"Did she say where's she been all this time?" Elizabeth asked.

"She never said, and I didn't want to ask."

"What? Why not?" Jack sputtered. "That would have been the first question out of my mouth."

"I just didn't want to put any pressure on her," she said, trying to hide her pleasure in the warmth of their attention. She took up her fork and knife and cut another piece of turkey.

"Did she tell you anything?" Ginny asked. "For instance, like why she left the way she did?"

"Not really."

"And you didn't ask?" Ginny said exasperatedly.

"Well I did, but all she said was there was a lot of tension." She saw Aunt Arlene's hands mask her face with a deep gasp, and suddenly she not only regretted the lie, but was trying to think of some way out of it. A quip, a burst of laughter before announcing the joke was on them, but how could she now when they were so taken with it, so intrigued and excited? They all watched her, none more intently than Uncle Charles. He knew. He always knew, had always seen through her lies. She had to end this before it got worse. "You know, because she was so young and it just all seemed so overwhelming to her."

Again, Aunt Arlene gasped.

"What about her sister here?" Jack asked, resting a hand on his mother's shoulder. "Did she ask about mother? Did she even care?"

"Oh yes! She asked about everyone, but especially you, Aunt Arlene." She smiled, and Aunt Arlene began to sob.

"There." Jack put his arm around his weeping mother. "There now."

"Oh, Mother! Arlene!" Ginny, Elizabeth, and Susan cried in unison. Bob Fay kept looking down the table as if imploring the Judge to set this right again.

Unaccustomed to seeing this calm, regal woman upset, no one knew what to do or say.

"I'm all right," Aunt Arlene sniffed as she stood up. "I'm fine, really!" She hurried into the kitchen and closed the door softly.

"Well," Elizabeth said, closing her eyes with a sigh. Rudy put his hand over hers and a flush infused her delicate features.

"I'll go see how she's doing." Ginny started to get up.

"She's fine," Uncle Charles said, motioning for her to sit back down. "She'll be all right. She just needs to be alone a minute so she can collect her thoughts."

In the kitchen the water ran full force, but not enough to muffle the sobs.

"I'm sorry," Fiona said, desperate for eye contact, but no one would look up, so acutely were they feeling their mother's pain. "I didn't think she'd be so upset. I thought she'd be happy."

"You do have an interesting sense of timing, Fiona," Uncle Charles said in a low voice as he took up his fork and knife. "I mean, why here, why now, tonight at Elizabeth and Rudy's dinner?"

"Dad!" Elizabeth said.

"No," Uncle Charles said. "There's a time and a place—"

"That's right, Dad, so come on!" Jack interrupted with his father glaring at him.

"No, I know. I shouldn't have," Fiona said, looking at each of them. "I mean, I should have waited. I'm sorry. I'm so sorry."

"Oh no, Fiona . . . It's all right . . . Of course you wanted to tell us . . . We understand," her cousins kept assuring her as they came and crowded round, patting her arms and shoulders. Elizabeth hugged her while she sat with her head bowed in shame at the cruel lie that in the midst of all this affection and love she could not now retract. It had always been this way. Hurricane Fiona strikes again, Uncle Charles used to laugh, but it had stopped being funny a long time ago.

A few minutes later Aunt Arlene emerged from the kitchen and took her place at the table. Her eyes were puffy, her nose red as she assured everyone that she was fine, just shocked, that was all. It certainly was a relief though to finally know that her sister was alive and well after all these years. She took a deep breath. "Fiona," she began in her most gracious tone. "If you should hear from your mother again, would you please tell her that I'd like her to call me—that it would mean a great deal to me. A very great deal." Her eyes bright with tears, she urged everyone to start eating again. There was a wonderful surprise for dessert.

"As a matter of fact, Fiona, it's your favorite," she said, smiling. "And yours too, Charles."

Blueberry pie, Fiona knew, though her uncle looked confused.

Later, when they were putting dishes away in the kitchen, Ginny asked if they'd heard about the Glidden baby.

"I know, it's such a shame," Aunt Arlene said. "But let's not talk about it. Tonight we're all together, so let's only have happy thoughts." She reached across the open dishwasher door for Fiona's hand. "I know it hasn't been easy, but thank you," she said softly. "Thank you for coming."

Fiona tried to smile. She felt not only afraid, but precariously displaced. Once again her aunt's kindness had managed to push her even farther out of the circle.

Chapter 4

She stared through the coffee shop window into the brilliant October afternoon. The leaves on the ground were as crisply orange and red as the leaves on the sun-washed trees. The very air seemed charged with shimmering particles of light. Looking closer, she saw waves of jewel-bright insects flying over parked cars and telephone wires, now rippling in swarms against the dusty plate glass. They were tiny orange beetles.

"Fiona!" Maxine tapped her shoulder. "The bell! Chester! Can't you hear it?" Maxine was a wreck. When Sandy had dragged in late again this morning, Chester had screamed at her not to bother, to just go back home. He didn't need her or anyone else for that matter because he'd had it up to here with the whole damn mess. In fact, they could all go home as far as he was concerned, every damn one of them, customers included, because he was sick of it. Goddamn sick of it! Humiliated, Maxine had locked herself in the cooler until Fiona finally convinced her that no one in the dining room had heard his bellowing. They had, of course, but the regulars were used to it.

"Your clubs're up," Chester said, patting his face with a towel. "You can't let hot toast sit on a cold plate. Condensation! I ring that bell, boom! You gotta come. Boom! Boom! Boom!" he said, ringing it three more times.

"We're being invaded by beetles." She picked up the sandwiches. "Orange ones with black spots. It's some kind of sign or something."

"They're Asian ladybugs." He slid a rack of dirty dishes into the dishwasher and pushed the button. "They come every few years."

"Come from where?"

"Well, Asia, obviously. And don't forget, it's bad luck if you kill 'em," he called after her.

"It's bad luck if you kill anything," she called back as she came into the dining room.

After she had served the men in the middle booth their sandwiches, she stood by the window and watched the ladybugs inch up the glass. In the distance a familiar figure had just turned the corner. It was Patrick Grady in his usual plaid flannel shirt and rumpled pants. He crossed the street in front of Town Hall, where he sat on a bench in the brick square. He folded his arms and stared into the street.

The little she knew about Grady had come from her aunt, who had described him as an angry, brooding young man. He hadn't been in Vietnam long when he was shot and burned in a freakish battle where an American miscalculation had killed all the men in his patrol. All but Patrick Grady. His first few months back had been spent in the hospital. Natalie was pregnant with the child conceived in their last days together. According to Fiona's aunt, there had been trouble between them when he left. When he came home from the hospital it only grew worse. Deeply depressed, he thought everything had changed: the country, the town, people he'd known all his life. With the baby's birth came violent bouts of paranoia. His tirades and bizarre accusations frightened Natalie. Finally, after yet another terrible scene, she wouldn't let him near her or the baby. He was convinced that she avoided him because she could not bear the sight of his ugly, scarred face. Leaving his house only at night, he would walk miles alone through the dark. He was in constant pain, and all the medication filled his head with strange ideas. He saw Natalie's own melancholy and confusion as proof of her betrayal. The more she tried to reason with him, the more convinced he became that Fiona was not his. His refusal to sign paternity papers came as the last blow. It was cold and rainy the day Natalie got into her car and drove away forever, leaving the baby to be raised by her sister and brother-in-law. Patrick Grady turned his bitterness against the world. "Poor Patrick," people would murmur when Fiona asked about him, then try to change the subject quickly, but she had been a persistent child.

One day when she was nine Aunt Arlene came into her room and sent Elizabeth downstairs. She said Fiona had to stop embarrassing people with questions about her mother and Patrick Grady. It was a family matter, and if she wanted to know about her mother she was to ask Aunt Arlene. But what about her father? she'd asked. Who would answer those questions? Beyond his obvious problems there was nothing more to know about him, her aunt said. She had already been told everything. He wanted nothing to do with Fiona. Nothing at all. She had to understand and accept that, and if she could not, they were afraid of what he might do. You mean to me? she'd asked in disbelief. Yes, her aunt said. To you.

Fiona looked up now as the front door opened. Two men came in and sat in the booth by the window. Disappointed that she hadn't been able to seat them, Maxine hurried to give them place settings, red calico mats with matching napkins she had made herself. Every night she brought home trash bags of soiled place mats and napkins to wash and iron. Chester insisted it was a waste of time and money, but she said she loved doing it. "Fiona will be your waitress," Maxine said, handing them menus before she left.

"Fiona?" said the stockier man, smiling over the menu as she set down his glass of water. "Now that's an unusual name."

She smiled.

"What does it mean?" he asked.

"It means beautiful, intelligent, sensitive, and anxious to take your order now since you're my last table."

"Egg salad sandwich," he said, laughing. His friend, a thinner man with red hair, couldn't decide between the egg salad or the shepherd's pie. Eggs were bad for his cholesterol and the shepherd's pie might be greasy. "I'll have a hamburg!" he announced, then snapped the menu shut.

"Excellent choice. Good and greasy and high in cholesterol!" she said, and both men laughed.

When she came out of the kitchen they were looking out the window at the scowling man on the bench. She began to scrub the table next to theirs.

"He was something, really something," the stocky man was saying. "I mean, one of those purely natural athletes. He could do anything, play any sport. I remember this one time we were all up to the quarry diving and everyone kept climbing to see who could dive and do the most flips from the highest point. And there was this one ledge, at least fifty feet up, this little narrow rim of rock way up the top that one time some guy'd supposedly jumped off of, but not dived! Nobody'd ever dived from it, and Grady's not only up there ready to dive, but he yells down that it's going to be a triple. 'No! No, don't!' we all yell back and the girls're all screaming and crying and begging him not to. 'Don't! Don't do it, Patrick. Please don't!' they're screaming and Jesus, I can still see it like it's happening right now. he raised his arms up over his head and off he goes, doing a triple, slow and easy like it was the simplest thing in the world."

"Is that so?" the thinner man mumbled, swallowing a yawn.

The stocky man sighed as he moved the salt and pepper shakers back and forth. "It's hard to put into words, but it was one of those moments you have when you're a kid. You know, those defining moments, like something goes click, and you realize there's Patrick Grady and then there's everybody else."

The other man chuckled. Glancing over at Fiona, he said his defining moment involved vomiting in his girlfriend's parents' bed.

Chester was ringing the pickup bell. She hurried into the kitchen, returning so quickly with their orders the hamburg slid from the plate onto the table. "I'm sorry," she said, trying to rearrange the scattered hamburg and chips and pickles. The paper cup of ketchup had landed upside down. "But I heard you mention Patrick Grady before," she said with a deft scoop of the ketchup blob. "And so I was just thinking you must have known his girlfriend too if you knew him."

"Natalie!" he said. "Yes. Natalie Range. We were all in the same class." His eyes widened. "You're related to her, aren't you?" He smiled. "I haven't been back here in years. I've lost touch with just about everybody, but you certainly do look like Natalie Range. She was the prettiest girl in our class. An absolute knockout," he told his companion, who was eating his hamburg.

"I'm Fiona Range." She held out her hand. "Natalie's daughter," she said with a surge of unaccustomed pride.

"Hal Meade. Good to meet you, Fiona," he said, still shaking her hand. "God, you do look just like her, now that I know." He glanced out the window. "Did she and Patrick end up getting—"

"No," she answered so quickly that he knew not to ask any more.

When she left work ladybugs were swarming on the back wall of the coffee shop and there were even some on the hood of her car. She drove around the corner into the sun, smiling as they began to fly away. Patrick Grady still sat in front of Town Hall. She pulled up to the curb and quickly got out of the car. As she walked toward him his eyes darted in the opposite direction. Her heart was racing and her mouth was dry, but she stood right in front of him and said, "If you don't mind, I'd like to talk to you. Just for a minute. I don't know if you remember, but I spoke to you one night at Pacer's. I'm . . . I'm . . . ," she stammered under his hard stare. "You know who I am! You do, don't you?"

"What do you want?"

"Nothing. I just want to be able to say hello at least, that's all. I see you around all the time, and it seems weird not to say hi or anything."

"Doesn't seem weird to me."

"I don't want anything from you if that's what you're worried about."

"All I want is to be left alone." He stood up.

"You know I know who you are." She stepped closer. "Everyone knows. That's why this is so ridiculous!"

He turned and started walking up the street. She hurried after him. "I just want to talk to you, that's all. Just for a minute."

"Get away from me!" he said with such a sudden slash of his arm that she cringed back, convinced he'd meant to hit her.

"Please!" She caught up with him again. People were probably watching, but she didn't care. "I just want to tell you something! I got a call last week from my mother, from Natalie, and I . . . I just thought you'd like to know!"

He stopped on the sidewalk. His mouth twitched as he stared, his gaze still and flat, almost lifeless. "You leave me alone. Do you understand? Just leave me the hell alone," he growled, leaning so close she could see the pores in his skin, the smooth, almost waxy scars that ribboned from his nose to his ear.

"You're afraid of me, aren't you?" she said so softly that for a moment it seemed he hadn't heard.

"No. It's you that should be afraid," he said, then walked away.

Last week's exams were being returned and Fiona tried to hide her confident smile. The test had been so easy that she had finished and left a half hour earlier than anyone else.

"Good. Very good. Interesting. Good," murmured Lee Felderson as she came down the row.

"Yes!" squealed Jen, the pale little blonde in the back row, when she saw her grade. She had taken the test stoned.

Without a word Lee Felderson placed Fiona's test facedown on the desk. Fiona turned back the corner and saw the red-inked D. Her face burned and her eyes stung. "Screw this," she muttered, squeezing the booklet into a ball. For a moment the only sound was the frantic tap of her foot on the tile floor. Everyone's eyes were on her. She felt like such an ass. Bitch, she thought, glaring as Lee Felderson sat down at her desk.

"Most everyone did extremely well," Lee Felderson said, "but a few of you . . . well I'm not sure what happened." She glanced at Fiona, who was sliding her notebook into her backpack. She wasn't about to sit here and be humiliated in front of everyone. She stood up and flipped the crumpled blue book into the wastebasket on her way out the door.

"Fiona!" Lee Felderson called from the doorway.

"Go to hell!" she muttered. Laughter burst from the classroom as she hurried down the stairs into the cool night air. Well so much for college, she thought as she started her car and turned out of the parking lot in a dusty squeal. "Who needs it," she muttered. She'd been kidding herself. At this rate it would take thirteen years to graduate.

She'd be forty-three and probably still be working at the coffee shop, and by that time who'd even care if she had a degree or not. She sure as hell wouldn't. Jack, Ginny, and Elizabeth had done it the right way, the way they did everything, on time and diligently. The pieces had always fallen into place for them, while Fiona Range could never do things the simple way, the right way. "God damn it!" She banged the wheel with both hands. "I'm so sick and tired of you," she yelled at her grim reflection in the rearview mirror. "Always thinking you're so smart. Always thinking you know all the answers. Jesus Christ, you don't know anything about anything!"

The streetlights blurred as she sped into town. She shouldn't have stormed out like that. She knew herself too well. After the first misstep the next one always came easier. If she didn't turn around right now and walk back into that classroom and apologize, then she'd never return to school. Just like telling the family that her mother had called. Sometimes she didn't know where all the lies and anger came from. She pressed down on the accelerator.

At first I couldn't believe it, she'd once overheard Aunt Arlene say of her mother. *Every car that came by I'd think was her. That whole first year I kept thinking she'd be back. Every holiday I'd think, Well, she'll change her mind. She'll come back.*

She was going too fast as she came down Main Street. In the distance the light had just turned red. She took her foot off the gas pedal, but didn't brake. She didn't care. If the light turned green or stayed red, either way, she'd just sail on through, keep on driving until she was miles and weeks and, before she knew it, years gone from this phony place. Half a block to go and the light was still red. The speedometer showed fifty miles an hour. If anyone stepped into the street they'd be dead because she wasn't stopping. She'd go find some warm place where the sand was always sifting onto streets lined with palm trees. She'd write back to say she was with her mother and they were both very happy. "Don't try to find us," she said aloud. "It's better this way." The light was still red. Please don't let there be any cars coming through the intersection. She held her breath, then suddenly jammed on the brake. Todd Prescott was coming out of the liquor store with a six-pack in each hand. He opened the door of Sandy's dented red

Chevy Malibu and got in behind the wheel. Fiona's tires squealed as she pulled into the lot next to him. She rolled down the window.

"Hey!" she hollered as he looked over and smiled. "What the hell are you doing with Sandy Rudman's car?"

"Buying beer?" he said, lifting up a six-pack. "She ran out."

"What the hell are you doing? What are you thinking? She's just a kid!"

"Oh, no, Fee, you're not gonna bust me, are you?" He laughed.

"What do you want with her?" she asked, even angrier now as his grin widened. "Jesus, Todd! Don't go messing up her life any more than it already is.

"Are you kidding?" he called, starting the car. "I'm the best thing that's ever happened to Sandy. I am the proverbial man of her dreams!" He winked, then backed up and drove out.

Poor gullible Sandy. No wonder she'd been so late for work every morning, and so tired, and so happy. She probably thought she'd died and gone to heaven now with rich, handsome Todd Prescott in her life.

Fiona glanced up at the clock on the corner of the Dearborn Savings Bank. Twenty minutes to go until class ended. If she got on the highway and drove really fast she'd make it in time to apologize to Lee Felderson. And then what? She'd still have a D. She couldn't have studied any harder for that test than she had. And it would probably be the same next time, or worse. Yes, flunking Fiona Range would probably be the high point of Miss Pisspot's year.

"Screw it," she muttered, then turned and drove down the hill over the railroad tracks to the pay phone in front of the 24-hour store. What she needed most right now wasn't going to be found at Dearborn Community. She got out and opened the telephone book, looking for George's number. She ran her finger down the page, then stopped at GRADY, Patrick, surprised he had a phone, much less a listed number. Maybe the only reason was in the hope that Natalie might call. She wondered if he'd felt like Aunt Arlene in the beginning, listening for every car, thinking each time the phone rang it might be her. She remembered his hard, slitted eyes, the seething anger when she said her mother had called. Maybe it wasn't anger at all, but hurt and resentment that she had received the call instead of him. Maybe he had avoided, ignored, and denied her all these years not because he believed her another man's child but because she was the image of the woman he had always loved. Poor Patrick Grady. For the first time she felt sorrier for him than she did for herself.

She moved her finger up the next row of names.

"George!" she said to the sleepy answering voice. "This is Fiona. You're not asleep, are you?" It was nine-thirty.

"Not anymore."

Apologizing, she told him to go back to sleep. No, no, he said, he was glad she'd called. He'd been getting up so early for this latest job that he was in bed every night at nine.

"You haven't been in and I thought, well, maybe you were sick or something." She cringed. She'd been afraid all week that he'd heard something about her and Brad Glidden.

"No, I'm fine. It's just I have to be at the site by five every morning."

"Oh. Well, you said to let you know when my schoolwork was done. So this is the call!"

"Great! Well when would you like to go out?" he said, and she heard bedsprings squeaking.

She smiled. "How about tonight?"

"Tonight?" You mean now?"

"If that's okay. I mean if you don't mind."

"It'll take me a few minutes and then I'll be over."

"No, I'll come over there. I'm right around the corner."

He opened the door as she came up the porch steps. Barefoot, he'd managed to put on jeans and was still buttoning his shirt in such haste that he'd missed a button; one side was higher than the other. "Is everything okay?" He turned on a light in the den. "After you hung up I thought maybe something was wrong."

"No, not really." She shivered as she sat down on the sofa, its black vinyl cold against the back of her legs. She hugged herself to get warm. "I was just feeling kind of alone, and I remembered what you said about, well you know, being whatever I might need, a friend, or a plumber, or whatever."

"So which do you need?" He smiled down at her.

"Well right now the thing I need most is to get warm."

"Oh, the heat, it's not on," he said, turning up the thermostat. It shouldn't take too long for it to come up, he assured her, suggesting some cocoa or coffee or tea in the meantime. She didn't feel like any, she said. He'd get her a sweater then, he said, explaining that he was so accustomed to working in the cold that he seldom noticed it himself.

She patted the cushion. "If you'd just sit down I'll be warm in no time."

He smiled and sat down, blushing. His earlobes were red. "Now how come I didn't think of that?" He put his arm over the back of the couch.

"Maybe you're just out of practice."

"No to be honest I don't really have too many moves. I'm kind of"—he made a chopping gesture with his free hand—"you know, right straight on."

She laughed and made the same gesture. "What does that mean, right straight on?" She pulled his arm down over her shoulder and leaned into him with a shiver.

"Well it takes me a while. I mean, I'm just not loose enough. You know, I don't want to come on too strong. I don't want to take advantage or offend anybody."

"George, what are you talking about?"

"Well like that other night, here—I wanted you to stay, but I didn't say anything, then after you left I just felt like . . . I don't know." He sighed and shook his head.

"Like what?" She reached up to pull his head to hers. "Come on, tell me," she said against his lips. "What'd you feel like?"

"Like what Elizabeth called me our senior year when I finally told her I wasn't going to go to college, that I wanted to be a plumber with my father. She said the only reason was because I'd always been afraid to take a chance or to stand out, that it was safer being a shadow."

"You don't feel like a shadow to me," she said, touching his eyes, his bristly cheeks, his mouth. She had forgotten about her cousin's need to manage and refashion those she cared most about.

"She sent away for catalogs and she even filled out all the applications for me." He sighed deeply as if he still bore the weight of Elizabeth's disappointment.

Fiona sat back. "She was always like that. She wanted everyone else to be as good and as happy she was. It's the curse of the Hollises. They were born to do good."

He looked so perplexed that she patted his cheek and laughed. "I on the other hand was born to feel good. What about you, George?"

"Yah . . . I mean . . . well, like that night I wanted to be with you. I really did, and so there we were, and all of a sudden I start thinking, well, maybe I'm just so anxious myself I'm misreading the whole thing, so maybe the thing is to just slow down and not rush anything. You know, just take my time, wait and see what happens."

"Um," she agreed, kissing him again. "Good idea, George, we can do that. So let's just take our time here and see what happens."

He was on top of her. The pillows had fallen off the couch and now the slippery vinyl cushions were sliding out from under them. The lampshade was crooked and her tossed skirt had landed on the recliner. His jeans were on the coffee table. She had never realized what a powerful man he was. The muscles in his back were thick as coiled rope. He was not only decent, but strong and sweet. He was everything she needed. He kept trying to tell her something. She begged him not to talk. He wanted her to go upstairs with him. She'd be more comfortable in his bed. She was very comfortable, she said. It would be better there, he said. Promise? she said, holding on to his hand as she followed him up the dark stairs.

Afterwards, they lay covered by a sheet. She stared up at the bright gashes of moonlight down the sides of the window shade. She felt strangely, acutely awake, as if every nerve ending in her body were being electrically charged. Her brain was a network of flashing, buzzing connections and long-ago voices. Why did you do that? Aunt Arlene was asking as she scrubbed grit from the raw cut on her knee. Children's shrieks burst into the room. Fiona was the one! She did it on purpose! She smashed the cold frame that sheltered Uncle Charles's seedlings. It was Fiona! She pushed the doll carriage into the pond. Fiona did it! She pulled down her underpants in front of all the boys. We told her not to, but she did it anyway! Fiona!

"Fiona?" George called from far away, and she turned, startled to see him on his side smiling at her. "Can I get you anything? Glass of water? Blanket? Pajamas?"

"Just hold me."

He pulled her close, and she buried her face in his chest, timing her breathing to his.

"I saw Elizabeth the other day," he said after a few minutes.

"Oh yah? Where?" she asked, easing back her head.

"I saw her driving down Main Street, so I hit the horn and she pulled over. I got out and then we talked for a while." He paused as if expecting a question. "Anyway, she looks good. A little too thin though. I almost said something, but then she said she's been training for the Marathon." Fiona rolled over and reached onto the floor for her underwear.

"She said you met her fiancé." He paused and cleared his throat. "Did you like him?"

"Yah, I did. He seems nice enough. A hyper kind of guy, but with a pretty good sense of humor." She stood up and pulled on her panties. "And he's crazy about her," she added, and his silence confirmed the nagging thought she'd had while they were making love: that it was Elizabeth he'd been thinking of the whole time.

Chapter 5

F iona glanced in the mirror as she ran by. She still didn't like the way she looked. Heaps of clothes littered the bed and the floor. She had tried on just about everything in her closet. Nothing felt right. Ever since Elizabeth had called her at work and invited her to dinner she'd had this tightness like a fist in her chest. There had been an urgency, a breathless edge in her cousin's voice.

She began to feel better though as she drove to the restaurant. She couldn't remember the last time she and Elizabeth had spent any time together. She turned onto Main Street and looked for a parking space near Verzanno's. Elizabeth had said one of the doctors Rudy worked with loved it. He wasn't going to dinner with them, but it would probably be like that all night: Rudy this and Rudy that, the same way Elizabeth had been with George: George likes peas; George thinks I should keep my hair long; George says . . .

Smiling, she backed into a space near the corner. She had been with George every night this week. He had called her at work this morning, but when she finally was able to call him back he wasn't there. She had left a message on his machine saying she was going to dinner with Elizabeth and that she'd be home after nine. He couldn't understand how she could live without a telephone. He had offered to help her pay off her old bill, but she didn't want the relationship to start with George deciding what she should and shouldn't do. The other night he had asked why she always wore such tight things, then seeing her eyes flare, tried to squirm his way out of it by asking, weren't tight clothes really uncomfortable? Not at all, she'd said, with a level stare. She liked the way they looked and the way they felt.

As she came down the street she noticed the ladder in front of the Wishing Well Gift Shop. Patrick Grady stood halfway up washing the small-paned picture window. He sprayed another pane, then leaned forward scrubbing intently. When his hand faltered then darted back to the glass, she knew he had seen her reflection.

"Hello," she called, but he didn't stop scrubbing or look back. "Looks good. You're doing a good job," she said.

He sprayed the next pane, set down the bottle, and began to work his rag into the corners. He hunched over the ladder.

"Oh, am I bothering you?" She went to the foot of the ladder. "Or maybe you can't hear me. I can talk louder," she said, voice rising. She cupped her hands to her mouth. "Is this better? Can you hear me now?" she called.

"Get outta here!" he said, turning, and her stomach weakened with his hateful expression. She thought of him years ago, handsome and fearless, poised on the highest ledge of the quarry while shrieking girls begged him not to dive. Had her mother been among them? Calling to him, begging him not to. Her aunt said Natalie had begged him not to go to Vietnam. Such a waste, all that loss and pain.

"It's a public sidewalk." She folded her arms. "I can stand here as long as I want."

He dumped his rags and bottle into a plastic bucket, then scurried down the ladder.

"What's the matter?" she asked as he yanked a rope that brought the top half of the ladder down with a metal-scraping clang. "Why can't you talk to me?" She followed him into the alley where he swung open the rear door of his old blue station wagon and tossed his supplies inside. "You said I should be afraid, but you're the one that seems afraid. Why? Do you think I want something from you? That I'm going to start calling you Daddy or something?" She laughed and followed him alongside the car. She asked if he had any idea how ridiculous this was after all these years. "I mean, I'm thirty years old."

He started the engine as soon as he got in. She leaned down at his window. "I just want to—"

"Get the hell away from me, will you?" he growled.

"I just want to be able to talk to you, that's all!" she was shouting into a cyclone of dust as he sped out of the alley.

Red candles flickered in wax-ribbed Chianti bottles. The low, arched stucco ceiling shimmered with light and shadows. The cavelike little dining room seemed even darker with its damp redolence of garlic and red wine. The minute she saw her cousin she felt better. Elizabeth sat at a small table in the far corner. She smiled as Fiona hurried toward her. "I know, late as usual," Fiona said with a hug, alarmed that Elizabeth felt so fragile. She drew back carefully, hand extended as if to catch whatever bones she had dislodged.

The waitress took their drink orders, a daiquiri for Elizabeth and a beer for Fiona. The minute she left Fiona blurted, "God, Lizzie, you're so skinny! What's going on? Are you all right?"

"Actually, I'm in training," Elizabeth said, grinning.

"For what, a death march?"

Elizabeth laughed. "I'm running the Marathon next April, so I'm getting ready now."

"April! Well at this rate you'll be in the wheelchair competition. If you're lucky," she added, reluctant to say more. There had always been the sense in the family that calling attention to problems only made them worse.

"Well there's just been so much going on," Elizabeth said with a weary sigh. "With Daddy being sick and trying to get Rudy settled. We finally found a place he likes on Salem Street. It's right by the hospital."

"What's wrong with Uncle Charles?"

"He was having chest pains so we took him into Boston. The General kept him a couple of days and ran all kinds of tests, and everything came up negative. Fiona!" Elizabeth leaned closer and touched her hand. "You should see the look on your face. The tests were negative. He's fine."

"I didn't know he was sick! Why didn't anyone tell me?" She was stunned.

"You don't have a phone, Fiona."

"You could have called me at work. You called me there today."

"But that's different. You know how private they are about things like that," Elizabeth said in a low voice. "And Daddy didn't want people to know."

"People! Is that what I am? Jesus Christ!"

Elizabeth's back stiffened, her fine blond hair swishing back and forth over her shoulders. Her delicate jaw sharpened to a point like her father's, who she resembled more than any of them. "You know that's not what I meant," she said.

"Then why didn't anyone tell me?"

"It was all so fast." Elizabeth explained that the pains had started late at night, after the engagement dinner.

"It was me, wasn't it? When I said that about my mother." That's why no one had told her.

"You mean your mother's phone call? Of course not! No, we were all so happy for you, you know that." Elizabeth leaned forward, intrigued as ever by the mystery of Natalie. "I'm dying to know. Has she called again?"

"Obviously not. I don't have a phone, do I?'

"Then how did she call before?" Elizabeth asked, watching so carefully Fiona knew this question had already been raised among the family.

"It was last summer. In my old apartment."

"Why didn't you tell us then?"

"When? At the family banishment?" Her voice rose. "If you'll remember, no one wanted to hear anything I had to say!"

"Oh Fiona. Fiona," Elizabeth coaxed, taking her hand. "Let's just be happy. Please? It's so much easier."

Yes, for some people, she thought, watching her cousin's easy smile as the waitress served their drinks. Even as a little girl when Fiona had been sent to her room, convinced that no one cared or understood, there was always Elizabeth slipping notes under her locked door. "Just be good," she would write. "That's all Mommy and Daddy want. Just try."

The waitress asked if they wanted to order now. Someone else was coming, Elizabeth said. "Rudy," she told Fiona. "I told him seven to give us some time alone."

"Oh." Fiona smiled to hide her disappointment. She should have known there would be the same lockstep marital intensity in this relationship as well. She still remembered walking by the barbershop once when they were fifteen and seeing Elizabeth primly reading a magazine like someone's mother or wife while George got his hair cut.

"I try and keep him busy," Elizabeth said. Even though Rudy insisted he was happy here, Dearborn had to be so boring after New York. "He's so intense. He's one of those high-energy people; you know, they don't walk, they run. He's always got to be doing something."

Fiona blinked with the image of him racing down from his car to bandage Todd Prescott's cut.

"In two days he not only built bookshelves, but he painted his entire apartment," Elizabeth said.

"His apartment?" Fiona interrupted. "Don't you live there too?"

"No, I'm still at home."

"You're kidding!"

"Well, I stay there sometimes."

"Conjugal visits, well, I hope so!" She laughed. Elizabeth's pinched expression drew Fiona forward to add softly, "I mean, after all, Elizabeth, you are engaged. And the wedding's not until next fall." Elizabeth stared at her with almost virginal discomfort. "Well, you're not going to be living at home that whole time, are you?"

"I might," Elizabeth said, an edge coming into her voice. "And I might not."

"But why? That seems so . . . unnecessary." Unnatural, she had almost said.

It was her mother and father, Elizabeth tried to explain. They needed her there. She couldn't put her finger on it; they weren't sick or anything, but they seemed tired, weary, older, sad. That was it. Yes, sad. "Sometimes they just seem so sad," she said.

Dreading the answer, Fiona refused to ask why. If she'd only be good. If she'd only just try. That's all they wanted. This summer had been an important lesson. She had told them the absolute truth, but they had assumed the worst. And it would always be this way. They expected her to fail, and always would.

Elizabeth was saying how much she loved being back, seeing old friends and familiar faces all the time. "Oh, and I ran into George last week," she said. "He said he sees you in the coffee shop sometimes."

George. Fiona grinned.

"He looked tired. Poor George, he always seems so alone." Elizabeth sighed.

"I wouldn't worry too much about poor George." She winked. "He does all right."

"I don't know. He looked so sad, I thought," Elizabeth said, and Fiona began to chew her lip. It would be her cousin's only vanity to assume that with her absence everyone's life had stopped. "Speaking of sad," Elizabeth continued, "yesterday I ran into Ann Lewis, and she told me that Krissy Glidden's moved back home with her parents." She leaned across the table and whispered, "Apparently, the night after their baby was born Brad got drunk and slept with some woman."

"Who was she?" Fiona held her gaze as the reason both for this meeting and the fiancé's delayed arrival became clear. Ann Lewis had been Elizabeth's best friend in high school. So now everyone knew. The family had sent their kindest emissary to deal with her most vile transgression yet. She recognized the plea in her cousin's anxious eyes. Why do you keep doing these terrible things? What's wrong with you?

"Ann wouldn't tell me." Elizabeth glanced at her watch. "But listen, before Rudy gets here, there's something I want to ask you." She took Fiona's hands in hers. Elizabeth's mouth quivered and her eyes glistened with tears.

Fiona's heart was racing. All right, she would tell the truth, not that it was any kind of excuse, but Glidden had taken advantage of her when she'd had too much to drink. No, better to just deny everything. It was her word against his.

"Fiona, will you be my maid of honor?"

"Oh Jesus!" she gasped. "Your maid of honor?"

"I know. I know how you feel about all that kind of fussing, but you can pick out any style dress you want, I don't care. Please?"

"Of course! It's just I'm so surprised. I can't believe you're asking me and not Ginny, your own sister. Or Ann even."

Elizabeth looked surprised. "Don't you remember our promise when we were little?"

"Yes, but . . ." Fiona's eyes filled so suddenly with tears that she didn't see Rudy Larkin until he'd pulled out the chair and was sitting down.

"Well, this looks like fun. Dinner with two weeping women!" he said, making them laugh and cry more as they blew their noses and tried to explain how happy they both were.

At first Rudy seemed bigger than Fiona remembered. After a while she realized it wasn't height or bulk so much as inner animation, a centrifugal energy that was both magnetic and expansive, like a rising storm that made one's hair stand on end as it gathered force. His rich, gutsy laugh immediately drew people's smiling attention. When he spoke his hands were in constant motion, drawing circles, arcs of pleasure and astonishment, a sudden right angle now as he grimaced with Elizabeth's plea to lower his voice. Gripping the table as if to contain himself, he apologized, genuinely concerned that he might have disturbed the other diners. In the wake of such exuberance Elizabeth seemed small and pale, though it was as clear here as it had been at their engagement dinner that she was very much in charge. She would let him get just so far, then with a sharp look or sigh could quickly subdue him. In a deft movement now she pushed back his hair and straightened his wrinkled tie.

"She thinks I'm a mess," he said, laughing.

"I do not!" Elizabeth cried, her voice just a little shrill, almost brittle with her second daiquiri. Fiona was surprised to see Elizabeth eating more than either of them. "I think you're just one of those geniuses who never spend any time on themselves."

"Well a smart mess, then," Rudy said with a wink at Fiona, and as if for emphasis a last slurp of his ginger ale.

"Then you're perfect for one another. Elizabeth is a born nurturer," Fiona said, and they both looked relieved. She had been quiet through most of dinner. The few times she had spoken, Rudy's attention became so acutely focused that she almost felt as if she were being studied. It was unsettling the way he could click so much ebullience on and off. And yet Fiona had often enough had to work herself back into Elizabeth's good graces to recognize the syndrome. For some reason the man was walking on eggshells. He seemed far more anxious not to displease his fiancée than he was to please her. But then again, she thought, it might be his clinical nature as well as the fact that they were drinking and he was not. She had assumed his sobriety was because he was on call tonight, until Elizabeth said he never touched alcohol. She watched him pop an ice cube into his mouth. Teetotalers made her uneasy, self-conscious about her own drinking.

"See, I knew that the minute I saw her," Rudy said. He began to tell Fiona about their first meeting. He'd been working nights at the City Hospital Clinic to pay off medical school loans. The clinic served the city's poor, the elderly, some teenagers, but mostly street people. It was a late Saturday night, and he had just stitched up a drunken woman's forehead when a volunteer from the Women's Shelter stepped into the room to see if he was done. She had been waiting to drive the woman back.

"'There she is!' the drunken woman bellowed." Rudy laughed. "'The one that did this to me! Call the police! I want her arrested and I'll be down first thing in the morning to testify.'"

"What did you say?" Fiona asked Elizabeth, against whose sincere and simple goodness irony usually collided with a dull little thud.

"I didn't know what to say!" Elizabeth said, shaking her head.

"She froze!" Rudy laughed. "She just stood there."

"Well tell her why!" Elizabeth insisted, eyes wide with feigned exasperation.

He shrugged. "All I did was ask the obvious question. I asked her why she'd hit this sweet old lady, and she just stood there, turning ten different shades of red, sputtering on about how it was all a mistake, and I didn't understand."

It had happened last winter, but it still made him laugh so hard he could barely speak. Fiona looked between them and smiled. In their life together he would tell this story hundreds more times to friends and acquaintances, to children and grandchildren. It was the same with Uncle Charles and Aunt Arlene, the story of their meeting, legendary, the intersection of two lives from which a family had begun; the struggling young lawyer who had fallen in love with his accomplished secretary, but fearing rejection spoke to her only when necessary, until the day the serious young woman walked in and gave her notice. When asked why, she said she couldn't work for someone who didn't like her. "Don't like you! I love you!" Uncle Charles had supposedly blurted to a startled and confused Aunt Arlene.

Now came Elizabeth's part of the tale. "And then he looked out into the hall and made believe he was talking to a policeman, calling him 'officer' in this loud voice, and he said he'd not only see to it that Wilma got safely back to the shelter, but he'd take her there himself!"

"Oh God, what a pickup artist," Fiona groaned, easily imagining Elizabeth's consternation.

"So I thought!" Rudy said. "But then all the way back to the shelter Wilma's sitting as far as she can away from Elizabeth, cringing and muttering how she better not touch her again, and it's a good thing I'm there to protect her. In fact Wilma's even starting to come on to me a little . . ."

"Tell her why!" Elizabeth prompted.

"Well, I was only telling her how she should just relax, that I wasn't going to let anything happen to her."

"So in other words what you had going was a double pickup, right?" Fiona pointed out.

"Well it would have been, except I finally got Wilma out of the car and into the shelter when Elizabeth here runs out to thank me and to tell me how she hadn't wanted to say anything for fear of getting Wilma all riled up again, but she wanted me to know she absolutely hadn't had anything to do with her injury. Can you believe it?" he said, laughing so hard that the people at the next table turned and smiled.

Elizabeth grabbed his hand. "Shh," she said. "Everyone's listening."

"I believe it," Fiona said, then recounted a similar tale of Elizabeth's naïveté years back when they were children.

"No! Oh no!" He laughed, and Elizabeth was laughing too, when she suddenly stood up and said she'd be right back. She hurried off to the ladies' room.

"She's not sick, is she?" Fiona asked, sensing Rudy's concern as he watched her go.

He took a deep breath as if to say something, then thought better of it. He began to crimp an empty sugar packet, as preoccupied with the tiny folds as she was with the awkward silence.

"So what do you think of dear old Dearborn?" she asked.

He looked up now with that odd sudden intensity that in anyone else would have seemed overwrought. "It's beautiful! I love it! I feel like I've lived here for years."

"Well, when you have, you probably won't think it's quite so beautiful."

"Why? Why do you say that?" he asked in great earnestness.

"Well, nothing's ever as beautiful as you first think. It's all on the surface. You just haven't noticed all the cracks and the mucky things yet."

"You're probably right," he said, chuckling. "But then don't forget, after you live with the cracks and the mucky things long enough you stop seeing them."

"I still do."

"Maybe that's because you're looking for them."

"No, that's because I'm a realist. I see things exactly the way they are," she said, irritated by his smugness.

"Well, don't you think most people do?"

"No! I know they don't."

"But most people accept the fact that everything's flawed one way or another. We all make mistakes."

So here it was. She glared at him. "And what the hell do you mean by that?"

He burst out laughing. "Well not whatever the hell you're thinking!"

"I know what you mean," she said in a low voice. "I know exactly what you mean. That day. That day of the dinner. In the field? I had handcuffs on? I think you remember, and that's what you meant, isn't it?"

He frowned and rubbed his chin. "You know, you may be right."

"All right, good! Then let's just get it right out on the table here and now. Have you told Elizabeth yet?"

"No. I haven't!"

"Are you going to? Because the thing is, I don't care if you do tell her, I really don't, as long as I know, but I don't want to spend the next ten years every time I see you thinking, okay, this is it, what's he going to say?"

He looked at her, shaking his head, eyes wide, and then he began to laugh so hard the candle on the table flickered and sputtered. The woman behind him turned to look.

"Can I help you?" Fiona asked, and the woman spun around.

He shook his head. "I'll tell you the truth. No, I'm not going to say anything, but . . . ," and now he was laughing again. "But I'm dying to know. Would you please tell me? Every time I think of it I crack up! I mean, one minute, there you are, cuffed to a cruiser, and then the next thing I know, we're being introduced like I've never seen this woman in my life before, and we're passing each other stuffing and gravy, and we both know what just happened."

"It's a long story," she said, laughing also, though not quite with the same relish. She told him about her stalled car and Todd offering to give her a ride in the car he said was his. "I guess the bottom line is I've always had too many jerks in my life." She glanced toward the back of the restaurant. "She's been in there an awful long time. Lizzie's not much of a drinker. Maybe I should go see." Just as she got up, Elizabeth appeared, walking quickly toward the table.

"We were beginning to think you went home." Rudy stared at her as she sat down.

"Now why would you think that?" she said with a bright smile.

After dinner they walked down Essex Street to Dusty's Grill. When they were seated, Elizabeth asked her to run with them at sunrise, but Fiona couldn't because she had to be at work so early. Rudy drank black coffee. Fiona and Elizabeth had both ordered Jack Daniel's and Coke, but Elizabeth's was almost gone. Elizabeth seemed to think she had to shout to be heard. She kept grinning up at Rudy and leaning her head on his shoulder.

"When we were in high school Fiona was the fastest runner on the track team and then she quit," Elizabeth told him, then peered across the table as if through mist. "Why'd you quit? I never understood that. You were so good."

"I don't know, I probably got self-conscious or something," she said. What she had gotten was thrown off the team for drinking on the bus after an out-of-town meet.

"Self-conscious! You?" Elizabeth said, pointing. "You don't have a self-conscious bone in your body, Fiona Range. She doesn't," she insisted to Rudy, who nodded pleasantly.

Fiona smiled, but under the table her foot tapped irritably as her thoughts reeled with images of dancing with Goldie the dog, then with Larry Belleau, and now she could almost hear the ratcheting clamor of Patrick Grady's ladder as he rushed to get away from her. She was tired. Soon everyone in town would know that she was the woman Brad Glidden had slept with. She took another sip. Screw it. He'd been the one married with the newborn baby. He was the one with vows to honor. Not her. He was the one who had done something wrong. Not her. Elizabeth asked how her class was going. Okay, she said. She wanted to go home. Now Elizabeth asked in a slurred voice if Lee Felderson was a good teacher. Fee Lelderson, she kept saying. She was all right, Fiona said. Elizabeth was trying to tell Rudy that Lee had been one of Ginny's best friends. It was hot in here, the music was too loud, and it was painful to see Elizabeth laboring at this. Rudy had grown very quiet, a faint smile the only trace of his earlier animation. He was stirring an empty cup. A surge of protesting voices rose from the bar and he craned his neck to see what was going on.

"Any of your friends in here?" Elizabeth asked, and the minute Fiona said no, she knew what was coming.

"Fiona used to be in here all the time," Elizabeth told Rudy loudly. "Once she got in this big fight with somebody and the bartender told her to leave, and she wouldn't, so they called my father to come get her. He couldn't believe it. She was only seventeen, but Fiona always had the best fake IDs, didn't you, Fee?" she asked, though it was Rudy she was beaming at as she tried to impress him with Fiona's misadventures.

"Only the best," Fiona said, looking down, as Elizabeth continued.

"Anyway, while my father was trying to get her out, the bartender called her a bad name or something, and my father grabbed him and said if he said one more word to her he'd have him arrested for serving a minor. I still remember that night. He was so mad. And then the next morning it was the same as always. Like nothing had ever happened. I never understood how you did that. How'd you do that, Fiona?" Elizabeth's heavy eyes were half closed.

"Charm," Fiona said softly.

"The least little thing and we'd be in trouble," Elizabeth went on. "Especially Jack. Poor Jack, he was always being lectured, punished, grounded, but not Fiona."

"Ah, the strange convolutions of family dynamics," Rudy said, with a quick gesture to the waiter for the bill.

"Rudy was an only child," Elizabeth told Fiona as she cocooned her arms around his. "It was just him and his mother. It's an amazing story. Most of the time he had to take care of her, she was in and out of mental hospitals so much."

"Elizabeth, stop. That's so personal," Fiona said. The waiter stood by the table while Rudy got out his credit card.

"But it's so amazing," Elizabeth continued. "I admire him so much. I think of it and I just want to cry. Can you imagine? A little boy and he had to go buy groceries and cook and just do everything, didn't you?" she asked, as oblivious to the waiter's leaving as she was now to his return.

"Deprivation has its advantages," Rudy said as he signed the slip. "We ate what I liked, and I could watch television all night." He looked up and smiled. "Days on end if I wanted."

"You poor thing," Elizabeth said, nuzzling her chin against his arm. "Poor Rudy."

"I came and went as I pleased," he said to Fiona. "And I never had a curfew."

"Lucky you," she said, annoyed to see Elizabeth as easily intoxicated by alcohol as by the sadness in his life. She wanted to go.

"I was." He laughed. "In my way. I still am."

"Wait!" Elizabeth said as Fiona started to get up. "What about

Todd?" Elizabeth looked around as if he might be here. "Have you seen him lately?"

"I try not to," Fiona said as Rudy tried to tell Elizabeth they should go.

"Todd's father owns the classiest furniture store in Massachusetts," Elizabeth said, ignoring him. "He and Fiona started going steady in junior high. My father had a fit. They were always together and he was just the wildest boy in town, but he had this big deal, important family, you know, so there wasn't much my father could do." She gave a little hiccup. "Was there, Fiona?" She giggled. "Nobody could tie Daddy up in knots the way Fiona could. None of us. No matter what she did. He'd get so mad, but he never seemed to know what to do, did he, Fee?" She laughed as if this were some remarkable achievement. "God, you always ran circles around my poor father." She closed her eyes and rubbed her head against Rudy's shoulder. "She still does, don't you, Fee?" she purred.

"Well if I don't," Fiona said, conscious of Rudy's uneasy smile, "the man's going to be taken straight up to heaven, body and soul. I just keep him human."

Elizabeth doubled over with laughter. "It's true. It's so true!" she gasped, then buried her face in her hands and burst into tears.

"Lizzie!" Fiona said. "I was only kidding!"

"I know! I know." Elizabeth wept. "Here I am with two of the most wonderful people in the whole world, and look at me. I'm a wreck." Elizabeth wept into her cocktail napkin. "I'm just a wreck."

"You're just a little drunk, Lizzie, that's all," Fiona whispered in her cousin's ear. Rudy had picked up Elizabeth's purse and now he was helping her into her coat.

"I'm sorry," Elizabeth said when they got outside. "I really wanted this to be a happy night."

"It was," Rudy said softly.

"It still is!" Fiona added, then saw the stricken look on his face and her cousin's frozen smile. The only sound was the dry rasp and drag of their feet through the fallen leaves.

■

There was a note from George duct-taped to Fiona's door. She winced reading it. She had completely forgotten the message she had left on his machine that she'd be home at nine. He had come by at nine, waited a while in his van, and then he'd driven to Verzanno's to see if she might still be there. He had come back here then and waited a half hour or so until ten-thirty. I'VE BEEN WORRIED, he had printed in bold letters. I'LL SEE YOU TOMORROW. GEORGE. She paused in the doorway, considering whether or not to drive to the 24-hour store and call from the pay phone, but she was too tired, and George was probably sound asleep by now. She waded through mounds of clothing and crawled into bed.

The doorbell rang at five-thirty. No. Not Elizabeth and Rudy. She squinted through one eye. It was still dark outside. She was sure she had told them she wouldn't be running. The doorbell rang again. Typically though, once Elizabeth got it into her head that something would be good for you she would not be dissuaded. Groaning and shivering in just her bra and panties, she rolled out of bed and groped her way to the door, which she opened the merest crack. "Just go without me. I'm still asleep. I'm sorry," she mumbled, closing the door.

"Fiona!"

"George!" She opened it quickly.

"I just wanted to be sure you were okay before I left for work." He was holding two small white bags.

"I'm okay," she said, teeth chattering with the early-morning cold. "I just have to get back to bed."

As he followed her into the bedroom he said that he had stopped at the bakery and gotten doughnuts and coffee. "But if you're too tired," he said, setting a bag on the nightstand, "you can have yours later."

"I'm not that tired." She crawled back into bed. "I'll have mine now." She smiled as he sat on the edge of the bed and opened one of the bags. "Cream or sugar?"

"Neither," she said, slipping her hand up under his shirt.

"Are you sure?" he asked, letting her rub his back while he unbuttoned his shirt.

"I'm sure." She watched him stand up to take off his dark blue work pants. He folded them over the back of the chair. He was so neat and the room was such a mess. He stood over the bed and she held up her arms. She was glad it was dark, glad he was on top of her now, heavy and warm, so freshly shaved his cheeks were smooth and soft and sweet. He was sweet, he was sweet, he was so sweet, she kept whispering in his ear as he said her name over and over again, panting it in that soft voice that now at the end came like tears, a ragged, pleading sob. "Fiona. Fiona. Fiona, oh my God, Fiona."

Just then the bedroom door opened and the overhead light suddenly came on as he collapsed against her.

"Fiona, we came . . . Oh, oh, I'm . . . I thought . . . ," Elizabeth cried, then slammed the door. Dazed in the sudden glare, Fiona and George both reached to cover themselves. George had grabbed a blue-and-white miniskirt, which he held to his groin, and Fiona hugged her pillow in front of her.

"I don't believe it," she groaned, getting out of bed. She grabbed her bathrobe and turned out the light. She opened the bedroom door and peeked out at Rudy and Elizabeth in running pants and sweatshirts. They stood by the front door.

"I can't believe it. I'm so embarrassed," Elizabeth whispered. Her eyes were closed and her fists were clenched in front of her.

"I told you not to barge in like that," Rudy said.

"Oh my God, oh my God, oh my God," Elizabeth gasped, shoulders heaving as if to vomit.

"Come on, stop that now," Rudy said, trying to face her, but she turned, cringing away from him. "Come on, let's go. Let's just go!" he insisted.

"Oh my God, oh my God."

"Elizabeth!" Fiona said. She closed the bedroom door behind her.

"I'm sorry," Elizabeth cried, then buried her stricken face in her hands. "Oh, I can't believe I did that."

Rudy touched Elizabeth's shoulder and she recoiled with a high bleating sound.

"For godsakes, will you stop it?" Fiona demanded, coming closer to her cousin, who was sobbing uncontrollably now. "I said stop it!"

Wincing, Elizabeth tried to look at her. "I'm sorry," she gasped, then glanced toward the bedroom door. "He must be so embarrassed. I'm so sorry."

"Then why don't you just go?" Fiona said in a low voice.

"Come on," Rudy said, taking her arm.

"But I don't know what to do," Elizabeth bawled. "I'm so sorry, and I don't know what to do."

"You don't have to do anything, honey," Rudy coaxed. "Just come with me, that's all."

"But I do. You don't understand. I do. I do. I do. I have to do something. I do! I do!" she cried, slapping one hand against the other.

"You could leave," Fiona hissed in disgust. "That'd help."

"Come on now," Rudy said, easing her into the hallway.

Fiona closed the door, then pressed her ear against it as Elizabeth's soft weeping dissolved down the steps and into the vestibule. "I don't believe this!" she muttered, returning to the bedroom where George sat on the foot of the bed with his head in his hands. Completely dressed, he had even attempted to make the bed. To hide the evidence, she thought, in case Elizabeth came charging through the door again.

"Jesus Christ." He looked up. His eyes were red-rimmed and bloodshot from being rubbed. "What just happened?"

"Well, let me see," she said, aggravated by the pain in his voice. "I think we'd both just climaxed when Elizabeth burst into the bedroom. What the hell do you think just happened?"

He chewed his thumbnail and stared down at the floor. "Was that him I heard, the fiancé?"

"Yah. Rudy. That was him, the fiancé."

George got up with a heavy sigh and shook his head. "That was awful." He walked past her into the living room, then stood by the door with his hand on the knob.

"The door must've been unlocked," she said. "Maybe I left it open. But still you don't just go charging into someone's bedroom like that."

"I never heard her that upset before." His eyes were dark and heavy with concern. "Never."

"Well I'd say this was probably a unique experience for Elizabeth."

She cleared her throat against the hysteria, this virulence rising in her chest. "Don't you think?"

"I think something's wrong, terribly, terribly wrong, that's what I think," he said almost angrily as he opened the door.

"And what's that supposed to mean?" she shot back. Seeing his blank look, she threw up her hands in exasperation. "What about me? How do you think I feel?"

He continued to regard her with vague perplexity as if trying to recall her name. "I know," he muttered with a distracted kiss on her forehead.

"George!" she called as he went into the hallway.

He looked back, then stopped at the top of the stairs when she said his name again. She ran and threw her arms around him, but he stood rigidly in her fierce embrace.

"I better go now. I'm sorry," he said, pulling away.

Chapter 6

The cold, rainy week had been like today's lunch hour, dreary and slow. "I don't know why you won't go to the walk-in," Maxine said, following Fiona into the kitchen. "You're just going to get sicker and make everybody else sick too. And it's probably some kind of code violation, waiting on healthy people when you've got the flu."

"I told you, it's not the flu," Fiona said. She pulled a chair close to the warm stove and sat down. All she wanted right now was to be left alone. For the last three days she'd had a headache and a shaky stomach made worse a while ago when she saw Todd Prescott dropping Sandy off at work. He had driven away in her car with the two little girls in the backseat.

"Oh, it's the flu," Maxine insisted. She knew five people with the exact same symptoms and they all had it. "You gotta get some penicillin or something. I'll give you a ride. I'll even wait in the waiting room."

"Maxine, look, I don't have the flu, I don't have insurance, so forget the walk-in. Please," she groaned, huddling close to the stove.

"Here." Chester handed her a mug of chicken broth. "That's better than penicillin."

"Oh good! You want to get sick too! Then what happens? Then what do we do?" Maxine said, sounding so panicky that Chester laughed.

"What? What're you talking about, I want to get sick?" he said.

"You must, or else you'd go get your free flu shot at the Senior Center," Maxine said.

Fiona sipped the broth and looked from one to the other. Her aunt and uncle's disagreements had always taken place quietly, in private. For the most serious discussions they would get in the car and go for a ride. If it hadn't been for the days of exaggerated formality that sometimes passed between them, Fiona would have sworn they never argued.

"I haven't been sick in twenty-five years," Chester said. "And I'm not about to let anyone inject me with live germs, no sir, thank you, ma'am!" he called as Maxine stalked back into the dining room.

"She thinks everything she touches is gonna turn to crap. Including me," he said as the door swung in and out.

"She just wants you to stay healthy."

"She just wants me to stay," he said.

"Same thing, isn't it?"

He glanced back irritably. "What're you hanging around here for? Why don't you go home?"

"I'm okay." She dreaded the thought of another lonely night in that cluttered little apartment. At least her phone was supposed to be turned back on today. She hadn't seen or heard from George since that miserable morning last week. She hadn't heard from Elizabeth either. She looked up now as a loud knock drummed on the back door.

"You should've called," Chester told the huge man in the doorway. Rain dripped off his enormous orange poncho, and when he pulled the hood back, Fiona recognized him as Stanley, the same red-faced man who had been in here two weeks ago talking to Chester. Maxine had been getting her hair done, and Fiona was supposed to let Chester know when she got back. Chester seemed even more nervous today. He kept glancing toward the dining room.

Stanley slipped a manila envelope from under his poncho. "I know. But here," he said, handing it to Chester, who put it on top of the refrigerator. "I didn't want to wait."

"Okay, okay, okay," Chester said, walking him to the door. "Give me a couple days though," he called into the rain rattling down on the tin canopy. "I'll call and let you know."

"What's that all about?" she asked when he closed the door.

"Nothing." He opened the refrigerator and stared into its bleak light.

"All right," he said, closing it. "I gotta tell somebody." He grinned. "That was Stanley Masters!"

"Who's he?"

"You know, Masters, the Bagel Master! The guy on TV! They want to put a Bagel-Master in here." He pulled down the limp, rain-streaked enveloped. "That's how bad he wants it. He brought it over himself, the purchase and sale agreement."

"What about Maxine?"

"I didn't want to say anything until I had something in writing."

"You think she's going to like the idea?"

Chester came close and tweaked her chin. "One look at this, and she's gonna love it," he said with a flap of the envelope.

Her head hurt even more. A Bagel-Master. It was mostly take-out business. High school kids worked in Bagel-Masters. The downhill track of her life was steepening. Yesterday a letter had come from Dearborn Community with Lee Felderson's name on the envelope. She had thrown it away unopened.

The door flew open and Maxine ran into the kitchen, grinning and gesturing for her to come. "Guess who's out there? Your uncle! Judge Hollis! He just came in. He wants to see you!"

"My uncle? What's he want?" The only other time Uncle Charles had come in was six years ago when she had first started. He and Aunt Arlene left her a twenty-five-dollar tip. A few days later he summoned her to his office and offered her a job as a file clerk in the courthouse. She told him she couldn't think of a more boring job than filing. At least as a waitress she met a lot of different people and the time went by faster. But waitressing, he tired to explain, was something one did on their way to something else. She certainly didn't want to be doing it all her life, did she? Why not? she said; she'd probably make as much if not more than a file clerk. But it wasn't just the money, he said; it was security and self-esteem. Whose self-esteem? she had said, noting that hers was fine so he obviously meant his own, which was his problem, not hers.

"He said just coffee, but I want to bring out something special," Maxine said, looking around the kitchen. "But don't say anything. He'll just say no, and I want to surprise him."

Uncle Charles was sitting in the window booth where Maxine always displayed her most notable guests. Still in his wet trenchcoat, he hunched over the table, as if this were the last place he wanted to be.

"Hello, Uncle Charles!" When she bent to kiss him his hand trembled as he set his cup clinking against the saucer. He looked deeply tired, as if he hadn't slept in days. There were circles under his eyes and his pale cheeks were mottled with spidery red blotches.

"Well you're certainly looking fine," he said.

Recognizing the tone, she tried not to be irritated. Accentuate the positive. If it's not right, think it, wish it, pretend it's right.

"Wouldn't have anything to do with you and George Grimshaw, would it?" he added with a nod.

"What? What do you mean?" she said, hands clenched in her lap. Elizabeth must have told him.

"Well, haven't you two been spending some time together?" He smiled. "Seeing each other? Dating? I'm not sure what the other euphemisms are nowadays."

How about screwing; that's one, she thought with an uneasy smile.

"I always liked George. He's a good, decent, hardworking young man, and believe me when I tell you, there aren't many like him around anymore."

"Yah, I know. He's a good guy," she said, then with the old provocative urge, added, "Of course, he'll never be rich like Lizzie's Rudy."

"It's decency and dependability, those are the most important things," he said.

"And love, right?" she asked, amused to see his neck flush.

"Well of course. That goes without saying."

As do most things, she thought.

"So tell me, how's school going?"

She stared at him.

"Your course at Dearborn Community."

"Yah, the history course." She squirmed, remembering the unopened letter. Lee Felderson must have called Ginny, who'd gone running to her father to report Fiona's latest failure.

"I can't tell you how much that pleases me, Fiona. You're extremely bright." He leaned forward and smiled. "There's never been any doubt about that. The problem is your impulsivity. And that's—"

"Hey! First let's talk about your problems, Uncle Charles," she said, and his head snapped back. She asked about his tests in Boston.

Everything was normal; nothing wrong, according to the doctors. Just a little stress, he said in typical blustery denial of any flaw or misfortune in his rock-solid life.

That was a relief, she said, an edge sharpening her voice as she explained that she hadn't come then or called because no one had bothered to tell her he was in the hospital.

"Well consider it a favor they did you," he said, cutting her off. "It was just a lot of commotion over nothing at all."

"But that's not the point," she said. "I mean, what if it was serious, what would they do, call me, and—"

"Excuse me, Fiona, but at the moment there's another matter that needs discussion." He glanced at Sandy, who had been staring at them over the register. Sandy smiled and gave a little wave.

"That's Todd Prescott's new girlfriend," Fiona said, startled by the deep sense of loss just saying it gave her. It wasn't that she wanted Todd back in her life; she just didn't want him in anyone else's. Especially not Sandy's. "She's got two kids, each one by a different guy. The Prescotts must be going out of their gourd, huh? They thought I was a bad girl!" She laughed, and he winced.

"Maybe it would be better if we went for a ride," he said with a painted little smile.

"I can't," she said, well aware Maxine would let them sit up on the roof if it would please the Judge.

He leaned forward and shielded his face with his hand. "I received a very disturbing phone call the other day," he said softly.

And in the brief pause, this moment, the ellipsis that conveyed his deep struggle, she knew without doubt or a scintilla of logic that the call had come from her mother. She grinned. Such irony. With that one senseless lie she managed to set the truth in motion.

"It was from Patrick Grady. He said you've been bothering him. Actually, the word he used was harassing. He said you've been harassing him, and it's got to stop."

She was shocked. "Harassing him! All I said was how it didn't make any sense not to ever speak to one another."

The kitchen door swung open, and Maxine rushed out with a plate of brownies and slices of banana bread arranged on a gold foil doily. She placed it between them, then with a glance over her shoulder wiggled her hand, Sandy's cue to refill the Judge's cup.

"No! No coffee!" Fiona snapped. Nothing in her life was her own. Nothing, now that he would discuss so personal and painful a matter in such a public place.

"Well just give a holler if you do," Maxine said, and Uncle Charles nodded with a sheepish smile. "But first I just want to tell you, Fiona here is our very best waitress." Maxine patted her shoulder.

"I'll bet she is," Uncle Charles said.

"Oh yah, everybody loves Fiona." Maxine laughed.

"I'm glad to hear that," Uncle Charles said, his smile strained and thin.

"She's got, like, her own customers. You know, like a fan club or something. And that's not even including the guys that are always hitting on her all the time." Maxine leaned on the table with both hands. "But then again, she doesn't mind telling them all where the dog died if she has to." Then seeing Fiona's set jaw and boiling eyes, she bent closer to add in a low voice, "And that's a compliment, young lady, so don't be looking at me like that."

Uncle Charles picked up a brownie and took a small bite, the price of extrication. "Thank you," he said, gesturing with it. "This is absolutely delicious."

"Oh. Thank you," she said, coloring a little. "They're homemade from scratch, right in my own kitchen." The secret, she confided, was pecans instead of walnuts, one and a half times the usual amount of cocoa, and a dollop of sour cream.

"That's why they're so distinctive tasting," he said.

Fiona squirmed, the cushion damp under her thighs. Sweat trickled down her chest. His control over his feelings had always amazed and irritated her. A newspaper reporter had once written that Charles Hollis was so highly regarded because of the respect he accorded every man, woman, and child he had ever encountered. His great dignity and wisdom were said to be surpassed only by his kindness. It occurred to her now that his civility sprang as much from a sense of his own superiority as from a profound and often painful awareness of his fellow man's utter baseness. Certain trials, certain admissions of clients or witnesses, even the actions of fellow attorneys would depress him and empty him of something so vital, as Aunt Arlene had tried once to explain, that for days he would eat in silence, often leaving the table abruptly to sit in his dim study with the door closed, listening to classical music until bedtime. A low time was her aunt's description of it, and yet with an unexpected visitor's knock at the door or a phone call he could not avoid, this affable mask would slip over his face and the dead voice would rise, warm with greeting.

Two women entered the coffee shop and Maxine hurried off to seat them. Uncle Charles put down the brownie and leaned forward. "You mustn't bother him." He spoke quickly. "You know he's not a stable person, and to keep this up is just asking for trouble. Trouble for everyone," he added, with a flicker of a smile for Maxine as she bustled by. "Do you understand?"

"No! No, I don't."

"He said he's told you to leave him alone, but you won't. He said you keep . . ." His struggle for the precise word seemed physically painful. "You keep confronting him."

"Because he's my father!" she said with such equanimity that for a moment he could only stare at her.

"But he's always denied it. You know that, Fiona. You've always known that. Why would you start . . . confronting him now?"

"Because I know he's my father, and I don't care what he says or what you say or what anyone else says about it."

He moved closer. "Well you had better care, Fiona, because he's very upset. He's angry and . . . and I'm afraid of what he might do."

"What?" She tried to laugh. "What do you mean, what he might do?"

"Please, Fiona, trust me. I thought long and hard before I came here to tell you this. I knew you'd be defensive. And . . ." He reached for her hand, holding it limply as he whispered. "And I knew you'd be hurt."

She pulled back, as offended by this token affection as by his words. "Well I'm not hurt. I'm just mad. I'm so damn mad. I'm thirty years old and I have every right in the world to, as you put it, confront my own father if I want." Again, she tried to laugh, but its brittle ring only made her uncle flinch, his face coloring as if he'd just heard something vile. "So next time he says I'm bothering him, tell him to get a restraining order. In fact, Judge Hollis, you could even give him one."

For days afterward her uncle's warning loomed in her thoughts. There were many things she regretted in her life, chief among them all the opportunities and years she'd wasted on Todd Prescott. She wished she had done better in school. She wished she enjoyed reading good books instead of falling asleep every night in front of the television. She wished she had more self-discipline. She wished that for once she could start something and see it through to the end. She wished she could get on with her life instead of feeling so hopelessly stalled all the time. But most of all, she wished she had someone in her life who cared about her.

At night her dreams were riddled with angry voices, and the most familiar, innocuous faces turned suddenly sly and sinister, leering, calling her the slut, the tramp. She woke up one morning wondering if that's why Patrick Grady was so repulsed by her. Had he heard the stories, many of which she herself had cultivated, the exaggerations and lies, and some of the truth? Was he rejecting her for the same reason he had refused to marry her mother? Because she was easy, because she slept around? As an antidote, she tried to remember everything she could about George, the sound of his voice, the way he smelled, the taste of his sweat, his thick shoulders and dazed, crooked smile as he rose above her. Her uncle had been right about one thing anyway. George was exactly what she needed, someone calm, good, and steady enough to keep her forever moored. In these last few days she had missed him, not with the frantic hunger she had felt toward other men she'd desired, but with the sad realization that she had probably lost the most decent man she'd ever been with, and she wasn't sure why.

It was late Friday afternoon. Chester had finally worked up his courage. There were no customers, Sandy had gone home, and the Closed sign hung on the front door. Fiona was wiping down the booths with a damp cloth when he called Maxine into the kitchen. Fiona hurried, hoping to get out of here before he showed her the purchase and sale agreement.

"No," Maxine cried. "Oh no!" She burst into tears and accused him of trying to rob her of the only happiness she'd ever had in her whole life. He tried to reason with her, tried to point out how much happier she'd be, a lady of leisure in a flowery muumuu in her own brand-new condo in Florida with enough money so they'd never have to work again.

"But I love to work," she sobbed. "I love this place."

"And I hate this place!" he told her. "For thirty-eight years I've hated this place."

"But you don't understand," she groaned.

"Sure I do," he said softly. "This is familiar, and new things are scary. I know! Because it's what's kept me here all this time. The same thing, fear of the unknown, being scared. Even though I hated it, it was easier coming in here every day instead of taking a chance on something else."

"No, no, no. It's not that. It's not the same for me. All my life I never had anything. I grew up on welfare. I raised my kids on welfare, and now I finally got something, Chester. It's like I always dreamed, you know, a nice home where you can have all your nice things out to entertain with, for people to see. I feel very important here."

"Important!"

"Yes, I do. People say it's like their home away from home. They tell me that all the time. They like that I dress up every day, that I treat them with all due respect like family."

"Like family! They're customers, that's all, goddamn, arrogant bastard customers!"

"That's not fair!"

"Fair?"

"You don't even see them!"

"Jesus, Maxine, get your head on straight, will you? I'm sixty-six years old and I'm never going to get a better offer than this. Never! So I've got no choice, do you understand?" he demanded, his voice rising.

"No," she said quietly. "No I don't."

"Well, I'm doing it. See? See?" he cried, and there was the sound of papers being unfolded. "Watch me, because I'm signing. I'm signing."

"Go ahead," she said. "But then I'm going home and packing up all my things and I'm leaving."

She ran into the dining room. She stood behind her narrow counter by the front door and sobbed with her face in her hands.

"It's okay," Fiona tried to console her. "And who knows, maybe after a while you can even talk Chester into opening a place up just like this in Florida."

"No." Maxine wept, her nose red and leaking. Inky mascara trickled down her cheeks. "It wouldn't be the same."

"Sure it would." Fiona handed her a wad of napkins. "And it'd probably be a hell of a lot nicer than this, all brand-new and everything the way you always wanted."

For a moment there was no sound anywhere as Maxine wiped her eyes, then blew her nose. She lifted her chin with an odd dignity. "It wouldn't be the same, because . . . because no one would know me there." She struggled for the words. "It wouldn't matter as much. Because here I can show people. Do you know what I mean?"

Fiona nodded and a chill cut through her. She knew exactly what Maxine meant.

They both looked toward the kitchen as the back door creaked open and one by one Chester began to hurl saucepans, frying pans, ladles, and spatulas crashing, clanging into the alley. Neither one smiled, though they both knew Maxine had triumphed. Chester loved Maxine more than all the money and freedom selling the coffee shop could bring him. And Maxine loved the coffee shop more than money, more than she could ever love Chester, and he knew this.

On Monday Fiona left her new telephone number on George's answering machine. When she called Elizabeth, Aunt Arlene answered. Elizabeth wasn't home, but Aunt Arlene seemed eager to talk. Elizabeth was at the PTO meeting until nine-thirty or so. She'd had an awful lot of these night meetings lately, but she didn't seem to mind. In fact she'd been so happy these last few days, it was like having the old Elizabeth back, cheerful and so full of pep, Aunt Arlene laughed, that she and Uncle Charles got tired just listening to her. Ginny was getting over the flu, which she'd probably picked up from one of the children. They'd all been sick in the nursery school. This was the first year she hadn't gotten a flu shot.

And then her aunt stopped abruptly, murmuring, "Let me see, what else is new now?"

Oh yes. Jack thought he might be transferred to one of the courts up this way. He hated the thirty-minute commute into Boston every day, and Susan had just been named executive vice president of her company, which meant a huge raise and a brand-new office in the penthouse suite on the thirty-fifth floor.

Again her aunt paused, this time with a little gasp. "Oh Fiona, I just can't keep it in a moment longer. Everyone else knows but you because Ginny wants to tell you herself. She's pregnant! She's almost eight weeks along. I can't believe it! After all these years. I'm finally going to be a grandmother!"

"And I'm finally going to be an aunt!" Fiona cried.

"Well, cousin once removed," Aunt Arlene added.

Her smile faded with the sting of Aunt Arlene's clarification. Why? she wanted to ask. Why not let her call herself aunt? Why was there always this specificity of relationships? Except, of course, when it came to Patrick Grady. And no one had ever dared try and pin him down.

Continuing in her spirited chatter, Aunt Arlene made Fiona promise to act absolutely surprised when Ginny told her. "And I'm sorry I didn't tell you about Uncle Charles," she added in an almost giddy-sounding rush. "But I couldn't leave such an alarming message, and then by the time we found out he was all right, there didn't seem to be any point in—"

"That's okay," Fiona interrupted, knowing she should be pleased to hear her aunt so happy. She was usually most effusive when trying to compensate for her husband's coldness or disapproval. "And besides, now that I've seen him I'm not worried. He looked tired, I thought, but not sick."

"When was that? When did you see him?"

"Last week. He came into the coffee shop."

"Well, that was nice. I'm glad," her aunt said in a sudden sea change from balmy to cold.

"Didn't he tell you?" Fiona asked.

"You know, I'm not sure now. He may have, but there's just been so much going on lately, I probably wasn't even listening."

Once again the gate clanged shut, and inexplicably Fiona found herself on the other side.

"Fiona?" her aunt said quickly. "Tell me, that telephone call. Your mother. Did she really call? Or were you just . . . teasing us?" She tried to laugh. "I know your wicked sense of humor."

She had called, Fiona assured her, adding that it had only been that one time, though.

"Did she say what she's been doing? Is she married or did she say where she is now?"

"No, I told you. It was all very quick. She just wanted to know how I was doing."

"Well maybe she'll call again now that you've got your phone in." She paused. "Fiona, if she does, that is, call again, would you ask her to please call me?" Her voice broke, then resumed in a low, anguished whisper. "Would you tell her that I've missed her, that I've missed her terribly all these years."

The next day another letter arrived from Dearborn Community College. Fiona dropped it in the trash basket as soon she came into the apartment. She smiled to see the red light blinking on her answering machine. There were two messages. The first was from Elizabeth, her message curt, brief: she would call back later tonight. The second was her friend Terry, saying she missed Fiona. She suggested they meet at eight tonight in Dunkin' Donuts after her lampshade-making class.

"So what've you been up to?" Terry asked, setting the tone as she slid into the booth. Tim's rudeness would not be mentioned.

Not much—work, still getting settled in the new apartment, Fiona told her. The usual things. "But what about you?" she asked. After her loneliness these last few days, Terry's tales of domestic chaos would be the perfect tonic.

"Oh, same old life—crumbs, cuts, and cucka." Terry sighed and leaned forward. "So how are things going with you and George Grimshaw?"

They'd been out a few times, she said, trying to make light of it. Even hearing his name hurt. She couldn't bring herself to admit that she hadn't heard from him in over a week. She'd left three messages on his answering machine.

"And what about Elizabeth? What does she think of this whole thing?" Terry asked, wetting her lips, eyes bright with an eager gleam.

"She's engaged," she said, and to hide her growing irritation, added, "to a doctor. Rudy Larkin. He's at Memorial."

"No, I know," Terry said, waving this off as stale news. "But I mean, it must be a little . . . well, weird, they went together for so long."

Just then two tall women came in and sat in the last booth. "Aren't those the Kendale sisters?" Terry asked. "The ones that live near you?"

"Well, they used to. Near my aunt and uncle, that is." Fiona leaned close.

"I heard they're trying to get their mother declared incompetent," Terry whispered.

"Oh, they're always trying to do that," Fiona said, grateful to have their friendship back in its old gossipy rhythm. "Lucretia's harmless. All she wants is a good time."

"A good time! She must be in her eighties anyway," Terry said with a shudder.

"Yah? So? I hope I still want to get it on when I'm in my eighties, girl," she said. "Actually, Lucretia's always trying to get me to go to Florida and party with her. The funniest though is at my aunt and uncle's parties. She hangs all over my uncle and he gets so flustered. He never knows what to do."

Terry had been staring at her. "Fiona, you know about Krissy and Brad, right?"

"Yes." Her eyes never left Terry's.

"Did you hear what happened yesterday?"

"No."

Terry glanced away. "Krissy tried to kill herself. She took a whole bottle of sleeping pills, but thank goodness her father got her to the hospital in time."

Fiona picked up the coffee-stained slip. She took two dollars from her purse. Her hand shook as she put the money on the table. "It was great seeing you." She stood up.

"What? What're you doing? Why are you leaving? What's the matter?" Terry sputtered. Her face was red.

"Look, why don't you just come right out and ask me?"

"Ask you what?"

"If it's true. If I'm the one that made their baby die and broke up their marriage."

Terry's face drained as Fiona put on her jacket.

"That's what you want to know, isn't it? That's why we're here, right? Or maybe you just like seeing me squirm. Is that it?"

Fiona bent so close to Terry that their cheeks brushed as she whispered, "I may be a stupid, easy lay when I'm drunk, but I'm not a witch. I don't cast spells or kill babies. And you can quote me on that." She stood up and zipped her jacket. "Which I'm sure you'll do," she added with a cold smile.

A sharp wind nipped her heels as she hurried to her car. A haze of thin yellow clouds hung in the starless sky, and she was conscious of an emptiness so ravenous and vast she felt as if she were being sucked headlong into its dark belly. She walked close to the buildings and stores. The friction of her fingertips grazing the rough brick fronts seemed to give her a sense of substance and being.

"Fiona!" a man's voice called out. "Hey, I thought that was you," Rudy Larkin called as he hurried across the street. His beaked nose was running, and his thin jacket collar was pulled up over his red ears. "How've you been? I was just going to stop for coffee on my way home, and I thought that was you!" he said, shivering and waving his hands to gesture from Dunkin' Donuts to where they stood. "So how've you been?" he said so uneasily she knew they were both remembering the same early-morning scene.

"Fine, after I stopped being embarrassed," she said with a flash of rising anger, misdirected as she knew it was.

"I know. That was awful. And Elizabeth got so upset."

"How is she?" she asked.

"Better, I think. But then with Elizabeth it's hard to tell sometimes."

"Yah? Well, I've called her three times and she has yet to call me back, so my guess is she's still upset—with me, anyway," she said with a forced little laugh.

"Actually, I haven't seen her either. I've caught her on the phone a few times, but that's been about it," he said. "This is my first night off in two weeks, but I guess she's been having a lot of meetings, parent conferences, things like that."

"Well, I better get going," she said. "I'll see you." She took a step back and waved.

"Wait! I'll give you a ride," he called.

When she explained that she was parked right over there in the municipal lot, he insisted on walking her to the car. As they crossed the street, she asked if small-town living had gotten to him yet.

"No, not at all," he said in a torrent of conversation now as she unlocked her door. Dearborn was certainly as quiet as Elizabeth had said; well, actually the better word was probably warned. Whenever he'd expressed interest in coming here, Elizabeth would tell him how small the town was, how quiet, how unfriendly people could be to strangers, which wasn't turning out to be the case at all as far as he could see. New Englanders might be cautious and reserved, he said, but no one had been unfriendly.

"She was afraid you'd be bored to death here," she said, getting into the car.

He laughed. "No, she was just afraid I'd come."

She didn't know what to say for a moment. "Elizabeth's not like that," she said.

"What do you mean? Not like what?"

"She's a very sincere person. And if she said this might be too quiet a place for you, then that's exactly what she meant."

"You think so, huh?" he said with the forced amusement of one who finds himself the butt of a very complicated joke.

"I know so. She's probably the kindest person I've ever known. In fact, I don't think in her whole life she's ever hurt anyone."

"No, you're right. With me, a little paranoia goes a long way."

"Yah, tell me about it," she said as she turned the key.

With the roar of the old engine he leaned closer to say he was glad he'd run into her. That was another good thing about small-town living: seeing the same people all the time.

"Actually, that's the worst of it," she called up. "You can't ever hide."

"Really? Well Elizabeth's sure doing a good job of it," he said, then closed her door, and waited, watching as she pulled out of the lot.

At the corner she glanced in the rearview mirror and saw him standing in front of the steamy, bright yellow window of the doughnut shop. She felt guilty. He was lonely, and she had brushed him off when all he'd wanted was to talk about Elizabeth, which was usually what George wanted to talk about when he was with her. Elizabeth. Dear, sweet Elizabeth. Well, she couldn't blame them. She loved her too. Her eyes shot back to the road, to the faded blue station wagon ahead. Patrick Grady's head bobbed from side to side with the beat of whatever music he was listening to. She wondered if he was on his way home or if he was going to meet someone. A woman maybe. Someone he would never commit to because he had never stopped loving her mother, had never stopped hoping she'd come back to him.

He turned onto Chestnut Street, so she turned. Halfway up the hill, he pulled abruptly into the driveway of a large gray house opposite the Bird Sanctuary. She drove slowly past, then as soon as she was around the curve and out of sight she made a quick U-turn and came back down the hill, slowing at the darkened house. But the driveway was empty. He must have seen her car and had only pulled in there to get away. She drove slowly, angry that she'd followed him, angry that she'd been caught at it, angry to find herself once again swept up in this hopeless fixation. But who did he think he was, complaining to Uncle Charles about her when it was such a personal matter between father and daughter, and no one else, no one else, no one else, God damn it. Her aunt and uncle, like a lot of other people, might be afraid of him, but she wasn't. She wasn't. No, she wasn't!

She drove out past the Industrial Park until she came to his neglected-looking little house. When she pulled into his driveway behind his car, she still didn't know what she would say. Before she could change her mind, she jumped out and hurried up the narrow front walk. The windows were dark with drawn green shades. The porch creaked with every step. A No Trespassing sign was nailed on the peeling door frame.

She raised her hand to knock and the door swung open. Patrick Grady loomed in the entryway shadows, head half turned, his angled stare incredulous through the dusty screen, and angry. "Now this is harassment, and if you don't get off my property this minute I'm calling Charles Hollis and telling him to get his ass down here and drag you off."

"I have every right to be here—"

"No you don't!" he howled, pointing so suddenly she jumped back as his finger stabbed a hole through the brittle screen.

"But I just want to talk." She couldn't swallow.

"What're you, crazy? Leave me alone. I don't need this shit! Just leave me the hell alone!" he bellowed, with such rage that the scarred mass sagging from his cheek so burdened and stretched the lid above the eyeball seemed to hang from its socket.

"Please, I just want to talk to you, that's all."

"Talk to me?" he cried. "Don't you get it? There's nothing to talk about. Nothing! Absolutely nothing!"

"But I just want to know about my mother, that's all."

"Well I've got nothing to say about that, do you understand?" He stepped back and slammed the door.

"Please!" she cried, hitting it. "Please talk to me. That's all I want! That's all I want! That's all I want!"

The inner door opened, then the screen door, which he pushed just wide enough to slip past onto the porch. A gust of win tumbled a beer can, sending it clattering across the porch floor. He snatched it up, crushing it as he spoke. "If you just want someone to talk to you, then you're really at the wrong place, because I got nothing to say."

"Could I ask you some questions then?" She shivered. She clenched her jaw to still her chattering teeth.

"What kind of questions?" He seemed amazed by her persistence.

"Well, how long did you and my mother—"

"No!" he barked. "I don't have anything to say about that."

"Was she—"

"Jesus, you don't get it. I said, not about that!" he growled, pointing his finger at eye level.

That. Not her, but That. His contempt made her cringe. "Were you born here in Dearborn? Do you have any brothers or sisters? Are your parents still living?" she asked in a rush of words, already knowing the answers. He had been born in Maine. His one sister lived in Texas and never came back here. His parents were both dead. "Do you have any relatives around here?"

He shook his head. "What do you want? Are you nuts? You got mental problems? What? What is it?"

"I just want to know. I'm really interested."

"Well don't be, because I'm nothing to you."

She stared back, determined not to be hurt or driven off by his cruelty. "You were my mother's friend," she said.

His head jerked back. "She had a lot of friends. Why don't you go bother them? Go ask them some questions."

"Most people won't talk about her to me. They get uncomfortable or something." She shrugged. "I don't know why." She looked down. She could feel his eyes searching for Natalie, maybe even for some part of himself in her.

"Maybe you just come on a little too strong for most people."

"Yah, well, maybe I do." She shuddered in the sharp wind and had to hold her hair to keep it from blowing across her face. "Maybe I take after my mother then."

He glanced at his watch. "Is that it now?"

"Do I? Do I take after her?" she asked quickly. "Do you think I do?" She smiled and held her breath, posing, waiting for the shutter to snap.

"I think you should ask them—the Hollises. Arlene, she'd know better than anyone." He opened the door, then stepped onto the threshold and glanced back. "I'm going in now, so you better go."

"Wait! Please wait!" she called, and he spun around.

"No! You be quiet!" he said, jabbing his finger at her. "I don't want this. I don't want any trouble, do you understand?" He kept looking up and down the road as if someone might be watching, though there wasn't a house, car, or anyone around for miles.

She nodded, her mind racing for a way to keep him out here. His fearful gaze drew her closer to the quickly latched door. "I won't cause you any trouble. I mean it. I'd never do that. I just like you, that's all. I like you a lot. I do, I can't help it, it's like this natural thing. It's like this powerful attraction to someone I really don't even know. I'm sorry. But I can't help it."

There! She had seen it: just the slightest shift, the briefest flicker deep in his eyes; she was sure of it.

"Will you go? Will you please go now?" he said.

"I will, but is it okay if I come by again sometime? Just to say hi," she added, and now as he stared at her she did not look away.

"No. Don't," he said, then went inside. He closed the door and the deadbolt clicked into place.

The first message on her machine was from Elizabeth saying she was sorry they hadn't been in touch. She had to go somewhere tonight, so she'd call back tomorrow night. Hoping the next voice would be George's, she smiled as the tape whirred to the second message.

"Fiona! This is Rudy. Rudy Larkin. I know I just saw you a few minutes ago, but when I got in I called Elizabeth and her mother said she wasn't there, so I'm hoping maybe she stopped in to see you on her way home, but anyway I guess you're not there either since no one's picking up. Well, sorry to fill up so much of your tape like this, but if Elizabeth should come by, would you tell her to give me a call since I have this very rare thing called a night off, and I miss her very much."

There was a pause. "Well, thanks," he said uneasily, as if realizing how pathetic he sounded.

Even though she'd vowed to wait until he called her, she dialed George's number. It rang four times before he answered. "Hello!" he called exuberantly, traces of laughter bright in his voice. "Hello?" he said again, and then in the background a woman gasped and said, "Oh, I didn't realize it was this late."

Fiona set the phone so precisely, so carefully, so gently into its cradle that it did not make a sound.

Chapter 7

No matter how brilliant the sun, a cold metallic sharpness now thinned each day's briefer light. The flowers had died and most of the trees were bare, but for the oaks and their tenacious brown leaves, some of which could hold on through wind and snow. Fiona shivered as she drove. The heater didn't work, and winter's icy talons were already ache-deep in her bones. She dreaded the short days and longer nights, the freezing months to come in front of the television. All she wanted was someone who cared how she felt and what she thought about the simplest things, someone who would know when she left the room and keep glancing at the door until she returned. Was that too much to ask?

Hurrying into the coffee shop, she was instantly calmed by the clatter of the warm kitchen. Water drummed into the large double sink as Sandy filled the pitchers. Chester was mixing pancake batter, the beat of his wire whisk against the side of the metal bowl steady as a pulse. Bacon strips and sausage patties sizzled on the grill.

The minute she came into the dining room Maxine told her that Todd Prescott and Sandy were living together. Sandy had asked Maxine to "break the news."

"Break the news! Like I'm supposed to be heartbroken or something?"

"She doesn't want to upset you," Maxine said.

"Upset me! Me? What about her kids? What kind of screwed-up life is this going to be for them? Doesn't she have a brain in her head? Clueless is one thing, but this is fucking negligence!" she exploded, startled by this dizzying, almost ungovernable rage. She looked around, desperate to fix on something that would pull her back, but the sight most vivid was the stained carpet's threadbare path from the kitchen past these empty chairs, empty booths, and empty tables that she had sponged off and set, served and cleared more times, with more diligence and care, than anything else in her wasted life.

The door swung open and Sandy backed out from the kitchen with a tray of filled water pitchers. Strands of hair strayed out from her ponytail onto her collar with an air of childlike innocence.

"He moved all his stuff in last night," Maxine whispered.

"Which means he's desperate. He probably got fired and he needs a place to stay." She moved closer to Maxine. "You know I can't tell her, but you can." As it was, she and Sandy were barely speaking. Last week when Sandy had mentioned that Todd liked to take the girls to the playground, Fiona warned her he might be using them as cover for drug deals.

"Oh, no. Sandy said he just got a big raise," Maxine whispered. "In fact, his father even called to thank her for being such a good influence."

"Oh, shit, he always does that," Fiona sneered, though her only phone calls from Mr. Prescott had been enraged demands to leave his son alone.

"I've never seen her so happy." Maxine watched Sandy hurry into the ladies' room.

"No," Fiona said. "Real happiness is what you do for yourself. It doesn't come from what some guy does for you."

The front door opened and Maxine's hand shot to the menu rack. She looked up with an expectant smile, but it was only Jimmy Leonard pushing in his milk-laden dolly.

"Good morning, ladies," he called loudly, then looked around, disappointed not to see Sandy, who flirted and brushed up against him whenever he came near. Today he wore a T-shirt, instead of his usual tank tops that showed off the ropy muscles that bulged and rippled with the slightest effort. He pushed his delivery into the kitchen, where his good humor was quickly squelched.

"If I've told you once I've told you a hundred times," Chester was shouting, "deliver back here. From the alley! Not the front when customers are eating."

"Hey Fiona," he said on his way out of the kitchen. "Weeze and me're having our Halloween party Thursday night. You're coming, right?" Their party, an annual event, had come to seem like a chore in recent years.

"I don't know, Jimmy, I'll try," she said.

"Everybody's coming," he said as Sandy came out of the ladies' room. Smiling, she had fixed her hair and put on fresh lipstick. "Hey, and you're invited too, Sandy," he said. "You and Todd," he added.

"But that's Halloween." Sandy looked perplexed.

"Hey, she doesn't miss a trick, does she?" Fiona winked, but Jimmy was still grinning at Sandy.

"Steve and Myrna want us to bring the kids over for trick or treats," Sandy explained.

Steve and Myrna. Fiona couldn't believe it. Dippy little Sandy Rudman, the bartender's daughter, on a first-name basis with the Prescotts.

"Besides, Todd doesn't like parties too much anymore." Sandy smiled, unable to hid her pride in his stability.

"What, are you kidding? Todd Prescott? I'll just ask him myself then," Jimmy called on his way out the door.

"Oh, I hope he doesn't," Sandy said under her breath.

"That's the worst thing you can do, try and put bars around him," Fiona said, and Sandy regarded her coldly. "Because that's what they always did, the Prescotts. It was like this sick game, like they almost wanted him to get in these horrible messes because then they'd have some control over him again."

"Well I guess that explains why they put up with you then!" Sandy said. She banged her tray down on the table.

Fiona wheeled around, so surprised she laughed. "As a matter of fact, they hated my guts."

"And they will do!" Sandy spat back triumphantly.

"Stop it!" Maxine demanded.

"Thank God. My integrity's still unblemished!" Fiona said.

"Your integrity!" Sandy scoffed as the front door opened. Two women entered with a gray-haired man in a three-piece suit. All three carried briefcases. "Your integrity!" Sandy whispered on her way to their booth with a water pitcher. "Oh that's good. That's really good."

Fiona stormed after her.

"Good morning!" Sandy said, pouring their water.

"Excuse me." Fiona tapped Sandy's shoulder, and Sandy looked back, startled.

"I don't like what you just said to me."

The two women and the man watched curiously.

"Fiona!" Sandy gasped.

"You better apologize."

"Fiona!" Maxine called nervously.

Sandy's round, dimpled chin trembled with shock.

"Did you hear me?"

"I'm sorry," Sandy whispered.

"I didn't hear that."

"I'm sorry," Sandy repeated in a choked voice.

"Thank you," Fiona said, then flashed a smile at the bewildered customers. "Be sure and try the corned beef hash. It's Chester's specialty."

It was early in the morning when George Grimshaw finally called. He offered no excuse or apology for his ten-day silence, but asked to see her that night. If she wasn't busy, he added quickly. Actually, she was busy, she lied, surveying her chaotic apartment. Tomorrow would be better. She ran around, picking up as much as she could, then after work she bought new mauve-colored sheets, their thread count so high they billowed like silk when she shook them open onto the bed. She tucked lacy rose sachets under the pillows. She raced home from work the next day with groceries, a new tablecloth, and curtains for the living room. "That looks really nice," she called down the hall to Mrs. Terrill, who was taping a faded crepe paper pumpkin on her door.

It was one of the decorations she had saved from her schoolteaching days. Halloween was her favorite holiday because she got to see so many children, the tiny old woman gasped as she stretched to reach the top of the sagging pumpkin. Fiona set down her bags and quickly taped the pumpkin. Grateful, Mrs. Terrill invited her in for cider. Fiona explained she was expecting someone for dinner and only had an hour before he came.

"Oh!" said Mrs. Terrill, grinning as she opened her door. "Well maybe the two of you can come then. I'd love that. I really would."

Fiona patted her thin arm and said she couldn't promise, but she'd try. Though she hadn't wanted to get the sweet old woman's hopes up, she was sure George would go with her.

The doorbell rang just as she was hanging the last sheer panel.

She hooked the rod onto the bracket, then jumped off the chair and dragged it back to the table. She grabbed the Halloween candy and ran to the door.

"Hello, stranger." She held out the bag. "Take your pick. Trick or treat."

George hesitated, then took a Snickers bar. "Thanks," he said as he stepped inside.

The apartment smelled of hollyberry potpourri simmering on the stove and the scented candles that threw ripples of light across the living room ceiling.

"Clever costume," Fiona said, disappointed that he still had on his dark blue work clothes.

"I figured I'd come straight here." He shrugged. "It didn't make sense to go home first and change." He swallowed hard and winced, as if that hadn't come out right.

She smiled, pleased he was this eager to see her. He looked wonderful, lean and muscular, but so nervous it was almost amusing. Hunched on the edge of her pink velvet couch, he kept folding his arms, crossing his legs, clearing his throat. She went to get him a beer. She peeked out from the kitchen and saw him tapping the candy bar on his knee and looking around as if someone else were in the room with him. She understood his edginess: it was the same desire she'd had in the pit of her stomach ever since she'd opened the door. This time there would be no rush, she reminded herself, no fumbling at buttons, and afterwards no remorse.

He drank half the beer in his first swallow. "I was thirsty," he said sheepishly, then set the mug on the coaster. Peering closely, he moved it first to the right, then a bit to the left, as if this precise placement were the very reason he had come. Suddenly the oven timer buzzed, and he flinched, looking toward the door with a startled expression.

"Don't worry, it's locked," she said and couldn't help smiling. "You must be hungry." She hurried into the kitchen to turn off the timer. The meatloaf and baked potatoes were ready. "Turn on the TV," she called as she bent to open the oven. His shadow fell over her just as the oven's heat stung her face.

"No, don't," he said from the doorway.

She gripped the counter edge a little dizzily as she stood up. He couldn't wait.

"I didn't come to eat. I . . . "

"But it's all ready."

"No. I have to talk to you. That's why I'm here."

"Well, you're a sharp guy. You can talk and eat, can't you?" She removed the sizzling pan, then the potatoes, conscious of his frozen silence in the doorway while his eyes darted everywhere but at her. Jimmy Leonard's Halloween party was tonight, but costumes and getting wasted on a weeknight just didn't do it for her anymore, she said as she gave the limp salad a quick toss. She had poured in too much dressing and now the spoon flew from her hand onto the floor. She didn't know why she felt so nervous. She set the bowl on the table that with its leaf up almost filled the tiny kitchen. She asked if he'd seen any trick-or-treaters on his way here. Maybe they're starting early, she said when he didn't answer. She wished some would come now. She pictured the two of them passing out candy and then, as soon as the door closed, bursting into laughter at the unrecognizable costumes. "Oh! I bought this really interesting wine," she said, turning with the corkscrew and the bottle. Seeing the grim set of his mouth, she decided he didn't know how to do it. It was a Spanish wine, she said, twisting in the screw then pulling out the cork, amused that its soft pop made him wince.

"George!" She put her arms around him and held him tightly. "Oh

George, I know how awful you must have felt that morning. I mean, how confusing it must have seemed. I know, because I felt the same way. And poor Elizabeth." She sighed. "I mean, it's just all so damn confusing, isn't it?"

"It's not that." He stared past her at the clock, at the molten brown mass of potpourri, the grease-moated meatloaf, and the two shriveling potatoes on the stove top.

"What is it then? Come on, George, tell me. You can tell me," she whispered at his ear, while with a child's perversity she kept her fingers knotted at the small of his rigid back, as she pressed her pelvis, bone hard against bone, into his as if by force, by friction, by the sheer intensity of her own desire she could reignite some flickering ember and will his limp flesh to stir so that everything would be good again.

"We're not right for each other," he said, so resolutely that she was certain he'd spent days repeating these very words in his van as he drove from job to job. "We're just two very different people."

"What do you mean, George?" She smiled at the heat of his face against hers.

"We were both kind of alone, so it just, you know, kind of happened," he said.

She knew by his uneasiness that he'd either already said it or intended to explain it exactly this way to Elizabeth. It fascinated her that his feelings for her cousin continued to be so pure, so worshipful that he'd never been angry or even resentful that she'd gone away and chosen someone else to love. Elizabeth was love in the abstract, while she, Fiona, was his reality.

"It? What's it? What do you mean, George?"

"You know. Us." He reached back and unpried her hands. "I'm sorry. But I'm just trying to be honest. It doesn't make sense not to be. I mean, I know I could just let this whole thing play itself out, but really what would be the point of that?"

"Well, I suppose one advantage would be the sex you'd still be getting," she teased with a pat on his cheek, and he shuddered, his head jerking back as if from a venomous sting. His eyes glazed with such affliction she didn't know what to say. She felt breathless and panicky.

How could she have been so stupid, and once again, so blind? She picked up a potato and juggled its heat from hand to hand. "But then you'd always be feeling weird around Elizabeth, right? And that's the real reason, isn't it?"

"This doesn't have anything to do with Elizabeth." He looked deeply offended.

"Jesus Christ, George, of course it does!" she roared, hurling the potato, smashing it into the tiled wall over the sink. "Admit it! She's the reason you asked me out in the first place! And now she's the reason you want to end it! Admit it, George! You've never gotten over her! You're so desperate, you're still trying to figure out ways to please her and make her happy and get her attention. But George!" she goaded, waving her hand in his face. "George Grimshaw, it's over! She's in love with someone else, and she's going to marry him! For godsakes, George, don't look so pathetic! Face the facts! It is over!"

He stared at her. "All right," he said with cold appraisal. "I didn't want to have to say this. But maybe it's the only way to make you understand. I know about you and Brad Glidden. About what happened."

"What?" Her head trembled as if from a blow. "What do you mean?

"I mean it changes things."

"Changes things! What do you mean? What the hell are you talking about?"

"I just can't have the same feeling for anyone who'd do that."

"Do what, George? Say it! Tell me! Tell me what I did! Go ahead!"

"I'm sorry," he said, with a deep shrug that buried his neck in his shoulders. "It's just I wanted to be honest with you. And fair. I mean, we've known each other for so long. And that's why I had to come and do it in person." He opened the door. "I'm sorry," he said softly, then hurried out.

She ran into the hallway. "Well aren't you the noble prick," she called over the railing as he raced down the stairs. "Thanks, George! Thanks for being so damn fair. I really appreciate it!" On her way back to her apartment, she was ashamed to see Mrs. Terrill's door closing down the hall.

She dumped the meatloaf into the trash, grease-dripping pan and all. She opened a beer and sprawled on the couch, staring at the television, oblivious to the packs of giddy children roaming the building now. A flurry of knocks banged on her door and she continued to ignore them. Footsteps stampeded down the hall to Mrs. Terrill's opening door. "Trick or treat!" the children screamed, and the old woman laughed. Fiona's half-eaten bag of Snickers bars lay warm and soft on her belly. She opened another one, balled up the wrapper, and tossed it into the growing pile on the coffee table.

"One, I said. Just take one," Mr. Clinch insisted from his doorway across the hall. he had begun the evening admiring the different costumes, but it was now nine-thirty and these foragers sounded like an older, greedier pack. "All right then, that's it!" he announced in a shrill voice. "Halloween's over! Go home! It's too late anyway!" His door slammed.

"But I didn't get any," a younger child whined.

Fiona opened her door and tossed the bag into the hallway at the feet of a charcoal-faced, startled boy in a baggy, patched tramp suit.

She put on tight red pants, a black lace top that barely covered her midriff, and gold spike heels. She laughed as she put on her makeup: shimmering red lipstick, thick black mascara on her lashes, and purple shadow that swept up from the corners of her eyes like the wings of an exotic bird.

"Trick or treat!" she said as Jimmy Leonard's front door opened into a narrow foyer lit by sputtering jack-o'-lanterns. A low cackle rose from the life-size dummy of a witch sitting on the bench.

"Fiona! I haven't seen you in so long," cried Louise, Jimmy's girlfriend, in a leopard costume. She flicked the long ropy tail she was carrying. "Jimmy'll be so glad you're here." The rest of her greeting was lost in the din of voices and music as she led Fiona into the crowded, smoky living room.

"Fiona!"

"Hey Fiona, how ya doing?"

"Fiona!" called people she knew, barely knew, or couldn't recognize behind their masks as she squeezed past.

"Bar's in here!" Louise shouted, pointing toward the bright kitchen. The table was covered with bottles and plastic cups. There were two kegs in the corner. The five people huddled by the counter were Jimmy's relatives, Louise said. One was dressed in black with a hangman's noose dangling from his neck. Blood leaked from his nose and the corner of his mouth. Jimmy was out on the side porch, smoking, Louise said, rolling her eyes. She taught at the junior high and couldn't risk having the smell of pot get into her clothes.

"Great costume," Fiona said, stroking Louise's spotted furry arm. Louise thanked her. She'd made it herself, she said, then assured Fiona she wasn't alone. A lot of people hadn't worn costumes.

"But I am in costume!" Fiona said.

"As what then? It's way too subtle for me," Louise said, looking her up and down.

"Oh, it'll come to you." She smiled as she filled a cup at the keg spout.

Louise grabbed a five-pound bag of pretzels and said she was going to refill bowls. Fiona edged closer to Jimmy Leonard's relatives, whose animated conversation about pickup trucks waned with her approach. She introduced herself. They said hi and no more. "Well, nice to meet you,' she said, then moved away a few feet into the doorway. A slow, sweet ballad was playing. She could feel someone staring at her. It was Sandy, sitting next to Todd, wedged into the corner of the sofa, looking miserable. In her lap was a gorilla mask that she kept folding and unfolding. Todd's Frankenstein mask hung loosely around his neck as he talked animatedly to Lynn Clarino, who sat on his other side. Fiona and Lynn had been friends in high school until the senior party at the town pond. Lynn had hated her ever since. Although Fiona had absolutely no memory of the incident, it had been retold so many times that by now she knew all the alleged details. Apparently she had stood on the dock and in a pitch-perfect stammer had recited Lynn's own plea, made in confidence just hours before, asking Fiona why nobody ever asked her out; was it her big thighs, her tiny tits, what was wrong with her? The laughter faded and no one could even look at Lynn, who crouched on the beach with her head in her arms, crying. Todd climbed onto the dock and pushed Fiona into the water while everyone cheered.

Well, she wasn't about to start mending that broken fence. Not tonight. Besides there were too many Lynn Clarinos in her life, all judgmental and too quick to take offense. Bored, she wandered back into the kitchen. She got another beer and went out to the porch where Jimmy Leonard and some couple were smoking. When she sat down Jimmy passed her his wet and shriveled joint. She took a deep drag, then held it as long as she could. She exhaled, then took another drag before returning it to Jimmy. She didn't feel a thing. The spike-haired woman's name was Gretchen. She laughed at everything her boyfriend, Pete, said. He was describing the crunch of his kid's turtle under his shoe.

"'Daddy, Daddy, he's jumping up and down and screaming. 'You're standing on Freddy.' 'No I'm not,' I said. 'Freddy's in the kitchen. I just saw him.' So off he runs in the other room and I reach down with my fingers and actually have to scrape turtle crud off my shoe and off the floor. And right then I hear someone coming, so I'm standing there with this mess in my hand, and it's his mother and she's screaming at me about the support payment being late, and then she hears the kid screaming he can't find Freddy so she takes off to look and her jacket's hanging on the back of the chair so I reach over and dump Freddy and his shit bits right into her pocket just as neat as neat can be."

The woman's head rolled on her arms as she gasped with laughter. Jimmy chuckled. "Man," he kept saying. "Man, oh man."

"Dick," Fiona said.

Pete looked at her. "Huh? What'd you say?"

"Dick," she repeated, getting up. "You dick," she said, leaning over him.

"No, not Dick," he called as she went inside. "Pete! The name's Pete." Gretchen and Jimmy Leonard giggled.

Talking to people she knew along the way, she ended up in the living room. Sandy had sunk deeper into the corner of the sofa, but now Todd stood by the stereo unit, talking to Bill Hatcher.

"Hey, cuz!" she said, joining them. Bill Hatcher's mother and her uncle Charles were cousins.

"Cuz!" He greeted her with a long kiss on the mouth. The joke had always been that he could kiss her romantically because they were related only by marriage. Hatcher's hand strayed to her backside and she gave him a good-natured swat.

"Hey, Toddie," she said with a poke in his ribs and a long lazy smile that made her wonder if she was high.

He had been telling Bill how much fun it had been taking Sandy's girls trick-or-treating tonight. He and Sandy had brought them to every house on his parents' street.

"That must have been quite the sight," she said. "Those little hellions running up and down Humphrey Street."

"They had a great time," he said. "They got so much . . ."

"That's Sandy," Fiona told Hatcher with a nod. "We work together. Not too bright, but cute, huh?"

"Umm," Hatcher agreed, then said he was going to get a beer. Could he get either one of them something?

"No thanks," Fiona said. "Don't bother. She's underage," she called as he started toward Sandy. "So," she said, turning back to Todd with a smile so dazzling it ached. "I hear you're quite the daddy now."

"They're a lot of fun. I really like being with them."

"Wow!" She staggered as if she'd been blown back.

"I always liked kids," he said.

"You did?"

"Kids're great. All they want is to have fun."

"Which is all you ever wanted, if I remember correctly, you bastard!" she whispered through a shaky smile. "You no-good bastard."

"Are you all right? What is it, Fiona?" he asked.

Afraid to speak, she kept trying to hold her smile.

He lowered his head and pretended to rub his nose. "Go on outside. I'll be out in a minute."

Facing the street, they stood together on the top step. His hands were in his pockets and he shuffled his feet to stay warm. She hugged herself against the cold and told him how everything just kept falling apart no matter how hard she tried. He apologized for last summer as well as the incident with Dexter Carey's car, and for any other way he'd messed up her life.

No, she said, it was her. Nobody else but her. "And the worst of it is never feeling anything. I mean, I know up here," she said, touching her temple. "But that's where it begins and ends. It's like this really quick process." She tried to laugh. "And then I don't give a shit, which is probably why I never learn my lesson, huh?" She peered up at him, then had to look quickly away from his sad half smile. "We've had this conversation before, right? Like a hundred times maybe in the last fifteen years? Oh, God!" She groaned in disgust. "What the hell am I doing out here with you? Of all people!" She threw up her hands and turned in a frantic little circle. "Am I nuts? I must be! What the hell else could it be?"

"Aw Fiona." He picked up a chip of paint and flicked it onto the sidewalk. "Shit, I know just what you're going through. I do! You see, the thing is, you've gotta find someone like I did. Like I found Sandy. Someone who needs you. Someone you've really got to make it for."

"Oh Jesus!" She burst into teary laughter. "Someone like Sandy! Yah, a cheap ticket to total disaster."

"But that's what you need."

"Well that would be you then, Todd," she said as she reached up and pulled his head down and kissed him. He put his arms around her. She squirmed against him. She needed to feel something. She wanted the burning to ignite behind her eyes, the breathlessness in her lungs like drowning, and deep in her groin the desire to hurt and to be hurt, please, please, please, but all she could feel, all she could think and feel and hear and smell was loathing for him, but most of all for herself now as his cold hands clawed her back, then slipped under her waistband. She opened her eyes. "Todd!" She tried to pull away, then closed her eyes again. "Why am I doing this? Why?"

He touched the side of her face, then her chin, his fingertips tracing her mouth. "You know why. We both do, don't we, baby? We always have. We always will," he murmured into her hair.

"No, that's not—," she started to say as the door opened.

Sandy looked out, then ran past them down the stairs, sobbing with her fist at her mouth.

"Shit! Oh, shit!" Todd cried, chasing her down the steps and around the corner.

The next morning, Chester was glumly chopping red peppers. He dropped them into the omelet sputtering in his black frying pan. A heavy-lidded nod passed between them, but neither one spoke. The last week had been difficult since Chester had rejected Stanley Masters's offer. Maxine worked with the rejuvenation of one who's just been told the positive biopsy had been a mistake, while out in the kitchen Chester dragged himself from stove to sink with weighted sighs, eyes casting about in panic as if he felt the walls shrinking around him.

As much as Fiona hated doing it, she would apologize to Sandy, explaining that she had been upset and that Todd had only been trying to comfort her. She took a deep breath, then tied her apron on her way into the dining room. It was filling up rapidly. "What the hell?" she muttered when she saw Sandy taking orders from the six rugged men jammed shoulder to shoulder into the largest booth. They cut trees for the Begler Company. They always asked for Fiona, who knew exactly how each one liked his eggs and who had decaf instead of regular. Fists clenched, she watched them joke with Sandy, who kept grabbing her sides and doubling over the table with laughter. "That little bitch," Fiona muttered and stormed toward the table, as shocked by the eruption of rage as by the giddy relief it gave her.

Ponytail bouncing, Sandy hurried by with their slip.

Fiona turned abruptly and followed her into the kitchen. She snatched away the slip.

"What're you doing?" Sandy cried, grabbing for it.

"That's my party. I always wait on them, and you know it," she growled.

"You weren't even here!" Sandy protested.

"I was out here talking to Chester." She could feel his eyes on her back.

"How was I supposed to know that?"

"Let's see now," she said, scratching her head. "Maybe you could've looked. That would've helped."

"They said they were in a hurry." Sandy looked to Chester, who continued ladling pancake batter onto the grill.

"Look, just get off it, will you, Sandy? I know what the hell this is all about!"

"What do you mean, Fiona?" Sandy demanded, spinning around to face her. "Why don't you say what you really mean!"

Fiona forced a smile. "Believe me, I do. I always do that," she said, desperate to stay in control.

"No, because you're so jealous—"

"Jealous! Yah, right!" She rolled her eyes and pretended to laugh.

"And that's why you were all over Todd last night, because you're so goddamn jealous you—"

"Listen to me, you stupid little dip!" She grabbed Sandy's arm. "Todd Prescott's going to ruin your life if you—"

"You tramp, that's all you do is ruin lives! You can't stand seeing people happy. You're poison, that's all you are, and everyone knows it!"

Fiona shoved her. Sandy tripped and started to fall, then caught hold of the shelf post. The pots and pans clanged into one another.

"Fiona!" Chester warned, scurrying around the bench.

"Bitch," she spat. "You stupid little bitch." She grabbed Sandy's ponytail and yanked her head back.

Chester snared her wrist. "What're you doing? What're you trying to do?" he snarled, squeezing her wrist until she let go. "What's the matter with you?"

"I'm sorry." She backed away with her hand out. He kept walking toward her. Sandy ran into the dining room, holding the back of her head. "I'm really sorry, Chester."

"Who the hell do you think you are?" he demanded, his face red with rage, fists clenched to his chest.

"Nobody. That's who I am. Nobody. Nobody!" she hissed.

"Well I got news for you, so's everybody. So the fuck what!"

"You going to fire me?"

"You want me to?"

"I don't give a shit what you do."

"But you want me to, don't you? You'd like that. That way everything falls into place, doesn't it? And you don't have to lift a finger to change anything. It just keeps getting shittier and shittier, doesn't it?"

"Oh Jesus, listen to you! Like you're really in charge around here, aren't you?"

"I do what I have to, and I don't let disaster and jackasses run my life."

"Yah, right!" She rolled her eyes.

"So you decide. You want to stay, then stay. You don't, you don't." He gave a weary laugh. "But I'll tell you one thing, it's not going to affect my life one way or the other. Because I've had it up to here with you and your crap," he said, hitting the bottom of his chin with the back of his hand.

She started past him and his arm shot out to block her.

"But you decide now. I want to know right now."

"Okay! I quit." She untied her apron. "There," she said, flipping it into the air, relief eddying through her as it swirled down onto the floor. "You happy?"

"No! Are you?" he shouted after her.

She jumped into her car. She had made the right decision, and it felt good to have somewhere else to go, to be on her way to the courthouse. She seldom came to Collerton, though it bordered Dearborn. A small city that had given refuge to generations of immigrants seeking work in its mills and homes in its sturdy tenements, Collerton had always seemed a grim, tired place to her. Uncle Charles liked to say its pulse might be a little fainter now, but its life force was still the same: opportunity and hope. A shadow darkened her window and she looked up amused to see two young Hispanic men whiz by on child-size bicycles. Across the street three teenage girls pushed baby strollers over the wide concrete bridge that spanned the Merrimac River. The old textile mills, many of them empty, some covering whole blocks. loomed over the city streets. Farther along were entire neighborhoods of three-deckers. Dotted among them were weed-choked vacant lots where abandoned buildings had burned, then been leveled by the city. As she waited for the light to turn she glanced over at a car being repaired curbside by two men. The engine lay on the hard-packed strip of dirt between the sidewalk and road.

Uncle Charles had been born and raised in Collerton. His father had been a mill worker, his mother a department store clerk. Their two-family home had been modest, but always meticulously maintained. Sometimes after church Uncle Charles would drive through his old neighborhood while he lectured them all on the value of perseverance and honest labor. To a stranger his tale of the millhand's son becoming a judge might have seemed boastful and self-serving, but anyone acquainted with Judge Hollis knew how deeply he revered his parents' values that had made his own success possible. The last time Fiona had seen his house it was a fish-and-chips shop, but then a few years ago Uncle Charles had seemed pleased to announce its latest transformation into a Vietnamese grocery store and tailor shop. Whenever she saw the plain little house she couldn't help comparing it to the gracious home a few miles away in Dearborn where her mother and Aunt Arlene had grown up. Once when Uncle Charles had been angry for yet another misdeed, he had told Fiona he would not tolerate such behavior in his house. She had delighted in reminding him that it was not *his* house, but her mother's as well as his wife's, and therefore as much hers as his.

She parked behind the courthouse, then hurried inside. The corridors were jammed with people. Spanish and English conversations rose in a dissonant babble that was at once comical and agitating: lawyers with briefcases, court workers shouting out names, sullen defendants, nervous litigants, sweaty-faced children, a wailing infant, and here now blocking her way a court officer trying to placate a sobbing young woman whose pregnant belly strained against her Patriots sweatshirt. He looked familiar, but she couldn't place him.

"He's going straight from here to prison, and the only ones he can see is family."

"But I told you, I'm family. I'm his wife," she cried.

"And I told you he's already seen his wife," the officer said with a weary smirk.

"But this is his baby," she said, hefting up her enormous belly with both hands. "This is his family. This!"

"I'm sorry," the officer said. "But there's nothing I can do." He smiled at Fiona. "Can I help you?"

She said she was on her way to see Judge Hollis. The Judge was in the middle of a trial, he said, stepping away from the woman. He asked if it was something he could help her with.

"You bastard," the woman erupted. "You're protecting him, aren't you? That's what you're doing!" she screamed before pushing past everyone to the front door.

"No, I'll wait in his office then," Fiona said, watching her go.

"Hey. I know you," he said, squinting. "You're . . . I know, wait a minute, don't tell me now. I know, you're . . ."

"Judge Hollis's niece," she said.

"Oh!" He grinned. "Leona, right? I'm Pete. Yah, Jimmy Leonard's party. You thought my name was Dick."

"Oh, sure. Pete!" She tried to smile. "Well, I better get up there," she said, heading for the stairs.

"I didn't know you were the Judge's niece," he called up after her. "I'll let him know you're here."

Both the outer office and waiting room were empty. She was flipping through a travel magazine when the door flew open.

"Fiona!" Uncle Charles rushed in, black robe billowing in his wake. "What is it? Is everything all right? They just handed me this note." His hand shook as he held it out, and she realized how upset he was. He hurried her into his office, then pressed a button on his phone and told someone he would return in thirty minutes.

She had forgotten how small his office was. The larger offices came with seniority, and though Judge Hollis had been sitting in the Collerton District Court for sixteen years, he preferred keeping his original office. She glanced around, both pleased and chagrined to see her high

school picture on the same top shelf with her cousins' college graduation portraits.

She apologized for alarming him. The note, she tried to explain,
had been the court officer's idea. Actually she would have enjoyed
watching whatever trial he was presiding over.

That, he told her, would have been even more startling—to look up
and see her sitting there. "You must have come straight from work," he
said, gesturing at her uniform. He glanced at his watch. "But it must
still be breakfast."

"It is. And that's why." She gulped nervously. "You see, the thing is,
I want a job, a better job, a really good job, and I was hoping maybe
you could help me. Find one, that is." She sat rigidly on the edge of the
chair.

"But you have a job, right?" he said, watching closely.

"Well, yah. That is, I did. But not now. I'm not at the coffee shop
anymore."

"Since when?"

"Well, let's see . . . I uh—"

"Since what?" He angled his wrist to show her the watch face.
"A half hour ago? Forty-five minutes? What happened? What did
Chester do, fire you?"

"No, he didn't fire me!"

"Then what did you do, quit?"

"Well, I—"

"What did you do, just walk out in the middle of the morning
rush?"

"Yes, but you don't understand. I—"

"What's to understand, Fiona? Isn't this standard procedure? You
don't like something, so you just quit, right?'

"No, what you don't understand is I want to make something of
myself. I'm thirty years old, and I don't want to be a waitress in a coffee shop for the rest of my life."

He studied her for a long, uneasy moment. "So what do you want to
be?" he finally asked, folding his hands at his chin, a foreboding gesture that always unnerved her.

"Well, I don't know." She glanced around the cluttered office, the stacks of law books and thick folders, like his somber pose, making her feel foolish and insignificant. "I'm not really sure, but maybe something with the court. You said once I might be good at it, remember?"

"Good at what? What do you mean?

"Well, you know, like a file clerk or something like that. I don't care," she said with a shrug. "Anything! Whatever jobs there are. I'm real flexible," she added with a laugh that seemed to resound with his stare.

"There aren't any jobs right now," he finally said. "And for every position that comes up there are thirty, forty, fifty qualified people waiting on the list."

"Oh, well, all right. That's okay. I just thought . . . " Her voice trailed off weakly. She'd thought he might be able to help her the way he'd helped Jack. She regretted coming here. She'd made the mistake of thinking the same loyalties and platitudes applied to her as they did to his children, and now she'd have to pay the familiar price: his weary castigation, his dour expression, the humiliating lecture, the heaviness she would drag around for days, the weight of all her failures.

"You don't think, Fiona. That's your trouble, you just explode, and then you need someone to pick up the pieces for you." He leaned closer and looked at her. "Things haven't been right for a long time with you, have they? And from what I'm hearing lately, they don't seem to be getting much better."

"What do you mean? What're you talking about? What things?" she demanded, half out of the chair.

It was clear he knew by her fury not to elaborate. "Actually I'm flattered that you've come here, that you still trust me."

"I want to know what things you're talking about," she said.

"Why? What's the point?"

"The point is, things get taken all out of context, and people lie and exaggerate, especially when it comes to me. I'm starting to feel like some frigging magnet for trouble and I'm sick of it!"

"Really? Well, would Lee Felderson be lying or exaggerating about you telling her to go to hell when you crumpled up your test and threw it at her?"

"I didn't throw it at her." She closed her eyes and groaned. "Don't tell me she came running to you with that."

"Ginny told me." He sighed. "Do you know why she gave you a D, Fiona? Why she had to?"

"Yah, because she didn't like my frigging attitude."

"Because you didn't finish the test. You skipped the whole last page. She tried to call you. She's even written you letters, but you reach a point and you just stop caring, right?"

She was stunned. She had never even looked at the back page. Well, still—it wasn't her fault. And why had she given her a D? Instead of playing mind games, Lee Felderson should have said something and given her a chance to make it up.

"I used to think it was our fault, Aunt Arlene's and mine. I used to think we'd failed you somehow, and now there's all this business about Patrick Grady. You even went to his house the other night, Fiona." He shook his head and lowered his voice to a pained whisper. "After I specifically asked you to leave him alone."

She jumped up. "That's none of your business, Uncle Charles! That's my business, my decision to make!"

"No. Because he came to me again about it. He wants you to leave him alone."

"Really? Well I don't care anymore what he wants or what you want!" She opened the door. "Why should I? Why the hell should I?"

"Fiona!"

It took all of her willpower not to slam the door. She hurried down the stairs. Just as she turned on the landing a man came around the corner with a metal bucket and rolls of paper towels in his arms. As they collided the paper towels flew up in the air.

"Hey! What're you doing?" Patrick Grady growled, chasing his bouncing roll down the stairs.

"No! What're you doing? You in here complaining about me again?" She bounded down after him and picked up one of the rolls. "Look, if you have a problem with me, you tell me yourself. You tell me to my face!"

"I did that." Grady turned and looked at her. "I told you."

"Fiona!" Uncle Charles called from the landing. "Fiona, would you come back up here, please. I'd like to talk to you."

"No. I think you already said everything." She saw Grady's gleaming eyes shift between her and her uncle. "But he's obviously got some more complaints he wants to make about me," she said with a flip of the paper towels at Grady.

Two women came up the stairs carrying cups of coffee. They immediately stopped talking.

"Please, Fiona. It'll only take a minute," Uncle Charles said, red-faced and clearing his throat as he tried to smile. He nodded at the passing women.

"I said no." She turned and continued down the stairs.

"Good morning, Judge!" she heard Grady call.

"Oh, yes, fine, Patrick. Just fine," Uncle Charles said, answering some unasked question.

She was working in the coffee shop again. Chester had taken her back, but was barely speaking to her. She had apologized to Sandy, who made a great point of looking away whenever she came near. Only Maxine would talk to her. She hadn't heard a word from George or Elizabeth. She could understand George not calling after her now regrettable scene, but it hurt terribly that Elizabeth continued to avoid her. Last night Rudy had left a terse, almost angry-sounding message on her machine that said he was trying to catch up with Elizabeth, and if she should stop by Fiona's would she please call him? With her hand on the receiver she had almost picked up the phone while he was recording. As much as she wanted to talk to someone, the last thing she needed was a conversation about Elizabeth.

Thanksgiving would be here soon, and she had made up her mind to spend it alone. The Hollises could believe whatever they wanted, whatever rumor they wanted to harvest from the already overladen vine. The breach would be complete. The other day she had torn an ad out of the paper for young people interested in working on a cruise ship. The minute she dialed the number she remembered Elizabeth's wedding and hung up. She couldn't leave now, not when she'd promised to be her cousin's maid of honor. No matter how upset Elizabeth might still be with her, she would be needing Fiona more and more as the day drew near. She had saved the ad though as a reminder. After the wedding there'd be nothing keeping her here. She could go anywhere she wanted.

The rush hour was over. When she came out of the kitchen a man was slouched in a booth, reading the newspaper.

"Good morning," she said, setting down a glass of ice water and the menu.

"Morning," Patrick Grady said, with a curt nod. His hands shook as he folded the paper. He sat with his scarred side to the wall. He wore his baseball cap so low on his brow that little of his face was visible.

"What do you want?" she asked coldly.

"Orange juice, muffin, coffee," he said without looking up.

"You know what I mean."

"I want some breakfast, that's all I want."

She leaned over the table so no one would hear. "Look, all I did was try and be friendly, but you had to go running to my uncle, so fine. Fine! But don't come in here now trying to play head games with me."

"I'm not."

"Then what do you want?"

"Orange juice, muffin—whatever kind you got, and coffee. Black."

"That's all?"

"That's all," he said, unable to meet her gaze.

"No, it's not. I can tell just by looking at you."

"You can?" His mouth twitched, whether with amusement or anger, she couldn't be sure. "Well then tell me why I'm here."

"Because my uncle sent you."

"Why would he do that?"

"Because he's probably sick of you bothering him at work about me." Or maybe he'd finally told Grady to do the right thing after all these years and acknowledge his daughter.

"The only reason you saw me at the courthouse is because I work there now."

Stunned, she asked how long he'd been there. A week, he said, watching her.

"Judge Hollis," he said with a slow, sour smile when she asked how he'd gotten the job.

Her uncle had helped Patrick Grady get a job, but he wouldn't help her.

"Can I have my breakfast now?"

She chose the biggest blueberry muffin and poured his coffee from the freshly made pot. She accepted his grunts as thank-yous. When he finished his juice, she brought him another.

He held up his hand before she could set it down. "I didn't ask for that."

"That's okay," she said in a low voice so Maxine wouldn't hear. "It's free."

"Oh." His taut lips parted, again in that odd twitch. "Then it'll taste even better then." He glanced at Maxine, who was still tallying register slips in a great show of industry.

He ate with the newspaper spread over the table. Fiona observed him from different parts of the dining room. She enjoyed being able to look up from the service hutch or the alcove outside the restrooms or the table she was setting and find him still here. She was so nervous she felt short of breath.

The door opened with a burst of female laughter and three middle-aged women entered. One of them said hello to Patrick as they followed Maxine to the last booth. He nodded. As soon as they were seated they all glanced back, then leaned forward in a buzz of conversation.

"What's the holdup?" Maxine whispered on her way back. "See if he wants his check." She meant Patrick Grady.

"He's still eating." Fiona was annoyed.

"No, he's not. He's done," Maxine hissed. "Give him his check and get him out of here."

Instead, Fiona refilled his cup. He looked up and she realized that his eyes were brown like hers. They had the same thick black hair, though his was straight and starting to gray. She wondered if he noticed that hers was wavy like her mother's. He drank his coffee quickly, then asked for his check. He stood up and fumbled in his pocket for change. She was about to say he didn't have to tip her, but was afraid he might take it the wrong way.

"You were in a rush yesterday," he said, stacking four quarters on the table.

"Yah, I guess I was."

"The Judge didn't seem too happy." He looked at her and again his mouth twitched. "You made him nervous."

"I didn't mean to." She followed him to the register.

"Well you did. You made him real nervous," he said, and now his twitch caught in a smile. "I'll tell him I saw you." He handed his check and money to Maxine, who picked apart the folded bills with as much disgust as if they were crawling with maggots. "Course he's such a busy man," he said, his hand open for his change. Maxine put the coins on the counter. He counted them before putting them into his pocket. "I don't like to bother him. Usually I don't." He turned now to look at Fiona, his head tilted, the odd twitch coy, almost playful now. "Unless it's really important." He looked at her so intently that she could only stare back. "Thanks," he said, taking a penny from Maxine's Good Neighbor cup and slipping it into his pocket.

"That's not what they're there for," Maxine snapped, but he ignored her and pushed open the door.

From the window Fiona watched him cross the street to his station wagon. He drove away, the black smoke from the tailpipe still in the air when he was gone.

"He's got a hell of a lot of nerve coming in here," Maxine said.

"All he did was have breakfast," Fiona said, adding, "I think he wanted to see me. To set things straight."

"That's not why," Maxine said in a low voice. "He's a psycho."

"He's my father." She couldn't help grinning.

"There's something wrong with him, Fiona. I mean really wrong."

"He just has a bad temper, that's all."

"No," Maxine said. "He likes to hurt people. He needs to. He looks for ways to do it. Believe me, I know."

When she went to clear his table she saw his quilted plaid jacket on the seat. She picked it up and folded it carefully. He hadn't forgotten it. No. He had left it behind for a reason.

Chapter 8

"Come on, come on," she muttered, only slowing for the STOP sign ahead. She had just left work and the car had already stalled twice. Folded neatly on the seat beside her was Patrick Grady's jacket.

She drove down the curving road, relieved to see his faded station wagon in the driveway. Not wanting to alarm him, she came quietly up the warped front steps and raised her hand to knock.

The door swung open.

"Oh!" she gasped. "You surprised me!"

"I just got in," he said, regarding her through the torn screen with an odd petulance.

"You forgot your jacket." She held it up and tried to smile.

"I would've gotten it tomorrow." He still didn't open the screen door. "Or maybe you were afraid I would, is that why?"

"I just thought you'd need it, that's all. Here." She held it up again, but he made no move to take it. "I'll just leave it here then," she said, trying to hang it on the pitted door handle, finally stuffing the collar through instead. She said goodbye and started toward the steps.

"You can come in if you want!" he called. He opened the door and looked out with a terror almost juvenile in its hope and dread.

The chill she felt entering the dark house seemed as natural and deep an emanation as the damp, gritty cold of dirt floors, and fieldstone walls, and caves. She kept rubbing her nose against the acrid smell of woodsmoke and wet ashes. She followed him into the small living room, where the rickety brass floor lamp continued wobbling after he had turned it on. Instead of a couch there was a sagging daybed covered by a torn brown quilt. Next to it was an enormous square upholstered chair, its flattened gray cushions dotted with crumbs and coins. The coffee table was littered with magazines and newspapers, and on top of these, beer cans, soda cans, and half-filled coffee mugs, which he picked up, two in each hand.

"Who's that?" she asked of the framed picture on the television.

"My mother," he said.

She leaned close to the black-and-white photograph of a stern-faced young woman. "You don't look like her."

"You think I always looked like this?" he said, with such uncoiling harshness that she jerked back from the picture.

"I meant the features," she said in a small voice. "Her eyes. She has curly hair, and yours is straight."

"I look more like my father," he said. "I used to, anyway."

She hugged herself, shivering. "What was your mother's name?" She followed him into the kitchen.

"Mary." He put the mugs in the sink, then grabbed a stack of envelopes from the table and stuffed them into a shoebox on the shelf above the stove.

"Mary," she repeated. Mary. Her grandmother. "When did she die?"

"Why? What does it matter?"

Because everything mattered, all the pieces of a heritage she had been denied. "I don't know," she said with as offhanded a shrug as could be managed with such hungry, darting eyes. "I just wondered." Wondered if Mary had known about Natalie and the baby, wondered how long he'd been alone in this dismal place, wondered what it would take to make him trust her. "You've got a message." She pointed to the red flashing light.

His answering machine was on the table alongside the remnants of a recent meal—a ketchupy plate, coffee mug, and empty bread bag. The gas stove was beside a small refrigerator, which was half obscured by the open door of a tall white metal cupboard, its sagging shelves jammed with dishes, glasses, cans, and boxes of food. There were no other cupboards, no countertops, no pictures on the walls. Not even a calendar. She tried to take it all in—the stiff, dingy bath towel on the chairback, the Mobil gas magnet on the refrigerator door, the envelope-filled gray shoebox over the stove. It wasn't right, she thought, touching the corrugated porcelain drainboard. He had been just a boy, brave and handsome, when they sent him off to fight a war. It was almost incomprehensible that he had given so much, and now had only this. This starkness. The chipped sink, with its exposed pipes plunging through warped green linoleum, seemed the embodiment of all that had gone wrong and been lost.

He leaned over the table listening, and she knew by the hitch of his shoulder as the machine clicked on that he did that every night, did not even turn on a light, but came straight in here with the mail to see if Natalie had written or called. It was painful to think her lie might have gouged old wounds or raised false hopes. Behind him the one narrow window was a tangled smear of hedges gone wild and gnarled vines.

The message was from Mrs. Latterly, complaining that she'd called three times and he still hadn't called her back. "Please call at once, Patrick," she ordered in a shrill voice. "Or I will have to get someone else to do the windows."

"You do that," he muttered.

"And you know I think very highly of your work," she continued to wheedle.

"Of my price," he muttered.

"So please call me just as soon as you get this message!"

"Yah, right!" He jabbed the rewind button and started out of the kitchen.

"Go ahead." She gestured to the still-whirring machine. "I mean, if you have to call her now."

"I don't." He stood in the doorway, scowling.

"That's Mrs. Latterly over on Sunset Rock Road, right?" She didn't want to leave yet. "I've been in that house. It's enormous. That must be a big job, all those windows and doors. What about doors? Do they count?"

"Count? What do you mean, count?" He stepped back into the kitchen.

"The same as windows. I mean the glass, you know, on a door. That is, if the door has glass, of course."

"What do you care?" he said, his scowl gnarling his scarred cheek into a fleshy, purple knot. She noticed how the scar pulled part of his lip up over his tooth the same way whether he scowled or smiled.

"Actually, I don't. I'm just trying to make conversation."

"About windows?"

"About anything. The point is just to talk," she said, her voice wavering as her eye strayed to the shoebox again. It might be filled with old letters her mother had written him in Vietnam. Maybe he kept them there to read at the table.

He folded his arms. "Okay, so then talk."

"Well, okay, let's see now," she mused, her mind racing, and for no good reason she began to tell him about her first bicycle. She and Elizabeth had both gotten them on their seventh birthdays. He leaned against the wall looking faintly amused as she described her great joy and Elizabeth's great disappointment with the bikes. She had been a daredevil and Elizabeth had been timid, hesitant to take chances, afraid to try new things.

"You still a daredevil?" he asked.

"Yes. But now it's mostly people I take chances on. I'm not the judgmental type. I figure everybody's got reasons to do whatever they do." She was relieved to see him smile.

"The judgmental type," he said. "Like good Judge Hollis, you mean?"

"Well that's his job."

"His fucking mission, you mean," he muttered, eyes roiling and bright.

She looked away, as uneasy with his contempt of her uncle as flattered by it.

"So what was that all about the other day? You have an argument with him or something? He was mad, wasn't he?" His crooked, ropy smile quivered.

She shrugged. "I guess you could say we don't usually see eye to eye on things."

"Oh yah? What kinda things?"

"Just about everything, really. I'm just different from the rest of them, you know, and it bugs the hell out of him."

"What do you mean, different?" He came closer and leaned against the sink.

"I don't know. Different! Like I said, I take people as I find them, but the Hollises, they all have to have rules, you know, for everything. But life's not that simple. It's not that easy. You can't just—"

His hand shot up for silence. "It was me, wasn't it? That's what happened, huh?" He stared at her with gleeful anticipation.

"Well, I . . . you see, he . . ." she stammered. "Well, yes, that's part of it. A big part of it," she added, warming to his obvious pleasure.

"And I told him," he said, snickering. " 'What am I supposed to do?' I said." His eyes widened. "I warned you, didn't I? I did, right?"

"Yes, but . . ."

"I told you there was nothing between us, right? No connection, nothing. Right?"

"I know, but it just doesn't make sense anymore. I mean, I'm a grown woman now. Whatever happened, I can handle it."

"You think so, huh? Well make sure you tell the good Judge that then," he leaned close and whispered.

"Why? Does he say things? Does he give you a hard time?"

He shook his head and laughed. "Oh no, he'd never do that, not the Judge. Uh-uh. You see, we have a very delicate relationship," he said, so suddenly somber that she understood: the relationship included her.

"I know, but the thing is, I don't want to cause you any trouble! Really, I don't. I'd just like to . . . to know you, to be able to talk to you." She took a deep breath and met his piercing stare. "Couldn't we just do that?"

"Why?"

"Because I like you. And I want you to be my friend."

"Well I can't. Because I'm not your father, no matter what the good Judge says."

"Oh no! He never said you were! He never did!"

He burst out laughing. "But he never said I wasn't, right?"

"Actually, it's never talked about. It's like the whole thing never happened. Like suddenly there I was and nobody knows anything. But you do. And that's the thing. I just want to be able to talk to you, that's all. Really!"

"Yah? Well, I don't do much talking."

"That's okay. This is great! I just like being here. Being with you! We don't need labels or names for anything, I mean, for us, for what this is." She put her hand on his arm. "I like you. I like you an awful lot. And all I want is for you to like me."

With his head half turned, he looked at her hand still touching his arm. His chest rose and fell with deep, labored breath. "You better go now," he said with a sudden yank of the string that turned off the overhead light.

They were driving down Chestnut Street in Patrick's station wagon. When she started her car the engine had stalled and she had to go back inside his house. That happened sometimes, she explained, but if he didn't mind she'd just wait and try it again.

"No, it might take too long," Patrick had said, making no effort to hide the fact that he wanted her out of there. He said he'd bring her car by later if he got it going. She was almost home. Her mind raced with all the things she wanted to know.

"So how old were you when you went to Vietnam?" She held her breath.

"Nineteen. Twenty when I came back."

"God, that's so young! Were you scared?"

"I was too stoned to be scared."

"You were a hero though. You got a Silver Star, right?"

"Right," he said with a bitter snort.

"Well you deserved it. I mean you were so badly—"

"Screwed," he interrupted. "That's where this came from." He touched the scar. "Somebody made a mistake, that's all." He glanced at her. "So drop it, will you?"

She didn't say anything for a moment. "I guess a lot of veterans don't like to talk about it."

"Because there's nothing to talk about."

"There must be. And I'm interested. I am. Really."

"Well don't be," he growled with a glance so sharp it stirred the air between them. "It's like going to the bathroom. Everybody knows why you went in, so when you come out, who needs details?"

She tried to laugh. "Well, me! Or anyone else who wasn't there."

"Why? You like to puke? You want to taste it and smell it like it's on you all the time? I don't think so," he said in a childish, singsong tone.

They were almost at the bottom of the hill. To beat the yellow caution light at the intersection, he accelerated and turned the corner on screeching wheels. Just then two teenage boys darted between parked cars into the street.

"Look out!" she yelled as he hit the horn and jammed on the brakes. Laughing nervously, the boys scrambled back to the sidewalk into the startled pack of teenagers milling in front of the drugstore. Patrick rolled down his window. "Stupid shits," he muttered, glaring at them.

"Hey, Patrick, slow down!" one called out.

"Yah, Patrick, Jesus, what's the big rush?" another called.

There was a high, piercing whistle and then a flurry of young male voices. "Hey, who's that?"

"That your girl?"

"Not bad, Patrick."

"Way to go, Patrick!"

"Hey I know her that's Fiona Range! Fiona hey Fiona!" bellowed a deeper voice.

"Fee-yona! Fee-yona!" the boys began to howl. "Fee-yona!"

With that he opened the door and stepped out. He stood in the middle of the street facing them, his hands on his hips. Two cars had come around the corner and idled behind them. "You want to talk? I can't hear you too good. Come here. Come here," he urged, gesturing.

They bunched closer as he advanced on them. They stared with the same horror Fiona felt. He was only making things worse. Cars inched by, the drivers glancing between Fiona and the scene on the sidewalk. Patrick seized the arm of the tallest, heftiest boy, and said something. The boy cringed and shook his head miserably. Groaning, Fiona slid low and covered her eyes.

"Leave him alone, will you?" a girl yelled.

"Jesus, it's just Larry," another yelled.

Turning, Fiona realized it was Larry Belleau in his blue-and-gold satin football jacket.

With the two girls yipping like small dogs at his heels, Patrick released Larry's arm with a disgusted flip of his hand. As he walked back to the car Fiona could see them all struggling not to laugh. Only Larry still looked troubled.

He got into the car and shifted into gear. "Little assholes," he grunted as they drove past. She looked back and saw them stagger into one another with hysterical laughter.

"No respect, that's the thing. That's what the trouble is." He looked at her, and she nodded uneasily.

"They were just fooling around, that's all." She watched him from the corner of her eye. "And Larry, he didn't mean anything. He's harmless."

"Yah, harmless as a frigging moose." He laughed. "And you know what you do when you gotta get a moose off the streets?" He raised both arms and squinted as if aiming a rifle over the wheel. "Pow, pow!"

The hair on her arms stood on end. "Poor Larry," she said.

"Poor Larry is right," he said through clenched teeth. "They never should've pulled him out. What the hell kind of favor was that?"

"It's not his fault."

"Nothing's ever anybody's fault, is it?" he said so angrily that she stared ahead and didn't say anything. He turned the corner, then looked over at her. "Were you and him friends or something?"

She nodded. "In high school."

"Yah, you used to be tooling around with Pretty-boy Prescott all the time."

She tried not show her joy with the realization he had been watching, keeping track of her all through the years.

"You and him still—"

"No!" she said quickly. "God, no."

"What about Grimshaw? How's he figure in this?" he asked.

She squirmed with the disgust in his voice. In this? In what? In this mess that was her life? Would he be asking next about Brad Glidden? "George is an old friend, that's all," she said, adding that he and her cousin Elizabeth had dated for years.

He didn't say anything, his silence as abrupt as the turn onto her street.

"How old were you and my mother when you first started going together?" she asked.

He jerked the wheel and pulled in front of her building. "I told you," he growled through clenched teeth. "You want to know about things like that you go ask somebody else."

"I'm sorry. I—"

"You go ask them. Ask your aunt and uncle; they'll tell you. It's got nothing to do with me."

"I'm sorry. Really, I am."

"Look," he said, both hands gripping the wheel as he seemed to pull himself, almost rocking back and forth, over it. "I gotta go. I just gotta go. I don't want to hear any more."

"Okay," she said, then told him not to worry about getting her car started tonight. She'd walk to work in the morning, then have somebody give her a ride out to his house later so she could get it. She thanked him quickly before closing the door. She paused on her front steps. The relief she felt as he drove down the street was like watching a violent electrical storm move on. One thing was clear. She would have to be more patient. There could be no mention of Natalie. Friendship would have to be enough. At least for now. It was better than nothing, better than being ignored, better than the hurt and humiliation of being cut cold all these years.

"Hey, Fiona!"

She turned to see a tall thin man running toward her. He wore a torn, baggy sweatshirt, and the brim of a baseball cap shadowed his face under the streetlight. "It's me, Rudy," he said, clicking off his watch. Sweat poured down his temples. He asked what she'd been up to.

"Up to?" She laughed. "You mean as in no good?"

"No, just that. As in what've you been doing since the last time I saw you?"

"Not much," she said; working, getting over a cold.

He gestured down the street. "Was that George Grimshaw?"

"No, that was Patrick Grady," she said, disappointed when his expression did not change. Surely Elizabeth had filled him in on all the nasty details of the family scandal. "My car died in his driveway so he gave me a ride home." She couldn't help smiling, though he seemed to have no idea who this Patrick Grady was.

"Fiona, I need to ask you something." He kept wiping his brow on his sleeve. "It's about Elizabeth. I don't know how to say this, but you know that morning? Well ever since then . . ." He held up his hands in exasperation. "I don't know, I feel like I did something wrong. I mean, really, really wrong, but I don't know what. Do you? Has she said anything?"

"Said anything!" She gave a bitter laugh. "I haven't seen her since then, but I think you're right. She is upset, but not with you. It's me." She told him she would call Elizabeth tonight and one way or another set things straight between them.

"I better get going." He seemed pleased, and yet she had the odd sensation of being the subject of an intense, troubled scrutiny. "Hey, I just thought. How about a run? I'll loop around the block while you get ready."

"I can't."

"Can't? What do you mean, can't?"

"I don't have any running stuff."

"Running stuff? All you need are some old clothes and sneakers."

"That's what I don't have. Sneakers," she lied, irritated with his persistence.

Looking down, he asked what size she was. Seven? The same as Elizabeth? She was an eight, she said. He was disappointed. Elizabeth had left her sneakers at his apartment, and if they wore the same size he would've gone and gotten them, he said, so eagerly that she laughed.

"Boy, you must really be hard up for a running partner then."

"Yah, well, actually I am," he said, clicking his watch back on as he jogged a few steps backwards.

"Well, thanks!" she called after him. "Thanks for asking me. Thanks a lot."

"Get yourself some sneakers, so next time you can come!"

"Maybe I will!"

"Hey, what street does George Grimshaw live on?"

"Elm Street."

"What number?"

"I don't know," she called. "But it's a little blue house with white shutters." Now that would be interesting, Rudy and George as running mates, she thought as she headed up the steps. She was inside her apartment when she realized that Rudy didn't want to run with George. He wanted to run by George's house to see if Elizabeth was there. That's why he had asked her to come, so she could point out George's house. He had probably run by her building any number of times tonight looking for her car, waiting for her to come home.

Was Elizabeth spending her free time with George instead of Rudy? She picked up the phone and called home, relieved when Elizabeth answered and not her uncle. She explained that she'd just seen Rudy out running, and she thought maybe Elizabeth might feel like doing something with her. Girls' night out, maybe go to a movie or rent a video. Elizabeth yawned and said she'd actually been on her way to bed. It had been a crazy week. Tomorrow night then, Fiona said. They'd have dinner together. Elizabeth didn't know if she could. There might be a meeting—

"Come on Lizzie, this is ridiculous," Fiona interrupted. "We have to talk. You know we do."

"What do you mean?" Elizabeth asked, breathless with dread.

Fiona paused. "The wedding, Lizzie! It's not that far off," she said, smiling when she heard Elizabeth's relieved voice agreeing, yes, it wasn't that far off now, was it; they'd have to get together soon, real soon.

"Tomorrow night," Fiona said.

The next morning she almost cried when she looked out the window and saw her car down in the parking lot. The note on her windshield said he'd put her key in the mail slot. A heady warmth rushed through her. Her father hadn't wanted her to have to walk to work.

They met at Verzanno's again for dinner. The waitress had taken their orders, and now Fiona waited impatiently for the conclusion of Elizabeth's detailed story about two of her first-grade students, twins who lived on a tiny, run-down farm with their grandfather. An old man, he did the best he could, but the girls usually came to school in the same soiled clothes. Last summer when their long curly hair got too snarled to comb he decided the simplest thing to do would be to start over, and so he had shaved their heads.

"Their hair's finally starting to grow, but they still look like shivery little goslings," Elizabeth said in a little-girl tone.

Fiona hunched on the edge of the chair with a forced smile. She had intended to talk about that morning with George as soon as they sat down, but Elizabeth wasn't giving her the chance. This bubbly chatter people found so sweetly guileless had always been Elizabeth's bell jar, the glass fortress that kept her irreproachable and safe.

The twins were always being pointed out and stared at, Elizabeth continued, her exaggerated pout suddenly more clownish than endearing. During the first weeks of school they would only speak to each other, but that was changing now, thank goodness. Elizabeth was picking them up for school every morning. She had bought them a few nice outfits, and Aunt Arlene was knitting them both sweaters.

"They're just the sweetest little girls. They get so excited with the least little thing you do for them. Daddy's been dying to meet them, so the other night we took them to Friendly's for sundaes. Every time Daddy said anything to them, they'd look at each other and giggle. Well, you know Daddy. He just melted. Now he wants to get them both bikes and new winter jackets."

Typical, Fiona thought. The dear, saintly Judge who had refused to help his own niece couldn't do enough for two little ragamuffins.

"Lizzie," she said quickly. "Not to change the subject, but . . ."

"I know, I know, the wedding. Mother called you, didn't she?"

"No!"

"She's a wreck because nothing's been done, but every time I even think about it my heart starts pounding. I don't know why things like that get me so worked up. Mother wants me to get a prescription like I had for Ginny's, but I told her, I said, what am I going to do, be on medication for the whole next year?"

"It's less than a year, isn't it? Next September, right?" Fiona asked.

"Oh God, yes. It is!" She closed her eyes and shuddered. "Oh, I don't know, it just all seems so crazy, all this commotion, and for what? I mean, when you think about it, it's just one event! One day! That's not the point, Mother keeps saying. I shouldn't look at it that way. It's not just some event, but my wedding, she says, and then I start feeling like I can't breathe."

"Lizzie!" Fiona reached for her hand.

"I won't even tell you how many people they want to invite. And then I think of the expense, I mean, all that money. And even though I know Daddy's—"

She stopped abruptly and sat back as the waitress arrived. Her pale cheeks were so suddenly red they looked stained and unnatural. Her eyes followed the wineglass's descent to the table.

"Lizzie," Fiona began the minute waitress turned away.

"But wait, let me just finish," Elizabeth said, the rim at her mouth. She took a quick sip, then smiled. "I can tell the way you're looking at me, I must sound like such a neurotic, but at least you're not all over me like Ginny has been, and God, Susan! She's made an appointment Saturday at this bridal shop in Concord for the three of us to go look at dresses. I can't do that! Especially not with Susan. You know what it'll be like. They'll flatten me. That's what they'll do. They'll just flatten me! I know they will! I'll never be able to stand up to them. Oh Fiona, I wish I were more like you, and I could just tell everyone to leave me the hell alone and let me live my own life. That's all I want. I just want to do things my own way."

"Then go ahead. Do it, Lizzie. Tell them!"

Elizabeth closed her eyes and shook her head. "I can't," she said in a small, pained voice.

"All right then, I'll go with you! It'll be fun! Just the two of us!"

"I don't know. They'll be so hurt." Elizabeth took another sip. "Oh, I don't know what to do."

"Lizzie, it's your wedding. Do whatever the hell you want. And besides, I'm your maid of honor, not Susan."

"You wouldn't mind?"

"Mind! No, I'd love to do that with you."

"What if I don't see anything I like? What if I hate everything there?"

"Then we'll go somewhere else. We'll just keep looking, that's all."
Elizabeth smiled.

"But there is one thing, Lizzie. Don't you think we better get the
whole George Grimshaw thing out of the way?"

"What do you mean?" Elizabeth's cheeks were scarlet.

"What do I mean? Lizzie!"

"Well, I mean, I know what you mean." She glanced around uneasily. "But I don't see any point in talking about it and making us both
feel . . . well—embarrassed all over again."

"Embarrassed? Lizzie, I was mad! I wasn't embarrassed."

"I was," Elizabeth said in a low voice.

"No, you weren't. You were upset."

Elizabeth looked down, and for a moment the other diners' voices
swelled around them. Somewhere in the distance a telephone was ringing.

"And that's okay," Fiona continued. "I mean, after all those years, all
that time you and George . . ." Her voice trailed off as Elizabeth's head
shot up.

"Yes, I was upset," Elizabeth admitted, eyes fast on Fiona's. "But not
in the way you think."

"What do you mean? What way?"

"Well, it's me, I'm . . . it's just such a confusing time right now,
that's all." She waved her hand back and forth, shaking her head, eyes
wide with the dread of tears. It wouldn't do for Miss Hollis to go to
pieces in Verzanno's. They had been such well-behaved children,
never crying in public, squabbling, or, God forbid, talking back to their
parents. Taking a deep breath, she forced a grim smile. "I'm so emotional. It's all this wedding business. The least little thing can set me
off. So anyway," she said, raising her glass with a perky tilt to her head,
"let's just talk about happy things."

Wasn't her wedding a happy thing? But watching Elizabeth sip her
wine, then move her tortellini into different patterns on the plate,
Fiona knew better than to ask. Elizabeth was even thinner now. Her
ivory silk blouse lay flat against her chest. Her breasts were practically
gone, Fiona realized with a sudden wave of revulsion. She struggled to

keep her eyes on her cousin's delicate face, the flawless white skin gleaming above the candlelight, her pupils so oddly dilated that her large eyes looked flat and vacant.

"Lizzie!" she blurted. "Why don't you and Rudy just elope?"

"Oh no, I couldn't do that." Elizabeth looked shocked.

"Why not?"

"I couldn't! I just couldn't, that's all."

"All right then, why don't you two just live together? Just put off the wedding and be together without any pressure, Lizzie. Have some fun! Enjoy each other! I mean, the way it is now, you never see each other. Rudy's miserable; you're miserable; what's the point?"

"Oh look, now I've got you all worked up too." Elizabeth patted Fiona's hand. "Don't worry, everything'll be fine. I just needed to talk, that's all."

Now Elizabeth began to tell her about Ginny's pregnancy, shifting gears as smoothly as ever. In their need to escape the fray, the Hollises were all like that, quick, not to forgive or explain, but to overlook transgressions, their own and everyone else's. Being considerate was far more important than coming to grips with a problem.

Elizabeth was describing the nursery her mother was decorating for her first grandchild.

"The nursery?" Fiona asked.

"Well, the old sewing room," Elizabeth said, adding, as if to remind her, that it had been a nursery once when their mothers were babies.

Fiona wondered why no one had ever told her that. But then why would they, when with any mention of Fiona's mother, Aunt Arlene would interject, "Best not to talk about that right now," making her mother seem as nasty a subject as distant cousin Hannibal Tooley who'd been arrested for exposing himself to little girls.

"Mother painted the old crib white, and she's doing these adorable stencils. Green and yellow elephants to go with the mint green carpeting." Elizabeth said that Ginny had just had an ultrasound, but she and Bob Fay didn't want to know the baby's gender.

"God, how can they do that? That's just so weird!" Fiona said, grateful to finally have a target for all her pent-up irritation with Elizabeth. "Now wouldn't you and Rudy want to know what your baby was as soon as you could?"

"Well, I don't know. I mean, I don't . . . I mean, I haven't really thought about it," Elizabeth stammered, her cornered look returning.

"Lizzie," Fiona said when she was almost finished eating. Her cousin's plate was still full. "I keep meaning to ask you. How come you left New York and came back home? I thought you loved it there."

"I don't know, I guess I just stopped liking it as much. And I missed everyone." Elizabeth put down her fork. "I wasn't the same person there as I am here. People don't want to know you in the city. They just don't want to be bothered."

Fiona laughed. "Sounds good to me!"

"It's all these here-and-now kind of superficial relationships," Elizabeth said with uncharacteristic bitterness.

"What about Rudy?" She watched the fine lines around her cousin's eyes deepen. "Did he feel that way too?"

"Oh no. That's where he grew up. He loves the city. That's why it took me so long to tell him I was leaving."

"What do you mean, so long?"

Elizabeth closed her eyes and sighed, wincing as she spoke. "I was all ready to go. I'd given my notice at school. I'd found someone to sublet my apartment, and I even had the new job waiting for me here, but I still hadn't told him. I just couldn't. And the longer I waited the worse it got."

"So when did you tell him?"

"Four days before I left."

"You're kidding!"

Elizabeth shook her head with an expression of such utter sadness that Fiona didn't know what to say. A little procrastination would have been understandable given her cousin's inability to hurt or even disappoint anyone. But Rudy hadn't been just anyone. He was her fiancé. They'd just gotten engaged, the first step in their shared life. Or had that been the precise problem? she wondered as Elizabeth touched the corners of her eyes with her napkin. Had the pressure begun to weigh on her then?

"It was awful," Elizabeth said. "He was so upset. I thought he was going to have a nervous breakdown. He kept trying to talk and he couldn't. He cried," she whispered, looking away as if from the still too vivid memory.

"You mean that was the first he knew of it?"

Elizabeth bit her lip and nodded.

"He had no idea?"

Elizabeth shook her head.

"God, Lizzie!" She couldn't imagine the energy it must have taken to maintain the loving lie. No wonder Elizabeth still seemed so drained and confused. "So what did you do?" she asked softly.

Elizabeth took a deep breath. "I left." She gave a little gasp, then could not look up. "It's probably the worst thing I've ever done."

"Yah, I think so," Fiona agreed. "At least the worst I ever heard you do."

"He drove here that same night, and the next day he'd gotten himself a job at Memorial, and a room at the Collerton Y."

"Well, I'd say that was pretty damn ballsy of him. God, I'd be so flattered if any guy ever did something like that for me."

"But that's part of the problem. He makes me so nervous. He's just too impulsive sometimes."

"Oh, and you weren't, just taking off like that?"

Elizabeth laughed, but so weakly that Fiona would later recall it as a sigh, a long, sad, hopeless sigh.

It was windy as they walked down the street, arm in arm, kicking their way through drifting leaves. Fiona was conscious of Elizabeth's bony frame leaning against her. They were singing their old Bubble Gum song, trying to remember the words so Elizabeth could teach it to her students.

Chew, chew, chewie, chew-chew,
And I know how to chew, chew chewie, chew-chew, do you?

"Yes!" Elizabeth shouted, raising her fist now as they made it through the last line without a mistake.

Fiona didn't know if it was the wine or the relief of finally being able to confide in someone, but Elizabeth was her old affectionate self again. The brisk autumn night was alive with stars, wisps of clouds racing past the yellow crescent moon, and the distant pungency of woodsmoke through the dark.

"Anyway," she said, clutching Elizabeth's arm. "Just so you'll know, the thing with George and me, it's—"

"That's okay," Elizabeth broke in. "There's no point in beating the thing to death." She continued walking, and though Fiona was right beside her it felt as if she couldn't keep up.

"No, but I want you to know. It's over. We—"

"I know. You don't have to say it. It was just one of those . . . those situations people find themselves in. You were both lonely, but you're just two very different people, that's all." Elizabeth stopped to face her, smiling sweetly. "And now that's done, so we don't have to talk about it anymore. Ever!" She threw her arms around Fiona, who couldn't help wondering if Elizabeth had not only known all along that it was over, but had coached George in his lines, with herself playing the role of Fiona until he managed to get it right.

Chapter 9

During the night the temperature had dropped below freezing. The minute the door opened the rush began and now every table was taken. It was so warm inside the noisy coffee shop that the plate glass window was dripping with steam. Three parties waited to be seated. Sandy and Fiona hadn't had a moment to catch their breath. When Maxine wasn't working the register she was refilling coffee from the pots she brandished in each hand, regular and decaf. She had given up any attempts at homey chatter. One side of today's elaborately plaited hairdo drooped over her ear.

Fiona backed out of the kitchen with four plates of omelets. The front door swung open and Larry Belleau barreled inside past the line of waiting customers. "Fiona!" he shouted, wading heedlessly between the crowded tables. "Fiona I gotta talk to you I gotta tell you something I have to really I do!" he announced, as he trampled one man's foot, jostled a woman's arm, spilling her coffee, knocked coats off the rack, now jarring a table as he bent to retrieve them. "Sorry . . . Sorry . . . I didn't mean to do that . . . excuse me . . . Excuse me," he said, finally reaching Fiona with the coats slung over his arm. Everyone stopped eating. All heads turned with his turbulent apology. He hadn't meant anything bad when he'd called out her name the other night. He'd never say anything bad about her. Never. Honest, he wouldn't. "Honest to God!"

"It's okay, Larry. I know. I know you wouldn't," she said, managing to slide the plates onto the table. With a firm hand on his huge arm she tried steering him toward the door.

"I like you." He kept looking back. "I like you a lot I always did and you know I do right?"

"And I like you too, Larry, but there aren't any seats," she said, moving him along.

"I don't want a seat I just want to say how nice you always are you're so nice you always are always!"

"Okay, good. Just keep going and you can tell me how nice I am outside."

"Yah and I never say bad things about you never!" he said, his voice rising.

"I know you don't," she said quietly, already dreading the words his contorted, earnest expression struggled to emit.

"And when you do bad things I never say anything I don't I don't really!" he shouted.

"That man's got my coat!" an elderly woman cried. "He's got my coat!"

"Oh, Jesus," Fiona said under her breath, as she tugged away the coats.

"So will you tell Patrick I didn't say anything bad please please Fiona because next time he said he's gonna beat the shit outta me." His hand flew to his mouth. "Sorry." He winced as he looked around the dining room. "Sorry I said that sorry."

After he left, she fled into the kitchen. Sandy was behind the bench, telling Chester what had happened. He shook his head and kept chopping celery.

"Poor Larry," Sandy sighed on her way into the dining room.

After that Chester had little to say, and Maxine barely spoke to her. Lunch was almost as busy as breakfast. By the end of the day they were all exhausted. At three-thirty Sandy's neighbor across the hall called to say that Todd hadn't arrived yet to pick up the children. "Something must've happened," Sandy said as she grabbed her jacket. "Todd just wouldn't forget them like that."

"Yah, right," Fiona said, watching her run up the street. "He's so dependable."

Maxine slammed the register drawer shut. "Why don't you just back off, Fiona?"

"What?" Fiona laughed.

"You can't stand it that they're happy together, can you?"

"That's happy?" she asked, pointing toward the street. "Do you have any idea what kind of life she's going to have?"

"Yes, a very nice one. Probably the best money can buy," Maxine said.

"That's disgusting!" she blurted. "That's so disgusting!"

The two women stared at one another, and it was Fiona who had to look away first.

She was hanging the Closed sign when Patrick Grady tapped on the glass. She opened the door. Her first impulse was to scold him for threatening poor Larry. She changed her mind when she saw how nervous he was. He kept wetting his lips and scratching the back of his neck. She wondered if he had an appointment somewhere. His hair had been cut and he was so freshly shaved that the nick on his chin still bled. He wore green corduroy pants and a red-and-white-striped shirt, dated and tight but a big improvement over his usual dark, seedy clothes. With some of the ragged edges smoothed, it was possible to see what a good-looking man he was in spite of his scars. And how handsome he must have been before them.

"No problem," he muttered when she thanked him for bringing her car back that night. She said she was disappointed, though, that he hadn't come in.

"It was late," he said.

But that would have been all right, she told him. It wouldn't have mattered.

"I figured you were sleeping. All your lights were out," he said, and she felt a little weak inside that he would even know which windows were hers. So he was at least curious about her, maybe even interested. Certainly more thoughtful than she'd been.

Until this moment she hadn't even wondered how'd he'd gotten back home. He must have had someone meet him there. A woman, which was probably why he'd gotten himself all spiffed up like this. He was on his way to see some woman and, illogical and absolutely bizarre as it was, she felt jealous. There'd already been too much time wasted to have to share him with anyone right now. Especially not with some woman who might try to keep them apart.

"So how'd you get home then?"

"Cab," he said.

"Oh you shouldn't have done that. Here," she said, pulling ten dollars from her pocket and putting it on the table. She had just cashed in her tips. "That must have cost a fortune to go all the way out there."

"I don't want that! Here, take it!" He shoved the money to the edge of the table and glared at her. "I said, take it!" His eyes widened, not with anger, but desperation that she let him do this for her.

"All right then," she said, returning the money to her pocket. "Thank you."

"It start up okay?" he asked.

"Yes! As a matter of fact it's been running great. Better than ever."

"The battery. There was a loose terminal. Plus all the corrosion. I taped it and got some of the crud off."

Her hand flew to her mouth. "Thank you! Thank you so much!"

He shrugged, his mouth twitching self-consciously.

"You didn't have to do that." She couldn't stop grinning.

"Yah, I did! I had to get it started, didn't I?"

"Well it's awfully nice of you. And I appreciate it. I really, really do."

He asked for coffee and a slice of blueberry pie. She was cutting it in the kitchen when Maxine asked who it was for.

"I said, who's the pie for?" Maxine repeated shrilly, and Chester's head shot up.

"Patrick," she said in a low voice.

"He better be paying," Chester called as she started toward the door.

She came back, not wanting Patrick to hear. "Of course he is," she said.

"That's not the point," Maxine told Chester. "You go out there and tell him to leave!"

"Why? He's not bothering anybody," she said.

"He knows he's not supposed to be in here!" Maxine said to Chester.

"But he's not doing anything!" Fiona said. "He's just waiting for me to finish up," she added, and couldn't help smiling.

"He can wait somewhere else! You go out there right now and tell him I said so," Maxine said.

"No. I won't."

"Then you tell him," Maxine demanded of Chester, who grabbed a towel and patted his forehead and jowls, his ritual before entering the dining room.

"No!" Fiona said before he got to the door. "I will." She couldn't bear the thought of him being humiliated when he'd come only to please her.

Patrick lowered the newspaper as she came out of the kitchen. "Where've you been? Out picking the berries?"

"No, baking the pie," she said.

He grinned. "So where is it?"

"Well, I've got some bad news, Mr. Grady."

"You burned my pie?"

"No."

"You dropped it."

"No. Worse than that. Much worse."

"What could be worse than that?"

"Well, it's Maxine," she said quietly. She wouldn't give her the satisfaction of hearing her tell him. "She's got a problem with you being here."

His grin wrenched to a trembling sneer. "What'd she say?"

"She wants you to leave."

"That bitch," he muttered, grabbing the paper as he stood up. He charged outside. He stopped at the curb, then turned abruptly and raced back to the doorway. He pointed toward the kitchen. "You tell that low-life bitch she better watch what she says about me," he yelled, hitting his breast so hard she winced with the hollow thumps. His chest heaved with thin whinnying gasps. Spittle frothed in the corners of his mouth. He teetered back and forth. "I don't have to take shit like this from her or from anyone. You hear me?" he yelled into the dim coffee shop. "You hear me? Who the hell do you think you are, you bitch, you lousy no-good tramp!"

The kitchen door swung open. Patrick's tormented face smoothed into an eager, glint-eyed grin as Chester ran toward him.

"You bastard, talking to my wife like that, you no-good bastard!" Chester bellowed.

"Don't! Please, don't," Fiona cried, trying to block the doorway between the two men. Maxine was holding on to Chester's arm.

"Come on, Chester!" Patrick taunted. "Come on, come on out and get me!"

"No, don't, Patrick, please. Please, just go," Fiona begged, pressing against him. "Please!"

"Yah, I'll go. I'll go," he shouted, lurching back. "But I'm not going to forget this, you son of a bitch. You're gonna pay for this, you no good motherfucker, you . . ."

Passersby darted aside. Shouting and jabbing his fists into the air, Patrick stormed down the street. The bell-bottom pants he wore were probably as old as she was. Poor Patrick. Had everything ended for him that long ago?

"Crazy son of a bitch," Chester muttered, watching him disappear around the corner.

"Don't say that," she warned, trembling herself now.

"It's the truth, and if you're smart you'll stay away from him," Chester said.

"He's my father," she said.

"He's never wanted to be," he scoffed.

"He's had a hard life. Nothing's ever gone right for him. Nothing."

"Which is just how Patrick Grady likes it. And given the choice I don't think he'd have it any other way."

"You don't know what the fuck you're talking about," she growled.

"And neither the fuck do you!" Chester growled back. "You think you've got all the answers. You think he's just poor misunderstood Patrick, and I used to too, until I heard what he did to Maxine."

"What?" She looked at Maxine, who was crying. "What did he do?"

Maxine shook her head. "You ask your uncle. And if he wants, then he'll tell you." She pulled a paper napkin from the holder and blew her swollen red nose.

"Why? Why can't you tell me?"

"Because I can't," she sobbed as she sank into a chair, head hung, her hand covering her eyes. Chester stood behind her, both hands on her shoulders.

"He beat her so bad she passed out," Chester said.

"Why did you do that?" Maxine gasped. "Why did you tell?"

"Because she should know," Chester said, leaning close to comfort her.

"But I never told anyone," she insisted. The Judge had asked her not to. It was the least she could do. She'd always be grateful. "He made sure every one of my bills got paid, and he even had a nurse come in after I left the hospital. Your uncle's a good, good man. As I long as I live I'll never forget how kind he was." She looked up and tried to smile, then burst into tears again. "But I can't ever forget what Patrick Grady did to me."

"I don't understand," Fiona said, though the minute she said it, she did. Her uncle had not believed Maxine's story, but typically, instead of challenging her, instead of getting to the bottom of what had happened, to the real truth, had done everything he could to placate her.

"Well, I gave my word, so I'm not going to talk about it. But you see, this is the evenest keel my life's ever been. I love it here. I'm so proud. It's like my own home in a way. And I feel the same way about you, hon," she whispered, taking Fiona's hand and squeezing it. "I really, really like you. You don't know how proud it makes me to have Judge Hollis's niece working here." She leaned forward. "So the first time he came in I tried to ignore it. But then to see him come in again now like nothing ever happened, like he hadn't done anything wrong—no. No, I can't let him do that. Because with someone like me, it's just all so iffy, you know, like any minute the least little thing—" she snapped her fingers— "and it would all be gone. People like me, we have to be so careful. Do you understand? Do you know what I'm saying?"

It was early Friday evening. Snow flurries glittered down through the cold night air of the supermarket parking lot. Fiona had only two grocery bags which she pushed in a balky car. She was tired. She hadn't slept well the last two nights. This morning she woke up shivering with a chill no layers of blankets or sweaters could subdue. More than the cold, it was a profound sense of aloneness lodged deep in her being. All day long she had dredged up every failure and disappointment, examining them with merciless scrutiny. She had spent her entire life pursuing dead ends. Here she was, thirty years old and she didn't have an education, a decent job, or even friends anymore. Most of the eligible men left were too young, and in only a few more years she'd be too old to have children. Like a dead star the life of the party had sputtered out. It had always been easier to act on whims than to discipline herself, easier to wade through the ensuing rubble into denial, this cold and quiet tomb safe from pain and remorse. But after enough years, denial's toxins had so deadened her pride and hope that there was little that could hurt her now, but even less that could make her happy.

When she got into the car she turned on the radio full blast, then sat staring out at the traffic, the shoppers, their children, the huge carts jammed with bulging bags, the tall skinny stockboy in shirtsleeves and earmuffs blocking her way now with the wobbly caravan of empty carts he was straining to steer back to the store.

"God damn it!" she shouted, banging the wheel with both fists. She should have driven back to her class that night to apologize and discuss the test with Lee Felderson, should have told the family her mother hadn't called, should have set things straight with George Grimshaw instead of losing her temper. It wasn't too late, she kept telling herself as she pulled into traffic.

His van was in the driveway, but the porch light was off. She hoped he hadn't gone to bed early. She was still ringing the bell when the door opened.

"Hello!" he called, his smile fading with his voice as she stepped nearer the light. "Oh! Fiona."

"George, I have to talk to you, to explain things."

"You don't have to do that," he said sheepishly. "You don't have to explain anything to me."

"But I do. I want to. Please. Can I come in?"

The flickering television was the only light in the den. He switched on a lamp. Barefoot, he wore sweatpants and a torn T-shirt. There was a blanket and pillow on the couch, and at arm's reach on the coffee table the portable phone. The minute she sat down she regretted choosing the swivel rocker that squeaked with the slightest movement. Eyes downcast and arms folded, George sat on the couch while she told him how Terry and Tim's party had been her first night out in two months. She told him about dancing with the aroused collie and kissing its mouth while everyone laughed, then dancing with Larry Belleau because no one else would dance with either of them, then waking up the next morning with a man in her bed.

"But it was dark, and I couldn't remember who he was." Her voice faltered and she closed her eyes. Never had she felt so ashamed.

"You don't have to tell me any of this, Fiona. I mean, I know how things can—"

"No, let me finish. Please." She took a deep breath. The rocker squeaked.

He winced and looked away.

"You see the point is, it didn't matter what I knew about him. What should have mattered, what should have made a difference, was that I knew who I was and what I was I doing, just like he knew who he was and what he was doing. He knew he was married. He knew his wife had just had a baby. I mean, I know it was wrong and stupid and disgusting to do, and it's been a real wake-up call for me. But the thing is, you can't blame me for his baby dying and his marriage breaking up."

"I don't," he said, so quickly she smiled. "It's just this isn't a very good time for me right now."

"Why, what's wrong?"

"Nothing!" he said. "I mean, no one thing. It's just everything seems kind of muddled right now." He shook his head and raised his hands in a helpless gesture. "I'm sorry."

"That's okay. I understand. Just take your time, that's all. No rush," she assured him with a little laugh as she stood up. "It's not like either one of us is going anywhere, right?" At the door she turned and kissed his cheek. "You call me, okay?" she said.

He looked at her, his somber expression never changing.

The snow was falling more steadily as she pulled into her parking space. Tomorrow was Saturday and Chester had given her the day off to go to the bridal shop in Concord with Elizabeth. She would get up early, exercise for as long as she could, clean the apartment, then pick up Elizabeth at eleven.

As she trudged through the slushy lot, she heard a car door open and close behind her, then her name being called. She turned to see Patrick Grady hurrying toward her.

"I need to talk to you," he said, blinking against the snowflakes coating his head and eyelashes. He wore just a blue plaid shirt. His hands were deep in his pockets, his shoulders hunched against the gusting wind.

"Sure. Yah, come on in. I stopped to get groceries," she said, almost breathless with excitement as he followed her up the stairs. She knew by his troubled face that he'd come to talk about the incident at the coffee shop.

"I thought maybe you had a date or something," he said, while she shifted both bags into one hand so she could work the key into the lock.

"No, no date," she said, coming into the chilly apartment. "Just another night with the clicker." She wanted him to have this image; the quiet, even-keeled life of his sensible daughter. She was not like her mother, and yet she was beginning to sense those moments when he was seeing Natalie in her. She had seen the shock of recognition often enough in others to recognize it now in his stare. "It's freezing in here," she said, turning up the thermostat. "Could I get you some coffee or a beer or something?"

"Coffee'd be good." He watched from the kitchen doorway as she started the coffee before putting away her groceries. "I wanted to explain about the other day," he said. "My side of it, that is."

"I appreciate that, but you don't have to," she said, touched. "Really. I know how sometimes things—"

"Just so you'll know. She's a no-good, lying bitch! Don't believe anything she says about me." He paced back and forth, his agitation mounting. "Anything!"

"I won't," she said softly to placate him.

"We just didn't get along, that's all."

"Well that's pretty obvious." She made herself laugh.

"She was always losing it and storming out on me. Now she's just going to keep telling lies about me. So what'd she say? What'd she tell you?"

"Nothing," she said.

He sank down into the chair. His head hung and his voice dropped as he rubbed his eyes. "I just don't want you thinking bad things about me."

"I don't," she said. Maxine not only had a flair for the dramatic, but a very short fuse.

"Well a hell of a lot do," he said with a mirthless laugh.

"That's because you go your own way."

He snorted at this and shook his head in disgust. "That was the whole thing with her, that bitch. And the crazy thing is, I didn't really even want her around. No-good bitch, driving me nuts," he muttered. "Always whining, whining, whining."

"That's what happens," she said quickly. He was getting angry all over again. "People can't stand it when they're not needed. When someone like you can just go off and do his own thing."

He leaned back with a bitter chuckle. "My own thing. Yah. I do my own thing, all right."

She poured coffee into her best mug and set it in front of him, noticing how he lowered his face to the steam and took a deep breath. She often did the same thing. "That's what's so interesting about you," she said, touched by the hunger in his quick glance. "You don't care what anyone thinks, do you?"

"What's to care about?" He held the mug with both hands and sipped loudly at the hot coffee.

"I know." She sighed. "All most people care about in this town is how much money you make and who your family is," she said, these last words uttered with a soft grunt as she jammed the rest of her groceries into the refrigerator.

He was quiet for a moment, and she held her breath, afraid she'd been too obvious. She turned to find him staring up at her. She smiled and sat down. "But then sometimes I think maybe I've just been here too long. I've never lived anyplace else. And I don't think that's very healthy, do you?"

"You're asking the wrong person. This is the only place I've ever lived."

Just then she jumped, startled by a loud knock on her door. Opening it, she was annoyed to find Rudy Larkin shuffling from foot to foot.

"Hey! Look what I've got." He handed her a shoebox. "Size eight women's running shoes." He had won them at the hospital raffle and of course he'd thought of her immediately.

He was the last person she wanted to see right now, but she invited him in, certain he'd say no when he saw she had company. Instead he went straight to the table and shook hands with Patrick, who remained seated. She knew if she asked Rudy to sit down he would, so they stood there talking. Patrick nodded grunts of acknowledgment as Fiona explained that Rudy was Elizabeth's fiancé, originally from New York, but living in town now and working in the hospital emergency room.

Rudy didn't seem the least bit uncomfortable with Patrick's sullen silence. He was telling them about the child he'd treated this afternoon. His mother had rushed him in because he'd swallowed a nickel. As it turned out, the boy's stomach was loaded with change. "A veritable piggy bank," Rudy said, and Fiona smiled. Patrick drank his coffee and didn't even look up. She asked how Elizabeth was doing. She knew if she mentioned their meeting the other night or tomorrow's shopping trip she'd never get rid of Rudy.

"Well to tell the truth, if I didn't have such a healthy ego, I'd think she's avoiding me." He laughed and put his hand on the back of the chair, wobbling it noisily back and forth. Afraid he was going to sit down, she thanked him again for the running shoes. "I can't wait to try them," she said.

"How about tomorrow morning then? Tell me what time and I'll be by," he said eagerly.

Patrick looked up at him.

"Seven," she said so he'd leave. She'd call later and cancel.

He headed for the door, advising her to dress warmly; it was supposed to drop way below freezing tonight, he said, rubbing both arms as if he were already cold. "Nice meeting you," he called to Patrick, who grunted.

"What's his problem?" Patrick asked with the closing door.

"My cousin Elizabeth."

"That night in Pacer's, you were with Grimshaw, right?"

"Yah, George. He's a real good guy."

"You and him, you going out or anything?"

"We're friends. Or something like that." She felt her face redden with his scrutiny. They'd had this conversation before.

"So when you go over there it's not like a date?"

"No, but I don't go there . . ."

"You were just there tonight," he said angling his head.

"Yah, that's right. I was. It was so quick, I forgot. I had to tell him something." She was as confused by her lie as by the realization he had been following her.

"That Larkin, the doctor, watch out for him. He's up to something," he said.

"Rudy?" She laughed. "He's harmless."

"No he's not!" He hit the table with his fist. "He's just biding his time, believe me, I know," he said so venomously that goose bumps rose on her arms and she felt afraid, but like a child did not know exactly what there was to fear other than the dark at the windows and the blood pounding in her ears as if she were running as fast as she could and getting nowhere. She did not take her eyes from him.

"It's how they do it," he said.

"Do what?"

"Stay in charge," he said, with a note of surprise that she would have to be told. "And then there's nothing you can do about it."

"No, Rudy's a good guy," she said, more to disrupt his convoluted reverie than to convince him.

"Yah, and you're going to have to go running with him tomorrow whether you want to or not." He was pointing, jabbing his finger at her.

"No I don't!" She tossed her head back with forced laughter. "And I never do anything I don't want to do!"

Smiling that disfigured smile, he stood up and tucked the shoebox under his arm. "And I'll make it even easier for you. I'll dump them somewhere on my way home."

"But they're brand-new," she protested. "And they're expensive. I don't have to go running, but I can at least wear them."

"Okay," he said disgustedly and dropped the box onto the table. "But I'll tell you something. He didn't win these. Believe me. He went out and bought them, the conniving bastard. That's part of it, the other way they do it."

Later that night Elizabeth called to say she didn't feel well. They'd have to postpone the trip to Concord. Maybe next week, she said in a small voice. Or maybe never, Fiona thought as she hung up.

The next morning she woke up to the ringing telephone. The minute she heard Rudy's voice she realized she had forgotten to cancel their run. It was six forty-five and he was telling her he wouldn't be able to make it at seven. There'd been a bad accident a few hours ago on Route 93, a truck and two cars. He'd been called in to the hospital, and he was till there.

"Don't worry about it," she said, closing her eyes.

"We can still go," he said quickly.

"No, that's okay." She yawned.

"I should be done in a half hour or so. I'll come straight over."

"That's all right. You'll be exhausted. Just go home and go to bed."

"But the thing is . . ." He paused. In the background a woman's voice droned a list of medical supplies. "The thing is," he continued, "I'd really like to talk to you. If you have time," he said, then added, "If you don't mind."

She agreed to meet him at Dunkin' Donuts. At least there she could get rid of him when she wanted to.

"You're not wearing them!" Rudy said, pointing at her feet when he got there.

"Because I'm not running, am I?" She was irritated. He was almost a half hour late.

"I haven't been out yet either. How about a run this afternoon sometime?" he asked.

She couldn't. She had too much to do, and now most of the morning was gone.

"I'm sorry," he said, dropping an ice cube into his coffee and stirring it. He looked tired. He was unshaven and a cowlick protruded from the back of his head. "I really hate bothering you—that is, I knew you didn't want to go out running, but I find myself in the ridiculous position of having no one to talk to." He sighed and cleared his throat. "Since Elizabeth won't. Talk to me, that is." He began to tell her how happy they'd been in New York and how not long after he had proposed she began to tell him how much she hated the city and how she missed her family and small-town life. One day after weeks of tearful silences she announced that she was going back home. She said she didn't want him to give up his whole way of life and go to Dearborn with her. Even though he insisted he wouldn't be, she said she knew he'd be miserable there. And then she said she was leaving in four days. When she saw how upset he was she couldn't even talk to him about it. Hours after she left the city he got in his car, drove straight up here and got a job at Dearborn Memorial. But then when he told her, she had the strangest reaction. Not at all what he'd expected. Instead of being pleased, she had seemed almost panicky, afraid.

"At the time I thought she was afraid she was affecting my life in some negative way. She'd get so nervous around me."

"She's always been that way with changes in her life," Fiona said. "Big events were the worst. It got so with Ginny's wedding they'd just tell Lizzie when and where to show up. The worst was our high school graduation party. She spent most of the night in her room, asleep from all the Xanax she'd taken."

He sighed, "Well, be that as it may, the light bulb has finally come on in this mush head here. The real reason Elizabeth left New York was to get away from me. Because she couldn't bring herself to say she didn't love me. Elizabeth can't bear hurting anyone. But then you probably know that better than anyone."

Fiona had been nodding. It might be true. Elizabeth had gone to New York without ever actually breaking up with George. The relationship had just faded away, and she might have hoped the same thing would happen with Rudy.

"Yah, well, like I said, it's big events, all the pressure. She just goes to pieces."

"I think she feels stuck, trapped with me here, so now she's taken to just avoiding me," he said with a shrug of resignation.

Once again Fiona found herself trying to explain her cousin's emotional tailspins over the years. "A lot of that may be making you think she doesn't want you here. Her own anxiety. She'd probably be shocked to know we were even having this conversation." She paused, watching him finish his coffee. "Have you said these things to her?"

"I've tried, but she doesn't want to hear it."

She wasn't surprised. Poor Rudy, drawn here by Elizabeth's genuine goodness, was now hostage to it. "So what are you going to do?"

"That's what I was hoping you'd be able to tell me." He tried to laugh, but it splintered into a painful sputter.

"Well then, maybe you should go back to New York. Let her come to terms with her real feelings without having to feel so . . . so obligated," she said, wincing. She didn't want to hurt him.

"I've considered that. Unfortunately I have a year's contract with the hospital. Jesus." He sighed, slapping the table softly. "I feel like such a fool." He leaned across the table and said in a low voice, "I know you're not going to believe this, but I'm probably one of the biggest losers you've ever met."

"You are not!" she said, surprised, then laughed when she saw him smile.

Off to the side the door opened and she was aware of three women entering. She still did not look their way, though she heard a faint gasp as one of them loomed over the table, her narrow chest heaving as she pointed in Fiona's face.

"You slut," she spat. "You disgusting pig, you slut you!" Krissy Glidden was still saying as her mother and sister managed to pull her back out the door.

Unable to move, Fiona sat with her eyes closed and her hand covering her mouth.

"Fiona?" Rudy said as the door opened and closed again and footsteps moved to the table.

"How can you just sit there? You should be so ashamed of yourself, Fiona Range," hissed Mrs. Soule, Krissy's mother, who had been her Girl Scout troop leader in third grade. "So very, very ashamed for what you've done! Do you have any idea how much unhappiness you've caused? How many lives you've—"

"Excuse me," Rudy interrupted quietly. "But this is no place to—"

"Krissy's right. You are disgusting!" Mrs. Soule declared before hurrying outside.

Fiona still hadn't opened her eyes.

"Let's go," Rudy kept saying. "Come on, Fiona, stand up now. Let's go."

It was two-thirty in the afternoon and Rudy was still with her. He offered to stay longer, but she insisted she was fine. She'd taken up enough of his time. Time was something he had plenty of, he said. She was relieved when he finally got up and went to the door. Unaccustomed to so much attention anyway, she found his hyperkinetic energy completely draining. He had left the apartment twice, once for Tylenol at the drugstore, and the second time to get them both pizza.

"I'll call in a while to see how you're doing," he said, his hand on the knob.

"You don't have to call. I'm fine," she said from the sofa where she sat shawled in blankets he'd taken from her bed. "Really!"

"You sure now?"

"Yes!" She couldn't hide her exasperation with him, with everyone. Mrs. Soule had been right. She was ashamed, and now she was angry.

"Well just so long as you don't dwell on it," he said.

"I'm not," she said, remembering what Patrick had said about Vietnam. It had happened. But it was over now and she wasn't going to keep smelling it and tasting it all the time.

"Good then," he said with a sharp nod. "Because from everything you've said it seems pretty obvious you were the one taken advantage of—not him."

"I know. That's what you said before."

"Well, just don't dwell on it, that's all."

"I'm not, but you are."

His hand fell from the door. "It's just that I hated seeing you so . . . so humiliated like that." He walked back to the sofa and stood over her. "I know how painful that can be."

"Yah, but what you don't know is how resilient I can be."

"If that's what it is," he said, looking so concerned that she laughed. "Of course that's what it is! I'm the queen of second chances. Everyone knows that."

"Kind of like your high threshold for pain. Is that what you mean?" he asked with an indulgent smile.

"Like I'm some kind of worm? One part breaks off, I grow another, no big deal? No! I just know I can't be afraid to live in my own life, that's all. I mean, it's the only one I'm going to get, right? So I better not be afraid to take a few chances in it. And if I screw up, then guess what?" Her voice dropped. "It's not the end of world," she whispered, thinking of Patrick now. Forcing herself into his life was the best thing she had ever done for herself. And if there were bumps along the way, then so be it.

Rudy stared at her, nodding. "You know something, you're right! You're absolutely right! This is ridiculous! I'm just going to come right out with it. Yes! That's what I'm going to do! Just insist that we get it all out on the table once and for all." He looked at her. "But then I don't want to be too hard on her right now either. She's been in such a fragile state lately."

"What are you afraid of, Rudy?" Fiona asked, saying his name for the first time. "You don't think Elizabeth's going to go to pieces on you, that she'll flip out or something?" She wondered if he thought all women were as emotionally precarious as his mother.

"I don't know." He looked genuinely perplexed.

"Well take my word for it, she won't."

"Fiona." He sat back down on the chair. "Would you do me a favor? Would you talk to her? I just don't want to force anything on her right now. I think it's me. I think I just keep making things worse."

Elizabeth's long dress hung in deep folds from her bony shoulders. With every breath, her clavicle ridged up against the cloth like some mechanical appurtenance about to come loose. Her narrow mouth and fine features appeared oddly sharp in the harsh light of the early-afternoon sun. They were sitting in the TV room. A fire burned in the small corner fireplace, and from time to time puffs of smoke blew back into the room. A cold wind had begun to sway the bare trees and rattle the old farmhouse windows. The first significant snowfall of the season was expected tonight. It would be nice to spend a night at home again, Fiona thought. They would make popcorn, each huddled under his own afghan, watch old movies while Uncle Charles dozed in his chair, his eyes opening wide with feigned astonishment every time Aunt Arlene, her needle slipping in and out of the bright canvas, suggested he go up to bed.

He was downtown now, doing his Saturday errands, the greater part of which was always lunch at Hegman's Diner with three or four old friends. Aunt Arlene was on a stepladder in the dining room, hanging the new, white curtains she had been ironing when Fiona arrived. Fiona asked if Aunt Arlene was getting the house ready for September.

"For September?" Elizabeth asked with a vague look around.

"The wedding," Fiona said. "Remember how with Ginny's everything had to be cleaned and changed? She even had us clearing out the attic, remember?"

"That's right," Elizabeth acknowledged with a weak smile.

"That's when she had all these made," Fiona said of the blue-and-yellow chintz slipcovers on the chairs and sofa. They were just beginning to fade. The four walls of what originally had been a grim back shed were now a wide expanse of pale walls and window glass that overlooked a sweeping lawn and a small pond whose newly frozen edges glistened with ice. Always a lovely home, the house's maintenance was less a chore for Aunt Arlene than dutiful pride. For the last few years the Hollis house, as it had come to be called after one hundred years of being known as the Range house, had been featured on one or another of the many house tours local women's groups ran to raise money.

"Do you think there'll be new ones for your wedding?"

Elizabeth looked around, startled. "Thanksgiving's in three weeks," she said. She pressed her glass of soda water against each cheek as if to cool herself. "You know how Mother gets around the holidays."

"That's right, Thanksgiving!" Fiona said. "Will Rudy be having dinner here? With us?" she added.

"Probably," Elizabeth said. "Unless he has to work that day."

"I've run into him a few times lately," Fiona said, struck by Elizabeth's impassive gaze. "He seems a little down. Unhappy is more like it. Miserable," she said when Elizabeth still did not respond.

"I knew he wouldn't be happy in Dearborn. I told him that before he even came." Elizabeth's eyes glistened, but her voice was as flat as if they were discussing a stranger.

"I think he's just lonely." Fiona paused, wanting the words to come out right. "He said he hasn't seen much of you lately," she explained, watching her cousin pick at her cuticle, then strip it away, exposing a long raw slice next to her thumbnail.

"I've just been so busy," Elizabeth said in a low voice. She closed her eyes and tears ran down her cheeks.

"Lizzie!" Fiona got up and sat on the arm of her chair. "Don't you love him anymore?" she whispered, and Elizabeth looked up. Just beyond the door they could hear the squeal of Aunt Arlene's stepladder being folded up, then dragged into the hallway closet.

"It's all just very hard right now," Elizabeth whispered. "It all seems so confusing." She shook her head.

"What do you mean?" Fiona leaned closer.

"He shouldn't have followed me. He shouldn't have come here. The thing is, I was trying to figure out what to do. That's why I came home. To see what I should do." There was something almost cataclysmic in the tremble of her exquisite jaw.

Fiona held her breath.

"And I thought I knew, so I tried to tell him," Elizabeth whispered. "I was, I was going to tell him. I thought it would be easier if I was here, but then he came!" She buried her face in her hands. "And so I never did. I never did anything," she sobbed.

"Oh, Lizzie." Fiona stroked the back of her cousin's head while she cried. They sat like that for a moment and then Fiona said, "This is the worst part, all this worrying and agonizing and not doing anything."

"But that's just it. I don't know what to do," Elizabeth said, looking at her.

"Just tell him the truth. That's all you can do. You have to tell him you made a mistake, that he's a really great guy and the problem isn't him, but you, and you're sorry, but you just don't love him.'

"But I do!" Elizabeth gasped, starting to cry again.

"Do what?"

"Love him. That's why it's so hard. It's all so complicated."

Fiona's sympathy was ebbing. There had always been this incredibly blind aspect to Elizabeth that could be so maddening. "Can I ask you something?" she began, explaining that she wasn't bringing it up again to hurt Elizabeth, but only because it might help her understand her own feelings better. "That morning when you and Rudy walked in on . . . on George and me . . ."

Elizabeth's eyes locked on hers. Don't, they seemed to warn.

"What was Rudy's reaction when you got so upset?"

"He understood," Elizabeth said.

"But I didn't," she blurted. "Okay, I can see if you were embarrassed, but it was more than that. I mean, you and George haven't gone together in years and the way you were acting it was like you'd walked in on me with your husband or something."

Elizabeth flinched. She bit her lip and took a deep breath.

"I'm sorry, but that's what it seemed like. That's how it felt to me," she said as gently as she could.

"And I guess you'd know something about that, wouldn't you?" Elizabeth said, her tiny tongue darting in and out of her mouth as if savoring the bite of each bilious word.

Fiona was shocked. She jumped up and Elizabeth's head jerked back. She remembered hitting her once when they were six or seven. Elizabeth's nose had bled, staining her shirtfront and shorts by the time they got into the house. "What have you done?" her aunt had demanded, shaking her. "What have you done?"

"I'm sorry. I'm sorry I said that," Elizabeth gasped now as Fiona threw open the door. It banged back against the wall.

"Bad enough being a hypocrite, but don't be a liar too," she said. "The only thing you're sorry about is that you waited this long to say it to me!"

"No, Fiona!" Elizabeth called, following her into the hall. "I shouldn't have said that without hearing your side of it."

"My side of it!" she roared. "Jesus Christ, that's good! That's really good! I'd like to know when the hell my side of anything's ever mattered around here!" she shouted at Elizabeth, who stood in the doorway.

Aunt Arlene paused on the stairs, a pot of yellow chrysanthemums in her arms. "Fiona! What's wrong? What's going on here?" she demanded, looking from her niece to her daughter.

Uncle Charles was coming up the porch steps. He opened the front door. "Fiona!" he said, his brief smile disappearing. "Is something wrong?" His wary gaze settled on his wife. "What seems to be the matter here?" he asked, peering over his gold-rimmed glasses.

"I'm not sure," Aunt Arlene said, coming the rest of the way down the stairs. She set the pot on the table, then picked it up again quickly. She kept looking around. All this discord would surely cease if only she could find the right spot. She continued into the dining room.

"Are you two headed out somewhere?" Uncle Charles asked with a gesture between them.

"No," they said in faint unison.

"I was just leaving," Fiona said, and Aunt Arlene hurried out of the dining room to kiss her cheek. Elizabeth muttered goodbye, and now her uncle was walking onto the porch with her. He asked what had just happened in there. Nothing, she said.

"I was coming up the walk, and I could hear yelling."

"It wasn't anything, believe me," she said, conscious of his slow, deliberate pace, his arm brushing hers. He stopped, turning, and she glanced past him to her dented, rusting car in the sweep of the gravel driveway.

"I heard what happened with Patrick Grady in the coffee shop the other day," he said.

She shrugged. "No big deal."

"Yes. I'm afraid it's a very big deal."

"He's a good guy. He just lost his temper, that's all."

"Believe me, there's nothing good about him. Nothing."

"Really? Then why'd you get him a job at the courthouse if he's so bad?"

"Do you want to know? All right, I'll tell you then. I was hoping that way I could keep him away from you."

"Or me away from him, you mean," she said with a bitter laugh.

"There are some things, Fiona, that can never be taken lightly." He stared at her. "You have no idea what you're dealing with here."

"I think I do. I know I do."

"No, you couldn't. You couldn't possibly. All you know is what you choose to believe, some fairy tale version of a terribly difficult time."

"Well," and again she shrugged with upturned hands, "until somebody wants to tell me what really happened, I guess I'll just have to keep trying to fill in the blanks myself." She started to walk away, more to make her point than to actually leave.

"You've been told. You've known since you were a little girl!"

She whipped around. "Known what? What have I known?" she demanded, charging back at him.

His pallor deepened to purplish red, his earlobes and the tip of his nose raw with uncharacteristic fury. "The truth, of course," he gasped. "The truth!" He paced a rigid path back and forth. "And now you're putting yourself in the most vulnerable position. You know he's unstable. You've always been told the truth about that. And yet you persist in this misguided notion that he . . . that he somehow matters in your life, that he cares, that he's someone worth caring about."

"He's my father. You're talking about my father, do you understand that?"

"Did he tell you that? Did he say he was?"

"He doesn't have to." She opened her car door.

"Fiona!" he called abruptly, but softly, with torso, arms, voice straining toward her as if he were being monitored by thousands of eyes in the spindly shrubs, the skeletal trees, the barn and house, the heavily massing white clouds. "Listen to me! Don't trust him. He's cunning. If he's being kind or attentive it's only because he wants something."

She closed the door, approaching him now, slowly, steadily, every inch his match, her own blood high, her head so clear she seemed to be breathing a vapor of such absolute clarity that she felt almost giddy. "Did you forget that my mother called me? I know what you told her. And I know why she left. You chased her off, didn't you? You and Aunt Arlene, the two of you. Because she was like me, wasn't she? Too much of a problem. Too embarrassing! Too, oh now I remember, yes, Ginny told me once, she said my mother was too trashy, and that's why she had to leave. Well, I'm sorry, Uncle Charles. Unfortunately for all of you I'm not only staying, but I intend to have a relationship with my own father. A perfectly normal relationship!"

Such willful pleasure it gave her, the slamming door, the roaring engine, the stone-spitting tires, his patrician face rigid with shock.

They had always tried to make her into something she could never be. She was proud to be the daughter of Natalie Range and Patrick Grady. Energy surged up from the accelerator into her body. There was a force at work here, and her uncle was powerless against it. Yes, she thought as she sped along the narrow road into town, she had struck a deep and vital nerve. Never had she seen him so shaken.

"I got these for you," Patrick said, handing her the gold-foiled box of candy through the door. She'd just gotten home. He must have pulled in moments after she had.

"Oh, Patrick," she said, taking the box and following him as he strode into the living room, looking quickly around. "Thank you. Thank you so much," she said, her voice hoarsening with tenderness. "But why? What's the occasion?"

"No occasion. I just did it," he said so gruffly she was afraid she'd offended him.

"Well I'm glad you did then. I love presents—especially when there's no real reason." Her energy subsiding, she felt childish and flustered.

"Has that guy, the one with the sneakers, been back?" he asked, glancing around again.

Rudy was probably at work now at Dearborn Memorial, she said, not mentioning their meeting in Dunkin' Donuts or their return here.

"He drives by here all the time, you know," Patrick said, flopping down onto the sofa. He sat with his arms over the back, looking up at her.

"Yah, well he doesn't live too far from here." She peeled back the thin gold foil. "Actually, just a few blocks away."

"Salem Street. That big gray house, the old one with all the apartments."

She couldn't remember telling him which house was Rudy's, but obviously she must have.

"He always slows way down," he said.

"Probably to see if Elizabeth's car is here." She held out the open candy box, but he pushed it away.

"He always looks up. Like this," he said, craning his neck forward. "Up at your window there."

"I guess he and Elizabeth are going through a tough time right now." She looked for his reaction. "But I guess that happens a lot right before people get married," she said carefully. "All the pressures and everything."

"A few times he even stopped, and then he just sat there staring up at your window."

"When?" she asked, conscious of how cold her apartment felt. "When was that?" She got up and turned up the heat.

"Mostly late. Like around midnight." He watched her switch on the two lamps in the darkening room. "The other night it was on his way to work," he said.

She reached around the corner and turned on the overhead light in the kitchen, the drizzle of light over the messy countertop oddly comforting. One of the few things Aunt Arlene had told her about her mother was that she was afraid of the dark. The only way she could sleep was with a light burning. For years pine trees had flanked the north side of the house, but when eight-year-old Natalie complained they made her bedroom too dark, her father had cut them down. Her aunt had related this with a note of wonder at the child's power even then over grown men, over her own stern father.

"So what the heck are you doing out that time of night?" She laughed. "Some kind of one-man patrol?"

"Sometimes I don't sleep too good," he said.

"So that's what you do? You go out and drive around?"

"Sometimes. Sometimes I just walk."

"Where? Where do you go?"

"All over. I got different routes."

"God, you must see some strange things that time of night," she said, growing a little sad to see his face brighten.

"I do. I sure do." He chuckled, and she leaned forward, smiling.

"Like what? What do you see?"

"I don't know if I should say." He bit back a grin.

"Yes! Oh come on, tell me!"

"Well . . ." He looked up, then patted the sofa cushion. "Sit down and I will."

"What?" She felt big and clumsy as she sat beside him. Her thighs seemed enormous next to his rail-thin legs. She was conscious of her breasts resting heavily on her folded arms.

There was a certain path he always took along a ridge high over the dirt road that led into the recreation park. From there he could see down and not be seen by cars below.

Her face was hot. Her eyes burned. She held her breath. How many nights had he seen her there, his own teenage daughter, legs akimbo, sometimes even dangling out the open window the way he was describing now. Or on hot nights on blankets spread frantically on the needle-covered ground, and as he spoke she was remembering the piney smell, the prickly cloth against her back.

"Sometimes it bothers me though. The ones that boom, bam, boom, buckle up and they're off. Like it's just one more bodily function, you know?"

She nodded stiffly. He knew. This was his way of telling her.

"Especially with all the diseases now. It's important to be with someone you care about. I been alone a long time," he said.

The back of her neck bristled and she tried to lean slightly forward, away from the touch of his thin, hairy arm.

"And I'm so used to being alone now that when I'm with a woman I say all the wrong things."

"Like what? What do you say that's wrong?" She held her breath. Finally he wanted to talk about her mother.

"I don't know. I just do." He shrugged. "You like the candy?"

"I love it. It's delicious." She took a chocolate, then offered him the box. He shook his head. He'd rather watch her eat them, he said. She swallowed, and though she felt a little queasy took another, mindful of the pleasure in his gaze as she chewed.

"Wait. You got some here." He leaned closer and wiped a smear of chocolate from her chin.

The doorbell rang.

"You gonna answer it?" he asked when she didn't move.

"It's okay. They'll go away." She knew by the way he kept looking at her that he wanted to tell her something about her mother.

"Answer it!" he demanded, glaring at her.

"But . . ."

"Then I will!" He jumped up and opened the door. It was Todd Prescott, glassy-eyed and grinning in at them.

"Patrick, my man!" he cried. He looked at his watch, then shaded his eyes, peering past to Fiona. "Whoa!" he said, holding out his arms for balance. "Where the hell am I? Am I at your house, Fee, or am I at Paddy's place? Jesus Christ!" He laughed as he came inside. "My two favorite people in the whole world. Fee," he said, throwing his arm over her shoulder and pulling her close. He put his mouth at her ear. "I'm in kind of a bind and I need some place to stay," he stage-whispered.

"Get out of here!" she said, jerking free.

He was so high he continued laughing as he swayed and teetered backwards. "But I love you, Fee! I've been missing you so much."

"Go! Just go!"

"I'll just be here a couple hours, that's all," he said. "Sandy locked me out."

"No, not even a couple minutes."

"But I have to!"

"She said no. What's the matter, don't you get it?" Patrick snarled.

"But I miss her so much. And you too, Paddy. I've been missing you too," Todd said, grinning. "Want some stuff? I got some very nice stuff here, Paddy."

Patrick's hand clamped onto the back of Todd's neck. He steered him out the door. "Come on, get outta here, you asshole," Patrick muttered as they went down the hallway. Their footsteps were heavy on the stairs as if one was stumbling. "What the hell're you tryna do?" she heard Patrick growl before the outer door banged shut behind them.

Chapter 10

■

The telephone was ringing. A man's voice came through the answering machine. Fiona opened one eye: ten of seven, Sunday morning. She pulled the pillow over her head.

"Hello, Fiona? Fiona, I hope you're there. This is Uncle Charles. Something has happened, and it's very important—"

"Uncle Charles!" she said, snatching up the phone. "What's wrong? What happened?"

"It's Todd. He was hurt last night, quite badly, I'm afraid," he said, his long sigh filling her with dread.

"Oh my God. What was it, an accident? Who was driving?" She closed her eyes. Something had happened to Patrick, and he didn't know how to tell her.

"It wasn't a car. Apparently he's been beaten. Badly beaten."

"Oh my God. Oh my God." She looked around in panic.

"His father just called me," Uncle Charles was saying. "It seems he was dropped off. Actually 'dumped' is what Steve said. And the only intelligible thing he's said so far is your name . . ."

She gasped. "Oh, poor Todd!"

"And Patrick Grady's!" he continued angrily. "I'm on my way down now to see him."

"What do you mean? On your way where?"

"The police station. They just brought him in."

"But why? He was just going to give Todd a ride. I don't under-stand. It doesn't make sense."

"Did you see them last night?"

"Yes. Patrick was here, and—"

"What?" her uncle said, shocked. "You mean there? With you? In your apartment?"

"Yes, he stopped in. He brought me a box of chocolates, and we were talking and then Todd came to the door. He was on something. I mean you could tell, he was so high, and it bothered Patrick, the way he was talking to me," she said, her voice softening. "So he made him leave. He said he'd give him a ride home."

"Oh no," her uncle groaned.

"But he must have dropped him off someplace," she said. "God, Toddie goes everywhere. He knows just about everyone in town, you know that."

"All I know is that Steve Prescott's convinced Patrick has beaten his son to a bloody pulp."

"Patrick didn't do that. I know he didn't!" she insisted, closing her eyes against the image of Patrick being pulled off the young man in Pacer's and the look on his face as he tried to get at Chester.

"Fiona, why do you think I told you to stay away from him?" he said, his hard, weary voice lodging in the pit of her stomach. "Because I was afraid something like this might happen."

For the past ten minutes Steve Prescott had been sitting on Fiona's sofa, hands tight on his knees as they awaited Judge Hollis's arrival. A slightly built man, he was always carefully dressed. Even this morning, after a night of trauma, he managed to look not just elegant in his French cuffed silk shirt, onyx cuff links, black cashmere blazer, and houndstooth slacks, but imperturbable. He had come "purely on im-pulse," an inclination so alien his lips had curled on the words as he stood in her doorway, wanting to know what had happened here last night. She explained that she'd be glad to tell him, but first she had to talk to her uncle. She didn't let on that the call she made was to the po-lice station.

"Uncle Charles," she whispered when he came on the Prescott's here."

"Don't say anything. I'll be right there," he said.

She could hear his footsteps now taking the stairs two at a time.

"Fiona," he said, patting her shoulder the minute she opened the door. "Steve!" Hand outstretched, he hurried across the room. Flashes of similar meetings came to her: the cold wet night in Rocky Point, Maine, when the men had arrived in separate cars to pick them up. At sixteen she and Todd had tried to elope, but the one justice of the peace they thought they'd conned into believing she was eighteen had told them to wait in the wedding parlor while he got his marrying suit on. While they held hands giggling on his musty maroon loveseat he had been on the telephone with the state police, who identified them as juvenile runaways from Massachusetts. She still remembered the monotonous tick of the mahogany mantel clock and its hollow *gonggonggong* as both men paid the justice for his time and trouble. She reached down now and took a chocolate from the box that was still on the coffee table.

"He's conscious, thank goodness," her uncle said, taking off his topcoat. When Prescott didn't reply, he turned to Fiona. "I was just talking to Rudy on my way over." He looked back at Prescott. "Rudy's Elizabeth's fiancé. He's on staff at Memorial."

"I want to know exactly what happened last night," Prescott said, ignoring him. There had been a time years ago when the men had been close friends. Their families had visited at each other's homes, celebrating birthdays and holidays together. One of Fiona's earliest memories was jumping into the deep end of the Prescotts' gunite pool when she was six because Todd was screaming for help and she thought he was drowning. For a few years the story had been told as an amusing incident, an example of their prankish natures, until they hit their teens, when it became the paradigm of mutual self-destruction, their negative attraction to one another.

"Nothing happened," she said, recalling the time of Todd's arrival, his condition, his brief stay until his language started to get out of line.

"What do you mean, out of line?" Prescott asked.

"Well, mouthy. Careless. You know how Toddie can get when

he's . . . well, when he's high; silly almost," she tried to explain because he was looking at her so blankly. "But mean too. He was right on the edge." Her chest felt tight, breathless in the stricture of her uncle's gaze.

"And so Grady got mad at him?"

"No, he didn't get mad. Todd wanted to stay here. I said no, and Patrick told him he had to leave, that's all," she said.

"So where'd you take him then?" Prescott asked.

"I didn't take him anywhere!" she said almost in unison with her uncle.

"Fiona didn't take him anywhere, Steve. She didn't say that," he said.

"So he did stay here then." Prescott's eyes narrowed with his struggle to understand.

"No, he left," she said.

"Alone? By himself?" Prescott asked.

"Think carefully now, Fiona," her uncle warned. "Be specific. This is very important."

"Well, Patrick went downstairs with Todd, to make sure he left," she began slowly, looking only at Prescott. "But then he came right back up here. I looked out the window, and I could see Todd going down the street. The whole time I watched him, he was alone," she said, fully expecting her uncle to leap up and demand the truth.

Both men stared at her. Her uncle's expression was gray, wretched with her lie and his loyalty to her.

"I don't believe you," Prescott said.

"I'm sorry, but that's what happened," she said.

"No you're not. You're not sorry in the least. Sandy told us what's been going on, how badly you've been treating her. And Halloween night how you even tried to seduce—"

"Get out of here!" she cried, jumping up. "You get out of my house right now!"

"Fiona!" her uncle said, also on his feet.

"She put Grady up to this." Prescott pointed at her. "I know she did! She's a no-good—"

"That's enough, Steve! That's quite enough," Uncle Charles warned. "You be careful what you say now. I know you're upset. I know you're worried, but you're speaking to a member of my family now, Steve. Do you understand?"

"Understand! I don't understand anything anymore." Prescott groaned, rubbing his face. He looked up. "I mean there's something deeply wrong here. Patrick Grady's a dangerous man, Charlie."

"Well, now," Uncle Charles began as Fiona glared at Prescott, "Patrick's odd, we all know—"

"Odd?" Prescott demanded. "He's way past odd, Charlie. I mean, think of it, think of all the trouble through the years, fights and drugs, all the strange and unexplained incidents. The Belleau boy!"

"That was a diving accident," her uncle said quickly.

"My God, your own sister-in-law!" Prescott said with a glance at Fiona.

"Let's not go off on tangents now. The important thing is how Todd's—"

"Tangents?" Prescott cut him off. "How can you say that? Charlie, what was it, twenty-nine, thirty years ago that Natalie disappeared, and the last anyone's—"

"Wait a minute! Wait just a minute now, Steve," Uncle Charles insisted. "Let's get the facts straight here. Natalie left. She left of her own volition, her own accord."

"And has never been heard from since," Prescott added with a look of astonishment. "Or is that just odd too?"

"No, now, as a matter of fact, Fiona's been in touch with her." Uncle Charles looked at her. "When was it that your mother called?"

"A few months ago. Last summer," she said, but Prescott was already on his way to the door.

"You didn't have to do that," Patrick said. He sat with his good side facing her.

"Well I could see what was happening," she said.

"I don't need you to lie for me."

"I know how the Prescotts operate. The more blame they can heap on someone else, the easier it is to keep forgiving Todd," she said, careful not to mention Mr. Prescott's accusations.

No charges had been filed against Patrick. Todd had a minor concussion and back injuries, but no memory of the attack itself. The last he remembered was begging Fiona to let him spend the night at her apartment. Patrick Grady had been there, but that was all he could recall. There were no marks on Patrick, nothing to implicate him as Todd's assailant.

"He said some really bad things about you," Patrick said, wringing his hands.

"Yah, well, considering the shape he was in I'm not surprised." She got up to pour him another cup of coffee.

"I told him to stop. I kept telling him," he said, looking up at her. "He thought it was funny."

"Well anyway, the most important thing is it's over," she said, setting the cup in front of him. "I'm sorry you had to get mixed up in it though."

"It was sick the way he kept laughing. Even when he was hurt, even when he was—"

"Don't. Please, don't." She touched his wrist. "Let's just not talk about it anymore." She couldn't bear to think about what had happened, not only because of the pain it had caused Todd, but because of the guilty pleasure she took in Patrick's desire to protect her.

"Okay." He sat very still, and when she drew back her hand, he took a deep breath. "But I just want to say how glad . . ." He swallowed hard. "How glad I am that we're getting to know each other."

He hadn't eaten since last night so she made him a sandwich, which he wolfed down as he watched television. A World War II documentary had just started. She made him a second sandwich, and now he was eating that one just as fast. He stared at the black-and-white images on the screen, unshaven soldiers inching their way onto a sun-washed farmhouse porch. One soldier nudged open the door with his gun. The door swung wide, and he jumped back against the wall. The three soldiers behind him froze. Seconds later they surged forward and began smashing the mullioned windows with their rifle butts. Soon, a white-haired man and toothless old woman shuffled out the door with their hands clasped over their heads.

"That's so pathetic," she said as a new scene flickered onto the screen, American tanks rumbling through the narrow stone streets of an ancient Italian village.

Watching closely, Patrick put down his empty plate. A slow grin seemed to trickle from his mouth.

"Was it like that in Vietnam?" she blurted, then was instantly ashamed for even reminding him of it.

He lifted the remote and turned off the television, then leaned forward and removed the cover from the box of chocolates. "What's the matter? You don't like them?" he asked.

"I do. They're delicious!"

"There's only three gone." He held out the box.

"I want them to last."

"You don't have to do that. I'll get you more." He took one and peeled away the foil. "Here. Try this one." He offered the chocolate nougat daintily between thumb and forefinger, raising it to her mouth with a look of fearful excitement.

She was still chewing when the phone began to ring. "Uncle Charles!" she said, trying to swallow.

He said he just wanted to see how she was doing and make sure everything was all right.

"I'm okay. Everything's fine," she said, conscious of Patrick's nearness. He put his arm over the back of the couch.

"I was just telling Aunt Arlene we'll have to get together, all of us, for dinner one of these days," her uncle said.

"Yes, that'd be nice."

There was a pause. "The other thing, Fiona, is I wanted to tell you that Todd's out of the hospital. He's home with his parents. It may take a while, but he should be fine."

"Oh. Good."

"Fiona, what is it? You don't sound right. You sound tense. Is someone there? Fiona, it's not Patrick, is it?"

"Yes. We were just having coffee."

"And candy," Patrick said with a quick squeeze of her shoulder.

"Put him on the phone," her uncle said.

"Why?" she asked, trying to sound pleasant.

"He want to talk to me? I'll talk to him," Patrick said, taking the phone from her hand with her uncle's voice still in the receiver. "Hello, Judge. It's me. Patrick. I just came by to make sure everything's okay here . . ." He looked at her, smiling as he listened. "No. No," he said. "She's not upset. No. She's fine. You're fine, aren't you, Fiona?" He listened, then burst out laughing. "I know. I know, but that was before we got to know each other. But now we're friends." He listened again, gleefully chewing his lip. "We're friends!" he repeated. "We're getting to be really good friends," he said with such a high-pitched squeal of laughter that he had to pass her the phone.

"Uncle Charles—"

"Fiona, get him out of there! You tell him I want him out of there right now!"

"No, I don't think so."

"Fiona, he's—"

"Goodbye, Uncle Charles." She hung up the phone.

Patrick was still laughing. "He doesn't know what to do, does he? He can't believe this is happening!"

"There's nothing he can do," she said quietly.

"No, I know. I know. That's the thing. There's nothing, nothing, nothing he can do!" he gasped, sagging against her in helpless laughter. "Nothing. Nothing at all, is there?"

Sandy hadn't been at work since Todd's beating. Maxine said Sandy spent all her time at the Prescotts' now, caring for Todd along with his mother and a nurse. The other day Maxine had seen Mrs. Prescott pushing Sandy's girls through the park in an elaborate double stroller made in England.

"You'd be doing everyone a real favor if you'd just admit Patrick did it," Maxine said.

"But he didn't," Fiona said as she clipped today's specials to the menus.

"She said the doctors think he was kicked." Maxine paused. Her voice trembled now as she began to speak. "I didn't tell her, but that's what he did to me. He hit me until I fell down, then he started kicking me. I rolled up in a ball, and then I passed out. He did the same thing to Todd. I know he did."

"My God, Maxine." Fiona sighed. "What powers of deduction! Let's see now, I wonder how many other people in this town have two feet. Hm, quite a few, I think." She looked up, shocked as Maxine grabbed her wrist and squeezed until it hurt.

"You think you have all the answers, don't you? Nobody can tell you anything. You won't listen to anyone, will you?"

"I listen. When someone knows what the hell they're talking about," she said, pulling away.

"I feel bad for you. I had to find everything out the hard way too, but at least I listened. I wanted to know how to do things right. You've had everything you ever wanted all your life, but you don't want any of it, do you?"

Aunt Arlene called to invite Fiona to go to the bridal shop in Concord Saturday with her and Elizabeth. Afterwards they'd stop for lunch at the Inn. Ginny and Susan had been there last week and the food had been—

"How come you're calling me?" Fiona interrupted. "Why isn't Elizabeth?"

"I know," Aunt Arlene sighed. "She's wanted to, but lately she hasn't had a minute to herself. Poor Rudy. I think he's talked to me more these last few weeks than his own fiancée, and now with everything else she has to do she's taken on the job of directing the school's Thanksgiving pageant." Aunt Arlene laughed. "Your uncle and I find ourselves in charge of haystacks, of all things. We have to make three of them."

"Tell her to call then if she wants me to go."

"Yes. Of course, dear. And I'm sure she will, as soon as she gets a chance," Aunt Arlene said.

An hour later Elizabeth called. Fiona pictured Elizabeth being handed the telephone the minute she came through the door, with Aunt Arlene's steely smile smoothing, nudging all things and everyone back into place.

"I'm sorry," Elizabeth said in a faint voice. "I'm sorry for what I said." She paused. "I mean that. I do. Really, Fiona. I'm so sorry. Tell me you're not mad at me, please?"

"All right," Fiona said stiffly. She'd never been able to stand being the cause of Lizzie's pain.

"So will you come with us then?" she asked. Elizabeth never minded being the first to apologize. What she could not bear was any base and sweaty grappling in an effort to understand who had been wronged and who had said what. There would be no further discussion.

"Well are you and Rudy back . . ." Fiona hesitated. "Are you back on track then?"

"I like that," Elizabeth said, a little too brightly. "Yes, that's a good way of putting it."

"Yes, Fiona thought, she would like that, would seize such a safe, bloodless phrase, and with its suggestion of convention, routine, and inevitability, make it her own.

The next call came from Uncle Charles, inviting her to dinner at the club Friday with him and Aunt Arlene and Ginny and Bob Fay. The campaign had begun, its mission to return her to the fold where she could be more easily monitored and managed. She might be disruptive and embarrassing, but at least he could jump in sooner before too many people were involved, before it hit the papers, before she offended or shocked half the town. "She said it's been ages since she's seen her little cousin," her uncle continued, his attempt at joviality failing.

"Not since the engagement dinner," she said, amazed as always by his ability to transcend discord. In their last conversation he had been shouting, demanding she get Patrick Grady out of her apartment. And now, only days later, not a word would be said about Patrick unless she mentioned him first.

"The engagement dinner. Well that's even longer than I thought," he said with a faltering chuckle.

"Sounds like fun, but I can't," she said.

"Please, Fiona. I just think it's time we got this family back together, don't you?"

"What do you mean?" she asked, bristling.

"Life is too short. We're a family, and when one of us in hurting we all feel it, and then none of us is at our best."

"Do you mean me?" she shot back. "That I'm the one that's hurting?"

"I . . ." He cleared his throat. "I mean any of us, all of us. We've all been in that . . . situation at one time or another."

"Situation? What situation?"

He paused. When he spoke his voice was contained and oddly hollow, as if his hand cupped the mouthpiece. "You know what I mean. You know exactly what I mean."

"No. I don't. I never know what you mean. How could I? I never have, and I probably never will."

"Because you choose not to! Sometimes I think you enjoy being difficult, you enjoy seeing the rest of us uncomfortable," he said.

"Well, on that note I think I'd better hang up now," she said.

"Oh, and Fiona!" he said, clearing his throat in a way that signaled Aunt Arlene's approach. "There's something else. I wanted you to hear it from me. It appears I'm being considered for a spot on the Superior Court bench."

"Congratulations," she said stiffly. "I'm very proud of you, Uncle Charles. I am. I mean it," she said, trying but unable to rise above this flatness she felt inside.

"Yes, well, thank you. I appreciate that, Fiona. I've tried very hard to live a good life and make my family proud."

Unlike you, he might as well have added for the way it left her feeling.

Aunt Arlene rang the doorbell again. The three women waited outside the small antique frame house on Concord's Main Street.

"Maybe they're not open yet," Elizabeth said, shivering in the early-morning chill.

"The lights are on," Aunt Arlene said. "They're open."

"Well, that's weird," Fiona said. "Having to ring a bell to get in a store."

"Serena's isn't your typical store," Aunt Arlene said. "It's by appointment only."

"Oh, of course." Fiona winked at Elizabeth, who smiled weakly.

"They only sell their own designs. And the gowns are all made right here on the premises," Aunt Arlene told them for the third time now. "Brides come here from all over the country," she added, giving Elizabeth a quick hug. The ride here had been strained, with Elizabeth staring out the window and Aunt Arlene's nervous chatter alternating between the wedding and the Superior Court judgeship for which Uncle Charles didn't think he had a chance, but he was flattered just to be mentioned.

"Maybe you should ring it again," Fiona suggested.

"They'll come!" Aunt Arlene said, the sudden quiver of her bright smile as irreversible a portent as a hairline crack in crystal.

"Maybe it's not today," Elizabeth said.

"You wish," Fiona said and laughed.

Aunt Arlene's finger shot to the bell. This time she held it in. The door was opened by a tall, deeply tanned man in a cornflower blue jumpsuit.

"Good morning, ladies. My name is Desmond, and I'd like to welcome you to Serena's," he said, sweeping them through an effusion of sweet cologne and the funereal scent of eucalyptus sprays. They followed him down a softly lit hallway with Fiona mimicking him, swishing her hips and gesturing with a flip of her hand every time he spoke.

"Fiona!" her aunt said under her breath. "Don't be so cruel."

She wasn't sure whether her aunt had said cruel or crude. Either way she was embarrassed. It was like being a child again, wanting to bring a smile to her cousin's somber little face and succeeding only in irritating everyone. Just then Elizabeth began to sneeze.

"God bless! God bless! God bless!" Desmond called back each time. Fiona burst out laughing. The tension was finally getting to her. Aunt Arlene's eyes burned into hers, and Elizabeth looked even more miserable.

"You'll be in the back parlor," he said, leading them into a pale pink room, where they were greeted by two elegantly dressed women.

With its oriental rugs and antique furniture, Serena's seemed more like a gracious home than a bridal shop. The lamp on the table reminded Fiona of the pair in Aunt Arlene's bedroom. "Belleek?" she said to please her aunt, who nodded stiffly. They sat in chintz-covered Martha Washington chairs, expectantly facing the wide expanse of rose moire that curtained the dressing room. The younger, more slender woman stood ready to draw back the draperies as soon as Elizabeth was trussed, hooked, snapped, and buttoned by the matronly attendant with her in the dressing room. Desmond had just returned with a silver pitcher of coffee and a tray of miniature pastries.

"Umm. They're so delicious," Fiona said with a delicate bite of a glazed tart.

"Yes. Nobody makes plum tarts like Henri's," he said, dipping low in front of Aunt Arlene with the tray.

"Oh, Henri's," Aunt Arlene murmured with a sharp look at Fiona. She took a tiny croissant from his etched tray and thanked him. Still smiling, she watched the door close softly behind him. Her eyes flashed at Fiona. The slender woman stepped behind the curtain to confer with Elizabeth's attendant.

"Please don't," Aunt Arlene whispered through her frozen smile.

"What?" Fiona asked in a low voice. "What am I doing?"

"Making fun of everything."

"I'm not!"

"Please," Aunt Arlene implored.

"I was just trying to be pleasant," she hissed back.

"This has been difficult enough."

"You mean Lizzie?"

Her aunt nodded. "You have no idea," she said, and Fiona couldn't tell if her bright blue eyes brimmed with anger or tears. Aunt Arlene sighed deeply and her angular body seemed to sag into the sheen of the mauve cabbage roses.

"Why? What's wrong?" Fiona asked, startled to see her aunt so troubled, this sedate woman who was always in control, who would never show anger or tears in front of strangers or even acquaintances. It was her aunt's fierce conviction that to burden others with one's pain and problems was selfish and rude. *We are here to make this world a better place:* Fiona had been raised on that dictum, though she had always considered it more her cousins' legacy than her own.

"Everything." Her aunt sighed, then sat up, eyes widening, smile fixed now as the slender woman emerged from the dressing room and pulled the cord. The curtains parted, revealing Elizabeth, pale and wanly smiling in yet another gown. The long-waisted, pearl-encrusted bodice seemed sculpted to her thin body, making her look even more delicate and fragile.

"That's beautiful," Fiona and her aunt both said.

"Is it?" Elizabeth said, her gaze oddly skewed as if she could hear, but couldn't quite see them.

"Oh yes!" they assured her.

"It's an exquisite design. Perfect for such a tiny shape," the woman said as she strolled around Elizabeth, pausing now to point out some detail to the kneeling attendant, who was trying to smooth a crimp in the lace hem. She sat back on her heels and peered up. "See? Too high! Too high!" the woman scolded. She pointed at the dress back, and the attendant wobbled as she labored to stand up. "The bra," the woman explained. "It's the wrong one. She needs a waist cinch."

Elizabeth shuddered as the attendant began to tuck her bra into the gown. Goose bumps mottled her arms and chest.

Aunt Arlene tensed forward in the chair. "What do you think, hon?" She bit her lip.

"I don't know," Elizabeth said, as the woman wheeled a gilded three-way mirror out from the wall. Elizabeth turned, glanced in the mirror, then looked back. "I guess I like it. It's heavy."

"They all seem that way at first," the woman said.

"It's a different feel," Aunt Arlene said, her big clenched hands white at the knuckles. "You wear such loose things most of the time."

"You just have to get used to it," the woman said.

"Yah, just wear it around the house for a few days," Fiona added, but no one laughed or even smiled.

Elizabeth continued to gaze in the mirror, not at the gown, but at her face. For a few moments no one spoke.

"So what do you think?" Aunt Arlene asked softly, gently, as if afraid of startling her.

Elizabeth looked at her through the mirror. "I don't know."

"They were all lovely on you, but this one is just beautiful," Aunt Arlene said, her whisper heightening the stillness in the softly lit room.

Elizabeth folded her arms, hugging herself so tightly that her bony shoulders and chest seemed to rise up from the beaded gown as if she were being squeezed out of it.

"It's my favorite," Aunt Arlene said.

"I can see why," the woman said back over her shoulder. She held up her hands as if framing a scene. "It's a fascinating elegance. Sophisticated yet ethereal."

"Like Grace Kelly," the attendant continued, trying to spark the same enthusiasm in Elizabeth. The hem would have to come up. The waist needed to be taken in. And if she liked, seed pearls could be worked into the hem, the woman told Aunt Arlene, for now Elizabeth had become a mannequin in this suddenly bustling, though awkward tableau. But wouldn't that make the dress even heavier? Aunt Arlene asked with a wary glance at Elizabeth, who stood perfectly still, waiting. Not at all, the attendant assured her. There would only be a few, a sprinkling, for the effect, just to bring the eye from head to toe. And maybe some on the veil to complete the look. To create the illusion.

The illusion that Elizabeth was a happy bride, Fiona thought.

"Well, what do you think, hon?" Aunt Arlene asked.

"I don't know," Elizabeth said slowly, blinking as if to extricate herself from another consciousness.

"Do you like this one best?"

"I'm not sure. How much is it?" She felt under her arm, but there was no price tag.

"Forget about that for now and just think about which one you like best," Aunt Arlene said in her low soothing tone.

Fiona was amazed. This from a woman for whom carelessness with money was not only a character flaw, but an almost unforgivable vulgarity.

"I don't know. I'm not sure. I can't tell," Elizabeth said in a tremulous rush that brought her mother to her side and Fiona to her feet.

"I know!" Fiona said. "How about if I try it on? That way you can sit back and relax, and I'll go through all the rigmarole for you." She took Elizabeth's clammy hands and tried to hold them, but like cold little fish they slipped away.

Fiona was in the dressing room now being buttoned, snapped, tugged, and tucked into the same pearl-embossed gown. She was enjoying the attention, having already modeled four other gowns to the admiring cries of the two women and Aunt Arlene's growing exuberance. However, Elizabeth's forced smile had faded. On Fiona's last trip out, Elizabeth had suggested they call it a day. She had a headache. She wanted to go home and think about it.

"Think about what?" Aunt Arlene said so sharply that they all looked at her.

"About the gowns," Elizabeth answered in a pained voice.

"Just one more then," Aunt Arlene coaxed. "The last one you had on."

The attendant groaned now as she stood up. "Okay, ready," she called at the curtain. When it had been drawn, she gestured with a slight bow for Fiona's entrance. Fiona walked slowly, heel to toe, hands clasped as if coming down the aisle.

"Ah," said the woman.

"Such a vision," Desmond said, pausing as he removed their empty cups.

"Like Audrey Hepburn," the attendant said. "The long neck and those big eyes."

"It's beautiful," Aunt Arlene said. "Isn't it beautiful?" she asked Elizabeth. And then, as if realizing an oversight, added that Fiona of course looked lovely too. Absolutely lovely. She had always done that, hastily making a point of including Fiona, who hadn't even realized she'd been excluded or overlooked in the first place.

Jaw quaking, Elizabeth stared at her. Fiona couldn't tell if she wanted to smile or speak. "So Lizzie, what do you think?" She turned slowly, hands out, palms upward.

"I don't know," Elizabeth gasped through a great struggle of catching her breath, sighing, widening her eyes, then shutting them tightly. Each word was released so slowly, from such a painful depth that no one could look at her. "I . . . I just don't know what to do," she said. Tears ran down her hollow cheeks.

"Then have Rudy come in with you, hon," Fiona said, bending to embrace her cousin, but with the gown bunched between them the most she could manage was a gentle headlock. "He'll help you decide."

"No," Elizabeth moaned softly, her head hung. "Oh no."

"He can't," Aunt Arlene said, sounding irritated. "It's bad luck if the groom sees the gown before the wedding."

"No, dear, you wouldn't want that." The woman made a clucking sound and shook her head.

"Then we can come back," Fiona whispered at her cousin's ear. "If you want. Just the two of us. Or we can go someplace else. Or maybe you two should just take off, Lizzie. Just run away and elope. Hey, I know a good justice of the peace up in Rocky Point, Maine." She lifted Elizabeth's chin. "I'll even drive you if you want."

Elizabeth tried to smile, then suddenly covered her face with her hands in tearful laughing hysteria that sent a chill through Fiona until she looked down.

"Your boobs," Elizabeth whispered behind her hands. "They popped out!"

"Jesus Christ, get back in there, will you!" Fiona muttered as she tried to stuff her heavy breasts back into the stiff empty cups.

"Oh dear, dear, dear, I'm out of here!" Desmond cried in his flight through the door.

Elizabeth kept laughing. Aunt Arlene was searching in her purse for a tissue. Now she was crying.

Chapter 11

Fiona was coming out of the bathroom when her bell rang. Patrick, she thought, tying her robe as she hurried to the door. She hadn't heard from him in days, and Uncle Charles was probably the reason why. Her eager smile faded when she opened the door.

"You were asleep," Rudy Larkin said, wincing. "I'm sorry." He started to back away. "Go back to bed," he said in a loud whisper. "I'll call you later."

"Why? What is it? What's wrong?" she asked, alarmed. Unshaven and red-eyed, he looked as if he'd been up all night.

"Nothing's wrong. Really. Nothing," he said, his exaggerated whisper irritating her even more.

Then what did he want? she persisted. He'd obviously come for a reason.

He had forgotten it was Sunday, he said. With his own schedule so crazy lately the days were just running together. "And I knew you and Elizabeth were looking at some wedding gowns yesterday, and I was just, well, you know, wondering how it went." In a gesture of abject discomfort he rubbed the back of his neck, then shrugged and held up his hands. "What you thought, that is," he said with a hard swallow.

"You mean of the gown?" she asked, then realizing he meant Elizabeth, invited him in.

Arms folded, he huddled over her kitchen table, talking while she made coffee. His thin jacket pulled tightly across his shoulders and hiked up his long arms. The cuffs of his chinos were frayed. His loafers were gouged, the top stitching so torn on one that his little toe protruded. He kept swiping hair off his forehead. She wondered how Elizabeth could stand his messiness when she was always so neat.

He and Elizabeth had gone out to dinner last night, and he had been anxious to hear all about their "shopping foray." They had no sooner been seated when an old friend of Elizabeth's stopped by the table. They invited him to join them for a drink. The friend wouldn't order anything for himself, but he somehow ended up sitting with them all through dinner.

"Well that's weird. No," she corrected herself, "that was rude." She poured the coffee, then sat down. "Who was it?"

"George. George Grimshaw." He watched closely, gauging her reaction.

"Who was he with?"

"No one."

"He was alone? George? In the Orchard House? By himself?"

Rudy nodded. "He had some explanation, but then in the middle of it he seemed to get all hung up. I don't know. It all seemed pretty murky to me."

"It must have bothered Elizabeth to have him horning in like that on her evening with you," she said, studying him now.

"Something was bothering her."

"That's too bad. She was looking forward to dinner with you."

"She told you that?" He started to smile.

"She's been so busy. I know it bothers her, the thought of you being alone so much." Actually only her aunt had mentioned Rudy yesterday.

"Really?" he said with an almost caustic laugh. "I've even taken on some midnight shifts. I figured that way I'd get to see her at least some part of the day. But that's not working."

"She just gets too involved. Lizzie's such a perfectionist! About everything!"

"Except me." He looked up with a sad smile. "Things got a little better after you talked to her, but now we seem to be going downhill again." He took a deep breath and kept rubbing the back of his neck. "I hate bothering you like this," he said in a low hoarse voice. "I can't tell you how stupid I feel."

"Rudy! What are you talking about?" She reached over and touched his hand. "You're getting married! Lizzie was trying on wedding gowns yesterday! It's the pressure, that's all. I told you before, things like this throw her for a loop. She thinks everyone has to be happy and everything has to be perfect. And if they're not, well, she's a wreck. She always feels so responsible."

"I wonder why," he said, frowning as he looked past her.

"She was always like that. Even when we were kids. I don't know, it seemed like the worse I acted, the better she tried to be. And when we got older it was almost like she was trying to make up for me or something." She laughed, but he was still staring. To get his attention she jostled his hand. "Remember what I told you about Ginny's wedding? Maybe she just needs to get back on Xanax or something."

Hearing the name of the medication seemed to strike a decisive chord. He folded his hands on the edge of the table. "Last night was no coincidence. George Grimshaw didn't just happen to be there."

"What do you mean?" she asked, scalp tingling, the closest she ever came to blushing. Had George been looking for her? Had he thought she might be joining Elizabeth and Rudy.

"He was there for a reason. It was almost as if he had some set speech to deliver, but then he and Elizabeth didn't even look at one another. They both seemed so uncomfortable, so I started doing all the talking. Then all of a sudden he said something odd. Something about 'enduring strength.' I kept looking at him. I didn't know what he was talking about, and then Elizabeth interrupted. She said the waiter was coming and that we should look at our menus, which he didn't even have. It was all so strange. He ended up staying almost through our entire dinner. Whenever there was even the briefest lapse in the conversation, he'd clear his throat as if he was finally going to have his say. But then Elizabeth would start talking before he could. I never saw her talk so much! By the end of dinner he was just staring at her. Actually, we both were."

When Rudy had tried to discuss it on the way back to his apartment, Elizabeth got upset and accused him of always being too suspicious. He said he laughed then and told her she could, with all justification, accuse him of being confused and lonely and maybe even possessive sometimes, but never suspicious—not until that night, anyway. When they got to his apartment he put his arms around her and she started to cry. His attempts at consolation only upset her more. Finally she told him she was sorry, but she needed to go home. She'd had too much wine to drink and she wasn't thinking straight.

"So I brought her home, then a couple hours later I went to work, and now here I am," he said with a dismal smile.

"You must be exhausted," she said.

"I don't know what I am." He watched her pad across the kitchen in her soiled scuffs to get them both more coffee.

She was remembering a summer night after Elizabeth's freshman year at Smith. George came to the house to tell Uncle Charles what Elizabeth could not: that they were deeply in love and couldn't stand being apart. They wanted to get married. They had it all figured out. Elizabeth would transfer to Boston University. George was doing well enough with his father to support them both and pay for her education as well. Absolutely not, Uncle Charles had said. After he sent George home he told Elizabeth that one day she'd thank him for saving her from a lifetime of mediocrity and dullness. What did he mean by that? Fiona had asked when Elizabeth climbed into bed sobbing. "He means George!" Elizabeth had bawled.

Fiona's hand shook now as she poured coffee into their mugs. She sat back down. Had George gone to the Orchard House last night to speak once again for Elizabeth? To tell Rudy what she couldn't bring herself to say?

"Want some toast?" she asked.

"That'd be great. But only if you're going to have some too. I don't want you to go to any trouble."

"Trouble? How could toast be any trouble?" she snapped, then tried to mask her annoyance with a quick smile. She had noticed before how grateful, how deeply pleased he always seemed for even the most ordinary consideration, the smallest kindness. By magnifying the gesture, his inordinate gratitude only seemed to diminish its worth. It made her feel hollow and false, as if she wasn't doing enough because he needed more, a great deal more than toast.

"I don't know." He laughed. "I guess everything's starting to seem a lot more complicated all of a sudden."

"Then don't be analyzing every little thing. Relax! Just let things happen. I mean, what's the big rush here? It's not like Lizzie's going to leave town or anything."

"No, she already tried that," he said with a rueful laugh.

As she moved around the kitchen, taking the bread out of the refrigerator, the butter, then dishes from the cupboard, she was conscious of his keen watchfulness, as if each domestic detail were freighted with meaning and, now, far greater significance than the struggle to open a jam jar deserved.

"This is awfully nice of you, Fiona," he said as she tapped the side of the lid with a knife until it turned. "I mean, letting me barge in here on a Sunday morning with all my . . . my . . . Well, anyway, this is good, just being able to talk. And if nothing else, I'm finding out just how inept I am at this whole relationship thing. I thought it was all going to be a hell of a lot simpler than this. You know, the logical steps you take from A to B to C, medical school, work hard, meet the right girl, get married. I missed a step. I must have. But I'll be damned if I know which one."

"Maybe you've just been too intense, that's all."

"Yeah," he said with a weak laugh. "Maybe that's why."

She thought of him fending for himself as a little boy because of his mother's illness. Knowing that, how could Elizabeth be doing this to him? It just wasn't like her to be so cold, so selfish. She turned to find him sprawled in the chair staring down at the floor.

"Don't look so morose."

"The thing is . . ." He took a deep breath. "Until Elizabeth I never had a serious relationship. I guess I haven't made it very easy for her. She wants out, but she doesn't want to hurt me. I keep thinking maybe I should be the one to break it off." He paused as if expecting her to disagree. "But what if I'm wrong? I don't know, what do you think I should do?"

"Right now? The same thing she's probably doing: drink your coffee, eat your toast, and listen to the music," she said, turning on the radio.

"You're right. You're absolutely right," he called over the music, grinning with such pleasure that she had to look away. Even his sincerity was turbulent and vast, a powerful wave in which Elizabeth must always be floundering and gasping for breath.

Honky-tonk piano music filled the tiny kitchen. Rudy's head bobbed and his foot tapped with the beat. "This is great. I love ragtime," he said, snapping his fingers.

"Why aren't I surprised?" she muttered as she got up from the table.

"What?"

"The paper. I'm going to go see if it's here yet." She opened the door a hair and peered out. The *Boston Globe* was in front of Mr. Clinch's door. She'd done this a few times, managed to read his paper, then put it back before he woke up. She slipped into the hall, closing the door quickly on the rackety music, then tiptoed across the way. As she bent down for the paper a shadow loomed over her.

"Fiona!" A hand clamped down on her arm, pulling her upright.

"Patrick!" she gasped as his face moved close with angry urgency.

"I have to talk to you!"

"Alright. Well, come on." She tried to turn, but he pulled her back.

"He's in there!"

"It's just Rudy, Elizabeth's—"

"I've been out here! I've been waiting!" he said, hitting his chest with each declaration.

"Well, I didn't know. Why didn't you knock?"

"I've been waiting for him to leave!"

"He will," she whispered to calm him. "Come on in."

"Tell him to go!" he said through clenched teeth. "Tell him to get the hell out!"

"I can't do that. He'll only be here a few minutes more."

"A few minutes! He's already been in there a half hour! What's going on? What're you doing in there?" he demanded.

"We're talking." She kept looking at his distorted mouth, red and so wet a thin trickle of drool glistened on his chin. "We're talking about my cousin, Elizabeth."

Just then the door to her apartment opened, and he let go of her arm.

"I thought maybe you got locked out," Rudy said, squinting and angling his head to see. "Is everything all right?"

"It will be when you're gone, buddy," Patrick said before she could even nod. He stepped past her and stood in front of Rudy. "What the hell're you doing here? What do you want? Yah! Don't answer! You better not, because I know what you want. I know!" he said, pointing at Rudy. "Always coming by, looking up at the window. How many times you go by here this morning, huh, you no-good son of a—"

"Patrick!"

His entire face seemed raw, a wound so ugly and frightening she could barely say his name. "Patrick . . . Patrick . . . Patrick."

"Look," Rudy said calmly. "I'm not sure what's going on here, but I don't think there's any need to—"

"Shut up!" Patrick roared, jabbing his finger into Rudy's chest. "Just shut the fuck up!"

Across the hall Ned Clinch's door opened the width of his lock chain. "Do you people realize that it's Sunday morning and some of us are trying to sleep?" he said, looking only at Fiona.

"I know. I'm sorry, Mr. Clinch," she said to the delicate little man who seemed more giddy than angry.

"That's my paper, isn't it? You've got my paper! And you took it last week, didn't you? I could tell. I thought the folds were all wrong."

"Here!" she said, pushing it in to him. "I just picked it up, that's all. You can close the door now. It's okay. There won't be any more noise."

"I'll close it when the damn hallway's empty, that's when I'll damn well close it!" Ned Clinch declared from the safety of his chained door.

"No! You'll close it now," Patrick cried, lunging as the door slammed shut. "You little fag!" He banged on the door. "You goddamn little creep."

"Fiona!" Rudy put his hand on her arm. "What do you want me to do?" he asked in a low voice, his face close to hers.

"She wants you to leave, buddy!" Patrick bellowed with a shove at his extended arm. "She wants you to get the hell outta here!"

Rudy stared at her. For all his usual agitation, he was in this moment so obdurately calm he might have been a brick wall Patrick was trying to move.

"So go! Just—"

"No!" she said. "You leave, Patrick. You have to go. I want you to go now!"

He took a faltering step back, looking confused, as if he didn't believe her.

"I mean it! You have to! Please! Just go! Go!" she hissed, waving her hand as if to shoo him away.

"I'll call you!" he said as if it were a threat. "I'm gonna call. I don't care what the fuck he says. You hear me?" He pointed at her. "I'm gonna call!"

She nodded. "Yes. Call. You call me."

"Are you all right?" Rudy asked when they were in the apartment.

She nodded as she dialed the phone. Mr. Clinch answered on the first ring. She apologized.

"Apology not accepted," he said, adding that this had been a nice, quiet place until she moved in.

"I'm sorry," she said again, praying he wouldn't complain to the landlord. "I'm so sorry. It won't happen again, believe me. I promise, Mr. Clinch. I give you my word."

"You'd better, because I tell you if I see that creepy man lurking around here again I'm calling the police."

"There was a misunderstanding. He wasn't lurking."

"He most certainly was! And he was here yesterday too! I saw him! He had his ear to your door. I knew you weren't home, so I said to myself, 'All right, I'll give the creep two more minutes then I'm calling the police,' but then he left."

She assured Mr. Clinch he wouldn't be back. "Oh God," she groaned after she hung up. Why was Patrick doing this?

Rudy sat down next to her. "Fiona?"

"Nice life I have, huh?" she said, looking up. "Let's see, first it was handcuffs, then it was screaming women in Dunkin' Donuts. And now this! Jesus, you must think I'm some real piece of work."

"Of course I don't. This is the way it goes sometimes. For everyone."

"Yah, right."

"It's true. And remember, 'when sorrows come, they come not as single spies, but in battalions.' "

"Where'd you hear that?"

"*Hamlet.*"

"Oh. Good. Hamlet. He was the crazy one, right?"

"Tormented, I'd say."

"That's what Patrick is. God!" She sighed, shaking her head to free herself from this nightmare.

"He's the same guy who was here when I brought you the sneakers, right?"

She nodded.

"Was he trying to hurt you?"

"No. No, he wouldn't do that."

"He's obviously in a bad way, Fiona. I mean, he was gone! He was drunk with rage."

"No, it's pain and disappointment. In his whole life he's never really had anything."

"That may be an explanation. But it's no excuse. Not for what I just saw out there."

"You don't understand."

"Fiona," he said, putting his hand over hers. "What if you're his target the next time he loses control?"

"I wouldn't be," she said, pulling away.

"How do you know?"

"Because he's my father," she said, unable to quell her smile.

On Monday the coffee shop stayed busy from breakfast to closing. Fiona was grateful. She didn't want to think. If yesterday had been bad, last night had been worse. Patrick had called late in the evening to apologize, but then became so worked up he began shouting that she was acting like a tramp, and he couldn't understand it, couldn't understand why she'd do that to herself. She threatened to hang up if he didn't stop.

"You better not," he growled, and her hair stood on end.

"I'm hanging up now. Don't call me back until you've calmed down. And I don't want you to ever come here again. Ever!" Her hands continued to tremble after she hung up the phone. He called back immediately. She left the receiver off the hook until morning. The minute she replaced it the phone rang again. She took it off the hook and left for work.

A mild turn in the raw November days had lured shoppers out of the malls. The downtown storefronts had been decorated for Christmas since the beginning of the month. With Thanksgiving a few weeks away, Dearborn's public works department was stringing tiny white lights in all the trees on Main Street. Lampposts along the way had been hung earlier in the day with large balsam wreaths and red bows.

"It's starting to feel a lot like Christmas," Donna Drouin sang with a glance out the window. She was the new waitress hired to replace Sandy, who had moved into the Prescotts' house. Sandy was pregnant. The Prescotts were hoping the baby would be Todd's wake-up call, Donna was saying.

Fiona swept the floor. She was already sick of Donna's brash voice. Donna hadn't stopped talking since she'd come in this morning. Mention a name and if she didn't know the person, she'd at least know the best friend or closest living relative. A stout woman in her late forties, Donna had worked just about everywhere in town. She had even worked here a few years ago until Chester let her go because she was so messy and talked too much. Last week, after days of running an ad that brought in scores of young single mothers like Sandy, Chester told Maxine to call Donna Drouin. Maybe he could handle her big mouth better now that he had Maxine out front, he had confided in Fiona. But Donna was already bothering the hell out of him. She and Maxine were quickly becoming fast friends. On Saturday she had given Maxine a perm. Her last job had been receptionist at Carlene's Cute Cuts.

"She's so talented. She can do anything," Maxine told Fiona.

"Oh yah? Well just remember it's not exactly rocket science," Donna's booming voice called across the empty dining room. The safety pins at the hem of her uniform glinted as she lumbered from table to table, refilling salt and pepper shakers. The coarse black hair on her unshaven legs was bad enough, Fiona thought, but today she had the worst body odor.

Maxine touched her dry, frizzy hair. "Now I need some highlights. Donna's going to give me a foil."

"No, don't," Fiona said too quickly, and Maxine's eyes widened with injury. "It looks perfect the way it is."

"How about you, Fiona?" Donna called. "You'd be a great blonde." She came over and lifted Fiona's chin, moving it from side to side. "I remember when your mother went blond, and you have the same coloring."

"She was never blond," Fiona scoffed, pulling back from the soiled fingers.

"Oh yes she was!" Donna said with a sticky pinch of her cheek. "For a little while anyway. Everyone said how great she looked, and I know because I was working at the drugstore then and I sold her the kit. And then the next time I saw her it was all raggedy and short like it had been hacked off or something."

"When was that?" Fiona asked, trailing her to the next booth.

"Right before she left. Sixty-nine or seventy. I don't know, seems like everyone was dropping out then. Sometimes I think that's what I should have done, just—"

"What do you mean, 'like it had been hacked off'? What happened? Didn't she say?"

"At first she tried to make it sound like it was some hot-shit, badass thing she felt like doing. But it wasn't; I mean, you could tell, it was so . . . so violent-looking. Like I said, hacked. Like, some places right down to the scalp. You could even see cuts from the scissors."

"Did she say what happened?"

"Yah. Patrick Grady did it. She said he got mad because she bleached her hair. She said everything she did made him mad. I told her she should go to the cops, but he already had enough problems, she said. But then she said she was going away anyway so it wouldn't really matter anymore."

With Maxine's approach Fiona started to leave before there could be any more badmouthing Patrick. She didn't believe Donna. She'd never a heard a word about Natalie bleaching her hair or Patrick cutting it off. Donna would say anything for attention.

"But I'll tell you one thing though," Donna called, anxious not to lose her audience. "She loved her baby girl. She was crazy about you, kiddo!" she said with a wink. "I never once saw her without you."

"Really?" Fiona turned back and couldn't help smiling.

"Yah. In fact that's why she was there. You were sick. She came in for a prescription. And that's how we got talking. She had to wait. Now that I think of it, that was probably the last time I saw her."

When she got home from work her uncle's gleaming black Lincoln was idling behind her building. Her stomach began to ache. He got out of the car and hurried toward her.

"Uncle Charles!" She tried to smile, but could tell from the ice in his eyes that he'd come about yesterday's disturbance.

"I have to talk to you."

"Oh yah, sure! Fire away!" Let me have it, she thought, folding her arms over the ketchup stain on her uniform.

"I'd rather not out here, if you don't mind."

She looked around the empty lot. "Yah, people might think that's a little weird, huh, seeing you and me talking."

His breath quickened on his way up the stairs. She'd left the apartment a mess this morning. More fodder for his Fiona disaster mill. Her entire body felt locked in a permanent cringe. They didn't speak until they got inside. She asked him to sit down, but he said he'd rather stand after sitting all day. Any other time that might have been a joke, but there wasn't a trace of humor in his handsome face that was now lined and gray. He took a deep breath to calm himself before he began.

"There comes a time—"

"Look, Uncle Charles, I know exactly why you're here, but first I just want to say it was all just a stupid misunderstanding, that's all," she said with a disgusted sigh.

He looked at her. "As I was about to say, there comes a time in each of our lives when we must face up to the fact that certain things are absolutely beyond our control," he said slowly.

"Exactly!" she cried with relief. And that's what—"

"Fiona! Don't interrupt me again. Please."

"Then let me tell you what happened!"

"We always do it that way, don't we? But this time you will listen to *me*. This time, I will speak first." He paused, his cold gaze ensuring her silence. "My mistake has been in continuing to deal with you and all your troubles as if they were the mishaps of a child. Always picking up the pieces and patching the holes. But you are a grown woman, and as such, the havoc you wreak is so serious, the ramifications so pervasive, of such duration, so continuous, that now I see you destroying people's very lives, and I can't continue on in the same way. I just can't!"

Without a word she got up and walked into the kitchen. She opened the refrigerator and took out two bottles of beer. She put one on the coffee table in front of him, twisted open the cap on hers, then stood with her head back as she drank slowly, deliberately from the bottle. Setting the bottle down, she wiped her mouth, then smiled. "So what're you going to do?"

"Why? Why are you doing this, Fiona? What pleasure does it give you to hurt us this way, to—" His hands shot to his face, but then he looked up quickly as if he dared not look away, could not risk even a moment's lapse. "To destroy us?" he gasped.

"Don't flatter yourself," she said. "Please! Whatever shit I happen to step in, I step in for one reason, and one reason only. Because I just didn't know it was there."

"Do you know what this will do to your cousin? Do you have any idea?"

"I guess not. Because I don't even know what the hell you're talking about." She raised the bottle in another long guzzle though she didn't even want the beer. It left her mouth tasting of cold wet metal.

"I'm talking about Elizabeth," he said, then looked wildly about the room as if for another presence he had suddenly realized was there. "Oh God! Oh my God," he said, gripping his head with both hands.

"Elizabeth! What does she care?"

He looked at her, mouth agape. "Of course. Now it all makes sense. Oh my God. Oh my God!" He lurched forward, then turned back. "Fiona, I'm going to ask you straight out, and I want the truth. The absolute truth. What is going on between you and Rudy Larkin?"

She banged the bottle down and beer spurted onto the table. She looked at him, kept looking while all the bends and turns coalesced into blurred, ghostly images and voices of a half-forgotten film. "Oh. I see. Now I get it! Of course. Naturally whenever there's trouble your first suspect would be me, right? Well, I wasn't going to breach the good doctor's confidence, but since you're thinking such nasty thoughts I guess I'd better. Rudy came here because he's afraid Elizabeth wants to break off their engagement."

"Why didn't he go to her?" he asked, watching carefully.

"He said he's tried. But she won't discuss it. Sound familiar?" she said, immediately regretting her sarcasm.

He stood with his head hung, looking so miserable that she touched his arm. "They'll be fine. Don't worry about it. You know Lizzie. She always lives happily ever after, and she always will. She's like you. She's a perfectionist, and sometimes things just get magnified all out of proportion, right? They do, don't they?" she added, trying to smile. "Uncle Charles!" She shook his arm. "It's going to be all right. Believe me. In the scheme of things this is no big deal!"

He regarded her now with a kind of horror. "No, nothing's a big deal, is it? Not even breaking up a marriage. I heard what happened with the Gliddens. What you did," he said, holding his head back as if from some vile odor.

"What I did? No. No," she said with a deathly calm. "I want you to leave. I want you to leave right now."

"This can't go on. It's too destructive. What can I say? What can I do? There must be something, Fiona, something that would make you happy. You're thirty years old! Is this the way it's going to be for the rest of your life? Turmoil and shame? Is that what you want?"

"I want you to leave."

"First you're going to listen to me. For once in your life you're going to listen. I've already talked to Patrick and I've told him I don't want him anywhere near you. He mustn't come here. He mustn't call you. You can't have anything to do with him."

"What? You can't do that! You can't tell me—"

"Fiona! I will tell you, and that's because I know exactly what's happening. There's a dangerous, dangerous game being played here, Fiona! And it's working out just the way he wants it."

"Oh for God's sake," she scoffed.

He held up his hand. "No. No, listen. Patrick Grady would like nothing better than to destroy this family. And now he's trying to do just that through you."

"That's ridiculous! You just don't know him the way I do."

"Oh Fiona!" he gasped. "If you've never believed a word from my mouth, believe what I've just told you. Please!"

Chapter 12

Patrick was on the phone. He wanted to come over, but the only way she would see him was at his house. She assured him it wasn't her uncle Charles, but her neighbors. She couldn't risk upsetting them any more than they already were. As it was, neither Mrs. Terrill nor Mr. Clinch would speak to her. She didn't dare tell him that Mr. Clinch had lodged a formal complaint with the landlord, a copy of which he had slipped under her door. According to Mr. Clinch she was "a troublesome neighbor, one who was attracting a most undesirable element to the premises."

"No, that's not it," Patrick said. "You just don't want to see me anymore."

"Of course I do. You know I do. It's just better if you don't come here, that's all. At least not for a while, anyway." She explained that the landlord had sent a registered letter threatening to evict her the next time she caused a disturbance in his building.

"What's his name, the no-good son of a bitch!" Patrick growled.

"See! You're mad again," she said. "I'm not going to see you when you're like this."

"No! No, I just feel bad, that's all. I feel really bad."

"Don't feel bad."

"Well I do. I can't help it, I do. So when are you going to come then? Can you come tonight? How about tomorrow then?" he asked when she said she was on her way to bed.

"Well, I don't know. I'm not sure I—"

"Why? You have a date or something?"

"No."

"Then why not? Why the hell can't you just say yes or no? That's all you have to say. Yes or no. I mean, don't do me any favors!"

"Patrick!"

"I don't need crap like that, you understand? You're either up-front with me or you're not!" he shouted as she listened in stunned silence. "That's the way I see it, so don't be telling me, you don't think, or you don't know, or maybe, you're not really sure, because I don't have time for shit like that, you understand? You want to see me, fine, I'm here! If not, then don't bother me! Don't fucking bother me, you hear what I'm saying?"

"I better hang up now, Patrick."

"Yah! You do that! You hang the—" he was still shouting as she put down the phone.

She grabbed her coat and hurried out of the apartment before he could call back. Let him cool down, she thought as she drove to the supermarket. They were so much alike, volatile and impulsive. Facing up to the consequences of her actions was a hard lesson, but she was trying. What Patrick needed was a daughter's softening love and attention. And patience. She was on her way into the Shop And Save when she saw Terry wrestling her loaded cart through the door. Her younger son sat in the child's seat while the older boy stood on the front, clinging to the sides.

"Fiona!"

"Terry!" she called, as they both paused in the electronic sweep of the opposite doors. She continued inside, then came right out again to walk with Terry to her car. Terry was gaining a lot of weight with this pregnancy. Her puffy, red eyes made her face looked faintly bloated. Her hair was pulled back with an elastic, and the loose ends hung in chunks over her ears. There was a button missing on her jacket and the black wool was pilled with lint and dog hair.

Terry said she was exhausted. Both boys had been sick with strep infections, and Tim was shorthanded at the store, so he'd worked every night this week.

Fiona helped load the groceries into the back of the station wagon while Terry put the boys into their car seats. By the time she got them both fastened Fiona had emptied the cart. Thanking her, Terry slammed the hatch door shut.

"I used to look forward to this. But now I hate it," Terry said as she wedged herself behind the wheel. "I hate it more than anything. Stop it!" She reached back and snatched the windshield scraper from the older boy, who had been tapping the window with it. Fiona asked if she could give the boys gum. Only if it had a sedative in it, Terry said.

"Must be a lot of work, huh?" Fiona said, handing them each a stick of gum.

"Dragging those two along doesn't help," Terry said. She thanked Fiona again, then glanced back at the boys and warned them to stay awake or else they'd have to sleep in the car all night. She had enough to carry in.

"Wait!" Fiona called before Terry closed her window. "How about if I give you a hand? I can help carry the groceries in."

No, Terry protested, Fiona had her own shopping to do. But Fiona insisted.

At the house she told Terry to take care of the boys while she brought in the bags. She emptied them onto the counter, smiling as running feet scurried overhead.

"Get back here!" Terry called in a strained voice. "Get back here right now." There were more footsteps, screams, then giggling, and the gurgle of water through the pipes in the wall. Fiona had assembled all the canned goods together, dry goods, cleaning supplies. The perishables were on the butcher block table next to the refrigerator. All the bags were folded flat. She filled the kettle and put it on the stove to boil for tea. She rinsed out the dirty dishes in the sink and opened the dishwasher. Seeing the filled racks, she unloaded the clean dishes and glasses and put everything away. She used to enjoy helping Sandy like this, until she realized Sandy had no problem letting her do everything for her.

When Terry came downstairs Fiona was at the table flipping through a home remodeling magazine. She got up quickly and poured the water for tea.

"Fiona, this is so nice of you. You didn't have to do all this," Terry said as she put away her groceries.

"Keeps my domestic muscles toned," she said. "In fact, I was just thinking, if you want, I could come help you with this every week."

Terry paused with a wistful smile. "And knowing you, Fiona, you probably would." She sighed as she sat down.

"Of course! In fact, I could even baby-sit while you go shopping. You'd probably like that better." She had forgotten how much she enjoyed being with her old friend. "I'm sorry I blew up on you in Dunkin' Donuts like that, Terry. It just all seemed to be coming at me at once. I mean, the whole thing. Of course it never should have happened, but it's not like I did anything on purpose."

"No, I know," Terry said, eyes alert as she leaned forward.

"And I'm not going to go into gory details, but you saw the shape I was in when I left here that night. Was he as drunk as I was? I don't think so."

"No, I don't either. Oh, Fiona." Terry sighed. "I don't know. I mean, what did Brad say? What led up to it?"

"So you do want all the gory details." Fiona stared at her.

"No!" Terry protested. "I just want us to be close again. That's all. And I'm sorry for even bringing it up that time. I just thought it would help for you to talk about it."

"Well, that's why we've been friends for so long. We were never afraid to say what was on our minds. But some things are just too . . . too painful."

Terry looked down at the tea bag she had been dunking up and down. "I haven't been too good a friend lately, have I?"

"You're busy. I know. It's not easy with two kids." Fiona tried to laugh. "And a husband who hates my guts."

"Oh no, Fiona. You know Tim, he's just had his pants on too tight lately."

"What?" Fiona gasped, laughing. "What's that supposed to mean?"

"Well, it was okay at first, being this hot chick—he liked that, but now that we have kids I'm supposed to be the Blessed Mother or something. Kids." She sighed. "That's when everything changes. Hey!" she said, suddenly dumping her tea into the sink. "I feel like a glass of wine. How about you?"

Fiona asked if it was all right to drink when she was pregnant.

"My doctor said an occasional beer or glass of wine is fine," Terry assured her.

An hour had passed, and they were still in the kitchen. They'd been talking about Todd Prescott and Sandy Rudman when Terry's face flushed with her sudden admission that this pregnancy had been a mistake. It represented a terrible financial setback. In her eighth week she and Tim had gone to an abortion clinic in Boston. "All the way in we didn't speak. We didn't even look at one another. It was like neither one of us wanted to have to actually do it. But then again, neither one of us wanted the pregnancy either. So we did all the paperwork, and then I went in this little metal stall to change. It was freezing cold, and I was standing there in just a johnny and paper slippers, and I started shivering so bad my teeth hurt from chattering. The nurse kept coming by to see if I was ready. 'Not yet,' I said. 'Almost.' And I'm just standing there hugging myself. Finally on her fourth trip she asked if I was all right. She said the doctor had already been waiting fifteen minutes. I started putting my clothes back on. 'I have to go,' I said. 'I have to see my husband.' And the minute I walked out Tim jumped up and put his arm around me, and he kept asking me if I was all right. Was I supposed to be walking so fast like that so soon after? I didn't want to tell him in front of everyone in the waiting room, so I waited until we got outside. I thought he'd be so mad, but instead he started crying, then I started crying. There the two of us were on Comm. Ave. surrounded by picketers, bawling our eyes out."

"That's beautiful." Fiona thought of her mother, unmarried and having to face everything alone. She had asked Aunt Arlene once if her mother had ever considered abortion. No. She never did, her aunt had answered, her clipped tone betraying the cold censure her mother must have endured.

"Except now we're both so nervous," Terry said. They both looked up at the sound of running feet. A moment later, Will, the younger boy, charged into the kitchen, crying, and leaped onto his mother's lap. He said his brother, Frankie, kept shutting the door and scaring him.

"Every time I think of it, I get so afraid. We both do," Terry murmured, her chin resting on the boy's head. "You know, it's like we went to the edge, like we tempted fate, so now anything can happen."

Fiona looked at her hugging her sweaty son, his legs tucked under his small body that was curved against his mother's big belly. "But anything can always happen," she said. Just as there were no guarantees in life, there were no safeguards either, she tried to explain. Not even an exemplary life could assure a person good health or good fortune. Lightning could strike anyone at any time. Saints got cancer too. And innocent children got hit by cars.

"Don't say that." Terry shuddered, looking down at her sleepy son. She got up and carried him around the corner where she laid him down on the sofa. "It just makes everything seem so . . . so kind of rickety," she said, coming back into the kitchen. "You know. Unsafe."

"But everything is!" Fiona said with absolute conviction.

Terry poured them both more wine. "You didn't used to be this bitter."

"It's not bitterness. I'm just being realistic, that's all. All my life I grew up hearing that good things happen to good people, but I kept seeing how bad things happen to good people too. Of course my own family—I mean the Hollises, that is—they do good deeds the way most people knock on wood. It's not so much to help the other person as it is to cover themselves, to make themselves feel better."

"But you don't mean Elizabeth. She's not like that, right?" Terry asked, watching her.

"Well, Elizabeth's a different version of the same syndrome. She always had to be good to make up for me." She laughed. "Kind of a good twin–bad twin thing, I guess." She set down her glass. The wine on an empty stomach had made her lightheaded. She hadn't felt this relaxed in a long time, she thought, sinking back into the comfort of their easy intimacy.

She was telling Terry about Rudy and Elizabeth's problems. She knew she shouldn't, but after what Terry had just confided, how could she not? This trading of secrets had always been their way of putting things right again. Terry listened intently, then asked what Rudy was like. To describe him Fiona told how they'd first met, after she'd been handcuffed by Jim Luty.

"Jim Luty! Oh my God!" Terry roared, holding her sides, while Fiona related the rest of the bizarre tale.

"And he never even told Elizabeth?" Terry asked.

"No! That's what I mean. He's a really genuine person. Obviously he's smart, he's a doctor, but he's got this other kind of intelligence. You know like from in here," she said, touching her breast. Yes, that was it, she thought. That was it exactly.

Terry watched her over a long sip of wine. "If I tell you something, can you keep it to yourself?"

"Of course."

"I mean you absolutely have to. Timmy would kill me if he found out I said anything."

"I won't. I swear! What?"

"But then you probably already know."

"What? How would I know?"

"It's about George." Terry leaned on both arms over the table. "You know how he said this was a confusing time for him right now?"

Fiona nodded, and in that instant knew what Terry was about to tell her.

Elizabeth and George were seeing each other again. Tim had dropped in on George one night and Elizabeth had been there. Tim said it was so obvious. George didn't seem to want him there, and then right before he left, Elizabeth came down in George's bathrobe. She was mortified. After she went back upstairs, George told Tim the truth. They wanted to be together, but Elizabeth still hadn't been able to break off her engagement. "She can't bring herself to hurt the guy—"

"Rudy," Fiona interrupted. "Rudy Larkin." He wasn't a guy. He had a name.

"Yah, him," Terry continued, "but what's even worse, according to George, is that she can't bear the thought of upsetting her parents. Apparently every time he brings it up she goes to pieces."

Fiona sipped her wine.

"So you didn't know," Terry said.

Fiona shook her head. "Not really. But now that you've said it I guess I just didn't want to know." She described their strange shopping trip for the wedding gown. Terry's eyes widened with intrigue. Her lips seemed to move with Fiona's, already practicing the retelling. Fiona knew she would feel guilty for exposing Elizabeth, but right now she felt too betrayed herself, and angry. A sourness rose in her throat. It wasn't kindness that motivated her cousin, but timidity and deceit, a cowardly mix.

In the other room Will cried out briefly. Terry peeked around the corner. "He's all right," she said, hurrying back. "So anyway, what happened when you put the gown on?" Terry's head jerked up as the back-door glass filled with the headlights of a car pulling into the driveway. "Shit," she muttered, grabbing the wineglasses. She was almost at the sink when the back door opened. Tim entered, laughing and talking over his shoulder to the shorter man behind him. "Hey honey, look who—" He stopped, glancing down at Fiona with a look of confusion. Brad Glidden had already stepped inside and was closing the door.

Terry stammered an explanation of Fiona's help with the groceries.

"What's this?" Tim took the wineglasses from her. He dumped them out into the sink.

"We were just talking." Terry glared at him.

"Hi, Tim," Fiona said from the table. She ignored Glidden.

"Daddy!" Will said, rubbing his eyes as he shuffled into the kitchen.

"Hey, big guy!" Tim bent down to pick him up. "Come on," he said to Glidden as he headed past the table. "We'll turn the game on in here."

Eyes averted, Glidden hurried after him.

"Asshole," Terry muttered as the television came on loudly, as if the volume could somehow shield them. "I'm sorry," Terry said as Fiona stood up and put on her jacket.

Her face felt hot. "That's okay," she said. She had to get out of here. From the corner of her eye she saw Tim carrying his son up the stairs.

"No, wait! You just wait here. I'll be right back," Terry insisted, hurrying after him.

She could hear their muffled voices upstairs. She opened the back door. "No, God damn it," she whispered, then turned and marched into the living room. Brad Glidden was huddled on the couch staring at the basketball players racing across the screen.

"Excuse me," she said loudly to be heard over the announcer. "But there seems to be a misunderstanding here."

"What?" His eyes flickered warily between her and the stairs beyond.

She picked up the remote control from the coffee table and clicked off the television. In the sudden silence she could hear little Will crying, then heavy footsteps near the stairs. "Tell me," she said, moving closer. "Did I do something bad to you?"

"I don't know what you mean," he said, his voice barely audible, his head tilted back in disbelief.

"Did I hurt you in some way? What did I do? Did I take advantage of you somehow? Did I attack you? Exactly what did I do?"

"Nothing," he gasped, shaking his head.

"It was just the opposite, wasn't it?" She felt herself not just looming, but towering, swelling over him.

"We both had too much to drink, both of us," he said quickly, in obvious dread of the details.

A shadow fell across the stairwell.

"Well, you better tell your wife that then. And your mother-in-law too! And you also better tell them that if they ever insult me again the way they did, I will take them to court and I will sue them for every penny I can get." She was trembling with power and rage. He ducked as she flipped the remote onto the table.

"I'm sorry," he said in a high wheezy voice.

"And I'm sorry your baby died, but you know as well as I do that it didn't have anything to do with me."

"Get out!" Tim shouted as he raced down the stairs. "You get the hell out of my house!"

"Yah, I will, but first I want to see Terry." She smiled, but her heart was pounding.

"No! You go now!" he demanded.

Brad stood up. "That's all right, Tim, I'll—"

"No. She's leaving! Not you."

Fiona gave a little laugh and went to the bottom of the stairs. "Terry?" she called up. "Can you come down a minute?" She paused. "Terry?" she called a little louder. "Will you please come down here?"

"She's not coming down," Tim said, smirking. "So why don't you just go?"

"Terry! Can you hear me? Terry?" She was almost shouting.

"You wake up those kids . . . " Tim warned with a clenched fist.

"Terry!" she called again.

Terry appeared at the top of the stairs. "Fiona," she whispered in a thin voice. "I think you better leave."

She called Terry the next day, not to apologize but to say she hoped she hadn't caused any problems between Terry and Tim. Seeing Glidden had just brought everything to a head.

"That's okay," Terry said so numbly that Fiona knew she had lost her last friend. For the rest of the day she kept thinking of Rudy. If she felt this isolated in her own hometown with her family so close by, then she could just imagine how alone he must feel. They might as well be lonely together, she thought as she dialed his number, but then hung up before it could ring. She felt afraid, but didn't know why. That was silly, she assured herself as she called again. This time she let it ring. What was there to fear? That he'd be busy or misinterpret her call or know by her tone that her cousin was being unfaithful to him? Finally, when he didn't answer, she hung up, surprised at her disappointment. And then when she realized that he was probably working, she was even more confused by the relief she felt.

Uncle Charles called a few days later to remind her of their fall party. It always took place the weekend before Thanksgiving, just long enough before everyone's nerves got frazzled from too much shopping and too many holiday parties. He made a point of telling her that Rudy would be there with Elizabeth. Then as if as an afterthought, he suggested that if she wanted to invite someone, that would be just fine.

"I don't know, I'll see," she said, amazed he could so easily overlook everything he'd said in their last conversation. But that was typical. Ignore it and it would go away.

"Yes. Well." He cleared his throat. "What about George Grimshaw?"

"What about him?" She recognized the captious tone. Once again ostracism hadn't worked. Anger and ultimatums unsettled him more than they did her. He could manage her better if he could keep her right under his nose.

"Why don't you ask George? It would be so nice seeing all you young people together again."

"Oh yah?" She couldn't help laughing.

"Fiona, I just want you to be happy, that's all."

"I am. I'm happy," she said coldly.

His voice dropped to a shaky whisper. "Then let's just start over again. Let's try. Let's both try really hard."

Aunt Arlene called the next day to ask if she might need some cash for "a pretty dress" to wear. Fiona thanked her, but said no. She said she didn't know if she'd be going. "Please come." Her aunt sounded genuinely alarmed. "Elizabeth will be so disappointed if you don't. She's counting on your coming. You don't know how much she's looking forward to it."

Strange, she thought as she hung up. Why would her cousin care if she were there or not? In a gathering of her parents' friends Elizabeth would be in her element, admired and petted.

The next call was from Elizabeth, suggesting that Fiona stay over the night of the party so she wouldn't have to drive home alone. Now the shepherding was complete.

"Maybe I won't be alone," Fiona said, with the phone propped on her shoulder while she painted her nails. "Maybe I'll ask someone."

"Yes, I think you should," Elizabeth said. She paused. "Do you have someone in mind?"

"I don't know. What do you think, Lizzie, who should I ask?"

"I don't know. Is there someone you're interested in?"

"Umm, maybe," she said, blowing on her nails. "I don't know."

"Well, who?" Elizabeth persisted. "Who would you ask?"

"Well, I was thinking of George. I mean, you know, just as a friend."
She smiled, listening to her cousin's shallow breath through the silence. Let her squirm. Poor Rudy. How long could she keep up the
charade? Soon everyone would know but him.

"I don't know, he's not much of a party person. He might feel uncomfortable."

"Why would he feel uncomfortable?" She shifted the phone and
began to polish her left hand.

"I don't know. I just think he might. It's been a long time since he's
been here."

"Oh, don't worry. I'll take care of him." Fiona sighed as she blew
her nails dry.

"So are you going to?" Elizabeth said after a pause. "Are you going
to ask him?"

"I don't know. Maybe," she said before she hung up.

When her nails were dry she began to fold the basket of laundry
that had been on the couch all week. She was halfway through when
there was a knock on her door.

It was Rudy. "Well, speak of the devil!" she said, inviting him in to
watch her fold clothes. He said he'd been going by and had seen her
light on so he decided to pop in on her.

"It's 'drop in,' isn't it?" she asked, resuming her folding.

"I don't know. Doesn't that suggest something aeronautical, you
know like down from the skies?" he said, gesturing.

"Maybe, but 'pop in' just sounds so kind of feminine, you know, like
something a woman would say."

He laughed. "So I'm a cross-speaker. My lord, Fiona, I thought you
were a lot more tolerant than that."

"That's what happens when you've talked to too many Hollises in
the past hour."

"I see," he said, nodding. He touched his chest. "Thus the devil to
which you referred."

"Actually, no. I was just talking to Elizabeth, but not about you. In
fact your name never came up."

"I'm not surprised," he said, then explained how Elizabeth had
called last night to apologize for the way she'd been acting. She'd had

a long talk with her father, who had helped her put things into per-
spective. Elizabeth and Rudy had agreed to slow down. For the time
being there'd be no more wedding talk. If it happened on schedule,
fine. And if it didn't, well then, they'd just pick another date. There
wasn't any point in rushing. They had their whole lives in front of
them. What they should be doing now was having fun, enjoying one
another, and helping Rudy feel more like a part of the family and the
community.

"So is that why you're here? You're trying to feel more like part of
the family? Or am I the community?"

"You're both!" He laughed.

"Well, under the circumstances you don't seem very upset," she
said, trying to hide her irritation behind a raised towel.

"What would be the point?" he asked.

"Well, to find out where you stand, at least."

"Why?" He chuckled. "I think I'm better off not knowing."

"What the hell kind of a life is that?" she blurted. For one so passionate herself, so short-fused, she was confounded by his calm acceptance.

"The only one I got!" he said, idly turning the pages of a magazine
on the coffee table.

"Well I think it's ridiculous," she said, watching him.

"I don't know," he mused. "It makes sense, I suppose."

"Well maybe to you!"

"The thing is, I've been alone a long time. I mean, a really long
time." He closed the magazine and looked up. "In certain respects I've
almost always been on my own. So when someone like Elizabeth came
into my life it was like I knew instantly. I just knew."

"Knew what?"

"That I didn't want to be alone anymore. That I couldn't let her get
away." He chuckled. "You know how you'll hear an expression all your
life, and you never give it a thought, and then one day it suddenly
seems so relevant. It becomes so meaningful, so personal. 'It's too good
to be true.' That's what I kept saying to myself. Every time I saw Elizabeth I'd think, my God, she is! She's so good. She's so sincere and so
kind and thoughtful. But then I'd get this strange feeling, and I'd

think, what if she is too good to be true? Is it possible? Can a person be too good? So kind and good they can make everyone else happy, but never themselves?"

"I don't know, doc, you got me there." She sighed. This had been George's mistake. By idealizing Elizabeth he could ignore the reality. "My problem's just the opposite. I seem to make everybody pretty miserable, and most of the time I don't even have to try."

Laughing, he got up and stood by the table. He watched her shake out a sheet from the laundry basket and hold it high in front of her. "You know why, don't you? Because you're too true to be good."

"Thanks, Rudolph." She folded the sheet into sections. "You could've at least pretended to disagree. It would have been the polite thing to do."

"But that's what makes you so interesting, Fiona. You're very real. There's such honesty about you. It makes you very comfortable to be with."

"Thanks," she said. "I guess I'm just so well broken in."

"I hope George appreciates you," he said, buttoning his jacket.

"George?"

"George."

"Oh! George."

"How's he doing?" he asked, as he bent to tighten his bootlaces.

"He's fine," she said, unable to even say his name for fear she might blurt out the truth.

"Your uncle said you're inviting him to the party."

"And how did he happen to mention that?"

"It just came up, I guess," he said with a shrug. "So are you?"

"I don't know yet."

"Don't tell me you two have a relationship like ours."

"No!"

"Well that's good."

"I mean, we don't have a relationship."

He seemed confused, unsure what to say next. He tied his scarf around his neck. He never looked warm enough, she thought. He said he'd better get going. He couldn't risk making her sick of him too, he said as he opened the door.

"Wait!" she called. "So what are you? Are you still engaged?"

He paused as if trying to decide. "I think so. I don't know."

"You don't know?"

"Well, I guess that's the whole point of taking it easy and giving Elizabeth some space, a little more time."

"A little more time!" she scoffed. "She either loves you or she doesn't! Have you even asked her that? Why don't you?"

He closed the door and stepped back in. "Why?" he said, his stricken look turning all her frustration with her cousin to anger. "Why are you getting so worked up?"

"Because I don't understand why you're putting up with it!"

"Putting up with what?"

"With the way you're being treated!"

For a moment his dark eyes held on hers. "What do you mean, Fiona?"

"What I just said."

"No. You want to tell me something, don't you? Please, I wish you would. I need to hear it." He stared at her. "That's all right," he sighed when she didn't respond. "I think I already know."

No, she thought, standing by the window, watching him hurry through the parking lot to his car. He couldn't possibly know and still stay.

Chapter 13

Patrick looked out the window then sat back down to finish the lasagna Fiona had brought. Clutching his fork in his fist, he hunched over the table. He glanced up, then looked away. He wasn't used to sharing his table. Her attempts at conversation had only made him more fidgety. He put down his fork with a little grunt, then pushed back his empty plate. Head cocked, he sat very still for a moment. "You hear that?" He got up again.

"No," she said as he peered out the window. She asked if someone was coming. Did he expect company? He was just nervous, he said. That's what he did sometimes when he was nervous.

"What, go look out the window every two minutes?" She laughed as she cleared the table.

"No, I just look to make sure no one's coming, then I feel better," he said.

"Same difference," she said, filling the sink with warm soapy water.

"It's a bad habit I got. Once I get started I can't help it."

"Speaking of bad habits, maybe you can tell me. Did my mother ever bleach her hair? I just heard that the other day. Is it true?" She looked back to find him staring at her and wished she hadn't said anything. Especially not tonight when he was so edgy. "Want some more coffee?" She reached for a towel. "There's some pie—"

"I think you should go now."

"Why?" Wiping her hands, she turned, startled to find him so close. "What is it?"

"It might snow," he said.

"I don't think so. It's not predicted anyway." She had to step aside to take off her apron. "But if you want to be alone, that's—"

"I don't want to be alone. It's not that."

"What is it then?" She stared back, waiting for him to say it hurt to talk about her mother. She could see it in his eyes, all that pain and longing. All those wasted years when he at least could have been close to his daughter.

His mouth opened, then closed as if he'd changed his mind. He shook his head. "I guess maybe that's it."

"That you want to be alone?"

He nodded and bit his lip.

"That's okay," she said quickly. She touched his arm. "I understand. I get like that. Sometimes I feel like some kind of rabid dog, that just wants everyone to stay away."

He looked at her hand, and she pulled back. He didn't want to be touched. Just because she was determined to have a father didn't mean he was ready to be one. He could only take her in small doses and then he needed to be alone. He'd begged her to come, but bringing dinner had been her idea, and now she was getting on his nerves. She regretted mentioning her mother. But that was all right, she told herself as she put on her coat. She could understand if he was feeling awkward. She did too, though she wasn't sure why. Everything felt strained; she had been trying too hard, laughing uproariously at things that were barely funny, exaggerating the simplest facts to get his attention. Her exuberance had made him self-conscious, then when she had tried to be quiet and let him eat in peace he had grown even edgier and more watchful. It was almost, she thought, noting his clenched fist on the knob, as if he had just realized how much he disliked her.

"I'm sorry," he said before closing the door.

The locks clicked as she cut across the frozen grass to get to her car behind the garage. She pulled down the driveway and waved before she turned onto the road. He was in the window, watching.

■

She hadn't heard from Patrick in days. In a fit of loneliness tonight she called Rudy, thinking he might have a few minutes to kill before work, but he wasn't home. She put on her jacket and hurried out to the car. A light snow had begun to fall, but was melting as soon as it hit the windshield. All the lights were off in Patrick's house. She was about to turn around when she saw the flickering glow of his television.

The house was a mess. She started to pick up empty beer cans from the floor, but Patrick insisted she sit down. The cheese-encrusted lasagna pan was on the coffee table, with a fork in it. She'd been here for almost an hour and he was still talking.

"College, yah. I tried, but I just couldn't hack it. I was a . . . " He hung his head, chuckling. "I was gonna to say I was a lousy student, but I was just lousy. That's what it was." His voice drifted through the half-darkness. "It was the same thing then too. Too many people, too many people, just too goddamn many people," he muttered, the words trailing off, dying like a feeble engine. He sighed.

The acrid sweetness hung in the air. He was stoned. He said he'd been smoking on and off all day. He hadn't gone to work since last week. He'd had a fight with the head janitor, and he was sick of it, sick of seeing people, talking to them, being around them, smelling their stink. "They just walk by, and these little bits and pieces fall off," he said, rubbing his fingers together. "It gets in the air, and nothing can wash it off. Nothing, nothing, nothing. I never talk to them, never ever."

"Why did you want to work there then?" She pulled her coat sleeves over her hands. It was freezing in here.

"Who said I wanted to?" he asked, grinning. He leaned close and whispered, "Maybe I had no choice."

"What do you mean?"

"Just that." He sat back.

"Well you asked for the job, didn't you?"

"Is that what he told you? Is that what the good Judge said?" He shook his head, laughing. "He just wants to keep me off the streets, that's all. Keep me out of trouble. Keep me near him." His eyes widened. "And away from you."

"Why did you take it then?" she asked guiltily.

"Because I hate it so much. I hate it. I hate their faces. I hate the way they look at me. Or maybe I just hate my own face," he hissed, the whispered intensity erupting in giggles.

She closed her eyes. She felt dizzy, oddly disoriented. The air around her swarmed with his agitated presence. He had never been this willing to talk about himself. But each reflection seemed to end in increasing bitterness.

"So what did you do after you left school?" she asked to return to a safer subject. He had gone to Boston College on a track scholarship. From what she could tell of his disjointed tale he had quit after three months. Though she knew better than ask right now, she wondered if he had returned to be near her mother. Natalie would have been a senior in high school that year.

"Came home, hung out. There wasn't much going on, I know that. I worked a few places, the gas station for a while. Then some snowplowing for a while." His hand trembled as he reached for the joint. He took a drag and the tip swelled in an orange glow. He inhaled with a gasp that sounded like a bone snapping in his chest. His head bobbed while he held in the sweet hot smoke. The only light came from the ceiling bulb behind them in the kitchen. She could see dirty dishes piled in the sink. He had been disappointed that she wouldn't join him, but the thought of sharing a joint with her father repulsed her. He exhaled with a wheezy cough that seemed to weaken him. His head dropped back against the piled pillows.

"I did deliveries. You know, in and out of Boston. Some kinda courier service you'd call it today. But then it was just, 'Hey, give Patrick a call. He'll run it in for you. He ain't got nothing else to do.' " He laughed. It was quiet for a few moments. He lay sprawled the length of the frayed divan. Afghans were heaped on the floor.

His shirt was torn, with most of the buttons missing, as if he had ripped it to get it off. She had to lean forward to hear him now.

"But hey. What the hey. What the hey, hey, hey!" he said with a dismal sigh. "Tell you the truth, I was bored out of my mind. I had a pretty low number. In the back of my mind I kept thinking, well, any day now they'll get to me, and I'll be outta here."

The orange tip flared in the half-darkness. He grew so quiet and still she was sure he had fallen asleep. She got up and peered down. "Patrick?" she said softly.

"Yeah?" He stared up at her.

"Oh! I thought you fell asleep."

"I was just thinking."

"About what?" she asked, relieved as she settled back into the chair. He didn't answer.

"Were you thinking about the war? It must have been such a shock, you were so young."

"I was thinking about your face."

"My face!" she said with a nervous laugh.

"I love to look at it. You're beautiful."

"Thank you. I guess I look like my mother. Or at least that's what everyone says." She winced, wishing she hadn't said that.

"You're better-looking."

"She was very pretty!"

"You've got a great body." He lifted his head to look.

"What was she doing when you came home from Vietnam?" she said in a rush of words.

"Natalie? What she always did, running around like some . . . " He sat up.

It was the first time she had heard him say her mother's name. "Were you still going together when you came back?"

"Came back? When'd I come back? From where?"

"From Vietnam. When you came home!"

"Home? Yah, that's right," he said, kneading the top of his head with both hands as if it hurt. "I came home. I did, didn't I? But just for the glory, that's all. That's the only reason." He chuckled. "You gotta have somebody to show your fucking medals to."

"You must have been proud," she said, not sure he had understood her question.

"It was all shit, that's all it was. Shit. Plain and simple. Everybody got a medal. It was the war to award all medals." He laughed.

"So you were still going out with Natalie then?" Maybe if they both called her Natalie, it would be easier for him.

"I was getting skin grafts, that's all I was doing."

She asked how long he was in the hospital.

"A few months," he said, staring at her.

"And how long were you in Vietnam?"

"The same. A few months."

"You must have come home though. I mean, you came for a visit before then, right?"

He shook his head, grinning. "People came to see me."

"Did Natalie?"

"No." He took another drag.

"Why? Why didn't she?"

"Why should she? I was nothing to her." He smiled.

"But she must have been pregnant then."

"Oh. Well maybe that's why then." He chuckled softly to himself.

She didn't believe him, but she would have to be patient.

The kitchen faucet was dripping. The refrigerator motor shut off, and the drip grew louder. His feet smelled. The few clothes he had were gray and dingy. Money was a problem, and yet he owned all this land, over thirty acres. Outside, the flurries had turned into sleet that was pelting the windows.

She asked what he did when he came home from the hospital.

"Same as now, lay here, smoke a little weed. Get up, go sit in my car, smoke a little weed. Come back in, smoke a little weed."

"What kind of car'd you have?"

He smiled. "A sixty-five Thunderbird. It was black."

"Sounds cool."

"Yeah. I got a picture here someplace."

"Could I see it? I'd love to see it."

"Yah, sometime. If I ever find it," he said with a dismal gesture at all the clutter.

"Do you have any pictures of Natalie?"

"No," he said, his voice so flat now she was afraid he was angry.

"That always seemed so strange," she continued quickly, hoping to arouse his sympathy. "Growing up with hardly any pictures of her around. In that whole big house there was only one out. Aunt Arlene said it just made her too sad, but that shouldn't have mattered. They should have thought about me, about my feelings."

He didn't say anything. His eyes were closed. The joint was dead in the ashtray. "Patrick?" she whispered. He was asleep. She brought the lasagna pan into the kitchen, filled it with water, and let it soak on the drainboard while she washed the day's old dirty dishes. As she scrubbed she kept averting her eyes from the bulging shoebox overhead. When she was done she stacked the dishes in the metal cupboard. She was tempted to organize the shelves, but he would consider it an intrusion. He had lived in this dilapidated house all his life, except for those months in Vietnam and the VA hospital. Thirty years had passed and where had he gone? What had he done? He never even went into Boston anymore. In a very real sense he had stopped living. What had happened to cause such emptiness? So much unhappiness? Had her mother hated him so much that she hated their child as well? "What a bitch she must be. What a cold, self-centered bitch!" she whispered, amazed by the exhilaration of her anger. For years she had fantasized the joyful embrace of her mother's return, but now that she knew Patrick she realized what a waste those years of yearning had been. No wonder people seldom talked about her mother. No wonder her aunt and uncle squirmed with her relentless questions, their vague replies purposely misleading. Natalie Range was no tragic, romantic figure but an immature, selfish young woman who had not wanted the responsibility of motherhood. She had done exactly what Donna Drouin had said: just dropped out and moved on. But she must have at least wondered about her daughter. Or about Patrick.

She looked back over her shoulder as she slid the shoebox from the shelf. She put it on the table. One letter, a card, a note. Anything. But these were mostly bills, some ten years old, judging by the postmarks on the dingy envelopes. One grease-flecked folder was thick with expired store coupons, warranties for a toaster, a clock radio, receipts for oil deliveries, old tax bills. She was closing the folder when she recognized

Uncle Charlie's handwriting on the back of the envelope from the town assessor's office. With a nervous glance at the unmoving form on the divan, her cold fingers fumbled at the flap. It was last year's tax bill, $4,784.00 for Patrick's house and thirty-four acres of land. Uncle Charlie's note said: *Patrick, Enclosed please find what you need. And if it goes up again next year, then we'll just take care of it. Don't worry about it. C.*

"What the hell're you doing?" Patrick demanded from the doorway. He was red-eyed and wincing in the light.

She jammed the folder into the box. "Pictures. I thought maybe there'd be some in here." She reached up to slide the box back onto the shelf, but he grabbed it.

"There's no pictures in here!" he said, slamming it onto the table.

"No, I didn't see any."

"Next time, ask me!"

"I should have. I'm sorry. I was just leaving. I didn't want to wake you up."

"I wasn't asleep. I was watching you." He stared at her.

"My uncle paid your taxes last year?" she asked, staring back.

"He does every year."

"Why?"

"Why do you think?" He was trying not to smile.

"I don't know."

"Then you should ask him."

"Why can't I ask you?"

"Because it's a secret," he said as he came closer. He put his hands on her shoulders. His whiskery cheek brushed hers. "I'm not supposed to say," he whispered in her ear.

"Why?" she asked, eyes wide with the heat of his breath in her hair.

"Why do you think?"

She stood very still and tried to pretend his belly wasn't at her waist, his chest against her breasts, but now with his deep sigh her anger was uncontainable. "Don't play games with me!" she cried, pushing him away. "Why won't you answer my questions? Why can't we talk without this . . . this sick thing happening?" There. She'd finally said what she couldn't bear to consider. She tried to look away, but there was no hiding it. She felt sick to her stomach.

His mouth opened and closed as he came toward her, his hands groping in air. "I love you," he finally said bewilderedly. "You know I do. I told you. I love you!" he bellowed with a fierce blow to his chest. "I love you!"

"No! You can't! Not that way! Jesus Christ, Patrick, you're my father!"

"No," he groaned. "I'm not. I'm not. I'm not. How many times do I have to keep telling you? Why won't you believe me? Oh God." He covered his face with his hands. "God, God, God."

"I'm going to go home now. Don't smoke any more. I don't know, maybe you're just way too stoned. Maybe that's what happened." She hurried past him to the front door. "You probably don't even know what just happened," she said, opening it.

"I know what happened," he snarled, his face twisting with contempt. "And you do too."

She stepped onto the porch and gasped as a gust of icy rain swept over her. Before she could close the door it banged back against the wall. He had her wrist. He was yanking her back inside. He pushed her up against the wall and slammed himself against her.

"Patrick! Patrick, please . . . ," she managed to cry before his lips closed over hers. She couldn't move her head. His hands were clamped around her throat, his thumbs pressing up into her jaw, forcing her mouth against his. He grunted. His tongue was making her gag. He drew back slightly, but kept his hands on her neck. He closed his eyes and ground his brow into hers.

"Now that proves it, doesn't it?" he panted. "Now you know. I'm not your father, and that's the honest-to-God truth." One hand fell from her neck and moved slowly down her side, to rest on her thigh. "I love you. You know I do."

"Patrick, please let me go. I have to go now." Her throat was so dry she could barely speak.

He stepped back quickly. "Wait!" he called as she darted past him onto the porch. "Do you believe me? Just tell me that."

She ran to her car and locked the door, but when she pulled onto the road she saw him still on the porch watching.

It wasn't until she got into town that she could finally breathe. She kept touching her throat. The rain was turning back to snow and the roads were slick. More than injury she felt a deep defilement, a violation of her most vital bond. She thought of Rudy. He would help her. She didn't understand what had just happened. She drove to Dearborn Memorial and pulled into the parking lot. She stared at the emergency room doors. She couldn't bring herself to go in. An ambulance idled by the entrance. Every time its dome light flashed red streaks on the wet windshield she winced with her own frightened reflection. She was so much older than her mother had been. She kept remembering what Donna Drouin had said, what she had refused to even think about. Had he done that? Had he hacked off her mother's hair? Had she run away in terror?

Everyone had warned her, even Rudy. But it wasn't really Patrick's fault. In his loneliness he had confused her need and her desire to please him with seduction. He had never wanted to be her father, and now only wanted to be her lover. She felt as culpable as her aunt and uncle, who had also taken advantage of his loneliness. Were Patrick's job and the payment of his property taxes the price of their guardianship all these years? The annual fee for his denial, for not interfering? They were stronger than he was. They had paid him to stay away. They had forced him into this vile pact. By taking advantage of his vulnerability, they had stripped him of pride and reduced him to bitterness and twisted self-hatred. *Alright, you can bring her up, but I need help*, he must have said. The price had probably risen over the years, and so in a very real way she had become Patrick's insurance policy. He couldn't very well tell her the truth, but he couldn't help loving her. Her mother's leaving had probably been subsidized as well. They were probably still paying her to stay away. She started her car and drove home.

The telephone was ringing as she unlocked her door. Certain it was Patrick, she grabbed the receiver.

"Oh! Fiona!" Elizabeth sounded startled. "This was going to be my last try. I've been calling you all night."

"I don't see any messages," she said, checking the machine. "You should have just left one."

"I hate to leave messages. I don't like talking to a machine."

"Oh, and everyone else does, right?" she snapped.

Elizabeth paused. "I'm sorry," she said. "I guess that is selfish of me, isn't it? Well, anyway," she continued with forced perkiness, "Mother's been after me to call. She thinks something's wrong because we haven't been in touch. But I told her it's the time of year, that's all. I've just been so busy with school and with running, and I know how busy you are."

"Me? I haven't been busy. In fact I've been bored stiff lately."

"Oh. Now I really feel guilty. But there've been so many night meetings, it seems that's all I've been doing these last few weeks."

"Oh really? Where do you have those?"

"The meetings?'

"Yah, whatever you call them," Fiona said, with no effort to hide her disgust.

"At school! Actually, it's the Thanksgiving pageant that's been taking up most of the time. But then that's what happens when you're low man on the totem pole. You're not asked. You're appointed." She sighed. "But it's fun! It is. I shouldn't complain. I love my class. They're all so cute. Especially the twins—I told you about the twins, didn't I?"

"Yah, you told me," she said, yawning. Rudy probably had to listen to this inane crap all the time. And yet it was exactly this simplicity, this natural sense of clarity, that attracted people to Elizabeth. Like fine crystal, she would be handled differently from everyone else, with unquestioning care and appreciation. Her sweet nature made her seem only more delicate. She was the kind of woman other women rolled their eyes at but secretly envied, the kind of woman men were afraid of damaging.

"Well, I won't keep you. You sound tired," Elizabeth said.

"I am," Fiona said.

"You haven't forgotten about the party Friday, right?" Elizabeth asked, and Fiona said she hadn't. "Good! Then we'll have fun!" she said with that shiver of brightness Fiona recognized as dread.

"Is Rudy going?" she asked.

"Yes. Well, he says he is anyway," Elizabeth said, explaining that at first he didn't think he could go, but now he'd finally gotten someone to cover for him at the hospital. She almost sounded annoyed at this.

"That's good. Isn't it?" she couldn't resist adding, as she stretched the cord as far as the bathroom mirror.

"Well, anyway," Elizabeth said, ignoring her, "Mother wondered if you need anything—money, clothes, a ride, whatever."

"Yes. A date, tell her." She touched her neck. It still felt sore. Looking closely, she could see only a few red splotches.

Elizabeth laughed. "Don't worry. There'll be plenty of old judges there. More than enough to go around, I'm afraid."

"Actually," Fiona said with a malevolent grin at her reflection, "I've decided to ask George." She paused. "You don't mind, do you?"

"Well, I . . . Well, if you really want to know, I wish you wouldn't."

"Why?" Cruel as it was, hearing her cousin twist and turn like this seemed the leveling balance she needed against what had just happened. She kept touching her throat, now her chin where it was most tender.

"I don't know. It'll just make me uncomfortable, that's all. There must be any number of people you could ask. You know there are."

"But why? You still haven't told me," she persisted, bristling at Elizabeth's real meaning: any number of men she'd slept with. "Why would it make you uncomfortable?"

"Well, not just me. Rudy too."

"That doesn't make any sense, Lizzie. I mean, what does Rudy care if George comes with me? Besides, weren't you three all together at the Orchard House last week? I mean, all I want is an escort." She paused. "Someone safe. You wouldn't deny me that, would you?" Listening into the silence, she could feel her cousin's fierce struggle against tears.

Elizabeth's small voice came from a great distance. "Why are you doing this?"

"What?"

"Putting me in this position."

"What do you mean?"

Elizabeth took a deep breath. "I think you know exactly what I mean." Her voice trembled. "And I'm surprised at you, Fiona. You know I've been having a hard time lately. A really hard time, but I'm trying to keep everything together. At least until the holidays are over. And Dad's judgeship's announced. And now that Ginny's pregnant . . . oh, I just want everything to be calm and happy for Mom and Dad. That's all I want."

Now Fiona paused. No one had even bothered telling her that Uncle Charles had gotten the judgeship. She wouldn't let herself be sidetracked. "Well maybe that's too much for one person to want, Lizzie. Maybe the only thing anyone can really do is make their own happiness. And then everything else will fall into place."

"If only things were that simple."

"They can be! But you have to be honest about your feelings, Lizzie. You're always worrying about everyone else. If you and Rudy are having a hard time, don't wait, deal with it. Get it out in the open. That should be the most important thing on your mind right now. Forget about the Thanksgiving pageant and all that crap. So what if the holidays are a bust? Who the hell cares! We're all adults! And what if it isn't a perfect sunshiney day when they announce the judgeship. So what? And what about Ginny's baby? So, she's pregnant; great, but that's their thing, not yours!"

"It's Bob. He and Ginny are having problems again."

"Yah? So?" she said with a little snort. "They're having problems. They always have. Probably always will. But what's that got to do with you, Lizzie?"

"It's Mom and Dad. They seem so nervous all the time, so stressed. Especially Dad. He worries about you."

"Well, that's his problem, now isn't it?"

"No, that's what I mean. It's not that simple. You have to think of other people, Fiona. It's like when you drop a stone in the pond. The hurt goes out in ripples, and it affects everyone."

"Everyone?"

"I mean all of us. We're all connected."

"All of you are, maybe, but I sure as hell haven't felt very connected lately."

"And who's fault is that, Fiona?" Elizabeth asked in a thin scrape of a voice.

"Wait a minute! So, the bottom line here is, it's all my fault."

"That's not what I said."

"Of course it is! Stones? Ripples? Jesus Christ, Lizzie! I mean, who made you the fucking family oracle? The way you tell it, I cause all the trouble, and you have to put it all back together again."

"That's not what I said."

"No, I just did. What you said was bullshit. Pure and simple bullshit, because you never say what you really mean, do you? I'm going to tell you something, Lizzie, I may be the family fuckup, but at least I'm honest about it! I don't try to avoid my own problems by focusing on everyone else's!"

"Alright, Fiona. I wouldn't expect you to understand. You never did."

"No, you're right, Lizzie! I never did, God damn you! God damn you all!" She slammed down the phone. What she didn't understand was why she kept ending up alone in this same cramped space. No matter how hard she tried she could only get so far before being yanked back by an invisible tether.

Chapter 14

She woke up to the rumble of trucks sanding the glistening streets. In the wake of the rising sun, trees, bushes, mailboxes, power lines, and Fiona's car were all glazed with ice. By the time she got the frozen doors open and a porthole scraped on her windshield, she was already late for work.

There was only one customer having coffee in the back booth. At the register Maxine and Donna Drouin giggled as they looked through a lingerie catalog. "Good morning!" they called in unison as Fiona reached over the counter for an order pad.

"Yah, I hope so," she muttered. The last thing she needed right now was a slow day and time on her hands.

"Well maybe if you'd put a smile on that sour little puss it will be!" Donna said with a wink.

She looked up from the pad. "And what the hell's that supposed to mean?"

"She's kidding!" Maxine said quickly. "You know Donna, she's just kidding."

"Yah, and you know Fiona, she's just not in the mood," she said.

"Bad night?" Donna asked, pouting with concern. She sidled closer. "You do look tired."

"I hardly slept," Fiona said, turning the page of their catalog. The models wore skimpy bras and bikini panties. In some poses they leaned back on their hands, their legs spread wide. Remembering what had

happened at Patrick's last night, she shuddered with a wave of com-
plicitous shame. She had spent as much time getting ready to see him
as she would have for a date. More than she had wanted to please him
with dinner and her complete attention, she had wanted him to be
pleased with her. She had wanted to be admired, wanted him to need
her, to feel his loss all these years so he would want her in his life now.
It had been a seduction, but emotional, not sexual, and it had gone terribly awry.

"So what's his name?" Donna asked in a low, sexy voice.

"Who?"

"The guy. The reason you hardly slept," Donna said.

"There wasn't any guy! I don't know what you're talking about."

"It was so obvious!" Maxine said in a shrill voice.

"My God! What's that?" Donna said, pointing. She bent closer.
"Your neck—it's all black and blue, and under your chin too!"

Fiona's hand flew to her throat. "It's just some weird rash. I don't
know what it is." Her shoulders and neck felt sore this morning.

"Those're bruises," Maxine said, coming around the counter. Her
mouth hung open. "They are! Look," she told Donna.

"What is he?" Donna moved her head back and forth, trying to see.
"One of those weird rough-sex guys? I just saw that the other day on a
show. You can die doing some of those things!"

"Don't be ridiculous! That's not what happened. I didn't have a date
last night. It's just some strange rash. I woke up with it," she said, conscious of Maxine's stare.

"That, or someone tried to strangle you in your sleep," Donna said,
laughing as she hurried off to check on her customer.

Maxine touched her arm. "Somebody did that to you, didn't they?"
she whispered, her mascaraed eyes tiny with fear.

"No! Of course not!" she scoffed.

"It was Patrick," Maxine said, staring at her neck. "He did that to
you."

A draft swept into the coffee shop as the door opened and three
men entered. Lawyers from the offices next door, they always asked to
be remembered to her uncle. They stood by the register taking off
their topcoats as they waited to be seated.

"He's crazy," Maxine warned. "And I'm not just saying that."

No, Fiona thought, watching her lead the men to a table. He wasn't crazy, just so lonely and confused he didn't know how to love, so he loved her in the wrong way. She couldn't just walk away. Not from her own father, not after wanting him in her life for all these years. Not when he needed her help.

When she got home from work there were two messages on the answering machine. In the first, Patrick's low raspy voice asked her to call him. And in the next made just moments later, he said he was sorry, "very sorry," then hung up quickly. She stood by the phone now, her hand twice going to the receiver, then pulling back.

It was late afternoon and already pitch-black outside. She hated this time of year, the damp, bone-chilling cold, the hard, dead earth. The shortest days were yet to come. The nights would grow even longer, the darkness deeper. Her hand brushed her throat, and once again she was filled with bitterness toward her uncle, toward all of them who had so much because they had each other. And yet it was all so false. Elizabeth would live a lie rather than upset her parents. In order for them to be happy, the truth had to be hidden, denied, subverted.

She turned on the light and dialed George Grimshaw's number, smiling when he answered so quickly. There was an edge to his voice when she said her name, a guarded disappointment. He must have been expecting a call from Elizabeth. When he didn't seem surprised by Fiona's invitation to the party, she realized Elizabeth had warned him, had probably ordered him not to accept. It would be perfectly platonic, Fiona said, reminding him of his past offer to be an escort should she ever need one. "And don't worry, it won't be a date. I'm just sick of always having to go places alone. You know what I mean?" she added.

"Yah," he said with a sigh. "Yah, I do."

"So what do you think?"

"I don't know. I wouldn't want to make Lizzie mad or uncomfortable."

"Why would she be uncomfortable?"

"Well, you know," he said so softly she could barely hear him.

"Hey, what happened, happened. Like you said yourself, George, it was circumstances." She tried to sound offhanded, but she was almost choking with anger. So that was the ruse, the reason given, that they had slept together, one betrayal checkmating the other.

"Well, I know."

"It doesn't bother me anymore. So you better stop letting it bother you. Otherwise, you know how Lizzie is," she said, pausing for emphasis. "This could drag on forever."

When he didn't say anything, she could feel him dangling. "You'll still be trying to avoid each other in the nursing home." She laughed. "I can just see the two of you, both shuffling around the corner at the same time on your walkers, then you both turn and try to shuffle away real fast."

He took a deep breath, but still didn't speak.

"I know! We'll surprise her," she said. "She'll think it's funny. You know she will. She'll be relieved that you're there and that she didn't have to do the actual inviting, or whatever, because you know she really wants you there. She does. I mean, jeez, you're such old friends," she said, rolling her eyes as she began to flounder in the circularity of her argument.

"But what about the fiancé?" George asked.

"He has a name, George."

"Yah, Rudy," he grunted. "What about him?"

"Why should he care? I'm the one inviting you. Besides," she added, wincing with the lie. "The last I heard he might have to work."

It was settled. She and George would go together. She assured him that Elizabeth wouldn't be upset, then bit her lip to keep from laughing. Rather than have to arrive in the plumbing van, she offered to drive to the party. Her hand trembled as she hung up, and for a moment she sat staring at the wall. What am I doing? she wondered, taking deep breaths to calm herself. Why had her giddy anger veered so sharply into this chilling dread? It's harmless, and in the end she'll be grateful, she told herself, trying to forget the look on her cousin's face that morning in her bedroom doorway. The phone began to ring. She switched off the answering machine in case it was George, calling back to say he'd changed his mind. The phone continued to ring. She closed her eyes, then picked it up suddenly, but no one was there.

She leaned close to the bathroom mirror, shocked at all the discoloration. Patrick had left more than the imprint of fingertips in her flesh. It was a tattoo of frustration and blundering force, their separation made visible, an indelible mark of his pain, repugnant proof of how little she should expect of him. "No," she murmured, then turned off the light. She wouldn't be rejected again. His rage might fend off the rest of the world, but not her. The bruises on her chin could be covered with makeup, but the ones on her neck were too dark to hide.

She needed to buy a dress with a high collar for Saturday night. She took off her uniform and quickly put on pants and a sweater to go to the mall. She grabbed her jacket from the closet. She had to get out of here. She needed to keep busy. She didn't want to think anymore about Patrick or her cousin. She looked up suddenly. Is that why she'd called George, because of what Patrick Grady had done to her? Did she want to hurt Elizabeth because she had been hurt? Was she that twisted and cruel? Of course not. She loved her cousin and had only been trying to help. She paused in the doorway as the telephone began to ring. If it was George, she would tell him he had been right. He shouldn't go. She ran back inside.

"Hello?"

"Fiona!" Patrick said with relief. "I want to talk to you. I need to. Can you come over? I need to see you."

"I can't. I have to do something," she said in as level a tone as she could manage. Her hands were trembling.

"Please, I'm sorry. I am. Please believe me. I'm so sorry."

She took a deep breath. "You scared me."

"I know. I'm sorry. I didn't mean to scare you. That's not what I wanted."

"Well you did, and you hurt me too." She touched her throat. "You should see the marks you made."

"I didn't mean to hurt you. I swear I didn't. I love you, Fiona."

"No! Don't say that! You can't say that!"

"But in the right way! The way you want, that's what I mean, that's all I mean."

"Then why did that happen? Was it the pot? I don't understand."

"Please! Please come."

"I can't. Not tonight. Maybe tomorrow."

"Why?" he demanded. "Why not? You have a date or something?" The way he spat out the word "date" made her hair stand on end.

"No. I have to go to the mall. I have to get something."

"Well, stop by here on your way home then. Please? Oh please, Fiona," he begged. "Just for a few minutes. You won't even have to take off your coat. You can stay on the porch even, if you want. I just need to see you. I have to!"

The pain in his voice disarmed her. Feeling guilty, she said she'd try. When? he wanted to know. Maybe around nine-thirty when the mall closed. But she could only stay a few minutes, she added quickly, then listened for his goodbye, but all she could hear was angry muttering as he hung up.

Her eyes burned, her back ached, and her hair was wild after trying on so many dresses, but she had finally found one with a high neck that she liked. It was black and short with an open back. She waited in line at the register in Filene's evening wear department. The announcement had just come over the loudspeaker that the store was closing in ten minutes. She had been shopping for almost three hours. She wished she hadn't told Patrick she'd stop by. Glancing at her watch, she realized she probably wouldn't even get there before ten. She was still too drained from last night for any more emotional encounters. She'd find a pay phone on her way out and call him. She'd see him to-morrow, on her way home from work. Before he had a chance to get too high.

After her dress was paid for she hurried down the escalator to the bank of pay phones by the exit doors.

Patrick got angry when she said she was too tired to come. He said he'd been counting on seeing her. For the past hour every time a car went by he had looked out the window.

"I'm sorry," she said, thinking maybe she could stop by just for a few minutes. She moved her bag out of the way as a group of shoppers milled closer, waiting for the security guard to unlock the door and let them out.

"Where are you?" he asked.

The anxious crowd was growing larger. Whether it was mall policy or this elderly security guard's own peculiar practice, he was refusing to open the door until some requisite number of people had assembled.

"I told you, at the mall," she said. "They're closing now."

"Who're you with?"

"Nobody. I mean, I'm near a bunch of people waiting to get out." She spun around as someone tapped her on the shoulder. Rudy Larkin smiled over an armload of bags. She waved.

"This is ridiculous!" a woman fumed, and others muttered agreement.

"Help! Help, we're being held hostage!" a teenage boy called in a loud falsetto, and people laughed.

"I'll come by tomorrow," she said, smiling back at Rudy. The bottom half of his shirt was unbuttoned and his hair was uncombed.

"That's all right, you don't have to," Patrick said.

"But I want to." She picked up her bag.

The security guard had been listening to his cellular phone. He spoke into it, then turned and unlocked the door. The waiting crowd surged past him into the cold, brightly lit parking lot.

"What time then?" Patrick asked.

Rudy tapped her shoulder again then waved goodbye. "Bye," he called softly. "See you at the party?" As he turned, she reached out and grabbed his sleeve. She held up a finger for him to wait. He stood there, listening while she assured Patrick she'd stop by right after work. It was obvious Rudy thought she was trying to arrange a date.

"And don't be calling at the last minute to say you're not coming. I don't need any more of this bullshit, you know," Patrick warned.

"Hey, miss!" The security guard pointed at his watch.

"What?" she demanded, turning her back to Rudy. She could feel her face redden. "What did you just say?"

"You heard me," Patrick growled.

She paused. "You're right. I did," she said, then hung up. She walked outside with Rudy. She felt strangely lightheaded, as if she had just been spun in a dizzying circle before being sent into this frigid night air. She and Rudy began to tell each other how tired they were and how much they hated shopping. Neither one had eaten tonight. In unison they announced how hungry they were. Well then, Rudy said, they should go somewhere and eat, right now. She suggested Pacer's. Rudy followed in his car. When they got there both the dining room and lounge were full. It would be a half-hour wait so they stood in the crowded vestibule, jammed shoulder to shoulder, shouting at one another in order to be heard over the smoky din.

Rudy seemed pleased that he'd just bought pants and a shirt, and a pair of shoes. He described himself as a pathologically insecure shopper. The few times he had ever gone shopping with his mother had ended with her fleeing the store to wait outside for him.

"Was she claustrophobic?" Fiona asked. "Or is it agoraphobic?"

He smiled. "Some kind of phobic."

"She'd be miserable here then!" she shouted.

"Actually, she probably would've liked this," he said, looking around. "It was decisions she had a hard time with, and having to deal with people individually."

Was that why he continued to be so patient with Elizabeth, because she reminded him of his mother? "I'm surprised Elizabeth didn't go with you!" she shouted at his ear. "She always—" She caught herself. "She's always enjoyed shopping." She had almost said that Elizabeth always went shopping with George whenever he needed anything. In high school everything George owned, even socks, had been chosen by Elizabeth.

Rudy said something, but she touched her ear and shook her head to show she hadn't heard. More people had come in, and the hostess was calling out names to be seated. "She was supposed to," he shouted, putting his hand on the wall above and leaning over her so people could get by. "But then she said she felt guilty for not helping her mother more!"

"She always feels guilty!" Fiona said with a big smile.

"What?" he called, lowering his face and closing his eyes as if to hear better.

"Nothing!" she said at his ear, conscious of her cheek grazing his. She drew back stiffly.

"She said she had a big long list! Things her mother needed to do and didn't have time for!" He straightened then and looked around, smiling. "The food must be pretty good here!" he shouted. "Judging from the crowd, that is!" He leaned over her again. "I'm starving! I haven't eaten since breakfast!"

"Then let's go someplace else!" she shouted back. "Why wait if you're starving!"

"No, this is fine! I like this! All the noise and the people! Makes me feel good!"

"That's right, I forgot. You're a big-city guy!" she shouted, and he laughed.

He was watching a tall young woman in cowboy boots and a fringed suede jacket snap her fingers and dance to the blaring music. "I like watching people dance!" he said, turning back now. "Can't dance a step myself, but I could watch it all night!" He put his hand on the wall again. "I'll bet you're a good dancer, aren't you?"

"Damn good!" she said, but he couldn't hear, so she moved closer. "Damn good!" she shouted her cheek brushing his again, and this time he grinned so happily that for a moment she couldn't bear to look away.

"Let me see! C'mon, show me some moves!" he said, snapping his fingers.

She held up her hands and turned with an exaggerated wiggle that made them both laugh.

He bent closer, with a look of concern. He touched her chin. "What's that?" He tilted her head slightly back.

"Oh, a bruise, I guess." She eased away. "I hit it at work."

"You've got one here too." He squinted, bending a little to peer from side to side.

"Yah, I know. Weird, huh?" She tugged her collar higher.

An hour later, their table was covered with empty plates. Neither could remember the last time they had eaten so much. She was full, her appetite fueled by the pleasure of his approving gaze. Her every fork-ful, word, and gesture seemed to delight him. He took a bite of her chicken fajita, then rolled his eyes and asked for another. She agreed, but only in exchange for another of the spare ribs he had been allotting one at a time until the gleaned bones were piled as high now in her plate as his. Laughing, he pointed to the sticky barbecue sauce on her chin. She told him to mind his own chin. It was turning competitive. He asked for seconds on wild rice, so then she did too. She ordered black coffee with a scoop of vanilla ice cream in it. "An oxymoronical beverage," he declared, ordering the same. The waitress brought dessert menus and they burst out laughing, then ordered two slices of chocolate cream pie.

"We better not do this again," she groaned, making herself waddle on their way outside.

"Why?" he asked, holding open the door. "Is something wrong?"

"No, it's just that I'd weigh two hundred pounds. You make it seem like too much fun."

"Well it should be, shouldn't it?"

"Maybe once in a while," she said, walking with her head down, trying to avoid patches of ice between the cars.

"Why? Why not have fun all the time?" he asked when she stopped at her car.

"Dr. Larkin! I'm shocked! I didn't know my cousin's engaged to a hedonist."

"I'm so far from being a hedonist, it's ridiculous," he said softly. He put his hand on top of her car. "I think I've laughed more tonight than the whole time I've been in Dearborn."

"Oh yah?" She looked up at him. "And why do you think that is?"

"Which part? Tonight? Or the whole time I've been in Dearborn?"

She shrugged. "Both."

With a bitter chuckle he thumped the roof three times. "Tonight was fun. Plain and simple, no hidden agendas. I never once worried that I might say the wrong thing or that you might burst into tears for no apparent reason." He sighed. "I think I just answered both parts." He patted her arm. "That's not fair. I'm sorry. I don't mean to put you in a difficult position."

"You're the one in the difficult position."

He looked at her, his mouth opening then closing frustratedly.

"We're just going to play it by ear, so to speak, Lizzie and me." He tried to laugh. "No pressure, that seems to be the watchword now. I'm just kind of here, you know, and I shouldn't have any particular expectations or . . . " He sighed and shook his head.

"Or what? Needs?"

He looked at her and nodded. "Something like that."

"Do you love her that much?" She stared at him. "Or have you really screwed up here big time?"

He tried to hold her gaze, but his eyes kept sinking closed. "I don't know," he said so softly she could barely hear him. "All I do know is that I feel stupid. I mean really, really stupid."

Now, she thought. Now was the time to tell him about George and Elizabeth. But she couldn't. For all the right and all the wrong reasons. "God, you must be freezing!" she said, shivering herself. "Come on, button up. Time to go home," she said, poking the snap on his jacket.

He laid his hand over hers. "But there's one thing I don't regret about any of this. And that's been knowing you, Fiona. I mean that." He laughed. "You don't know how many times lately I've picked up the phone to call, and then I think, 'What the hell am I doing? I can't do this.'" He squeezed her hand.

"You should have," she said, her heart racing. "In fact, why don't you come over now? I'll make coffee." She had made up her mind. He deserved to be told. Elizabeth might not want him, but there were plenty of women who would.

"I can't. I'm on duty in less than an hour. It's this awful double shift I'm taking so I can go Friday." He said goodbye, then stood watching her back out of the space. As she rolled down her window to call goodbye again, he ran up to the car. "Wait!" he said. "I'll follow you home. Make sure you get in all right."

She drove slowly, glancing at his reflection in her rearview mirror. When they pulled into the lot behind her building, he got out of his car and waited while she parked. He walked her to the entryway door and once again she invited him up for coffee.

"I wish I could, but I don't trust myself," he said.

"What do you mean?" she asked, her heart going too fast again.

"Well, when I was driving back just now I was thinking of all the talking we did, and then it hit me! What did we talk about?" He laughed. "I couldn't remember!"

"Well, so much for my image of myself as a scintillating conversationalist," she said as he held open the door.

"No, you are! That's what I mean. That's the point. You're just too easy to be with."

"Too easy! Oh great," she said, rolling her eyes.

"I mean you're very comfortable to be with. It felt so natural that I . . . " Here now, he shrugged as if at a loss for words. "Fiona!" He grabbed her hand and held it in both of his. "I've still got a half hour. McDonald's is just down the hill. We could eat a hell of a lot in a half hour. A few Big Macs, some fries, some shakes. We could do it. I know we can."

She laughed, and as he brought her hand to his lips and kissed it with his eyes closed she kept laughing.

She stayed in the doorway, watching until he turned out of the lot. Below her the headlights came on in a car parked in the row to her right. Patrick Grady's faded blue station wagon squealed as it backed up. She ran down to his car and opened the door while he was still shifting.

"Patrick!" she said, shocked by his cold stare. "I didn't see you. I didn't know you were there." She slid onto the front seat, but left the door open. "Patrick, what're you—"

"Get out!" he growled, then jumped out himself and ran around to her side. "Just get out!" He grabbed her arm.

"Patrick!" she gasped, shrinking back.

"I was waiting for you!" He leaned in closer. "You knew I was waiting."

"But I called. I told you I wasn't coming."

"But I was waiting," he said through clenched teeth, his face level with hers. "I was waiting." He seemed confused, shaken, as if he knew he made no sense, but was stuck, unable to get beyond a certain point. He let go of her.

"I'm sorry," she said, sliding from the car. "I didn't mean to upset you."

"You lied. You had a date. You lied to me." His voice broke.

"No, I was shopping. And after, I ran into Rudy, that's all. He's on his way to work!"

"You said he's your cousin's fiancé," he said, glancing in the direction Rudy had turned.

"He is!"

"He kissed your hand." His face twisted with disgust.

"It was a joke! He was kidding." She thought of Todd's beating and a queasiness came over her. Patrick might be her father, but he was a deeply troubled man and she was confusing him and agitating him beyond his own limits of self-control. She had lanced the boil, but neither of them could stanch its poisonous ooze.

"It's almost midnight," he said. "Where've you been all this time?"

"We stopped for coffee." She spoke softly to calm him. He kept shaking his head. "We were talking about Elizabeth and their—"

"No! It's just like with the sneakers," he spat. He grabbed for her arm, but clutched her sleeve instead, pulling her so close spittle sprayed her face. "He's using her to get to you. But you act like you can't see it. Like you don't know what's going on."

"No. No, he's—"

"It's you he's after. It's you he wants, and don't think I don't know it," he growled, then jumped back into his car and roared out of the lot.

As soon as she got inside, she tore through the phone book until she found the number for Dearborn Memorial. The operator connected her to the emergency room. She could hear Rudy being paged.

"Rudy! It's me, Fiona," she said, then realized how upset she must sound. She took a deep breath.

"Fiona? Are you all right? Did something happen?"

"Oh, no, nothing's happened. I'm fine, but I . . . I was worried about you," she said lamely. She had to be careful. She didn't want to cause Rudy any harm, but also couldn't risk inciting Patrick more than she already had.

"You're worried about me?" He laughed. "Why? Do you think I'm still eating?"

"I don't know. I just wanted to make sure you were careful, that's all."

"Careful, huh?" He paused. "Careful about what?"

"I don't know. I thought I saw a car following you. And so I just wanted to tell you."

"Tell me what?"

"About the car! Just forget it, Rudy," she said, shaking her head impatiently. "It was weird. I shouldn't have called."

"No, I'm glad you did. What kind of car should I be on the lookout for? Who's driving it?" He sounded amused.

"I don't know. Never mind. It was just a funny feeling I got, that's all."

"You should listen to your feelings. Not enough people do."

"Yah, well," she said with a bitter laugh, "I haven't had very good luck with that kind of thing lately." She paused. "Anyway, I'll let you get back to your emergencies."

"Fiona!" he said with an urgency that made her press the phone to her ear, listening so carefully the hum between them seemed like a roar. "I just want to say what a great time I had tonight. I mean, a really great time."

"Good!" she said, managing to sound cheerful. "Well, maybe next time you can bring Elizabeth."

"Maybe next time we'll do something else," he said.

Hours later her eyes opened in the dark, and she was still trying to figure out what he meant.

It was early morning and Fiona had just finished showering when her bell rang. "Lizzie!" she cried, tying her robe as she opened the door. "Is everything all right?" She glanced at the clock. Quarter of six.

"Yes," Elizabeth said, following her into the kitchen, where Fiona started to make coffee. Elizabeth watched from the table. "Everything's fine, aside from the fact that I have a million things to do today. That's why I'm starting off so early. You won't believe Mother's list," she said, shaking out a folded piece of paper.

"I can imagine," Fiona said, amazed at how smoothly her cousin could skim over the choppiest seas.

Elizabeth looked even paler than usual. It was hard to tell if she had lost more weight or if she just seemed so lost herself under all the layers she wore, her long skirt, the oversize shirt, the long bulky sweater. There were dark circles like smudges of ash around her eyes.

"Five bags ice—round cubes, not square chunky ones," she read, glancing up at Fiona. "Silver plastic cocktail stirrers. Bettelman's usually has them. White silver-edged cocktail napkins—again, try Bettelman's first. Two cans silver spray paint. Five pounds walnuts." She glanced up. "There's more." She sighed, folding the paper. "And this is just today's list."

"I know Aunt Arlene's organized, but she doesn't need that stuff right now, this morning, does she?" she asked. If Elizabeth hadn't come in search of an apology or to apologize herself, then why else was she here so early? She squirmed, remembering George.

"No, these are my after-school chores," Elizabeth said.

"God, the details!" Fiona said, pouring the coffee. "It's like a treasure hunt, isn't it? But then that's why her parties are always so perfect."

"This one might not be," Elizabeth said. "Ginny and Bob are separated. It happened two weeks ago. Apparently he's been seeing the same woman this whole time so Ginny told him to leave."

"Two weeks ago? Why didn't anyone tell me?" she said, shaking her head.

"I know. That's why I'm here. To tell you," Elizabeth said with a sigh. "They didn't tell me either until last night, and I live in the same house. I think they were hoping things would, well, you know, work out."

"Work out! Jesus Christ!" Fiona sputtered, and Elizabeth's cheeks colored.

"Well, settle down anyway," Elizabeth said softly.

"Don't tell me they want her to take that creep back just because she's pregnant!"

"No, they just want to keep things, well, you know, calm, and . . ." She forced a smile. "Upbeat!" she said as if that would be everyone's most desirable goal in difficult times.

"Upbeat? Let's see, Ginny's pregnant, and her husband, Bob, who everyone knows is an asshole, is screwing some other woman, his twenty-year-old secretary if that even matters, because the most important thing here is for everyone to be upbeat. Nobody should get sidetracked. It's business as usual. Life goes on, we endure. Don't anybody cry or get mad. This too shall pass. Did I get that right?"

Elizabeth winced. "I'm worried about Daddy. He just looks so stressed all the time. He doesn't want anyone, especially Mom, to know, but he's having those pains again. I asked him and he finally admitted it."

"Jesus Christ!" Fiona jumped up. "Then he should see a doctor and stop trying to play God in everyone's life!" She paced back and forth as Elizabeth stared at her folded hands. "Why not just lay things out on the table? Here's the crap, here's the dirt, deal with it! Why does everything have to be so damn perfect? Why does he think he has to control everything? That he has to be the one to make everything right?" she demanded, thinking of Patrick's tax bills and the twins in Lizzie's class and Jack's job and the countless people telling her through the years how grateful they were to her uncle.

"He's not, he . . . ," Elizabeth said so hesitantly that Fiona stopped suddenly and bent over the table as the reason for this visit became clear.

"He sent you here, didn't he? What?" she demanded, snatching the list from her cousin's hand. "Am I on here too? 'Tell Fiona to please stop embarrassing the family!'" she pretended to read before balling up the paper and throwing it down. It rolled off the table onto the floor.

"I'm worried about him, Fiona. That's the only reason I'm here," Elizabeth said as she bent to retrieve her list. She smoothed it out on the table.

Fiona looked at her cousin, who once again was begging her to be good, please be good, Fiona. How had they maintained such power over this one dutiful child, and not the other? Was Elizabeth simply kinder, more sensitive? Or was it because she had always been the one more loved?

"Lizzie, things go wrong in people's lives. It happens all the time. Everywhere, to everyone. But Uncle Charles and Aunt Arlene can't face that. They won't accept it, and now the same thing's happening with you, isn't it?"

"I don't see anything wrong in trying to make them happy," Elizabeth said, her porcelain features fired into a hard white knot, as tight as it was unyielding.

"Well how can they be happy if you're not?" Fiona said, attempting to soften her tone. Cornered, Elizabeth would be, as always, intractable.

"I am. I'm happy." Elizabeth's hesitant smile brightened with steeliness. "Especially now that I don't have the wedding to worry about," she said, briskly stirring her coffee though she had added nothing to it.

Fiona's distress rose with the insistent click of the spoon, its tinny peal as chilling as Elizabeth's dismissal of her wedding and fiancé. Poor Rudy, she thought angrily. He had no idea how caught he was between Elizabeth's desire to please her father and her feelings for George. In the name of goodness, it was such devious cruelty; under the banner of kindness such invisible selfishness. By knowing all the bloodless ways to excise a heart, they had perfected the art of an admirable life with their careful composition of pleasant features, she thought with a sudden bilious exhilaration. Watching carefully, alert to any sign, the slightest quiver, sagging shoulders, downcast eyes, she began to tell her cousin how she and Rudy had run into each other at the mall last night, then gone to Pacer's for something to eat. She was amazed to see only pleasure in Elizabeth's expression. And relief.

"Oh, so that's where you were. Well, that's good. I'm so glad. I was feeling guilty thinking of Rudy all by himself, but I was helping Mom. All her little details, and that's when she told me about Ginny, so naturally I wouldn't leave them alone like that. Actually, I called you a couple of times, but you weren't home, and, I'm sorry, I know you think it's quirky, but I'm not good about leaving messages, and then it got too late to keep trying, so that's why I thought I'd leave a little early this morning and try to catch you before you left for work. It's just all starting to come too close together. I mean . . ." Her voice broke and she took a deep breath.

Fiona continued to stare.

"Fiona, I asked you not to invite George, and now I find out you went ahead and did anyway. I don't understand it. I mean, things are complicated enough now. I don't need George there. I don't want him there! I absolutely don't!"

"What do you mean, Lizzie? What's George got to do with anything else?"

"It's what I just told you. It's everything that's happening. And Mother and Daddy are going to have all those people there, and it's just all too much tension. They don't need that!"

"Tension! Because George comes to a party there's going to be too much tension? What the hell are you talking about, Lizzie? What do you really mean?"

Elizabeth's mouth trembled. She sat with her head bent. "Please tell him not to come," she whispered.

"No," Fiona said, shaking her head. "Not unless you tell me why."

"Please. Please, I'm begging you, Fiona." She buried her face in her hands. "You don't understand. It's just all too much. It's all piling up, and I don't know what to do," she gasped.

Fiona touched her shoulder. "Why don't you try just being honest?" she said softly.

Elizabeth's delicate face shot up from her hands, the perfect, chiseled features cold, tearless, inviolate. "Everything's always been so easy for you, hasn't it? You just do what you want, say what you want, go where you want, and you never look back. So you never know how much you hurt people. You have no idea how much damage you do or the harm."

Fiona picked up her coffee and stood over her. "Get out, Lizzie! And get out fast unless you want this added to that thirty-pound costume you're wearing."

Chapter 15

L ate afternoon now, it had been a brilliant day, but cold, with an un-relenting bitter wind. Fiona looked up to see Larry Belleau getting out of Patrick's car that was parked at the curb. Larry leaned back down and said something to Patrick. He turned, then, nodding vigorously, hurried into the coffee shop. He wore only jeans and a T-shirt. His nose and plump cheeks were red from the cold, and he rubbed his big hands together with glassy-eyed excitement. "Fiona! Fiona!" he called, though she stood directly in front of him. "Patrick says come outside quick he wants to talk to you."

"Larry, what are you doing with Patrick?"

He shrugged. "Nothing."

"Have you been drinking?"

"No!"

Maxine came into the dining room. She glanced warily between Larry's agitated bulk and the rumbling car in the street, then hurried back into the kitchen.

Fiona stepped closer and lowered her voice. "Have you been smoking or anything?" she asked, certain she could smell the sweet musk of pot.

"Patrick says come out to the car now I'm supposed to tell you that," he said with a nervous chortle that exploded like a volley of hiccups. "He just wants to talk he said to tell you that he just wants to talk that's all that's all he wants. See?" he said, nudging her to the front door. "He's right there that's his car right there."

"I thought you didn't like Patrick."

"Well I don't not when he's mean I don't not when he's mad, but he's not mad now see? See?" Larry waved, but Patrick didn't wave back.

"Now we're friends we're friends now me and Patrick." He leaned against the window and waved again. Patrick's hand lifted in a reluctant salute. "See I told you I told you we're friends," he cried, close on her heels as she hurried outside.

Grinning, Patrick rolled down his window. The car reeked of pot.

"Get in! Get in!" he called. "You'll catch cold."

She couldn't, she said, shivering and hugging her arms. She had to help Maxine close up.

"Screw Maxine. I just need to tell you something, that's all. Just a coupla minutes of your time, that's all I want."

"I can't now, Patrick. I have to finish," she said, gesturing behind her.

Larry opened the passenger door and Patrick's head spun around. "You wait out there! I said wait!" he ordered with a slash of his hand.

"But I'm cold I'm really cold," Larry said, his head and one foot still inside the car. "I'm freezing cold Patrick."

"Look, I'll call . . . ," she started to say.

"I said wait! You wait!" Patrick roared, backhanding the side of Larry's head. "This'll only take a minute!" he implored Fiona. "You can give me that much, can't you? A minute?"

"Hey!" Larry hollered, both hands poulticed against his head. "What'd you do that for I didn't do anything you said you wanted to be friends!"

"You didn't have to hit him," Fiona said. "He's just cold, that's all."

"I know! I know! I'm not thinking straight." Patrick raked his hands through his unruly hair. "I just need to talk to you, that's all. And then I'll be all right. I need to explain. You see it's not the way you think."

Larry stood on the sidewalk shouting that if Patrick wouldn't let him in the car, then he was leaving. "And you can go find out stuff yourself so go ahead just go find out and don't ask me anymore!"

The coffee shop door opened and Chester rushed out, wiping his hands on his stained white apron. Maxine watched wide-eyed through the window.

"What the hell's going on? What's all the yelling for?" Chester glanced between Fiona and Larry, who rushed forward to tell his side of the story. He begged Chester not to call his parents and get him in trouble the way everyone else did. "Don't please don't I didn't do anything honest Chester I didn't I really really didn't," Larry insisted at his elbow. "Oh boy oh boy oh boy oh boy," he began to chant as Chester shouted at Fiona.

"What're you tryna to do to me?" Chester demanded. "I told you. I don't want that son of a—"

"Go inside. Please, just go inside," she said.

"No, you go inside!" Chester howled.

Patrick's door flew open. "Hey Chester!" he called over the top of the car. "You got a problem, you talk to me not her. She didn't do anything. She's got nothing to do with this."

Chester stepped closer. "Why don't you just get the hell outta here!"

"Hey, I'm not bothering anybody, least of all you, Adenio!" Patrick called, jaw clenched, his eyes narrow and hard.

"Yes you did you bothered me!" Larry howled. "He did he hit me he did!"

"You hit Larry?" Chester shook his head in disgust.

"Look, just go in, Chester, please," she said. "I'll take care of it."

"Take care of it?" Chester scoffed, throwing up his hands. "Jesus Christ! You can't even take care of yourself!"

Patrick charged onto the sidewalk. Unshaven, he wore the same buttonless plaid shirt and soiled pants as the last time she'd seen him. "Here's your chance. C'mon, you've been wanting this for a long time, so here! Here you go. C'mon!" He put his hand on Chester's shoulder and pushed him. Chester teetered backwards a few steps.

"Oh my God, I don't believe this!" She grabbed Patrick's arm.

With the phone at her ear, Maxine banged frantically on the plate glass window.

"She's calling the police! Patrick! See! She's calling the police!" Fiona had to shout before he seemed to comprehend.

He stared at her for a moment, his eyes dull and roiling like the sky before a storm.

"Just go!" she said. "Get in the car and go! I'll call you. I promise. I will. Just go!" she called as she backed toward the coffee shop.

He drove off, tires screeching, his exhaust fumes like cold, oily metal in her mouth.

Maxine still held the phone, though she hadn't actually called anyone. A police car out front would have been too mortifying.

"It's the only thing that ever seemed to scare him," Maxine said when they came inside.

Larry begged Chester not to call his father. "Please don't please don't please don't," he wheezed, hounding Chester's every step.

"All right, look, how's this?" Chester spun around and pointed. "If you don't shut up, I will call him. You got that?"

Larry looked confused. His face bloated with tears.

"He's not going to call your dad, Larry, but you have to be quiet," Fiona explained. "Just don't talk, okay?"

Nodding, Larry chewed his lip to hold his silence.

She told him to go sit down a minute and then she'd give him a ride home. He scurried into the shadows of the last booth, as far away as he could get from Chester's tirade.

"That's it!" Chester cried, flinging a napkin dispenser the length of the room. He threw a stack of menus, and now the place mats Maxine had just folded. He was sick and tired of this place, sick and tired of having to put up with everyone's troubles all the time. "And what do I get?" he bellowed, pounding his chest. "I ask you, what do I get?"

Maxine locked the front door and turned the Closed sign. "I'm so sick and tired of that long sad face of yours always trying to make me feel guilty," she said as she advanced on him. "You think you're the only one that gets tired? You think you're the only one that works hard? Well guess what. I do too. But I'm sick of your attitude, Chester. I'm damn sick of you acting like you're doing me some kind of a favor by keeping this place open. So if you want to sell it, you just go right ahead. You just go do what you want, because I don't care anymore." She swung on her fur cape and stormed into the kitchen. The back door slammed.

"Oh boy oh boy oh boy," Larry moaned, biting his lip.

"Shit!" Chester said.

"She's just upset, that's all," Fiona called as he stalked grimly into the kitchen. He was wiping off the workbench when she came in a few minutes later to tell him the front was closed down and all the prep work was finished.

"And I helped too I did," Larry said, following her in. "I helped clean so don't be mad please don't be mad at me please Chester." He had wiped down the booths and swept the floor.

"Just get the hell out of my kitchen, that's all I want," Chester said.

She tossed Larry her keys and told him to wait in her car, she'd be right out.

Chester looked smaller. His pants sagged in folds from his belt. She realized his hair was completely white. The veins in his arms bulged in thick blue knots as he scrubbed the grill. "Aw c'mon, Chester. Don't be mad, please." She tried to hug him, but he stiffened and drew back.

"Tell me something. What is it with you? How come you can't listen to anybody? You think you were born with some kind of special knowledge or something nobody else has? People tell you something out of the goodness of their heart because they care about you, but you don't listen!" He shook his head in amazement. "You don't ever listen! What are you trying to prove with him anyway?"

"I'm not going to talk about this with you," she said.

"Good, then maybe you'll listen for once, because I'm going to tell you something. Stay away from Patrick Grady! He's going to hurt you!"

"Come on, Chester!" She rolled her eyes. "It's the not same as Maxine. He's my father, for godsakes!"

"It doesn't matter who you say he is, or who he says he is. What matters is what he is. And that's evil."

"He's not evil," she scoffed. "He's just all messed up. It's from the war. He can't help it."

"I was in a war! I was in the fucking Korean War, in a Chinese prison camp! Jesus Christ! I mean there's still times I wake up and I'm so scared, my heart's pounding. I just lay there looking around all confused because I don't know what the hell's going on or where I am. All I can think is, maybe I'm still there, how do I know? But Christ, I always get a fucking grip on myself! I mean, who the hell's he?"

"But they were two different wars. It's not the same."

"No, it's the same! I don't buy that whiny, weak-kneed crap!"

"But there's certain things in Patrick's life he just can't get over no matter how hard he tries."

"Yah, like beating on women." He stared at her for a moment. "Tell me something, did you ever think maybe the reason your mother took off was because of something he did to her? And that's why she stayed away all this time. You ever think of that?"

"What? What do you mean, something he did?" She had to keep wetting her lips.

"Like maybe he hurt her or something." The blackened steel wool dripped grease each time he dunked it into his pail of ammonia water.

"What do you mean, hurt her? Hurt her how?"

There was only the steady grate of metal scraping metal as he kept scrubbing.

"I don't know," he finally answered. "I don't know what I mean. All I know is one day Natalie Range was here and then she wasn't." He turned. "I've never seen anybody so scared as Maxine is of him. She told me once, that time he beat her so bad, she knew he was trying to kill her. He started choking her and he whispered how easy it would be, how all it would take was just a little more pressure and then it'd all be over. I keep thinking of that."

"Yah, but you're forgetting one thing." She wagged her finger and forced a smile. "I talked to my mother. She called me. I told you that. Last summer."

Chester took a deep breath, his heavy eyes probing hers; they seemed to know, to ask, but did she? Did she really, Fiona?

"So you can just forget about that sick idea." She sighed and pulled her coat off the hook, believing the lie now herself, because she had to, because for everything to work and all the parts to fit, it couldn't be any other way.

"I wish I could." He resumed his gritty scrubbing.

The Belleaus had moved from Dearborn to Middleton a few years ago. Larry didn't like it there because of the way people treated him, like he was retarded or something, so whenever he wanted to see his friends he always had to hitch rides into Dearborn, he was telling Fiona now as he bent close to her radio and fiddled with the dial. He was trying to get WBZN because the Rude Dog Boys were supposed to be on at five-fifteen. "You like them?" he asked, his ear pressed to the speaker. He'd almost had the station.

"I don't know," she said absently. Chester's words swirled in her head. She kept thinking of Patrick's hands on her neck, but he'd been trying to kiss her, not hurt her. Donna Drouin said he had chopped off her mother's hair, so brutally hacking it there had been cuts on her scalp. But if that were true, why hadn't anyone ever told her before?

"There! There! Can you hear them? Listen!" Larry sat back, grinning as hoarse wails filled the car with indecipherable lyrics and pounding music. High school music, she thought, as his hand kept time on his beefy thigh. After the first song she turned it down.

"Hey!" he protested. "This is my favorite one." He began to sing. 'Doomsday's the good way. Doomsday's my one way . . .'" He turned and pointed. "'To die for you!'" he sang so loudly he was shouting. "'Die! Die! Die, you foolish fool!'"

"Nice!" she called over to him. "Nice creepy song, Larry."

He gave her a sullen look. "They're good," he muttered. "Just 'cause you don't like 'em doesn't mean they're not good you know."

"That's true," she said. She patted his hand and smiled.

He grinned. "I like you, Fiona."

"Thanks, Larry. I like you too."

"I know you never act like I'm a jerk or anything."

"Well, you're not!"

He laughed. "Yah well I am," he said, nodding in time to the music. "I didn't used to be but I am I am now!"

"No, you're not. But sometimes you just try too hard, that's all. You don't have to make people like you, Larry. They either do or they don't."

"Listen!" He leaned forward as the next song began. "This is the best one the one I love this one's my favorite favorite one."

In high school Larry had been one of the sharpest guys in the class. When a lot of other people distanced themselves from Fiona and Todd, pronouncing them druggies on a downward slide, Larry had stayed a good friend, straight as he was. There had been more than a few nights when they were both so stoned or smashed that Larry had to drive them home.

"There that's the one!" he cried, pointing to the sign ahead. "That's my street."

"Larry," she said, slowing before the turn. "You still haven't told me. What were you doing with Patrick?"

"Nothing!" he said quickly. "Just riding around that's all and Patrick likes the Rude Dog Boys he does he likes them now I told him all about them and now he likes them too."

"So what were you two talking about?" she called over the music.

"You." He slapped his thigh with both hands now and rocked back and forth.

"Me? What about me?"

"He asked me about the party that time at Tim and Terry's." He looked away.

"What? What did he want to know?"

"You know." He stared down at his lap.

"No. No, I don't. Tell me."

"He asked me if you were in the pool without any clothes and I said 'I don't know I think so.'" He glanced at her. "'Maybe,' I said so then he said 'Well what about you, Larry, did you have any clothes on?' And I told him I said 'I think so.'" He winced and his jowls quivered as he shook his head. "But we didn't did we?"

"Of course we did." She felt queasy. She stared over the wheel, suddenly remembering the gleam of wet breasts bobbing in the water as she floated on her back, the churning laughter as Larry's flabby arms thrashed toward her, the hairy white breach of his huge buttocks as he dove under her.

"Well anyway," Larry continued as he thumped his leg to the music, "I said we were kissing and then I said we were tryna dance but the dog kept humping us and then he said you let Brad Glidden—"

"No, that's not true!" she interrupted. "You know it's not, right, Larry?" She pulled to the curb in front of the small white cape. The front door opened and Mr. Belleau was halfway down the front path in his red slipper socks before Larry saw him.

"Oh boy oh boy oh boy," he muttered, frantically fumbling with the latch when his father threw open the door.

Fiona hadn't seen Mr. Belleau in years. He looked like an old man, but his voice was the same deep growl she remembered. He ordered Larry out of the car, but then stood in his way berating him. He had been gone since early morning. Couldn't he have at least called to say where he was or when he'd be back? "Your mother's been a wreck, just a wreck all day!" Mr. Belleau said. Mrs. Belleau watched from behind the storm door.

"I'm sorry I'm really really sorry Daddy," Larry said with his head hung.

His point made, Mr. Belleau's gaze shifted. His eyes flashed with recognition and disgust. He sniffed and leaned closer. He lifted Larry's right hand and smelled his fingers. "You've been smoking pot again, God damn it!" he cried, flinging Larry's hand back in his face. "Get out of this goddamn car and get in the goddamn house!" He watched his bearish son shamble up the front walk. Larry's wide jeans hung so low on his hips the cuffs dragged under his heels. He glanced back and waved. "C'mon! C'mon! Hurry it up!" Mr. Belleau barked, and Larry tried to run, but his feet tangled and he stumbled onto the first step, catching himself on the wrought iron railing. The door opened, and his tiny mother rushed out to help him. With her hand at his elbow she guided him into the house.

Fiona looked away.

"Tell me something, what's in this for you? You think it's funny? You get some kick out of turning him on like this?" Mr. Belleau was saying. "He's damaged goods, he doesn't know any better. But what the hell's your excuse?"

"No," she tried to say, but he wouldn't listen. He kept talking.

"If it weren't for the fact that your uncle's been so good to us, I'd go in there right now and call him. But I won't. Not now anyway. But be forewarned, Fiona Range, the next time he comes back like this, I won't bother calling your uncle. I'll just have you thrown in jail!"

That night she let the machine answer every call. They were all from Patrick, either begging her to call him or angry she wasn't there. The phone was ringing again now. She sat up in bed trying to read the biography of Abraham Lincoln she had started last fall. She just couldn't get into it, but she suspected the fault wasn't so much with the book as with her. It was like everything else in her life. "What's your excuse?" Mr. Belleau had asked. Chester said she thought she had all the answers, when the real problem was that she never had the right questions. The ringing stopped and the answering machine message began to play. She looked toward the living room where Patrick's disembodied voice filled the darkness.

"Please call me," he said, breathless as if from some strenuous activity. "It's very important, Fiona. I have something for you. Something I want to show you."

She threw the book aside and ran to the phone. She stood over it, waiting while he also waited, listening for the click, for the receiver to be lifted. There was only the rise and fall of his labored breathing. This was all her fault. She had provoked this anger and confusion that neither seemed able to subdue.

"God damn it," he muttered. "I know you're there. Why do you make me keep calling? Why are you doing this to me?"

She jumped as the phone crashed down at the other end of the line.

It was Friday. She was supposed to pick George up at seven. She had almost called to say maybe he shouldn't go to the party after all. But then Elizabeth had called, leaving a strained, conciliatory message reminding Fiona that the party started at seven-thirty and to please call if she needed a ride or anything. Because there was no mention of George, Fiona assumed his coming had been worked out between them.

Patrick had called twice in the morning, then three more times this afternoon. Hearing his voice in the stark slant of November sunlight made her cringe. It was the low, hungry way he said her name, turning it into as much of an intimacy as a warning. Would she please call him soon. He wanted to make things right. And to do this, there was something he needed to show her. It would help clear the air, he said. At five-thirty the phone rang again as she stepped out of the shower. She shivered in the cold clutch of Patrick's raised voice informing her from the other room that he was at a pay phone. He had just driven by her apartment and seen her car so he knew she was there; knew, in fact, that right now at this very moment she was standing there, listening to him. "Why are you doing this?" he shouted. "Why won't you let me explain? What are you trying to pull here? What the hell are you up to? What the hell do you want?" He paused. "Please, Fiona, please pick up. I'm right around the corner. I just want us to be friends. That's all I want." He paused again. "All right. I guess I'm getting the message here. I won't bother you anymore. Is that what you want? Is that what the hell you want, God damn it!" He slammed down the phone.

He was falling apart and by doing nothing she was only making it worse. No matter how painful it might become, she had to confront the truth. She couldn't abandon Patrick the way she had everything else in her life.

A moment later the phone rang again and she ran to answer it. She tried to hide her disappointment when she realized it was Rudy. He asked if he could stop in before the party. No, he couldn't; she was trying to get ready now, she said, anxious to hang up so Patrick could call back.

How about if he gave her a ride then? That way neither one would have to come home alone.

"Actually, I won't be. I'm picking up George," she said.

"George? Oh! Yes, George." He sounded confused. "Grimshaw, right?"

"Yah, I ended up inviting him," she said quickly so he wouldn't think Elizabeth had.

"You did? Well, I didn't know that. Obviously," he said with a self-conscious laugh. "I guess I was just assuming you'd be going alone."

"Yah, well, so much for false assumptions," she said, and for a moment he didn't say anything.

"Fiona, if I could just come over . . . I mean, I know there's not much time, but it's important."

"I'm sorry, but I'm really running late here—"

"I just need to tell you something," he interrupted.

"I'll see you at the party. You can tell me there." All about you and Elizabeth, she thought, as she hung up and dialed Patrick's number. He didn't answer so she left a brief message: she wouldn't be able to call later because of her aunt and uncle's party, but she'd call him first thing tomorrow.

The minute she pulled into George's driveway he hurried out of the house.

"Can't wait to see me, huh?" she said as he got into the car. It irritated her to think he had rushed out before she could get inside his house.

He didn't answer. At first his seat belt had been caught in the door, but now that it was out he couldn't attach it.

"Here," she said, reaching, her hand over his to guide it into the buckle. "What happened?" She laughed as she backed out of the driveway. "All of a sudden you're mechanically inept?"

"No, just socially." He kept swallowing and wetting his lips. He tugged at his tie again to straighten it. He took a deep breath and tried to smile. "I can't remember the last time I went to a party." He looked at his watch. "So are we early or late? I couldn't remember if it starts at seven-thirty or eight."

"Seven-thirty. We're going to be fashionably late."

"Oh," he said, then they drove in silence for a while.

She heard him sigh a couple more times. "Hey, you look really sharp, George. I like that jacket." She had forgotten how handsome he really was, especially dressed up.

"Thanks, and you look very nice too." He looked at her. "I like that coat."

"Oh, you do, huh?" She laughed. "I've only worn it for the last five winters, but wait'll you see what's under it."

He looked out the window. "Going to be a lot of people there tonight?" he asked quickly.

"I think so. This is probably their biggest party ever, now that Uncle Charles has been nominated for the Supreme Court."

"Superior Court," he said. "Or at least that's what someone said."

"Oh yah?" She paused to hide her annoyance. Ever since they'd been children, he'd been informing and correcting her about events in her own family. "So what about Elizabeth? What did she have to say?"

He glanced over uneasily. "Same thing: Superior Court."

"I mean about tonight. You know, about your coming with me."

"Well, not much really, she . . . I mean, it was one of those quick conversations. We didn't have much of a chance to talk," he said, loyal as ever.

"So it's okay with her then if you go tonight." She looked at him. They were almost there. "Go with me, that is," she added.

"Well I certainly hope so!" he declared with a blustery laugh that only seemed to irritate his throat. He coughed softly into his hand, then took out a handkerchief and blew his nose.

She pulled down the long driveway, then turned so she'd be facing out. Both sides of the road were already lined with cars, all the way down to Lucretia Kendale's property. She smiled to see the gracious old house she'd grown up in blazing with lights. Theirs had always been the first house decorated for the holidays. The red-ribboned wreaths on the glittering windows filled her with giddy excitement as she remembered how wonderful this time of year always was.

"Before we go in, there's something I want to ask you," she said.

He stared miserably over the dashboard.

She kept looking at him. There weren't many choices with George, just black or white. He made it too easy. "Do you love me, George?" she blurted, unable to resist, then burst out laughing to see his mouth gape open. "No, no, no. I'm only kidding. It's a joke! It's a joke! It's a joke, joke, joke," she cried, wincing. "No, really. What I was going to ask you was, is this okay? Are you sure Elizabeth won't be upset? I mean, I don't want her having an anxiety attack or anything in the middle of the party."

"She knows I'm coming," he said, looking up at the house with surprising defiance.

Chapter 16

Across the room her uncle was surrounded by admiring friends. Tall and slender, with bright blue eyes and pure white hair, he was a uniquely handsome man. There had always been an unusual sheen to his skin, a glow, as if of some rare inner vitality that both set him apart and drew people to him. Aunt Arlene was telling her about last night's announcement at the Chamber of Commerce dinner dance. Judge Hollis had been named this year's winner of the Dearborn Citizen of the Year Award.

"He must be pleased," she said.

"He should be, but you know your uncle," her aunt confided. "He says they scraped the bottom of the barrel to get to him."

He threw back his head, laughing at something a younger man in the group was saying, then suddenly turned and looked at her. He excused himself and hurried to greet her.

"Well, look at you!" he said, holding her hands at arm's length. "Doesn't this young lady look pretty special, Arlene?"

"Yes, she does," her aunt agreed, smiling at her. "Beautiful, just beautiful."

"I can't get over it," he said, leaning to kiss her cheek.

"What?" Fiona stiffened. "What can't you get over?"

"How nice you look," he said with quiet guardedness, his smile as quickly blurred as a ripple in water, his eyes fast on hers.

"You seem so surprised. What'd you think, I was going to show up in a G-string or something?" she said, already hating herself and wanting the words, the moment back, but of course, as usual, once again, it was too late.

"Fiona, your uncle was only complimenting you. And I think you know that," her aunt said softly.

"I'm sorry."

"To answer your question, Fiona, I expected you to arrive looking every bit as lovely as you do."

"Thank you." She was thoroughly ashamed.

"Well! See you in a bit," he said in the flat, wounded voice only she could provoke. Someone had called his name. Aunt Arlene followed him to the door.

As a child Fiona had adored him, but then with adolescence began to sense his discomfort around her. There came to be invisible limits, wordless signposts, rules unarticulated beyond the flash of his eyes or his tightening grip on her arm. Uneasiness grew into almost constant disapproval. She would glance up to find him regarding her with the same aversion as he might any chronic offender in his courtroom. Her aunt tried to mediate the many clashes by getting them to at least acknowledge the fact of their opposite natures. Uncle Charles would try to be more patient and understanding, but knowing she could agitate him in ways no one else could became too heady an empowerment. She took pride in her cousins' shock each time she crossed the line or stood her ground. It seemed proof not just of her strength, but of her very identity, her role in this close-knit family. Central to their growing conflict was the fierce need she sensed in him. It was almost as if he were so desperate for her happiness because everyone else's depended upon it. There was little one could ever do to please the other. Her willfulness had always set her apart. If she could not have her own mother, she could be just like her. And yet the harder she tried to be different, the more deeply she resented his pained acceptance of it. She was the flaw in a seamless life, the foundling he could neither abandon nor love the way he did his own flesh-and-blood children.

Tonight he and Aunt Arlene looked every inch the happily unpretentious couple they had always been. They wore the same clothes every year. She had on the long, shapeless red velvet dress and he wore the holly green blazer, red suspenders, and red Santa Claus tie he would wear to all the parties between now and Christmas. Aunt Arlene had paused by the laurel-swagged mantel to talk to a vaguely familiar overweight man and his tiny wife. Fiona wondered what she could be saying to make them laugh so uproariously. She had never considered her aunt a particularly clever woman, certainly not a witty one. Her life's greatest concern was the well-being of her family and countless friends. Women were always telling Fiona how much they adored Arlene. She was the kindest person, and so considerate, just the sweetest, dearest thing. She was forever writing thank-you notes, messages of encouragement, congratulations and condolences, sending flowers, baskets of cookies she'd baked, delivering casseroles for mercy meals. For all her charity, there was little she could be given back. For all her affection, it was the hard bony protrusions that Fiona would remember most of an embrace. There was a remoteness about her, not coldness but an almost regal inviolability. And as is often the way for women said to have grown into their looks, simplicity had become her most attractive feature, her plainness its own stark adornment. She had never colored her wiry steel-gray hair. Even tonight her only makeup was pale lipstick, her jewelry a thin strand of flawless pearls.

Every room downstairs was filled with guests. Red-vested waiters were passing hors d'oeuvres on small silver trays. The bar was in the TV room and the buffet was being set up in the long, narrow dining room. Ham, tenderloin, lobster pie, pastas cooked to order on small portable burners, salads: it was the holiday party by which all others would be measured. Fiona wandered from room to room, enjoying her brief encounters. She hadn't seen most of these people since last year's party. She paused now at a circle of women to admire Lily Tyler's jade necklace and earrings, which everyone agreed were the same green as her eyes. Aunt Arlene had asked Fiona earlier to make a lot of her old friend if she could. This was Lily's first night out since her husband's death in August. Lily hugged Fiona and told her how beautiful she looked. Fiona returned the hug and compliment, then slipped away to the study. She had forgotten how good she was at this, how deftly she cold flit into a group, weave herself effortlessly into the conversation, then float off to the next one. So many people, the close hum, the gloss, the fragments of words as she passed, the flickering candle flame—it all shimmered around her like an enormous bubble. She could feel herself growing more and more animated, and she hadn't even had a drink yet. She loved the commotion, loved parties, loved to laugh, knowing all the while she was being watched and envied by other women who wished they could be as clever, as amusing, as natural in this contrived setting as she was. She truly was.

She looked around for Elizabeth, who was probably hiding upstairs. This was always the one night when Aunt Arlene really appreciated Fiona's spirited nature, her indefatigable determination to have a good time. But not her uncle of course. He would try to keep her in focus all night long to make sure she didn't drink too much, laugh too loudly, make any inappropriate comments to her elders. She wondered what Patrick was doing. No. She didn't want to think of him now when she was surrounded by so much festivity. Poor Patrick. She didn't want to feel guilty again tonight.

She didn't know where George had gone. She hadn't seen him for quite a while now. When she and George had arrived, Rudy and Elizabeth had been in the kitchen; Elizabeth in a corner white-faced with tightly folded arms and downcast eyes as Rudy stood close talking to her. His deep concern and her cousin's cold misery angered Fiona again now as she thought of it. She regretted bringing George. She tried to remember why she had even asked him. She should have thought it through first. Because of it Rudy was miserable. Once again she'd been too impulsive. She fanned herself with her hand. It was getting warm in here.

She stepped around the corner into the TV room and ladled the tart punch into a crystal cup, which she drank quickly, then had another. As she came down the hallway she saw Uncle Charles returning to the living room now with Rudy. They joined two men in the corner, Dr. Costello, her uncle's physician and old friend, and Dr. Preston, who had delivered her three cousins here in town. Fiona had been born in Boston, delivered by a doctor no one knew. Aunt Arlene said that had been her mother's choice. Given the circumstances, anonymity had been more important than the comfort of a familiar setting and face. Fiona wondered how many babies Rudy had delivered. It gave her a strange sensation to picture him in the hairy spread of a woman's stirruped legs. He was being introduced now. Her uncle's pride in him was obvious. The sleeves of Rudy's new tweed jacket were too short, she noticed, and his pants were too long. His attempt to turn up the cuffs had left thick rolls of fabric bunched above the top of his shoes. Wanting to go over and unroll them, it was all she could do to stand here. Uncle Charles patted Rudy's shoulder and leaned close to listen. Rudy's hands flew. Whatever he said was making the men laugh, Uncle Charles's laughter heartiest of all.

George must have gotten Elizabeth off alone somewhere. It had been at least twenty minutes now since Fiona had seen either of them. She headed toward her cousin Jack and his wife, Susan, who stood by the wingback chair talking to Bill Hebert, the balding lieutenant governor, and his tall, big-haired wife, Ann. They had been talking about golden retrievers, which Ann raised. "Speaking of little mutts," Jack said, putting his arm around Fiona, "I'd like you both to meet my very favorite cousin in the whole world."

Susan stared at him, then glanced imploringly at Fiona, who would have been insulted had it come from anyone else. When Jack drank he tried to be as clever as his father.

The lieutenant governor asked what she did for work. She said she was a waitress in a coffee shop in Dearborn.

"Now that's a hard job," Ann Hebert declared.

Oh, it was, she agreed. And it didn't pay much, of course, but then again it was an extremely challenging position.

"Oh yes, I'm sure," Ann Hebert agreed with an earnest nod. Only the lieutenant governor smiled. Jack looked confused, Susan concerned.

"What about you?" Fiona asked the lieutenant governor. "Do you find your job as stimulating as I find mine?"

"The truth? Not very often. Being a stand-in can be pretty draining," he said.

"We should trade then. You can get your batteries charged, and I can get off my feet a little," she said.

"Sounds good to me," he said, laughing. "But I should warn you, there's a lot of night work." He explained that was mostly when he had to stand in for the governor. Dinners, parties, testimonials, things like that. When she said that sounded more like fun than work, he pointed out that it was work, and of course that meant no drinking on the job. Did she still want to switch?

"Wait a minute!" She held up her hand. "So in other words, you're working tonight, right? You're not really enjoying yourself."

"No, no, no," he said quickly. "This is personal tonight. This isn't work. Your uncle's an old friend of mine. We go way back."

She dipped her pinkie into his drink, then tasted it and grimaced. "So how come you're drinking soda water then?"

He winked.

"Oh look, Fiona, Ginny just came in! Will you excuse us a minute?" Susan said, taking Fiona's arm and guiding her toward the front hall. "How could you do that?" she said through a wide smile, nodding at people as they went. "How could you put him on the spot like that?"

"Susan," Fiona warned through an even wider smile. "You're treating me like a real asshole, and I don't like it!"

"People can hear you," Susan said, still smiling and nodding.

Ginny looked exhausted. Dark, pouched circles hung from her eyes. "I'm here, but I'm not," she was telling her mother when Fiona and Susan reached her.

"Maybe this will take your mind off things," Aunt Arlene said, hugging Ginny with a pumping motion as if that might infuse her with cheer.

Fiona hadn't seen her cousin since early fall. As overbearing as Ginny could be, she was always fun at a party, because she was so easily amused by people's foibles and quick to laugh.

"Oh, I'm so glad you're here," Fiona whispered as they brushed cheeks. "Susan's got her decorum whip out tonight."

Ginny tried but barely managed a smile. Her wide, toothy face was puffy. She had gained a great deal of weight.

"You look wonderful!" Susan cried, throwing her arms around Ginny, who seemed to shudder.

"I won't be staying too long if you don't mind," she told her mother, who said of course she didn't mind. It was wonderful she'd even made this much of an effort. "Where's Daddy?" Ginny asked, looking around, then went with Susan in search of her father.

"Poor thing," Aunt Arlene murmured, giving Fiona's hand a quick squeeze. "I can't believe this is happening to her."

"She'll be all right," Fiona said, squeezing back, their arms and shoulders leaning into one another. "She'll get over it." She couldn't help smiling with her aunt's nearness.

"It don't know," her aunt sighed. "Being betrayed like that, it's so painful. And right now she's so vulnerable."

"It was bound to happen," Fiona said. "I always said he was a creep, but no one ever believed me."

"Well, the important thing was loyalty—for Ginny's sake," her aunt said, slipping her hand away. She smiled as their neighbor Lucretia Kendale and another elderly woman passed by looking for the martinis they'd set down somewhere only moments ago. "Good evening, ladies," Aunt Arlene called after them.

"No," Fiona said. "For Ginny's sake we should have told the truth." She reminded her aunt of the dinner when she'd been reprimanded for asking Bob Fay what he wanted. Nothing, he'd said quickly. Then why did he keep jamming his leg into hers, she had asked. Perhaps if she moved her chair Bob would have more room, Uncle Charles had said, his icy stare at niece and son-in-law freezing everyone into silence.

"I know. I know," her aunt interrupted. "But anyway, dear, I just want to say how pleased your uncle and I both are, not just that you're here tonight, but about you and George."

"We're just friends," Fiona said.

"Well I can't think of a better friend for you to have," her aunt said as she adjusted Fiona's pearls, turning the clasp behind her neck. "Or," she whispered at Fiona's ear, "a better better-friend should it turn out that way."

"Which it won't," Fiona said.

Elizabeth was in the dining room with the Matleys, a short man with bright red hair, and a heavy woman in a white crepe suit. Laura Matley taught with Elizabeth, and John was an accountant.

"In fact, he's George's accountant now," Elizabeth said, then with a wink at John Matley added, "I can't tell you how glad I am. He's been keeping his own books these last few years. I can just imagine what shape they're in."

Fiona was astonished by the change in her cousin since she'd last seen her in the kitchen. Elizabeth's eyes sparkled with almost feverish happiness.

"Well, we'll get him all straightened out in no time," John Matley said, looking around. "By the way, where is George?"

"In the kitchen," Elizabeth said with a broad smile. "The caterer was having a fit. One of mother's burners is out, so George said he'd fix it."

John Matley asked where the kitchen was; George might need a hand.

"Knowing George, I doubt it," Elizabeth said, eagerly leading the way.

Fiona asked Laura Matley how long she'd been teaching at the Crane School. Just a few months, Laura said. She had started in September with Elizabeth. She and John only knew a few people in town. He had been nervous about the party tonight, but Elizabeth had really wanted them to come. She thought it would be a good way for him to meet people. "She's just the sweetest person," Laura said. "I felt as if I've known her all my life. Everyone at school, we all say the same thing. We're just crazy about her. She's always bringing pastry in and little things she knows people will get a kick out of. Or if you're down that day, you'll go in to your desk and find some sweet little poem she wrote. Haiku, she calls it, and origami; she makes these delicate birds by folding little pieces of paper. Her students just adore her. She can't take a step without a bunch of them like little ducklings right behind her." Laura laughed. "Of course you probably hear that all the time." She looked toward the living room. "Now which one's her fiancé?" she asked. "I still haven't met him."

"Over there," Fiona said, pointing just as Rudy turned around. She gave a little wave, but he looked anxiously past her.

"Oh," Laura said, sounding surprised. "Isn't that funny. I pictured him looking entirely different."

"Like what?" she asked.

"Now that you ask, I don't really know," Laura mused with another glance back.

"He's probably more handsome than you thought he'd be," Fiona said, watching her.

"Well maybe," Laura said with a polite little laugh as Rudy made his way toward them, looking awkward and ungainly with his ill-fitting clothes, spikey cowlick, and somber expression.

Excusing herself, Fiona met him in the hallway. "Hey, I know what you're after. A big plate of spare ribs, right?"

His weak smile deflated in a sigh. "Do you know where Elizabeth went?"

"She's in the kitchen. George and his new accountant are trying to fix the stove."

In the kitchen George was on his knees with greasy stove parts laid out on a towel on the floor. Clearly annoyed, the caterers kept trying to work around him. Arms folded and also in the way, John Matley and Elizabeth stood over him watching. Elizabeth introduced Rudy to Matley by name only, Fiona noticed.

"He's her fiancé," Fiona added in the awkward silence that seemed to follow.

"Oh, yah! Sure!" John Matley said.

Rudy stared at Elizabeth, but she wouldn't look at him. Her jaw quivered and the cords in her long, thin neck were as taut as steel wires. The uneasy quiet was broken when John Matley said he'd better go see where his wife was.

"Yes, we've already left her alone for too long," Elizabeth agreed, hurrying after him.

"So how's it going, George?" Rudy asked after they left.

"Actually, I'm almost done. I think it's just blocked," he said, peering down a long metal tube.

"I meant you, how things are going with you." Rudy stood over him with his hands on his hips.

"Pretty good," George said, looking closely as he poked a steel skewer into the tube. "I can't complain, anyway."

"No, I guess you can't," Rudy said. "Much as you might want to, right?" he added, staring.

Fiona nervously popped a chocolate-dipped strawberry into her mouth and Darrin the caterer glared at her. She had worked for him once, but had quit in the middle of a wedding reception he was catering because he kept screaming at his waitresses. He couldn't stand her, but the Hollis party was one of his best references. She took another strawberry.

George's earlobes were bright red. He wiped the skewer on a paper towel, then stood up. "Excuse me," he said, squeezing past Rudy. He slid the tube into the well of the front burner and fiddled with the knob, but it didn't light.

"Need a hand?" Rudy asked.

"No thanks," George murmured, removing the tube. "I should have it clear in a minute."

"You wouldn't mind then if I borrow Fiona for that particular minute?" Rudy asked, and she looked up surprised and smiling.

"Of course not." George sounded relieved. "Whatever she wants."

"Yah, well don't anyone get the wrong idea. I'm kind of a free agent here." She laughed and took another strawberry.

"There was something I had to tell you, remember?" Rudy said, looking at her with such intensity that she was sure he was angry with her for bringing George when Elizabeth had asked her not to.

Just then the door began to open and close into the dining room as the chafing dishes were being carried in. In the midst of it all Aunt Arlene hurried into the kitchen. "There you are!" she cried, snaring Rudy's arm. "A very old friend of ours is waiting to meet you," she said, as they entered the bustle that was growing louder and more boisterous. More guests had arrived. The laughter and happy voices wafted in and out with the opening and closing door.

"George, what the hell are you doing?" Fiona blurted as he picked up another part.

"The tube was blocked," he murmured, bending over the stove.

"Yah? And what're you going to do when you're done, go sit on the cellar stairs?" She saw his back muscles flex as he stiffened. "You know what I mean. You came here to prove something, and now you're just hiding out in the kitchen."

He continued tightening screws, a bolt, now the burner itself. He turned back, wiping his hands on the soiled towel, his steadiness, as always, an almost irresistible goad. "You don't understand," he finally said.

"What? What's to understand? That she can't make up her mind? Isn't that why you came? To show her she has to?"

The two waiters by the sink kept glancing back to hear what was being said.

"She's afraid," he said in a low voice.

"What's she afraid of?"

He shook his head. "Herself, I think."

"Then that's her problem and she has to deal with it, instead of jerking everyone around, especially poor Rudy."

"There's too much pressure on her," he said. "There always has been."

"That's bullshit, and you know it as well as I do."

"No. I'm telling you," he said quietly. He stepped closer. "I'm worried about her. I know the hell she's going through. She hides it. Nobody else sees it. But I do!" His voice choked with concern.

"Boy," she said, shaking her head. "Has she ever got your number, George. All our numbers actually."

"I'm telling you, she's in a bad way!"

"Then if she can't, you better take charge, George!" she said, and once again his jaw clenched in grim resolve.

The door swung open, and now Uncle Charles came into the kitchen. "There you two are." He put one arm around George, the other around Fiona. "Come on out and enjoy the party," he said, walking them toward the door. "Listen, George, when we need a plumber you're the man we call. But not tonight. Tonight, you're here with Fiona," he said with a squeeze that made her shoulders ache. "And I just want you both to know how pleased I am about that." He looked from one to the other. "It just makes sense," he continued. "You two have been such good old friends."

"Actually, sir," George said, his face reddening, "I'm not here as—"

"Uncle Charles!" Fiona interrupted, and even as she spoke didn't know why she said what she did beyond the fact that in front of her uncle she wanted no part in George's revelations about himself and Elizabeth. "Actually George wants to do this for free," she said, taking George's arm. "But I was just telling him that's not how you like to do things, that you always insist on paying. That you have to, being a judge."

"Well of course. Yes, that's right. I always do."

"Oh no, sir," George began. "That's—"

"He usually gets forty dollars an hour," she continued. "But then again this is a night call, isn't it, George, and that's what? Time and a half, which comes to sixty dollars an hour."

"Certainly." Her uncle pulled out his wallet. "That's more than fair, especially having to work in the middle of all this ruckus!" He held out three twenties to George, who shrank from them.

"No sir. I don't want that. That's not why I'm here," he insisted.

"No, no, I know," her uncle said quickly. "But here, get me off the hook and take this." He laughed. "Otherwise I'll have to deal with Fiona later." He tried unsuccessfully to slip the money into George's jacket pocket.

"Absolutely not!" George said.

Uncle Charles smiled and shook his hand. "Well thank you then. Thank you for everything," he said, his nod toward Fiona meant to convey gratitude for George's care in matters far more sensitive than a balky stove.

Irritated, Fiona grabbed George's arm and leaned against him. "That Elizabeth. She can't keep anything to herself, can she?"

"I think she's hoping you two are as happy as she and Rudy are," her uncle said.

"Well, we're sure as hell trying, aren't we, Georgie?" She smiled up sweetly and felt his arm go rigid in hers.

Uncle Charles shook his head with a benevolent sigh and kept his eyes fast on hers. "Perhaps you'll have better luck getting her to watch her language. Lord knows I've tried." He patted George's shoulder and opened the door.

George pulled away. The door swung back and forth, fanning the audible breeze of bright voices in and out.

"That wasn't the least bit funny," he said.

"I wasn't trying to be. I was only trying to help." She pushed open the door.

"No," he said, blocking the way with his arm. "You wanted to see me squirm, didn't you? You're enjoying this, aren't you?"

"Of course not!" she said, stung as much by the accusation as by the knowledge that it was true. There was a certain satisfaction in seeing other lives in turmoil. But it wasn't enjoyable, so much as self-redeeming and energizing. All of her senses felt alive, her instincts primed. She knew what had to be done, knew what a man needed and a woman really wanted. The jagged peaks and crevices were always more nimbly scaled when they were someone else's troubles. Years of chaos had left her step sure and quick, far steadier through an avalanche than on a quiet path. "I can't stand seeing what this is doing to Rudy," she tried to explain. "But that sure as hell wasn't the time to break it to my uncle."

He shook his head in exasperation. "What this is doing to Rudy! What do you think it's doing to me?" he said, voice raw with a startling bitterness. "She keeps begging me to wait. 'Please wait,' she says. She can't stand the thought of hurting him or upsetting her parents."

"Maybe what she can't stand is having to make a commitment to either one of you."

"I've thought of that," he said, shaking his head as if to dislodge dust and doubt. "Sometimes I think she'd live here forever if she could. Because then she'd only have to be one thing—a dear, devoted daughter."

Voices swelled with the opening door. Fiona felt drained. Her only concern was Elizabeth. That's all. She didn't enjoy any of this. Not a bit of it. Of course she didn't. All she wanted . . . all she wanted—she didn't want anything, she thought, looking around, trying to see where Rudy had gone. He had to tell her something. She moved from room to room, smiling and nodding at anyone who looked her way, but now they stayed clumped in their little groups and had no interest in anything she might have to say. But if she could only find Rudy it would be all right, and this pounding in her chest would stop. Her throat was so dry it hurt. She got a beer from the bar and drank most of it standing there, but the hard tight throb stayed with her.

The Matleys were still with Elizabeth. George headed in their direction. Ginny and Susan were talking to the lieutenant governor's wife and one of the two female judges from her uncle's courthouse. She never knew which was which and they were both here tonight.

She came down the hallway and saw Lucretia Kendale talking to the heavy-set man she hadn't recognized earlier. It was Stanley Masters, she realized now as she joined them.

Though Lucretia Kendale lived next door, her elegant old house was a good two miles down the road. Well into her eighties she still dyed her long, wavy hair a dramatic bluish black. She leaned on a mahogany cane, looking top-heavy with her thick false eyelashes, full crimson lips, and deeply rouged cheeks. Lucreita owned most of the land for miles around. The better part of her visitors these last few years were couples who had been driving by or builders hoping to buy house lots, or a few acres, or even, as she was now trying to tempt Stanley Masters, "the whole kit and kaboodle."

Most local developers knew this cat-and-mouse game was Lucretia's amusement. It afforded her hours of earnest discussion in which she provided her "guests" with leisurely tours of the house and grounds along with the detailed history of her colorful life. Closets would be opened, old gowns held up, feathered hats swept on. Her photograph albums were always strategically placed on the tables and sofa cushions. It was with genuine eagerness and delight that she served her visitors brewed tea and cookies. None would have guessed that once, in a busier, more socially selective time, her dogs would have been set upon them without the slightest qualm. These visits would be followed by the further diversion of legal consultations while she mulled over the offers and counteroffers she had no intention of accepting.

Lucretia scribbled her number on a cocktail napkin. "And please bring your wife," she said, handing it to Masters.

"Mrs. Kendale," Fiona said, "would you actually want a bagel warehouse in your backyard?"

"I happen to like bagels very much," Lucretia said. "In fact, when I was younger I was probably one of the few in my crowd who had ever even eaten a bagel. You see, in those days they were considered quite

Jewish. Which obviously," she added with only the briefest look of concern at Masters, "meant nothing to me."

"Mrs. Kendale was always ahead of her time," Fiona said.

"It's the zoning," Masters said, easing away. "With all the trucks, I need industrial."

"Trucks," Lucretia mused, fanning imaginary fumes. "Well, you and your wife can come look, but I don't know about trucks."

"Nice talking with you." Masters turned to go.

"I know where there's land!" Fiona said quickly. "I think it's just what you're looking for. I'm not sure exactly how many acres, but I know it's quite a few. And it's right near the Industrial Park, so it must be the right zoning."

"Well, not necessarily, but anyway, where is it?" he said, stepping back.

"Do you know Patrick Grady?" she asked, undeterred by his weary nod. This could be just the boost Patrick needed. That land was only a burden. If he sold enough of it he could fix up his house, buy a new car, assuage his bitterness.

"Actually, he was one of the first people I went to," Masters said. "But Grady wouldn't even let me in the door. He said that land'll never be for sale."

"That doesn't make sense. I know he needs money," she said.

"Just typical Grady from what I hear." Masters tossed his head back to drain the last of his whiskey.

"Patrick," Lucretia murmured. "Oh! You mean Patrick who does my windows. Natalie's Patrick. What a handsome boy. In fact, what a handsome young couple they were."

"Maybe if I talked to him," Fiona said to Masters. She smiled at Lucretia, who was one of the few people who would ever talk about her mother. "Maybe I could get him to at least consider it," she added quickly. Uncle Charles was coming toward them.

"Sure." Masters shrugged. "But what are you, his agent?"

"Fiona is most probably his daughter," Lucretia said with the pluck of old authority. "Not that I ever saw a resemblance. Wouldn't you agree, Charles?" she said as he joined them. She stared at Fiona, studying her face. "To me you were always the picture of your mother. Her mother, Natalie Range," she informed Masters, "was without doubt the peppiest, prettiest girl in Dearborn."

"I always thought you were the prettiest girl in Dearborn, Lucretia." Uncle Charles bent to kiss her pancaked cheek.

"No small compliment, coming from the most handsome man in town," Lucretia said at his ear. She grabbed his tie to keep him near. "Remember, Charles, all you have to do is call. My bag is always packed, ready and waiting."

Fiona burst out laughing, and her uncle put his hand firmly on her shoulder.

"Well, Stan," he said. "I see you've met our neighbor here. Lucretia Kendale, the incorrigible siren of Timony Road."

"Yes," Masters said, "and your daughter here was just saying how she could maybe talk to Patrick Grady for me about selling some of that land of his."

"Fiona is my niece," Uncle Charles said slowly. "Her mother and Arlene were sisters."

"Which they still are," Fiona interjected.

"Natalie Range, a beautiful girl," Lucretia was telling her elderly lady friend who had just joined them. She had her martini in one hand and a plate heaped with food in the other. "Shiny black hair. Big, dark eyes. That milky white skin you never see anymore. Stunning, really."

"Oh, I remember her. Arlene's sister. They pretty one," the lady friend said, nodding.

"Here, let me hold that and then you can eat," Uncle Charles interrupted, taking the plate and holding it out for both women to eat from while he continued talking. "Stan and I are co-chairmen of the Y's building fund drive. Though I'm embarrassed to admit that he's been doing the lion's share of the work. Now that's something you'd probably be interested in, Lucretia." He turned to Masters. "The Kendale family was instrumental in getting the original Y built in Collerton."

"I could use all the help I can get," Masters said. "Same with the Grady thing," he said with a nod at Fiona. "Go ahead, talk to him, to your father. And tell him I consider that premium land. Very, very premium."

"I will!" she said, grinning in spite of her uncle's glare. "That'd be great!"

"I don't think so," Uncle Charles said, his grip tightening on her shoulder. "Patrick's not interested in selling. He never has been."

"But he needs the money," Fiona said as the two ladies wandered away from the empty plate her uncle still held. She looked at him. "He can't even pay the taxes on it."

"I'd certainly pay him what it's worth," Masters said excitedly. "Ever since I came here I've had my eye on that land."

"Actually it's mostly all ledge out there," her uncle confided. "The drainage is a horrible problem. And from a legal standpoint the quarry's a huge liability. It's an accident, a tragedy just waiting to happen. I hate to even think what a suit like that could cost."

Masters nodded thoughtfully. "I never did walk it. The way it's posted I didn't dare."

"But you could drain the quarry," Fiona said, ignoring her uncle's cold stare. "They were talking about doing that a few years back." She gave Masters a quick synopsis of Larry Belleau's accident.

"The cost of draining the quarry would be absolutely astronomical," her uncle interrupted. "Which is precisely why it wasn't done then."

"Except," Masters said, waving his index finger back and forth, "there's probably cheaper ways to do it now."

"Yah!" Fiona said, as if she already knew exactly what the ways were. "It'd be a whole lot cheaper now."

"I'll tell you what," her uncle said, turning so that he stood between her and Masters. "Grady's had proposals in the past, and so far he's always been adamant. But who knows, maybe this time it'd be different. If you'd like I can . . ." His voice trailed off as the two men walked into the hallway.

Fiona was trembling. Sweat trickled down her back. She hated him. This was the way she'd always been treated. By him, by all of them. She didn't belong here, she thought, watching Susan surrounded by an admiring group of Aunt Arlene's friends. Susan was clever and accomplished. Quality attracted quality. Like the best linen and china, she was sure to be brought out for special occasions, while everyone had to keep a close eye on Fiona, the wobbly chair that could collapse at the worst possible time.

"Fiona?"

She turned, startled.

"I was just talking to a neighbor of yours," Rudy was saying. "Apparently she owns the last, best house lots in town."

"Yes. Lizzie'd love that, right down the road from Mummy and Daddy," she said, surprised when he laughed.

"Yeah, I thought of that too," he said. "But anyway I told her I'm too much of a city boy. She wouldn't want me as a neighbor. I'd have to cut down all the trees and hot top everything."

"And what did Lucretia say? 'Why don't you come on over some time and let's talk about it, you big handsome city boy, you.'"

He shook his head in astonishment. "That's exactly what she said." He looked both ways then leaned close and whispered. "She wants me to be her doctor."

"Did she tell you it's been years since she had a really thorough physical?"

"My God. How did you know? Wait! Don't tell me. I was just being propositioned by the neighborhood harlot, wasn't I?"

"No, because I'm the neighborhood harlot."

"Then you've got some pretty savvy competition in that old gal," he said with a nod in Lucretia's direction. She was with the lieutenant governor and Crosby, a selectman in town.

"Oh yah? Why?" Fiona asked, turning back.

"She knows exactly what she's doing. She's got some real moves."

"And I don't?"

He held up his hands. "I never said that!"

"Well I don't. Not anymore, anyway." She sighed. "So what did you want to talk to me about? You said you wanted to tell me something."

"Where did George go?"

"Somewhere. I don't know. Where's Elizabeth?" she added with a shrug.

"Isn't there some game called 'Where in the World is Elizabeth Hollis?'"

"If not, there should be."

"Maybe she's helping George fix the furnace or something."

"Ooh, that was nasty. Or is that just your paranoia kicking in?"

"Nasty, paranoid, tired; what you see is a complete emotional disintegration taking place right here, tonight, before your very eyes."

"I can see tired and paranoid." She peered up at him. "But I don't see nasty."

"It's there." He started to put his hand on her arm, then drew back self-consciously. Instead, he moved closer. "I need to talk to you," he whispered. "Can we? Please? Right now?"

"You're serious, aren't you? Rudy, what's wrong?"

"Me! I looked around a minute ago, and everyone was laughing and talking, and I kept thinking this one thought over and over again."

"What was that, the one thought?"

"That I don't belong here. I kept thinking, what am I doing here? My God, what the hell am I doing here?"

"Well, welcome to the club. As a matter of fact, I was just getting the meeting started!"

"No, I mean it." He touched her wrist. "I need to talk to you, Fiona, because I'm feeling really screwed up here." He swallowed hard and tried to smile. "It's like I'm caught in something I don't even care about. And then there's the other part of it that I'm afraid to care about. The part that I can't have." He closed his eyes and sighed. "I've had some tough situations along the way, but I've never been in such a mess as this."

She squeezed his hand. "Poor Rudy." She glanced across the room. Her uncle had just returned and was talking to his old friends the Jorgensons. She told Rudy to leave a moment after she did and meet her at the top of the stairs. His pain filled her with guilt. She never should have brought George here tonight. She leaned over the railing, wondering why her heart was beating this fast again. Why was she so excited? Had George been right? More than the party, was it everyone else's misery she was enjoying?

Rudy looked up as she climbed the stairs, and she gestured for him to follow. She tiptoed to the door at the end of the second-floor hallway. Opening it, she gestured again. He followed her up the steep brown-painted treads to the cold, dark attic. She switched on the overhead bulb and saw him blink in surprise at the clutter of boxes and mirrors and pictures and all the old ice skates and roller skates hanging by their lace loops from ancient rusty roofing nails. At the far end of the attic was another door. She switched off the main light and turned on the dim bulb in the large, windowless, cedar-walled closet she and Elizabeth had long ago emptied of woolen storage, declaring it their secret room.

"We used to play dress-ups here." She closed the door. "See." She opened the rickety old rattan hamper and took out a wide-brimmed black hat. She put it on and smiled at herself in the mottled mirror. "This was my mother's. I used to pretend I was her."

"I have to tell you something," he said now as she extricated a musty white wool shawl from the hamper's tangle of cast-off clothing.

"Oh. Poor Rudy," she said with a shiver, tossing it over her shoulders. It was freezing up here. "I feel so guilty. I should have told you, but I kept thinking she would."

"I don't think we're talking about the same thing, Fiona."

"You're talking about Elizabeth, right?"

He shook his head no and his hands flew. "It's why I wanted to see you before the party tonight. So I could tell you. That is, so I could at least just say it. One time, anyway," he added.

"Say what?"

He stared at her for a moment. "That I love you."

"Rudy!"

"I know. I'm sorry. I apologize. I couldn't have picked a worse possible time and place, could I? I mean, all this time I've been hiding it and denying it and avoiding it, and then tonight I kept looking for you and watching you and every time you'd leave the room, I'd get this sinking feeling inside. Oh God, I'm sorry. This isn't fair. I shouldn't be doing this to you. I know I shouldn't."

"Rudy!" she said softly. She took off the hat and sank down onto the cold, damp divan. It sagged with the ancient rusty squeal she remembered. She felt the shawl slip down her back, but she couldn't move.

"I know." He held up his hands in a forlorn, hopeless gesture. "I'm so sorry. I know how you feel about Elizabeth and how she feels about you." He sighed. "But oh God, I know how I feel about you. I'm sorry. But I had to say it." He started to open the door.

She got up and threw her arms around his waist and pressed her face into his back. "Don't leave. Don't leave," she kept saying.

He had to unpry her hands so he could turn around.

"Please don't leave. Don't leave me. Please don't leave," she begged as he kissed her eyes, her temples, the tip of her nose, the soft underside of her chin, her mouth. He sank onto the divan and was kissing her breasts through her dress. He kissed her arms, her rib cage. Whispering his name, she pressed his head to her belly.

"Every night I dream of you," he whispered against her. "I dream of this." He watched her as his fingertips grazed her flesh, tracing a line down each inner thigh.

"Rudy. Oh, Rudy," she moaned.

"I know. It's all got to be right first," he said, getting up and kissing each part of her face again.

"We'll make it right. This is my favorite place. It always was," she said slipping her hands up under the back of his jacket.

"How could it be? This is the first time you've ever touched me." He laughed in her ear.

"I meant here. The room. This was our secret place."

"Oh. I thought you meant me."

"Well, that too," she said, laughing.

He leaned back and held her at arm's length. "But is it all right that I love you?"

She nodded.

"Could you ever feel the same way about me? Do you think you could?" he whispered.

"I already do."

Grinning, he started to pull her to the door. "Come on, let's get out of here. We'll go somewhere. Someplace warm and private."

"No." She laughed and turned off the light. "We'll stay right up here, right on top of them, and they'll never know what we're doing," she said as she undressed.

He sat on the edge of the divan and kept reaching out through the dark to touch her.

"It'll be our own private party." She groaned as he pulled her with him onto the cold, flat mattress.

He was the most passionate lover she'd ever been with, and the gentlest. When they were finished she lay with her head in the crook of his arm, the prickly shawl pulled over them. She had no idea what time it was. She wasn't sure if they'd come up here two hours or twenty minutes ago.

"Now what do we do?" he said, putting his open hand on her damp belly.

"I'll go down by the back stairs, then you come a couple minutes after. They'll all be at the front of the house."

"I mean about Elizabeth."

She sat up and rolled over on top of him. "Well, I think the first thing we have to do is get ourselves down from here without being seen."

"We could just stay up here, then leave tomorrow when everyone's at church," he said.

"Okay." She lay back and, closing her eyes, fell asleep. She woke up to the muffled sound of a car's engine starting down in the driveway. "Rudy!"

"We better get dressed," he whispered. He raised himself up on one elbow.

"I thought you said we could stay till tomorrow."

"I was just trying to be clever and romantic," he said, his mouth against hers.

With a sigh she reached up and turned on the light. He sat up, then looked back, alarmed. He pointed to her neck. "Those marks, they're down both sides of your neck!"

"It's from a scarf," she said, touching her throat. "It was this thing I did. When I was trying to tie it. At the coffee shop," she added, remembering she'd already told him that the bruises on her chin had happened at work.

"I've seen marks like those before. They're from someone's hand, Fiona." His jaw dropped open. "Was it Grady? Did he do that?"

"No!" she said, meeting his stare. "Of course not."

"Than who did?"

"Nobody!" she said, shivering as she pulled on her stockings. She was freezing and suddenly very nervous about going downstairs.

"I know what they are, Fiona," he said, buttoning his shirt. "And I know the kind of pressure it takes to make them."

She spun around. "Look! Don't do this to me! It was just this random thing that happened, and it has nothing to do with you, okay?"

He started to say something, then nodded instead.

She went downstairs first. The party had quieted somewhat. Most of the food had been eaten, and there was coffee brewing in the kitchen. Elizabeth, Susan, and Ginny were sitting on the back sofa in the living room. Elizabeth looked anxiously past Fiona as she came into the room.

"Where's George?" Fiona asked quickly. "I've been looking all over the place for him."

Elizabeth said he'd left with the Matleys a little while ago. "He said to tell you he was sorry, but he was really tired."

"Doesn't he know he's supposed to leave with the girl that brung him?" she said, trying to look annoyed.

"He thought you left. I'm the one who told him to go with the Matleys," Elizabeth said, staring at her.

"You look tired," Ginny said, getting up. She patted down the side of Fiona's hair, then held the back of her hand to Fiona's cheek. "And you're so flushed. You feel like you've got a fever."

"It got so hot in here," Susan said, wondering aloud if she should tell Arlene to turn down the thermostat. No one answered, and she didn't move.

"Have you seen Rudy?" Elizabeth looked past her again.

"Maybe he left with the Matleys too," Fiona said with a foolish grin, unsubduable even under Ginny's scrutiny.

"I feel so bad. He hardly knew anyone," Elizabeth said. "He probably had a miserable time."

"He seemed to be enjoying himself when I saw him," Ginny said.

"Yah, he was when I saw him too," Fiona said, then burst out laughing. They looked at her. "Please ignore me," she said, waving her hand. She covered her mouth and took a deep breath. "I think I've had just a little too much fun tonight." She was laughing again. She knew by their quick glances they thought she was drunk.

"Speaking of fun things, I was just telling Elizabeth about this new account I have," Susan said. "They're wedding consultants. They do everything. Find the right gown, plan the menu, the flowers. They even—now get this—send out the invitations."

"Really?" Fiona said, then had to cover her mouth again.

"Look who's here," Ginny said as Rudy came around the corner. "The missing fiancé."

Elizabeth hurried over and took his hand, holding it in both of hers while she spoke to him. He nodded.

"Poor thing. He looks so confused," Susan said.

"Mother thinks our little Lizzie's giving him a run for his money," Ginny said, watching them. "I asked her what was going on, but Lizzie says it's just his crazy schedule. She says he works so many hours she never gets to see him anymore."

"Fiona," Susan said in a conspiratorial tone. She leaned closer. "I just heard the good news."

"What good news?"

"You and George. That you're . . . well, going out," Susan said with an uncertain glance at Ginny.

"Well we're not," Fiona said, but they hadn't heard her because they both began to talk at once as Elizabeth led Rudy over to them.

"Rudy!" Susan said.

"We were so worried," Ginny said. "My father said the last he saw you were talking to Lucretia Kendale."

"Yes and believe me, she's quite the lady," he said, raising his eyebrows.

"We figured you were getting the cook's tour," Susan said.

"Oh, so that's what it's called!" Fiona blurted with a bawdy laugh.

"Rudy's going to be leaving now," Elizabeth said.

"Yes," he said, looking at everyone but Fiona. "I've got an early shift tomorrow."

"You look exhausted," Susan said.

Fiona picked up a magazine and flipped through it. To keep from smiling she chewed the inside of her mouth.

"I was just reading an article about interns and how stressed out they get having to work eighteen and nineteen hours straight," Ginny said.

"Well I don't do that anymore," he said. He glanced at Fiona and she grinned.

"Rudy's not an intern," Elizabeth said.

"No, I know," Ginny said quickly. "But when I read it I couldn't help thinking of you. Elizabeth's been telling us about your crazy schedule and how you—"

"So on that note I guess I better get you home," Elizabeth said to Rudy, turning to go before Ginny could say any more.

"But I thought you drove here," Fiona said, looking at him puzzledly.

"Elizabeth picked me up. She got sent to town on a last-minute errand," he explained with everyone looking on.

"Oh." She nodded. An errand that must have been her aunt and uncle's way of getting Elizabeth into Rudy's bed tonight. "Well I can give him a ride. I'm going right by his house," she said to Elizabeth.

"Oh yah, sure," Rudy said, and Elizabeth looked relieved. "That makes sense." They smiled at Fiona and spoke at the same time.

"Are you sure?" Elizabeth said.

"If you don't mind, that is," Rudy said.

"No, of course not," she said, smiling back broadly. "If I minded, would I have offered?"

There were in the front hall, putting on their coats. Her arm brushed his. They glanced at one another and tried not to laugh. Her heart raced, and her ears were filled with a sound like running water. So acutely conscious was she of his nearness that her cheeks tingled. She dropped her glove, and he picked it up, then held it open. As her hand slipped into the leather it felt as if she were reaching into some soft deep part of him.

The hallway door opened. "Oh!" Uncle Charles said, emerging from the candlelit shadows of the kitchen, where the last guest lingered over coffee. "There you are. Arlene just said you were on your way." His head moved as if with the slightest tremor. "I didn't realize you were leaving together."

"I'm going to give him a ride home."

"She's giving me a ride home."

They answered in unison, each not daring to say the other's name.

"Can't Elizabeth? I mean, is everything all right? I didn't see you for a while there," her uncle said to Rudy.

Fiona couldn't help smiling. She let Rudy explain that she was going right by his apartment, and this way Elizabeth would be spared the drive back alone.

"But I'm sure she doesn't mind," her uncle persisted.

"No, and I don't either," Fiona said with an irrepressible giggle as she kissed Uncle Charles goodbye.

"I don't know, Fiona, you've been drinking," he said stiffly. "Driving's probably not such a good idea."

"I've had one beer!" she said.

"Well, why don't you both stay over?" he asked, looking at Rudy. "Get up in the morning, have a big country breakfast."

"He can't."

"I can't. But thank you."

They couldn't look at one another. She wondered if her eyes were as bright with desire as his.

"Oh God," she groaned as they came down the path, arms folded, careful to keep a good space between them. She could feel her uncle watching them all the way to her car. She started the engine and pulled onto the narrow road. The half-moon was a patch of ragged haze in the cloudy sky. When she turned at the intersection they burst out laughing. She put her hand on his thigh, and he ran his hand through her hair.

"Your ears are cold." He stroked the lobe between his fingers. He was quiet for a moment. "You won't go near that guy again, will you?"

"What guy?" She tilted her cheek against his hand.

"The one who hurt you."

"I told you. No one hurt me," she said, lowering her eyes for a moment as blinding headlights filled her rearview mirror. There was a car so close on her bumper that if she stopped it would hit her. She looked in the mirror again but all she could discern through the glare was the shape of a man's head. She drove slowly, glancing back, then blinking to focus on the road ahead.

"Can I sleep with you tonight?" Rudy asked in a hoarse voice as he ran his finger along the curve of her chin.

"No, I don't think it's a good idea," she said.

"I mean just that, to sleep. I want to be with you, Fiona. I need to be with you."

"No. Not tonight. I can't." And now as she looked in the mirror, she saw what she feared. It was him. He'd been waiting for her to leave the party, and he was following her back. Their eyes met in the rearview mirror; hers, startled and confused, and Patrick Grady's, glowing with rage.

Chapter 17

It was the first Saturday she had worked in a long time. Maxine had called at six to say that Donna Drouin was sick with the flu and couldn't come in. Twenty minutes later Fiona dragged through the door, wet-haired and shaky with sleep. The coffee shop stayed busy throughout the day. With bright sunshine and temperatures unseasonably in the sixties, people filled the downtown streets and stores. The hectic pace kept Fiona's mind off her anger with Patrick, and now in the afternoon's unrelenting glare, her guilt and confusion over what had happened last night with Rudy.

Sandy had just come into the coffee shop with her daughters, who were dressed in patent leather shoes, matching wool coats, and velvet jumpers. One wore cranberry and the other green. Sandy hadn't expected to see Fiona working instead of Donna. Her eyes were irritated and her nose was red as if she'd been crying. Fiona had heard that Todd was better and back working at the store. He'd probably started running around again, she guessed, judging by Sandy's weariness. Fiona told the girls how pretty they looked. She was surprised when they not only thanked her but told her she looked very pretty too. The last time she'd seen them they'd been squabbling at one another to shut up. She asked if they were all dressed up for a party.

"Nonnie likes us to wear pretty dresses," answered Brandy, the older child.

"Who's Nonnie?"

"Todd's mother," Sandy said. "It was her idea, instead of Grammie or Nana."

"Cute," Fiona said. Todd's mother wouldn't want anyone thinking she was the actual grandmother of the little Rudman bastards.

"Yah, it is, isn't it? Like a kinda, 'Oh, I'm this special person in your life, but we can have fun too, you know?'" Sandy said, jiggling her head and wiggling her fingers.

My God, Fiona thought. She must be driving the Prescotts right out of their minds.

The girls ordered hot dogs and french fries. They asked for chocolate milk, but Sandy told them it wasn't on the menu. Fiona said she'd make some up, special, just for them.

"That's awful nice of you," Sandy said when she returned with crayons and paper place mats for the girls to color on. "Girls, you thank Miss Range for being so nice to you."

"Thank you, Miss Range," both girls chimed back as they began to draw.

"You're so very welcome, Brandy and Mandy," Fiona said, smiling. They were beautiful children. "Except for one thing," she said, bending close. "Please don't call me Miss Range. You never used to. We're old friends! So you just call me the same name your mommy does."

"I can't. I'll get in big trouble," Brandy said, not looking up from the tiny eyes, nose, and mouth she was adding on to the huge misshapen head she had drawn.

"No, you won't, honey. Not if I say you can," Fiona assured her.

"Can I?" Brandy asked with a skeptical glance at her mother. "Can I say it too? Can I say 'that bitch'?"

"Brandy!" Sandy cried and smacked her hand. The crayon flew onto the floor. Brandy's eyes closed with quiet sobs as her mother told her that wasn't nice. Nice girls didn't say bad words. Only bad girls said things like that. Did she want to be a bad girl? Is that what she wanted? To be a bad girl and have no friends and have everybody going around all the time saying, oh, don't play with her, that Brandy Rudman, she's a bad, bad girl. "Is that what you want? Is it? Is it?" Sandy hissed.

"Sandy, come on." Fiona sighed and shook her head. "Poor kid, it's not her fault. I mean—"

"She knows better!" Sandy said, her own mouth trembling and her eyes wide and wet. "She knows how she's supposed to act. She knows!"

"But she's only four, Sandy. I mean, it just doesn't seem fair to blame a little kid for telling it like it is. Come on." She squeezed Sandy's shoulder and now Sandy lowered her head and sniffed, trying not to cry.

"You look tired," she said when she returned with their lunch.

Sandy said she'd spent the last two days packing. "Oh!" Fiona said, hoping it didn't sound as vulturous as it felt. So that's what was wrong. Dumb, trusting little Sandy had finally gotten the big kiss-off from the Prescotts.

Sandy explained that she and Todd were moving into their own house.

Fiona gulped. "You're buying a house?"

Well, renting one, with the Prescotts' help, Sandy said Todd's mother was just too strict with the girls. With all her antique rugs they couldn't even wear shoes inside the house. They couldn't come out of the bedroom before seven-thirty in the morning, and they had to be in bed for the night no later than seven.

"It's just getting to be way too much," Sandy said. "She's like so wicked strict."

"Yes, it shows," Fiona said, the barb lost on Sandy.

"Yah, we were even thinking about getting my old place back, but then Myrna got all upset, and she kept begging us to stay. Next thing I know she's bringing me to see this house. It's got three bedrooms and this finished cellar kind of playroom. It's really cute."

"But Todd says it's a dump," Brandy said, glancing up from her scribbling.

"It just needs a little work, that's all," Sandy said with pointed exasperation. "Nonnie says it'll be good practice for Todd—you know, for someday when we do buy our own house."

Forcing a bright smile, Fiona tried to tell herself the twinge in her chest was pity, not envy. Maxine was at the table now asking about the wedding plans. Sandy said the wedding had been moved up to next month. "Myrna says there's no sense in waiting. All it does is give Todd more time to fred."

Maxine looked puzzled. "What do you mean, fred?"

"You know, worry," Sandy said.

Fiona rolled her eyes as she headed into the kitchen on her way home. It bothered her to still have these feelings for Todd. It wasn't that she wanted him for herself. She just didn't want to know that someone else had him. That's what Elizabeth must have felt seeing George in her arms. And now there was Rudy. "My God," she muttered as she hurried out to her car. "What the hell have I done? What's wrong with me? Am I nuts? Jesus Christ, I must be!"

It was getting dark. She didn't notice the paper under the windshield wiper until she started the car and turned on the lights.

I NEED TO SEE YOU. I HAVE SOMETHING FOR YOU. PLEASE COME. IT'S VERY IMPORTANT. PATRICK

There was no answer, so she knocked again. His car was in the driveway, but the house was dark inside. She hit the door with her fist. "Patrick!" she called, banging on it. When it finally opened, he stood there, glassy-eyed and disheveled, but grinning. He squinted into the porch light and explained that he'd fallen asleep, but he'd been hoping she'd come. He'd been waiting all day.

"Come in!" He opened the door even wider, but she still didn't move.

"You followed me last night! I can't believe you did that!" she said angrily. "You waited for me, and then you followed me!"

"Please come in," he begged, gesturing into the darkness behind him. "And then we can at least talk."

"No! The last time I was in there you hurt me."

He took a deep breath and shook his head. "You don't understand," he mumbled.

"No, but it's my fault, and I accept that, but now it's got to stop. You can't be waiting when I go someplace and then follow me. It's weird. It's all just getting too strange."

"I'm sorry," he said, shrugging. "But I had something for you. I was going to give it to you when you came out, that's all. That's why I waited." He hung his head.

"But don't you understand, you can't be following me like that. It's frightening."

"I know. I'm sorry. I won't do it again. I promise," he said so morosely she was taken aback. After all, she had been the first pursuer. She tried to explain this, pointing out how overwhelmed he must have felt to have her forcing her way into his quiet life. "So I can see how things could get so out of whack," she allowed, her mind racing, afraid to say what she really meant, that it was all so hopelessly twisted, only wanting what belonged to someone else, what she could not have, including Patrick, so naturally the lines had gotten blurred. "I confused you. I know I did, because I'm so—"

"You didn't confuse me!" he interrupted. "You think I feel this way because I'm confused?" He stood so close now she was conscious of his chest rising and falling. "Because I don't know what I'm doing?"

"But you saw things one way, and I wanted them to be my way. So I kept putting pressure on you," she said softly to calm him. "I shouldn't have done that."

"But I'm glad you did. You saved me," he said with a slow smile. "I didn't have anything before you. I was frozen, I was dead inside, and you saved me."

"You just kept to yourself too much, that's all," she said, choosing her words carefully.

"I didn't have much choice. Until now."

She didn't say anything.

"Do you know what the hardest part of a lie is?" he asked. "It's always trying to remember the truth."

"What do you mean?" she asked.

"I mean you."

She smiled, certain she understood, though to explain it right now would have been impossible.

"I've been alone a long time. I'm tired of being alone," he said.

"I know, because you're so isolated here. Sometimes it seems you don't even like being here," she said, pained by the misery glinting in his eyes. His mouth twitched as if he needed to speak, but couldn't. "But you feel stuck, is that it?" she asked softly.

He kept looking at her. "I hate it here!" he finally cried. "You have no idea how much I hate it!"

"Then sell it, Patrick! You don't have to stay here." She told him about Stanley Masters's interest in his property. "You should call him! At least hear him out," she coaxed.

"And then what do I do?" He began to pace back and forth, his eyes darting between her and the road, as if Masters's fleet of bagel trucks idled out there now awaiting her signal.

"Whatever you want!" she said. "Anything! Move into town! Go somewhere! Travel! You're still young, Patrick. There's so much you can do."

He stopped suddenly. "Would you go with me?"

"Well . . . I don't know. I . . . I mean . . . I could come visit you!" she said with a hopeful smile. "Why? Do you have a place picked out? Do you know where you'd go?" she asked, laughing a little.

"Alaska!" he declared, pacing again. He spun around. "But the thing is to not tell anyone. To just go! You know, just disappear." He kept looking at her.

"Well I don't know. I kind of have this prejudice against disappearing," she said with an uneasy shrug, but knew the significance of her quip had eluded him.

"Will you think about it though?"

"Alright—if you'll think about calling Stanley Masters." She glanced at her watch and said she had to go. She had to straighten things out with Rudy, she thought, with the sickening realization that she had progressed from sleeping with her friend's husband to seducing her cousin's fiancé.

"What's the big rush?" Patrick asked, insisting he owed her a dinner. He'd run out and buy two steaks, then do all the cooking while she relaxed and watched television. "Why?" he demanded, incensed when she said she couldn't. "You have a date? You're going to see that guy again, aren't you? The one you were with last night."

"I told you. I gave him a ride home. He's Elizabeth's fiancé."

He leaned closer. "Yah, and I told you, it's you he's after. It's you he wants, not your cousin," he whispered in her face.

"Don't say things like that," she said, shaken. A bitter taste rose in her throat. She remembered Patrick grilling Larry about her.

"I can tell by the way he looks at you. His eyes, they get hot. They—"

"That's ridiculous," she said, fumbling to button her jacket.

"You know what he wants, don't you? A little something on the side, that's what. A diversion," he said, lifting hair from the side of her face. He held it at her temple and watched her. "I don't imagine your skinny-rag cousin's all that much . . . well, fun, if you know what I mean," he said in a low, sibilant whisper. "She's more like her mother, isn't she? Finicky, I'll bet—fussy about things. Certain things." He paused for a moment. "And then he meets you and he knows whatever happens you'd never say anything. You'd never betray him. Because you love your cousin too much. You'd never want to hurt her."

"That's sick," she said, cold with fear of Patrick and that it might be true.

"I'll tell you what's sick," he growled, his brow at hers, his hand still clutching her hair. "Sleeping with every man who comes near you like it's nothing, like it doesn't mean a goddamn thing."

"What're you talking about?" She could barely breathe.

"You know." He stared at her for a moment. "Don't you care? I mean, your friend's husband. She just had a baby. How could you do that? And now your cousin's fiancé?" he asked, his voice breaking.

"You're hurting me!" she warned as his fist tightened in her hair. "Is that what you want? You want to hurt me? Because I look like her? Is that why? Am I like her? Am I?"

His eyes closed as if against some vile yet mesmerizing sight. His grip loosened, but he didn't let go.

"You hurt my mother like this," she said as quietly as she could. He seemed to be nodding. "You did, didn't you? You cut her hair. You chopped it off, didn't you?"

"No," he whispered, shaking his head.

"Yes you did. You know you did. You scared her. You made her run away." She pushed his hand from her hair. "You stand back now. Don't," she warned as he reached out. "Don't touch me again. I have to go!"

"No! You wait! You listen to me!" He grabbed her arm. "You keep asking me about your mother. Why? You want to be more like her? With no self-respect? Ruining everything she ever touched? Is that what you want?"

"I said, I'm going now," she said, straining back.

"Well you're not!" he said, pulling her closer. He touched her cheek, then drew his fingers around her mouth. "You're not like her. She was too stupid and trusting. And you're not." He smiled. "She was spoiled rotten. Whatever she wanted she got. So she thought things would always be that way. But how could they? They couldn't." He sighed and let go of her arm. "Not the way she wanted."

"What did she want? What things? What do you mean? What are you talking about?"

"I don't want to talk anymore." He looked at her and shook his head. "I can't. So you go. Go ahead. Just go. Wait!" he called as she opened the door. He reached into his pocket. "Here." He took her hand and in her palm placed a small gold locket. "You keep it."

The ornately filigreed locket was engraved with the initials DRS. "What is it?" Fiona asked, still frightened, but confused and painfully touched that he would give her his mother's locket. Opening it, she saw two miniature baby pictures inside. She stepped under the light. Details of the plump little faces were almost lost beneath webs of tiny cracks.

"It was your mother's," he said, and her head shot up. "You want it?"

"Oh! Yes," she said, closing it. "Thank you."

"She used to wear it." He pointed to her neck with an awkward gesture.

"DRS," she said, examining it more closely. Of course. Diana Skillings Range, her grandmother's name. The locket must have been hers before it was handed down to her daugher, Natalie. She peered at the tiny mottled faces that had to be pictures of her mother and Aunt Arlene. It was probably all he had that had been Natalie's. "Did she give this to you?" she asked, holding it out. His eyes widened, and though he did not move it almost seemed that he had jumped back away from her. "I mean, you don't want it?"

He shook his head. "I want you to have it. That's why I was waiting last night. So I could give it to you. Don't be mad at me, Fiona. Please, don't be mad," he said, starting toward her.

"All right, but I have to go now." She opened the door and edged slowly back. She wondered if he could hear the pounding in her chest.

Still in her uniform, she was slipping one of her own chains through the locket when Rudy came. When she opened the door, he just stood there grinning. The sport jacket he wore over his green scrubs was the same one he'd had on last night. She tried to smile, but Patrick's words rang in her head. *Sleeping with every man who comes near you, that's what's sick.*

"You look even more beautiful than you did last night," he said, closing the door.

"Damn it," she muttered, trying to snap the clasp into place.

"I'll do it," he said, standing behind her. He fastened the clasp on his first attempt, then kissed her neck. She stared at herself in the mirror. Patrick was right. They both needed the same thing and knew neither would betray the other to Elizabeth.

"I've been calling you all day," he whispered, turning her to face him. "I thought you said you had the day off." He kissed her brow, her eyes and nose, the space above her mouth, and now his lips moved against hers. "I got worried. So I came right over from the hospital. I was starting to think you were avoiding my calls."

"I wouldn't do that," she murmured against his mouth. His hands were kneading her back. They sat on the couch. If she closed her eyes she would sink into a deep sleep.

"You wouldn't?"

"If I don't want to see someone, I tell them straight out."

"That's good," he whispered, kissing her. "That's so good."

Her eyes closed heavily. She was skidding down a sandy embankment, now sinking, falling through a great watery depth. She held on to the back of his head, his mouth so hungrily at hers their teeth kept scraping. They had slipped from the edge of the couch to their knees.

They were trembling. So sensitive was she to his touch that her skin ached, her eyes burned, and her ears throbbed with growing pressure. She dug her nails into his arms. She wanted to hurt him. She fell back and pulled him down.

"Not here," he groaned. "Let's go in on the bed."

"No!" she cried so angrily that he tried to laugh, but could only moan with her demand that he help her, chanting it over and over, begging him to help her now, as she began to cry. "Please, please, please help me, help me, help me, help me," she sobbed, and was filled with such loathing for needing this, for wanting it so much that she wanted to die, to just die, and never have to feel anything again.

"I will! I will! You know I will!" He kept assuring her that he was trying, that he would. He would. He would do his best. Whatever she wanted, he would do. Anything. Anything. Anything, because he loved her. "I love you! I love you!" he panted, then collapsed onto his side. He stared at her. "Did you hear what I said? I love you," he whispered, touching her face.

"No you don't," she said, removing his hand.

He laughed and buried his face in her hair and told her again that he loved her.

"No. You're just so grateful, you'd say anything," she said.

"What do you mean, grateful?" He propped his head on his hand and watched her sit up.

"Twice in twenty-four hours? When's the last time you scored like that?" she asked as she stood up. She grabbed her clothes and hurried into the bathroom. When she came out she was irritated to find him still sitting in the dark. She turned on the light and began straightening up the room. He watched for a few minutes without saying anything, then suggested they go out to dinner. He'd worked straight through today, so he could be with her tonight. "All night," he said, watching her gather another armload of clothes. He picked up a dropped sock and held it out, but she pretended not to see it.

"I don't think so," she said, carrying everything into the bedroom. "I'm pretty tired."

"Then we'll stay in," he said from the doorway, watching her put away her clothes. "I'm a pretty good cook," he continued, swinging the sock. "All right, I'm being modest. I'm an excellent cook. How about Mexican? Do you like—"

"Actually, what I really need is to be alone," she said, her back to him. She froze, wincing. She could tell he hadn't moved, he was watching her. "I'm sorry," she said. She turned and met his gaze. "I am."

He tossed the sock onto the bed. "Boy, I really missed something here, didn't I? Something really big, and now I'm feeling like an absolute dolt because I don't have a clue what it is."

"You don't?"

He shook his head.

"Well here's a hint. It's called fucking my cousin's fiancé," she said.

His mouth dropped open. "But there's nothing there. There's nothing between us," he insisted. "You know that!"

"Well, let's see. You're engaged. I'd call that something. A little bit of a relationship, anyway."

Not really, he said, then tried to explain that he hadn't broken it off before because he'd been so rattled and confused, as much by Elizabeth's mixed signals as by his immediate and powerful attraction to Fiona. But now it was so clear. Now he knew what he had to do, he said, pacing back and forth. "And you're right. You're absolutely right!" he declared. "It's not fair to do this to you, to put you in the middle like this." He would do what had to be done. He would go there right now and tell Elizabeth it was over, that he loved Fiona. "So you just wait. You wait right here," he said, starting to open the door.

"No!" She grabbed his arm. "Please don't. Please."

He put his arms around her and kissed the top of her head, assuring her it would be all right. "I've spent my whole life looking for you," he whispered, and she pulled angrily away.

"But you found Elizabeth first," she said.

"And then I found you!" he said as if it were all so perfectly logical.

She laughed. "Found me! Found me? Like that's some rare achievement? Do you know how many men have 'found' me? I don't think you realize how easy I am to find. A few beers, a sweet guy, that's all it takes." She laughed again. "I mean, you saw me yourself, right there in that very bed with George Grimshaw. And all that took was a cup of coffee!"

"I know what you're trying to do, Fiona—the hard shell, the wise mouth. But it won't work." He shook his head with an indulgent smile.

She threw down the sweater she'd been folding. "Oh! I forgot! Your mother. You've had so much experience with screwed-up women, that what, you'll put up with anything, right?" He flinched, and she hated herself.

"I love you. I love everything about you. Everything!" He stared at her. "It's that simple."

"Simple!" She threw up her hands. "Jesus Christ, things couldn't get more complicated."

"But that's why I know this is right. I love you, and with that as the standard, everything *is* simple. Nothing else matters and that's all there is to it."

She had been shaking her head. "No, that's just the problem here. I've been so damn screwed up for so long that I keep messing up everyone's life, and I've got to stop. I can't do that anymore."

"Fine! But why not just kill the fleas? You don't have to get rid of the damn dog too, do you?" He tried to put his hands on her shoulders, but she wiggled free.

"I can't! I can't have them looking at me the way they do. Like I've just confirmed their worst fears. I can't do that to my aunt and uncle. They've been too good to me. But most of all I can't do it to Elizabeth."

"You won't have to. I'm going over there now to tell her." He started for the door.

She spun around. "To tell her? To tell her what?"

"What she and I both know. That it's over."

"You do whatever you want, Rudy. Whatever you have to do. But not because of me. Don't fool yourself about what happened. There's no mystery here. You were lonely and I was there."

"No. I loved you, and you were there."

She laughed. "Don't you get it yet? I'm always there! Always! For anyone who wants it." She stepped closer. "Can I make it any clearer? How's this? Rudy, I don't love you."

He studied her for a moment, as if she were one of his more vexing patients. "You don't want to love me, that's what you mean." He stepped into the hallway and closed the door quietly.

She buried her face in her hands, then suddenly fearing what was about to happen, ran down the hallway, to the top of the stairs. "Rudy!" she called, leaning over the railing, and he looked up from the lobby, his smile fading with her caustic warning. "Don't you mention my name! Don't! I'm warning you—because if you do, I'll hate you! I'll hate you forever!"

As she came back down the hallway, Mr. Clinch's door was closing. She stopped and knocked on it.

"Yes?" came his faint voice.

"Mr. Clinch, can you open the door? It's me, Fiona Range. I've got something for you."

"Oh! Oh dear, what is that now?" he said from inside, fumbling anxiously with chains and bolts. He opened the door and peered out.

"Something you've been looking for. There," she said as she grabbed his crotch with a good, hard squeeze. "It must be so boring to always have to do it yourself."

She had to be careful. She squinted, turning the locket slowly under the light. The thin gold clasp was fragile, its tiny hook so worn it barely clicked. She had been opening it all night to look at the miniature faces. She closed it again now, gently. It felt cold against her skin. She eased against the pillows and circled her thumb over the engraving as if for some message from the women who had worn it before, the women she had never known. Earlier, she had painstakingly pried out the brittle pictures, disappointed to find nothing hidden behind them, not an address, phone number, or secret wish for her daughter's happiness. She couldn't believe Patrick had merely found the locket in his house. She had called him a little while ago to see if her mother might have asked him to give it to her someday when she was old enough to understand.

"I don't know what you're talking about," he had said, sounding cranky and half asleep.

"Why she left. I mean why she had to, or—"

"Look. I told you, didn't I? I just found it, that's all."

"I know, but how did it—"

"That's it! I don't want to talk about it anymore! You woke me up!"
He had slammed down the phone.

She reached up and turned out the light. She held on to the locket
with her eyes wide in the dark. This ache inside wasn't loneliness or
even regret, but a profound disappointment in herself. She had been
right to send Rudy away. The red numbers glowed on the clock.
Eleven-fifteen. He had left five hours ago. Maybe he was on his way
back to New York. She rolled over and lay with her back to the clock.
She was glad he hadn't called. It would be easier, better for everyone if
he left Dearborn. He shouldn't have hounded Elizabeth by following
her here. Love didn't make anything simple. By putting a false glow on
pain it allowed terrible cruelties to be committed, then overlooked or
excused. Never again, she vowed, turning onto her stomach and
pulling the pillow over her head. The locket dug into her breastbone.
If she was lucky she'd never have to see him again, and no one would
know.

"Oh God," she moaned, flinging the pillow at the wall. Her life was
filled with men she couldn't bear the sight of. Maybe she should leave.
She could start over somewhere else. It wasn't just time she had
wasted, but so much of herself. All that spent energy and nothing to
show for it, nothing, nothing at all, not even friends were left. Thank
God she had come to her senses with Rudy. If she hadn't her family
would have abandoned her forever. She sat up and turned on the light.
She opened the locket. The picture of her mother looked like herself
at three or four. The opposite face resembled Ginny as a child.

"Yes. Yes," she whispered as she touched the slender hinge joining
the sisters' oval images. What had been the point of her struggle all
these years? For the life of her now she could not recall. It had taken
Patrick to bring her to this. Because this is what lasts, she thought,
searching her mother's miniature face, then her aunt's. Yes. Once this
is right, the rest will follow and be resolved. Her pursuit had been not
just of Patrick, but of the very thing she held in her hand, its tangled
knots and deeply clenched roots continuing to sustain her. She closed

the locket. Her grievances seemed puny and selfish compared to her family's great patience and kindnesses through the years.

The phone rang, and she leaped across the bed, then caught herself. Hand poised, she waited until the fourth ring before answering.

It was Rudy. "Did I wake you up?"

"Yes," she lied, yawning.

He had just left Elizabeth, and he needed to talk to her. Now, if he could.

"It's too late."

"I won't stay long. It's important." He sounded upset.

"What is it? Tell me now."

"I'd rather come over if it's all right."

She closed her eyes. "No," she made herself say. "It's not all right. If it can't wait till morning, you'll have to tell me over the phone."

"I'm coming over."

Rudy didn't take off his jacket. He slumped on the edge of the chair, his long bony legs looking even thinner under the wrinkled scrubs. He gestured as he spoke, pointing, now jabbing his chest with anger and regret that he hadn't seen this coming. He should have. All the signs had certainly been present. But that's what happens when you're too close. Even her own parents weren't sure what was happening. Her mother thought she had some virus that was draining her energy. She was sure a few days bed rest would get her back on her feet in time for school on Monday.

"Well, you're the doctor. Did you tell her?"

"I said it was obvious she was deeply depressed, and that I wanted her to see someone right away. Elizabeth said she only wanted me to help her."

"I meant my aunt!" Fiona said, unable to hide her impatience. "Did you tell her?"

"Elizabeth asked me not to. She doesn't want to upset them."

"God!" she groaned. "How could you just leave it at that? I mean, do you usually let your patients call their own shots?"

"She's not my patient. That's the problem."

She nodded. "Your fiancée. I forgot."

He described Elizabeth sitting in bed in her darkened room where she'd been since the party. She wouldn't let him turn on the light. He apologized for barging in on her. He offered to come back later when she felt better, but she said she was glad he was there. They needed to talk. She said he deserved a better woman than she'd been. She begged him to forgive her. She said she'd been so confused about George that she'd misled him and ruined his life. He tried to tell her that she hadn't ruined his life—in fact, quite the opposite, because he was happier here than he'd ever been anywhere. He had no regrets, none at all.

Elizabeth had burst into tears. "Don't. Oh, please, don't," she had cried. "I've just been so selfish and I'm sorry. I'm sorry. I'm sorry," she kept sobbing into her cupped hands as she rocked back and forth, insisting she had ruined everything for everyone, and she hadn't meant to. "In a hundred thousand years," she had gasped, "it's the last thing on earth I ever wanted to happen."

Would he please, please at least believe that, that she'd never meant to hurt anyone.

Of course he knew that, he said. She wasn't selfish, he told her, just confused and pressured, and that was his fault for pursuing a relationship she clearly hadn't wanted. After a while, when she seemed a little calmer, he told her that he understood her unresolved feelings for George, and that it was all right.

" 'No, it's not,' she said. It was a terrible thing she'd done, but she wanted me to know it was over between them. She swore it was. 'No,' I said. 'You don't have to swear to me.'

" 'Yes, I do!' she said. 'Because I need to know you believe me.' She said she'd had to be sure about her feelings for George, and now she absolutely was. She said she's going to get herself together and prove to me that I did the right thing by coming to Dearborn. 'Elizabeth,' I tried to tell her. 'You didn't make me come. I came because I wanted to. I needed to.'

"She said, 'You came because I wasn't honest with you.'

" 'Then let's be honest with each other now,' I said. 'I am,' she said, and she . . .' "

"She told you that she loved you," Fiona said, and he nodded.

"Good." She sighed. "Bittersweet story, happy ending. My favorite kind." She sat across from him on the couch, both of them aware of the enormous stillness between them. Outside, gusts of wind whistled, and the bare branches lashed the window.

He kept biting his lip. "I'm sorry," he finally said. "But it obviously wasn't the right time to tell her."

"Sorry? Why be sorry? I told you, didn't I? This is the way things have to be." She stood up, wanting him to go.

"But they're not going to be this way. Of course they're not," he said, looking up at her. "Elizabeth just needs to be thinking more clearly, that's all."

She laughed. "No, Rudy, you're the one who's not thinking too clearly. Elizabeth's made her decision, so things should be pretty simple from here on in."

He stood up, and she was relieved. She was tired, tired of him, tired of men, but more than anything, tired of always trying to justify her mistakes. She had blundered—terribly. They both had, but why waste a moment more on it? They both loved Elizabeth, and that was that. "So good night and goodbye." She started to open the door.

He held it closed. "I love you. I care about Elizabeth, and right now she's falling apart. I'm worried about her, I am. But it's you I love, Fiona, more than I've ever loved anyone in my entire life." He reached to touch her chin, but she turned her head.

"You know how I feel, so would you please go? Please?" She tried to open the door again.

"Tell me how you feel. Look at me and tell me."

"I already did."

"Then tell me again. Look at me and tell me." He tried to smile.

"I'm sorry, Rudy, but I don't love you," she said, smiling back.

Chapter 18

As Fiona came down the walk Sunday, Elizabeth's covered windows were a jarring sight. Shades drawn in daylight had always been considered a character flaw here. Industrious people with nothing to hide raised their shades first thing every morning. What a waste of time, she thought. All that fastidious attention to detail, not only raising the shades every morning, but positioning each one precisely parallel to the third mullion so that seeing such symmetry passersby would know that this was a house where order prevailed.

In the late gray light of the chilly afternoon the house seemed as dormant as the tall leafless lilac shrubs her great-grandfather had planted by the door over a hundred years ago, some as thick as small tree trunks now. She thought his name had been Phillip. Aunt Arlene would know. She and Uncle Charles had always had a great sense of history, ancestry, roots, and belonging, which they had instilled in their children. For Fiona, however, caring had seemed futile with her own heritage such a painful confusion of dead ends and denial. She had been little interested in their dinner-table tales of a feisty great-grandmother who raised pigs and chickens and her shrewd, tobacco-chewing husband who, when denied a loan by the local bank, started his own, the Collerton Co-op, which was still doing business to this day.

Surprised to find the door locked, she rang the bell three times before anyone came.

"Fiona!" Aunt Arlene pulled her close in a grasping embrace.

"What a nice surprise!" She stood back, smiling. She picked a fleck of lint from Fiona's sleeve, then apologized for fussing. "I'm so glad you're here. I was just thinking how right about this time on a Sunday afternoon you'd start telling us your head hurt or how much your belly ached." Aunt Arlene laughed. "Laying the groundwork for Monday morning."

"Except it never worked," Fiona reminded her.

"No, because I was on to you, lady," her aunt said, wagging her finger. "You know, just a little while ago, I said to your uncle, do you remember how noisy Sundays used to be when the children were all home? He used to complain that he couldn't hear himself think, and I'd remind him what my mother always said, to enjoy it, because someday it'll get so quiet, all you'll be able to hear are your bones creaking."

"Is that why the music's on so loud?" Fiona shouted over the keening of an Irish ballad that spilled out of the den into the drafty hallway.

"Charles!" her aunt called through the door.

A huge log blazed in the fireplace. Besides the fire the only other light in the cozy room shone low and diffuse on Aunt Arlene's empty chair and her hurriedly dropped needlepoint canvas. Uncle Charles dozed with his head back in his maroon leather chair and his slippered feet propped on the ottoman. His jaw sagged open. Discarded Sunday papers were fanned out around him on the floor.

"Charles, wake up. Look who's here! Fiona just came!" Her aunt turned off the stereo.

With the abrupt silence his eyes opened wide, darting between wife and niece. His hands gripped the chair arms. "What is it? What's wrong?" he demanded in a hollow voice.

"Nothing. Nothing at all, dear," Aunt Arlene said with an affectionate pat on his leg. She picked up her needlepoint and sat down. Reminding Fiona how cold the old house got late in the afternoon, she urged her to come sit close by the fire. Fiona said she would, but not right now.

"Why? Why not now?" Uncle Charles challenged with pursed lips, truculent as ever in his first minutes roused from sleep.

"Charles," Aunt Arlene warned with a stern look over her half-glasses.

"I'm going to go up first and see how Lizzie's doing," Fiona said.

Her uncle said she was probably still asleep. She'd been sleeping most of the day. "That's what she needs most right now," he added, peering up through the flickering shadows.

"If she is, then I'll be right back down." It wasn't her cousin's sleep he didn't want disturbed, but Elizabeth herself. He regarded Fiona now with the same vile apprehension she'd seen the other night when she'd left the party with Rudy. "I just want to see how she's feeling. Make sure it's not the old Sunday sickness," she added with a laugh.

"Well, I hope that's all it is," her aunt said, plucking her needle from the brightly threaded canvas in which a blood-red rose was being stitched on white trelliswork. "Because nobody needs a break from school more than your cousin, and will you please tell her I said so." She clipped off a fuzzy strand of red yarn, deftly knotting it. "Talk about giving one's all," she continued in that bright, delicate voice that had always reminded Fiona of the sunporch mobile with its tremulous glass birds, shimmering and clinking with the slightest turbulence. "It's time Elizabeth took care of Elizabeth now!" her aunt declared, the forced gaiety not only hanging in the air, but touching every surface, leaving Fiona and Uncle Charles nowhere to look but into the sputtering flames.

Upstairs, Fiona tapped lightly on Elizabeth's door, then opened it and peeked in. The dark air through the crack was warm and stale. "Lizzie?" she whispered.

"I'm awake," answered the frail voice. Elizabeth sat propped against pillows.

Opening the door wider, she saw Elizabeth's head jerk away from the hallway light.

"Please close it!"

"Hey, what's wrong?" She sat on the edge of the bed.

"I'm tired. I just feel so drained," Elizabeth said.

Fiona put her hand over Elizabeth's icy fingers. "Do you know why you feel like that?"

"No."

She wanted to turn on the light, but Elizabeth said it bothered her eyes. She was sorry, she said, but she just felt better in the dark.

"This is better?" Fiona asked. "What was it like then when you felt worse?"

"I don't know," Elizabeth said with a sob she kept trying to choke back.

"Lizzie!" Touching her, Fiona was shocked by the bony shoulder knob beneath the nightgown flannel. "Don't cry," she whispered, forcing herself closer to the sheeted, musky sourness. "It's all right. Everything's going to be all right. You don't have to cry."

"I know," her cousin sobbed. "I shouldn't be. There's not even any reason, I know, but I can't help it." Forearm across her face, she sank back against the pillow. "What I really need right now is to sleep. And then I'll feel better."

Fiona said Uncle Charles had told her that she'd been sleeping all weekend. Elizabeth scoffed, with a stuffy, bubbly-nosed sound, and said she couldn't seem to sleep for more than minutes at a time. Whenever she heard footsteps she pretended to be asleep.

"You were always so good at that!" Fiona said. "I'd start smiling or one eye would twitch, or I'd have to swallow, but you could always pull it off. You never got caught!" she said, laughing.

"I know," Elizabeth gasped, then gave a long wrenching sob.

Fiona waited. "But you feel caught now, don't you?" she said softly.

It took a moment for Elizabeth to catch her breath enough to reply. "I'm not feeling much of anything right now. I guess I'm just too tired."

"It's more than being tired, Lizzie." She touched her hand again.

"I don't know. Maybe."

"And the longer you stay up here in the dark with the door closed the worse everything seems."

"I just need to rest, that's all. I'll be all right."

"No you won't, because you're not just tired, Lizzie. You're depressed." She paused. "Do you know why you're depressed?" Elizabeth didn't answer so she plowed on. "Did something happen the other night with George?" She waited. "It did, didn't it?"

Elizabeth's hand slid free of hers.

"You can tell me, Lizzie." She sighed. "What? You think it was all a big secret about you and George? I knew. And now I'm sorry, but I'll admit, that's why I brought him to the party. I know, it was another one of my diabolical schemes you always used to accuse me of. But it just doesn't make sense. I mean, why wouldn't you want to be with him if you love him?"

"But I don't! I never should have seen him again! I almost made a terrible mistake!"

"I don't believe that." She switched on the table lamp. Elizabeth cringed in the glare, her eyelids raw and swollen from crying. "And I don't think you do either." Fiona held out the hand mirror, but Elizabeth covered her face. "Look at yourself! You're on the verge of a breakdown."

"No I'm not." Elizabeth looked up slowly. "I'm just very tired and . . . very . . . sorry for all the pain and all the trouble I've caused. You see, I was always too connected to George, and him to me. So I came back to make sure it was over, but then Rudy came too, so I knew it had to be over. And I thought it was until I saw George and you, and then it all got so confusing. But now I know, and the other night I told George what it was. That it was a connection, like a long, deep habit between us. But that it wasn't love. And that I knew what the right thing was to do. I told him I finally knew what I had to do, that if I didn't marry Rudy I'd hate myself forever."

"Why?" Fiona asked through clenched teeth. She could barely breathe in the trapped, dead air. The radiator under the window was clanging. "Why would you hate yourself?"

"Because he's . . . he's so good and . . . and . . ." Elizabeth was crying again.

"And because you love him? Because you love him so much?"

Elizabeth nodded, and the trembling between her sunken cheeks seemed more a leer than a smile.

Fiona stood up. She had to leave before she said something she would always regret. When she got to the door, the light went off, and Elizabeth sighed. Fiona turned suddenly. "Yah, go ahead, Lizzie, stay in bed! And then you can have everything the way you want it!"

"What? What do you mean? Fiona!" Elizabeth called as the door closed.

It took every effort not to slam it. Returning to the den, Fiona forced herself to sit with her aunt and uncle, answering questions about work, how her car was running, her apartment.

"Oh, and by the way." Her aunt glanced up mid-stitch. "That was so nice of George to spend all that time fixing the stove the other night. Uncle Charles said he tried to pay him, but George wouldn't hear of it, so we were thinking of maybe sending him a gift certificate to a restaurant he might like. You know, some really nice place the two of you would enjoy. So, do you have any ideas?" She shrugged uneasily. "Or suggestions?"

"No."

"Well, my first thought, naturally, was the Orchard House. My favorite. But Uncle Charles seems to think young people don't like it there, which I don't necessarily agree with. I mean, I see young people there. I see them all the time!"

"Occasionally, yes," Uncle Charles said. "But nothing like it used to be. Now just about everyone in there's our age!"

"I wonder what happened," Aunt Arlene mused, looking at him.

"Well, for one thing," Uncle Charles leaned forward and said, "all the older people we knew have died."

Their cheery banter was oddly comforting. She knew it well, words to fill the gaps in the barricade, its very banality meant to convey the richness and depth of their union. Surely if this was their greatest concern, then they were without cares and above most common woes. They had made a great success of their life together. Upstairs their daughter sat in darkness.

"And?" Aunt Arlene prodded. "What's the other thing?"

"We're the older people now!" He chuckled and picked up his paper.

"Oh, Charles!" She looked at Fiona and shook her head in mock dismay. "Well, in any event, we'll just pick out some nice place. Which I'm sure will be fine, since George Grimshaw never did have a fussy bone in his body. He's never changed, has he? He's always the same, always so sweet and dependable. Such a dear young man."

"One of the best," Uncle Charles added with a wide-eyed look at his wife.

"Oh, Fiona, before I forget!" Aunt Arlene said. "You're probably not interested, but I told Lucretia Kendale I'd ask. She wants to know if you might like to drive her down in her car to West Palm Beach and stay—"

"No," Fiona said. "You were right. I'm not interested."

"Yes, well, that's what I thought." Aunt Arlene took a deep breath.

"She wants to go right after Thanksgiving," Uncle Charles said. "It's a brand-new car she's got, a Cadillac, and I know you don't like the winter too much . . ."

"I never said that."

"Well, not in so many words maybe, but, I mean it's so cold up here, and I know how hard things can get when you're not making all that much, especially with an old car and—"

"What do you mean?" Fiona interrupted. "What are you really trying to say?"

"Just that! I just think it's a wonderful opportunity, that's all," he said.

"Well I'm not interested. Not in the least."

"But you should at least consider it, Fiona," he said, the old irritation nettling his voice. "There comes a point in life, you know, when opportunities like that are very few and far between."

"Driving down to Florida with Lucretia Kendale? You think that's an opportunity? Are you serious? An opportunity for what?" she asked, trying not to sneer. "Early senility?"

"An opportunity for a fresh start!" He stared over his glasses.

"God, you're insulting!" Before she could stand up, her aunt caught her hand and held on to it.

"Oh, Fiona, please. That's not at all what your uncle meant. Did you, Charles?"

"I know what he meant," Fiona said.

"No, you don't understand," he said.

"I'll tell you what I don't understand, and that's how you two can just sit down here and pretend nothing's wrong with Lizzie."

The flames reflected on their face as they stared at the fireplace. The enormous log sizzled and spit.

"Lizzie's having a bad time of it, we know that. She's exhausted. She's just overdone everything," her aunt finally said.

"Rudy thinks it's more than that. He wants her to see . . . someone," Fiona said, so conscious of her uncle's darkening eyes that she couldn't bring herself to say 'psychiatrist.'

"I know." His jaw clenched.

"Well, of course, if she's still feeling like this tomorrow or Tuesday," her aunt said. "In any event, Rudy's coming by later tonight to check on her," she added. "Maybe by that time she'll even be up and about. You never know with these viruses."

"Tell him to call me," Fiona said, enjoying her uncle's watchful silence.

"May I ask why you want him to call you?" he said, folding the paper he'd been holding.

"So I can tell him how I think Lizzie's doing."

He took off his glasses and bit the stem. "How's that? How do you think she's doing?"

"Not good," she said with blade-point enunciation of each consonant as they stared at one another.

"Fiona!" Her aunt leaned forward and angled her head as if trying to locate something in the fire-stirred shadows. "What's that?" she asked, rising from the chair, hand outstretched. "That locket. Where did you get it?"

Fiona held it out taut on its chain.

"Oh my God," her aunt said, bending to open it. "Yes. This was my mother's. She gave it to Natalie. These are our baby pictures."

"I know. That's the other reason I came. I wanted to show it to you. I almost forgot." She drew in her chin to see the locket in her aunt's hand. "I think it's so beautiful."

"Yes," her aunt said. "Natalie did too. She wore it all the time. Sometimes she'd forget and wear it swimming. She said it wasn't the reason, but I know that's what happened to the pictures, how they got so cracked. Did you just find it somewhere? Don't tell me it's been upstairs all this time."

"Patrick gave it to me."

"Patrick? Why would he have it?" her aunt asked, shaking her head in bewilderment.

"I don't know. I guess he just happened to come across it."

"Where?" her uncle asked.

"He didn't really say. In his house, I guess."

Aunt Arlene closed the locket, then eased back into her chair. She picked up her needlework, but did not slip the needle from the canvas. She stared forlornly, as if she had just seen a flaw in the half-stitched petals but hadn't the heart to rework it.

"She probably left it there once. It probably got wedged down behind cushions or something," her uncle said.

Fiona realized he was speaking to her aunt.

"That was thirty years ago," her aunt said quietly.

"Yes, and knowing Patrick, there's probably very little that's been changed there in all that time," he said.

"Excuse me," her aunt said, getting up. She went into the kitchen.

Fiona rose to follow, but her uncle asked her to wait.

"Fiona, how did Patrick happen to give you that locket? What exactly were the circumstances?"

"I don't know what you mean. He found it, and he gave it to me."

"It was that simple? That uncomplicated?"

"Yah!" She wasn't about to admit what had really taken place.

Her uncle continued to look at her with a kind of horror—as if he already knew.

"Why?" she demanded. "What other reason would there be?"

He stared up at her, head back on the chair, his gaze flattened and empty. "None, I would hope. But with Patrick you never know."

"He's always been pretty up-front with me."

"I'll say what I said before, Fiona. He's unstable and he can be very cruel." He was almost whispering.

"But it's more than that, isn't it? You don't trust him, do you?"

"No. No, I don't."

"So is that why you pay his taxes every year? What is it, some kind of payoff so he won't admit he's my father?"

"He didn't say that, did he?"

"Not in so many words, no."

"Well I would hope not, because it's really quite simple. From time to time Patrick has needed help, and I've given it to him when I could."

"Why? Why would you?"

"It's a difficult situation. He's so filled with anger and bitterness and self-pity he can't seem to ever help himself for long."

"Well, do you blame him? I mean, not only does he get fired his second week on the job, but then you tell him he can't ever even go near the courthouse again. Do you know how humiliating that is?"

"He's lucky that's all that happened. They almost arrested him."

"Arrested him! Arrested him for what?" she said, unable to hide her irritation.

"For assault." He explained that Patrick and his supervisor, John Zender, had argued and then Patrick had pushed him. Seeing her shrug, her uncle added that Zender had a club foot. When Patrick pushed him he fell halfway down the stairs and hurt his back.

"Patrick said it was an argument. In fact he said the other guy shoved him, but because of you he just walked away from it."

"Well." Her uncle sighed. "What can I say, Fiona? Why would I lie about it? What would be the point?" The flames glowed on his face as he leaned forward to retrieve a newspaper from the pile.

"I just feel so bad for him," she said. "He's so lonely. I hate seeing him so alone."

At this, all her uncle's features contorted, mirroring the contempt in his voice. "He made his own bed, now let him lie in it."

"What does that mean?" she asked weakly, not really wanting an answer.

"He doesn't deserve your pity. And he certainly doesn't deserve your good heart."

There was nothing to say back to that, nothing she could do, but try not to smile on her way into the kitchen. A good heart. She had no idea her uncle thought that of her.

Aunt Arlene was peeling oranges and grapefruits. She cut them into chunks which she put into a glass bowl. Fruit salad was the one thing she could always get Elizabeth to eat, she said. Part of the reason she had gotten so run-down was her diet. She hardly ate anything. "I think that's part of her trouble with Rudy," she confided. "She was falling back into her old eating habits. And she couldn't fool him, of all people—I mean a doctor, for goodness' sake! So she started, I think,

avoiding him. Which of course she will hotly deny and blame it on all
her school commitments. But I'm sure it's all tied in. She just pushes
herself too hard. She always has and I don't know why. I've never understood it. I don't think there was that much difference in the way the
two girls were raised. And why Elizabeth thinks she has to be such a
perfectionist is beyond me." She put the cutting board and knife into
the sink and turned on the faucet. In the light her wiry hair was silvery
gray. Her hips and rib cage were no longer defined by any discernible
waist. She leaned forward to scrub the cutting board. All she had ever
wanted was her family's happiness.

"Maybe that's just it," Fiona said softly. "I mean, the more trouble
she saw me get into, the harder she tried to be good."

Her aunt turned. She wiped her hands on a towel, then threw her
arms around Fiona. "Oh, I didn't mean you, hon. I meant Ginny, so
don't go thinking you're the cause of any of this. Elizabeth just has to
learn to relax and pace herself a little better."

Once again, however benignly, her aunt had managed to accentuate
her flimsy status here. Fiona said she'd better be going. Her aunt told
her to be sure and come early Thanksgiving Day. As Fiona said she
would, her aunt's eyes shifted to the locket.

"Have you ever gotten another phone call?"

It was a moment before Fiona realized what she meant. "No." She
hesitated. "Aunt Arlene, I made that up. I'm sorry. My mother never
called me. I think I was trying to get attention or something. I never
thought how it'd make you feel."

Aunt Arlene smiled and assured Fiona that she understood. And of
course she wanted attention. "Don't we all at one time or another?"
She sounded almost lighthearted now as she filled a plastic container
with fruit salad for Fiona to take home. "Thank goodness I never had
to worry about your eating habits. You've always had such a wonderful
appetite." She handed Fiona the container and her gaze fell to the
locket.

"Does it upset you, that I'm wearing it?" Fiona asked.

"Oh no! Of course not! It's just such a surprise seeing it again after
all these years, that's all!" She patted Fiona's cheek.

"Here." Fiona reached back to undo the clasp. "You should have it. It was your mother's, and it's got your picture in it."

"No," her aunt said, stepping back and shaking her head. "It was your mother's and your grandmother's, and now it belongs to you."

It was Tuesday morning.

"Congratulations!" Maxine cried from the front of the dining room as Fiona came through the swinging door, tying on her apron.

"Hey, what'd I win?" Fiona looked around. The three seated parties were all smiling at her. "Okay, then what am I having, a boy or a girl? Twins? Who's the father? And when are we getting married?"

"It's your uncle Charles!" Maxine announced loudly enough for everyone to hear. She leaned on both arms over the newspaper and read aloud. "Yesterday Governor James Proctor announced the appointment and elevation of the Honorable Charles H. Hollis to the Superior Court bench." The article listed her uncle's many accomplishments, professional affiliations, and went on to say that he would be sworn in after the first of the year. Fiona peered over Maxine's shoulder as she read, following her magenta fingernail from line to line. "Judge Hollis is married to Arlene Range Hollis, and he is the father of three adult children, John Hollis, Virginia Hollis Fay, and Elizabeth Hollis." Maxine looked up, pouting. "But your name's not here!"

Fiona laughed. "Because I'm not an adult!"

"They should have a retraction," Maxine said, scanning the article again to be sure she hadn't somehow missed it.

"Correction, you mean," Fiona said, reaching under the register for an order pad.

"Yes!" Maxine said, slapping the page. "And they should put your name in! I mean, the Hollises brought you up with their own kids. You were raised like one of their own and . . ."

"Maxine," Fiona said quietly.

". . . my lord, I mean, the judge comes in here all the time to—"

"Maxine!"

"What?"

"I already know this. Who are you telling, me or them?" she asked, rolling her eyes in the direction of the quiet dining room.

"Well I just think your name should be here too," Maxine insisted with genuine disappointment.

"Well it's not," Fiona whispered. "And if I don't give a shit, why should you?"

Maxine's face drained of color.

For the rest of the morning Fiona worked quietly. Customers kept congratulating her.

"Thanks, but I didn't do anything," she said each time.

"It's just everyone's so proud of him," Reese Fogarty, the pharmacist, said, grinning over the BLTs she'd just served him and his clerk, John Dale.

"And the really neat thing is," John Dale added, "most good people, people like Judge Hollis, never get any recognition at all."

"Especially when there's politics involved," Fogarty was saying as she headed back into the kitchen. Her aunt and uncle must have known when she'd been there Sunday night that the announcement would be made the following day, but neither one had said anything. It was so typical of them. Never call attention to yourself. Keep a low profile. Don't rock the boat. She'd heard versions of the same message all her life. Their reserve was incredible, even with one another. In all her years at home she couldn't recall ever hearing them argue, though she was probably still the only person who could make Charles Hollis raise his voice.

She wondered if Elizabeth had felt well enough to go back to school. Not the most fortuitous time for the judge's daughter to be flipping out, she thought, as Chester put up her orders. When she came into the dining room two more parties were waiting to be seated.

"Fiona!" called a man's voice from the last booth. "Come here come here come here quick!" Larry Belleau panted. He was hunched so low his chin was almost touching the table.

"Larry!" She backed up and rested the edge of the crowded tray on his table. "Can I get you something?"

"I need to see you I have to now Fiona please please please!" He

clutched the front of his shirt and tried to catch his breath. His ruddy
cheeks glowed with sweat.

Promising to come right back, she hurried to the next table, where
the two older women groaned when she served them. Their tuna
plates were wrong. They wanted tuna without mayonnaise. She returned them to the kitchen and had to endure Chester's diatribe
against "health food screwballs" and herself for not getting the order
right in the first place. When she finally came back out, Larry was sobbing quietly with his face in his hands. A mound of napkins grew in
front of him as he kept wiping his nose. She slid next to him into the
booth. "What is it? What's wrong, Larry?"

"I'm in trouble I'm in big trouble really big trouble." He burst into
tears and cried so hard the table shook against his trembling body.

"What happened? Calm down now, and tell me what happened."

"It wasn't my fault I didn't mean to . . . all the guys we were all just
fooling around that's all and they kept saying 'Yah, you think you can
but you can't you're big but you're just a pea brain Larry that's all that's
all you are' so I just pulled on the trash thing the basket part hard as I
could and it did it came off the pole but then it went *whoom!*" he said,
throwing his hands back over his head. "Right through the fucking
window Fiona oops bad word I'm sorry," he gasped, covering his
mouth. "Sorry sorry I didn't mean to say that but I'm scared I'm so
scared Fiona!"

"That's okay, Larry, but what window did you break?"

"The drugstore." He winced.

"CVS?" It was the largest expanse of plate glass on Main Street.

He nodded. "Yah the whole front smashed."

"When did it happen?"

"Just now."

"And what'd you do, come right in here?"

He nodded. They both looked toward the street now as a police car
flashed past the coffee shop. Its siren sounded a few short bursts to
warn pedestrians out of its way. She asked where everyone else had
gone. He said they all ran away when the window broke.

"Did anybody see you come in here?"

"I don't know!" he cried, shaking his head as another cruiser flew by. "But I don't want to go to jail Fiona I didn't mean to do it and now I'm going to be in so much trouble," he bawled.

Maxine and Donna were both at the table now.

"Stop it! Stop it!" Maxine hissed, jabbing her finger into his massive arm as if to find the button that would turn him off. "You just stop that right now!"

"Come on, Larry." Fiona held his hand. "I'll take him out back," she told Maxine, who kept demanding that he be quiet or leave. He was disturbing her customers. All eating and conversation ceased. Every head had turned toward his frantic bleating.

"I know his father. We used to work together down at the sneaker plant. Ed'll be pissed, but I know how to handle him," Donna told Fiona, who had finally gotten Larry onto his feet. "Don't worry, Larry. I'm gonna go call your dad," Donna said.

"No!" Larry groaned, pulling away. "No no don't don't do that please please don't."

"She won't," Fiona assured him. "Just come in the kitchen with me. Come on, Larry. We'll get this all figured out. Come on now, Larry," she coaxed, leading him by the hand into the kitchen.

Seeing the enormous sobbing man, Chester threw down his towel and began to laugh. "This is some kinda joke, right?" he cried in a high shaky voice. "What're you tryna do, push me all the way over the edge here?"

"I've got to call my uncle!" She raced past him and dialed the courthouse, praying he hadn't gone out for lunch. "It's an emergency," she told his secretary.

"Fiona!" Uncle Charles said, seconds later. "What's wrong? What happened?"

She told him about Larry. "He's still crying. He's so upset. The police are right down the street. I know I should bring him back out there, but I can't stand the thought of him having to go through all that alone, that's why I called."

"Tell him not to worry. I'll be right there. We'll work it out. We'll take care of it," Uncle Charles said, and she smiled down at Larry.

He was there in ten minutes. Fiona watched him lean over Larry with one hand on his shoulder, assuring him that everything would be all right. There'd probably be a fine and he'd have to pay to replace the window, but he was not going to jail, Uncle Charles said, and that was a promise.

Maxine hovered behind them. Chester gestured for her to get the Judge something to drink. Arms folded, Larry rocked slightly in the wooden chair, wide-eyed and nodding eagerly at all he was being told. Maxine hurried back in and gave the Judge a glass of ginger ale. He handed it to Larry, who gulped it down, belched loudly, then sheepishly apologized. Chester gestured for her to go get another one.

"So you come with me now, Larry. We'll go down and explain what happened," Uncle Charles said.

"No! They're gonna yell at me in there the manager he hates me he's always throwing me out of the store."

"I meant the police station. We'll go down to the station and we'll tell them what happened and we'll call your dad—"

"No!" Larry said. He shrank back. "Don't call my dad please don't call him please don't call him."

"We have to," Uncle Charles said softly.

"No!"

"I'll talk to him, Larry. And I'll tell him how scared you are and how it was an accident. He'll understand."

"No! He's gonna be so mad he's gonna yell and swear I know he is." As if straitjacketing himself in place, he crossed his arms over his chest and locked both hands on the back of the chair.

"I'm going to be honest with you, Larry. He'll certainly be mad, but if you want, I'll stay there with you while you talk to him. And I'll tell him how you didn't mean to do it. It'll be hard for a little bit, but then it'll get better, Larry. You'll see. The hardest part is right now, just sitting here and worrying about it, but as soon as we do something, you won't be so scared. So come on," he said, holding out his hand. "Let's go take care of it now."

"Can you call my mom can you tell her to come instead?" Larry asked, wiping his runny nose on his shoulder.

His mom was getting over heart surgery, her uncle reminded him, and Larry sobbed.

Fiona knelt down and took his hand. "Larry! We're not going to let anything bad happen to you. We're your friends."

"That's right." Her uncle leaned closer. "Listen to Fiona now, Larry."

She looked back and suggested it might be best to call Mr. Belleau now before they went to the station. "At least get that over with. He seems more scared of that than anything."

"Good idea," her uncle said, and Chester brought him to the phone by the cooler door.

Maxine got Larry another ginger ale while Fiona continued talking to him. Her uncle came back and told Larry his father was glad he wasn't hurt. He promised not to yell, but Larry had to get up right now and go to the police station. Larry stood then and followed her uncle to the door. Fiona gave Larry a hug. "My uncle Charles'll take good care of you. You know he will, so don't worry."

"That's right," her uncle said with a pat on Larry's sweaty back. "I'm going to take good care of you, Larry," he said as they went through the door.

"Phew! Who was that masked man?" Chester sighed, wiping his face with a towel.

"Don't even kid," Maxine said, shaking her head. "He's got to be one of the kindest people I've ever known. Not many men would do that."

No, they wouldn't, Fiona thought with such an unaccustomed surge of familial pride that for the rest of the afternoon she felt transported by a quiet buoyancy. A deep calm settled over her. There was so much to do, and it all seemed so simple, the layers of obfuscation suddenly so transparent. Sunday night her uncle had spoken of her good heart, his brief acknowledgment not just high praise but, finally, validation.

Chapter 19

O h, hi, Uncle Charles! It's Fiona." Her smile faded with the silence
at the other end of the line. "So. How're you doing?"

"I'm fine, Fiona. Thank you," he answered stiffly.

She said she wanted to know what to bring for Thanksgiving
dinner.

"Arlene," he called away from the phone.

"But wait! Uncle Charles!" She asked what had happened to Larry
Belleau, which was really why she'd called. She'd been waiting to hear.

"Nothing, really." His voice was clipped and distant. "His family's
paying the damages and the drugstore's agreed not to press charges."

"Oh, that's good." She was relieved, but hurt that he hadn't let her
know. "I've been wondering what happened. In fact, I was thinking of
calling the Belleaus to find out."

"No, don't. Don't call them," he said quickly. "Ed Belleau doesn't
want you bothering Larry."

"What do you mean, bothering him?"

"He said you get him all riled up. That you enjoy doing it."

"What? What the hell's that supposed to mean?" she snapped.

"He mentioned some party last fall. He said you and Larry were
swimming together. Without anything on," he added in a muffled
voice.

"And you believe that?" she asked, cringing and holding her forehead.

"It's hard sometimes to know what to believe, Fiona." He handed the phone to Aunt Arlene, who was asking if everything was all right. "Fiona just wants to know what to bring for dinner," he said as her aunt came on the line.

"Well, that's easy!" Arlene declared. The same cranberry mold she'd made last year, her aunt told her. It had looked so elegant on the table, shimmering red under the candlelight.

Except no one had eaten it, Fiona reminded her.

"They most certainly did," her aunt insisted. "Oh, and by the way, if you'd like to bring someone to dinner, Fiona, please do. Feel free."

"Really? Well maybe I'll ask Patrick then."

"Please, dear. Now you know that's not what I meant. Actually, I was just thinking of poor George and how alone he'll be feeling. This'll be his first Thanksgiving without his dad, you know. I bet if you asked him he'd be thrilled. And please tell him he doesn't have to bring a thing. His good company is all we need."

"I won't be asking him."

"Oh, but why?"

"Because I don't want to."

"But I know it would mean a lot to him. He's always enjoyed it here so much," her aunt persisted. "And now that you and he are—"

"Aunt Arlene," Fiona interrupted. "It's Lizzie who should ask him. Not me."

"Well. In any event we may be having two other guests with us. The little Buelmann twins from Elizabeth's class. Their grandfather's in the hospital and might not be out in time for the holiday."

"Oh! So Lizzie's feeling better then." She must be if two of her students were coming to dinner.

Fiona's longing for Rudy had become a constant ache in her chest. When she woke up this morning she had dialed his number, expecting she would know what to say by the time his machine came on. He answered on the first ring, sounding rushed and irritable. She had hung up.

"Actually, she's not." Speaking slowly, her aunt seemed to examine each word as if it might be a coin too valuable to spend. "That is, not as quickly as we'd hoped. But then, it took her some time to get this run-down, so I guess it's going to be a while before she's back to her old self again."

"Has she seen a doctor yet?"

"Rudy's up there now with her."

"I mean a psychiatrist." The word fell like a club between them. "She should be on antidepressants or something."

"But she won't," her aunt said quickly. "She's afraid of the connotations, the fallout. You know, with her job and everything."

"The fallout'll be a whole lot worse if she ends up having a breakdown."

"Well, yes, and that's pretty much what we're all working on here," her aunt said, as voices grew in the background. "Time and rest, I guess that's what she needs most right now. Yes, and a lot of good food, Rudy's just telling Uncle Charles now."

Rudy. Fiona asked to speak with him. She heard him clearing his throat on his way to the phone.

"Hello?" he answered uneasily. "Fiona? Are you there?" he said when she didn't speak right up.

"Yah, I'm here." Her eyes were closed.

"How are you doing?" he asked in a low, toneless voice. "Everything okay?"

"Oh yah. Everything's fine. Great. As a matter of fact, things couldn't be better."

There was a pause. "Are you sure? You sound . . . well, you sound a little congested."

"Do I?" She dabbed her eyes and wiped her nose.

"You do. You sound as if you've got a bad cold there. Do you need anything for it?"

"I don't know. What do you think?"

"Well, probably the usual regimen: rest, liquids, and Tylenol."

"Anything else?" she asked.

"No, that usually takes care of it," he said.

With her shoulder hunched against the phone, she was picking through cranberries while she listened to Patrick. His third call tonight, and they were having the same conversation again. She was right, he was telling her. The more he thought about it, the more convinced he was now. If he was going to have any kind of a life he had to get out of here. There wasn't any point in waiting. But what about selling his property? she asked. No, he said, it would take too long. But he needed the money and that was valuable land, so why not be patient and just wait a while? It probably wouldn't even take that long, and she was sure once it became a reality Uncle Charles would help expedite matters. No! Absolutely not. Hollis couldn't know anything about this. He'd made up his mind. He had to leave now, and that's all there was to it, but she had to promise not to tell anyone. They wouldn't have to take much. He was working himself into a frenzy again.

"Patrick," she said as gently as she could. "The whole idea is for you to get away. Not me."

"No. That's what I'm saying. I keep trying to tell you. I can't. I mean, it won't work that way. You have to come with me. You have to! It's the only way!"

She closed her eyes and shook her head. She was trying to be patient, but there was no reasoning with him. He had gotten on this bizarre tangent and couldn't seem to get himself off, and she had only herself to blame for suggesting it in the first place.

"I can't just go and leave you behind," he kept insisting. "I can't!"

"Why? Why can't you?"

"Because I can't, God damn it, I can't! I can't! I can't!" he bellowed with a thud as if he'd hit something with his fist.

Her doorbell rang. "I better hang up, Patrick."

"Why? Somebody there? Who is it? Who's there?"

"No, it's the oven. The bell's ringing. I've got to take something out."

"But I've got to talk to you."

"I'll call you back."

"When?"

"In a while. It shouldn't take too long."

She opened the door, amazed to see George Grimshaw. He apologized for barging in like this, but he had just come from seeing Elizabeth. He had to talk to someone, to someone who loved her the way he did.

"I've never seen her like that," he said. "She'd cry and then she'd try to talk, but then she'd just start crying." He sat on the edge of the chair with his head in his hands. "I can't get the sound of it out of my mind. Like she was in pain, this deep, deep pain that kept pouring out of her." He looked up with panicky eyes. "What can I do? I have to do something!" he said, hitting his hand with his fist.

"Why? Why do you have to do something?"

"Because this is all my fault!" he gasped.

The phone rang. The minute she picked it up, Patrick began to talk about leaving again. She said she was still in the middle of cooking and couldn't talk right now. She'd have to call him back. This time she left the phone off the hook. She had never seen George so distraught.

Frantic, he was on his feet, pacing now. "I never should have tried to get her back. I should have left her alone, but I couldn't. I was so lonely, I couldn't stand it. I kept calling her and calling her. The whole time she was in New York I'd call and we'd just talk, you know, like friends—or that's what she thought, then this one time she called me. It was a couple weeks after my father died, and I told her how much it meant that she'd called me. But she said she had to tell me something. She said she was engaged, and I just lost it. I told her no, she couldn't; she couldn't do that. I told her how alone I felt, how she was all I had left. I begged her to come home, to at least give me a chance. I said after all our years together she at least owed me that." He paused. "And I couldn't believe it. She said, all right, that she would. That she'd come back and see."

Fiona listened in amazement as he described Elizabeth's return. Overwhelmed with joy and the realization of how close they'd come to losing one another forever, they had slept together her first night back. But then a few days later, to Elizabeth's shock and dismay, Rudy arrived. She found herself trapped between everyone's expectations. Unable to tell Rudy the truth about her feelings, she stopped seeing George.

"Okay, let me get this straight now," Fiona said. "So that's when you started hitting on me."

"No. No, no, I was very fond of you, Fiona. I—"

"Fond of me!" She grabbed a magazine, and he ducked as she threw it. "Fond of me, you phony, uptight son of a bitch, you fucked me, remember? Me? In there?" she said, pointing to the bedroom door.

He closed his eyes. "I know. I'm sorry. I'm really sorry. I am. I've made such a mess out of everything."

"Well you weren't working alone, George, believe me." She shook her head with a bitter laugh. "In fact I thought we had some kind of special thing going there for a while."

He covered his face and groaned.

"Aw, c'mon, George. It's not that bad."

He looked at her. "She's always been so good, and I . . . I took advantage of that."

"No you didn't!" she said.

"Yes. I did. I did," he said with a helpless, sickening squeal.

"Come on now, George, she's a grown woman. She knew what she was doing."

"But I made her hate herself. I made her do something so against her nature that now she's destroying herself." He sobbed.

"But that's not something you did." She got up and sat next to him on the sofa. She watched him for a moment. He couldn't stop crying. Poor George, he was as caught in the web of Elizabeth's kindness as Rudy was. "George! Lizzie's . . . well, the truth is, she's always been a little neurotic! About certain things, that is. Like right now, she'd rather lay up in that bed than tell the truth or come to any decision about who she really is and what she wants."

"All she wanted was to be a good person. That's all she wanted," he gasped. "And I knew that."

"No, George, that's where you're wrong. Don't you see? It's not the being good that matters to Lizzie. She just can't bear the thought of anyone *thinking* she's not good." She put her hand on his arm. "George, you can't beat yourself up like this. It's not your fault."

"No, you don't understand."

"Yes I do. Because I love her too, so I know how you feel."

"No, you don't understand. You know that night you went to Verzanno's? Well, I ran into them." He looked at her. "No, the truth is

I followed them. He didn't know me, but I knew who he was. They'd just dropped you off, and she was so nervous she never even introduced us. I offered to buy them a drink, but Elizabeth said she had to get up early to run with you. So that's why," he said in a hoarse whisper. He kept trying to look at Fiona, but couldn't. "Do you know what I'm saying? I came here on purpose that morning. I even left the door open. I wanted her to see me with you. I knew that would hurt her more than anything, and I wanted to hurt her so badly. I wanted her to know what it felt like every time I saw her with him. How it would feel for the rest of our lives," he sobbed.

"You bastard."

"And that first night, the night we went to the Orchard House. They were supposed to be there that night, but she saw my truck in the driveway, so she said she was sick." He still hadn't looked up.

"You son of a bitch. You no-good son of a bitch."

"I know. And I'm sorry. But she was mine. I mean, I finally had her back after all that time, and I couldn't lose her again. I just couldn't."

"Get out, George. Just get the hell out, will you?"

He nodded, but didn't move. "But I just want you to know, Fiona, it was the worst, most disgusting thing I've ever done. Believe me."

"I believe you. Oh God, do I ever!" She burst out laughing, and didn't stop until he was gone.

Thanksgiving morning was cold and bright with sunshine. The phone rang while she was getting dressed. She ran to answer it. Her hand jerked back. Patrick was shouting into the answering machine. "Fiona! Pick up the phone! Pick up the goddamn phone!" he demanded. "I know you're there. You're listening to me, aren't you? You didn't call last night, did you, because that fucking Grimshaw was there, right? I saw his truck. I almost went up there. I should have. And next time I will, so you listen real careful now because I'm sick of this. I'm sick of your little games. I'm sick of this shit and I'm not putting up with it anymore. You said you'd call. We have to talk. You know we do. We have to do this, and I been up all night, waiting, and now I need to talk to you, so pick up the phone! Pick up the goddamn—" The tape clicked and cut him off. Her stomach was queasy. After George left she had fallen asleep on the couch. The phone began to ring again now. She hurried out to her car. She was upset with Patrick, and George had made her feel used and worthless, but it was with Elizabeth that she felt most angry.

It was windy, with sudden raw gusts that swirled papers and funnels of leaves across the road. Even with the heater on high she was still shivering when she pulled into the driveway. She knew by the cars that everyone was here—everyone but Rudy. He must be working, she thought, deeply disappointed. She could hear her aunt and Susan laughing as they finished setting the table in the dining room. Before she did anything, she made room in the refrigerator for her cranberry mold. She had gotten up at five this morning to make it, but it still wasn't firmly jelled. As she hung up her coat, she thought she smelled smoke. She opened the oven to make sure the turkey wasn't burning. Peeling back the aluminum foil, she saw that it was golden brown. The door to the back stairs opened and Ginny came into the kitchen carrying a tray of half-filled glasses and cups.

"Oh good. You're here," Ginny said, setting down the tray. She'd been tidying up Elizabeth's bedroom. Elizabeth didn't feel well enough to come down for dinner, but Ginny had just told her that everyone's day would be ruined if she stayed in bed. "She asked if you were here yet, so why don't you go on up and see her. She'll come down for you. I know she will."

Fiona said she'd rather not. What was the point in forcing her to come down?

Because, Ginny explained, her parents would be devastated if she stayed up there. "Mother's a wreck," Ginny whispered, with a glance toward the clatter of silver being laid out in the dining room. "I've never seen her so worried, and Daddy too. He's just so distracted. He even forgot to open the flue before he started the fire. Jack's trying to clear out all the smoke. They've got all the windows open. It's freezing in there."

"Ginny, what do you think is really wrong with Lizzie?" Fiona watched her cousin closely.

"Stress, I guess. Mother says she's just taken on too much all at once," Ginny said with another glance toward the dining room.

"Oh, so at least they've dropped the virus theory."

"I know," Ginny agreed. "But what else can they say? They have to!" she added, seeing Fiona's smirk. "I mean, they can't very well go telling everyone she's having some kind of breakdown now, can they?"

"They would if it was me!" Fiona sputtered. "Nobody'd have any qualms about that!"

"You really think that?" Ginny asked, and Fiona rolled her eyes.

"Well they wouldn't," Ginny said. "I know they wouldn't. Of course they wouldn't.'

"Are you kidding? Do you think for one minute they'd put up with that from me? You think they'd let me curl up in a ball and hide in the dark like that? No! You know damn well they wouldn't!"

"Fiona!" Aunt Arlene said, coming in from the dining room, carrying a stack of plates. Susan followed.

"Happy Thanksgiving!" Susan greeted her with a quick pass of her cheek. She took the dishes from Aunt Arlene and began putting them into the dishwasher. They'd gotten the table half set before realizing the china was dusty.

Jack rushed in next looking for matches. "Now Dad's fire keeps going out," he explained as he opened drawers and pawed through pot holders and tea towels.

"Jack!" his mother said. "Say hello to Fiona."

"Sorry, kiddo." He gave her a hug. He'd always been this single-minded when on a mission for his father, so anxious was he not to fail. His mother handed him a book of matches. "Dad wants to get the fire started before Rudy gets back," he said on his way out.

"Gets back?" Fiona blurted, grinning. "Why? Where'd he go?"

"To get the Buelmann twins." And once again Aunt Arlene explained that they were Elizabeth's students whose grandfather was just days home from the hospital and still too frail to cook.

The gaps were being filled. They were fortifying the barricades against chaos and disruption, this litany of detail as appeasing as prayer, each repetition confirming their goodness and deep connections to one another. When Fiona had done something especially calamitous an exchange like this Song of the Buelmann Twins could reach fever pitch around her: Elizabeth's running the Downtown 10K to raise money for the Dearborn Hospice. Aunt Arlene's up to three quilts a month for HIV babies. Jack's cooking at the Collerton Soup Kitchen every Wednesday night, while in their hearts they were really imploring her to: *Be like us. Don't keep wasting your life on messes. Be good. Help people.*

Yes, their kind of help that allowed Patrick to spend Thanksgiving Day alone. For all their works of charity, Fiona's poor, bitter father was the last person they wanted at their table today. It was always safer to help strangers. She thought of Patrick smoking and watching television all day in that cold, drab house. She should have talked to him when he'd called instead of rushing here to be with people who weren't as close to her as he was.

"Imagine, being alone and sick on Thanksgiving. That poor man." Her aunt sighed.

"Rudy'll make sure he's all right. He'll see if he needs anything," Ginny said.

"Well at least the poor man will have a nice hot turkey dinner. Rudy's going to bring one later when he drops the twins off," Susan said with a dramatic swish of her long plaid taffeta skirt back into the dining room.

"I thought I'd put a plate together for Patrick later. If that's all right," Fiona said.

"Oh," her aunt said a second later. "Yes, well." She paused, looking briefly flustered. "I hope Rudy remembers to tell him dinner's coming."

"Oh, he will," Ginny assured her from the stove as she whisked the gravy.

"I hope so." Aunt Arlene sighed. "For such a bright young man, he amazes me with his absentmindedness. I mean, look in the front closet at all the jackets and sweaters he keeps leaving behind."

"Maybe they're George's," Fiona said.

"George's? No, I don't think so," Aunt Arlene said.

"No, that's right. She usually goes there, and Rudy comes here. I got it mixed up."

They both turned. Aunt Arlene looked confused. Ginny took a deep breath and shook her head.

"Why don't you go up and see if you can coax Elizabeth down here with us," her aunt said, and Fiona headed out of the kitchen. "But don't say anything about the twins. It's supposed to be a surprise!" she called after her.

Elizabeth sat on the foot of her bed drying her hair with a towel. The mirror reflected her wan smile when she saw Fiona peek through the open door. Fiona came in and sat beside her. They looked at one another through the mirror.

"I'm trying," Elizabeth sighed when Fiona asked if she were feeling any better.

"Well that's good." Fiona was determined not to apologize for anything she'd said Sunday might. With the silence, their eyes caught and Fiona couldn't help smiling. "You still do that," she said as Elizabeth combed her lank wet hair. She'd worn it this same way all her life—straight, chin length, parted in the middle with bangs.

"It's the only thing that works," Elizabeth said.

"How do you know? You've never tried anything else. Here," she said, taking the comb. "Let me try something." She drew the comb along Elizabeth's pink scalp, making a part on the side. She combed the hair back over her ears, then pressed the sides into deep waves. "There. I like that! It's more sophisticated." It made Elizabeth look more her age, less like a child. She realized that Elizabeth's eyes were closed. "Are you crying?" she asked softly.

Elizabeth took a deep breath and shook her head. "I'm trying not to," she whispered.

"Why?" Fiona demanded angrily. "Because I did that? Because I changed your hair?"

"I just need to be alone for a minute, that's all," she said, raking her fingers through her hair until it was straight again.

Fiona jumped up and started for the door.

"I'll be all right," Elizabeth whispered in a small, choked voice.

Fiona turned and came back. "You're coming down though, right?" she said, standing over her.

"I really don't want to," Elizabeth said, her head bowed. "I really don't."

"But you have to!" she said. "You understand that, don't you?"

Elizabeth looked up then.

"Don't you?" Fiona repeated, and Elizabeth nodded, her eyes such stagnant pools of misery that Fiona took her arm and shook it. "Lizzie! You've got to stop it. You can't do this anymore. You've got everyone walking on eggshells. Your mother's a wreck down there and your father's just as bad. Can you smell that smoke? He almost burned the house down!"

"He did?" Elizabeth tried to smile.

"Yes! And George is in a bad way too."

"He's not here, is he?" she gasped, hand at her chest.

"No! But he thinks this is all his fault." She paused, looking for even a stir in that dull gaze. "But it's not, is it? We both know it's not, right, Lizzie?"

Elizabeth stood up. "I'll get dressed now. And then I'll be down. I promise."

"You won't even talk about it! How selfish is that? You're waiting for everyone else to work this out, aren't you? And you don't really care who gets hurt in the meantime, do you? Not even if it's me, right, Lizzie? Or maybe especially if it's me. Why? Because I deserve it? Because I brought it all on my trashy little self. Is that what you think? What did you do, write out that noble little speech for George so he could get rid of me? So I'd stop chasing him? So I'd leave him alone and stop trying to get into his pants all the time? Well, did he tell you what really happened? Did he tell you how he set us both up? How he used me to get you back?" she whispered, leaning close, amazed that Elizabeth's only reaction was to close her eyes. "But you don't really care, do you?"

"I do care. I hate him for that. For what he did to you and to me. And I told him. I never want to see him again. Ever!"

"But Lizzie!" The corner Fiona had backed into was closing around her. "Lizzie, tell me, tell me the truth now. Do you love Rudy? Do you really love him?" She waited, hands clenched, as Elizabeth stared back. It was so obvious that she didn't. "It's all right. You can tell me." She leaned closer and took her dear cousin's small hand. "You don't, do you?"

"Yes!" Elizabeth raised her chin. "I do. Of course I do."

When Elizabeth finally came downstairs she was dressed in baggy slacks and a shapeless black sweater. Rudy had just arrived with the twins.

"Miss Hollis!" both girls cried, rushing toward her.

"Margaret! Lucille!" Elizabeth said, kneeling to hug them. She told them how surprised and happy she was to see them.

"Are you all better? Everyone misses you so much! Lucy told Mrs. Matley we're not gonna go back to school until you come back," Margaret declared in a defiant tone. The taller of the two, she was the more outspoken.

"Oh, but you mustn't do that now, girls!" Aunt Arlene laughed as she tugged off their jackets. Fiona knew from her aunt's scrutiny of the soiled sleeves that both jackets would be washed and dried before the children left.

"An ultimatum!" Uncle Charles said, smiling and patting their heads. "Well, Lucy, I guess we'll just have to spend the day getting Miss Hollis healthy and ready for school again."

"Actually Maggie and Lucy could use some Tylenol, and I promised them both juice," Rudy was telling Aunt Arlene. In the car one complained of an earache and the other a scratchy throat. "Oh! Thanks," he said, his first acknowledgment of Fiona when she handed him the Tylenol bottle.

"Oh! You're welcome," she said, echoing his surprised tone. He glanced away.

The twins had opened the bottom drawer of the sideboard and were pulling out coloring books and crayons. Rudy broke a tablet in half. Elizabeth poured two glasses of cranberry juice, then watched in amusement as Rudy tried to convince the girls to swallow the halved pills. Gagging, they ran to the sink to spit them out. Elizabeth broke another pill, which she crushed on teaspoons and mixed in sugar and juice, a concoction the girls quickly swallowed.

"Obviously I'm not needed here," Rudy said, leaving the kitchen.

The twins announced they had to go to the bathroom. Fiona offered to bring them, but they ran off saying they already knew where the bathrooms were. Stepping into the hallway, Elizabeth said she was going to see how her father was doing with the fire. A moment later there was a creak on the back stairs. Elizabeth was tiptoeing back to her room.

The twins raced into the kitchen with a deck of cards and Chinese checkers from the den closet. Their casual familiarity with everything irritated Fiona. Aunt Arlene was rinsing lettuce leaves and dropping them into the spinner.

Jack pushed up his sleeves and sat down at the table to play cards with the girls. "Go fish!" he said to Maggie's request for a queen.

"For what?" Maggie giggled, hand poised over the cards. "Trout or for perch?"

"She can't. She don't have any worms!" Lucy cried, and Jack burst out laughing.

"Doesn't," Fiona corrected from the stove where she was ricing the boiled potatoes.

"What'd the lady say?" Lucy asked Jack.

"Doesn't," Fiona repeated. "You said it wrong. It's supposed to be 'She doesn't have any worms.' "

For a moment there was only the sound of Aunt Arlene's knife striking the glass board as she sliced cucumbers.

"She was only kidding," Maggie informed her sister, then glared up at Fiona. "It was a joke, that's all." Maggie turned back to Jack and asked, "What the hell's her problem?"

"What?" Fiona said, trying not to laugh. "Wait a minute now!"

"Yes dear," Aunt Arlene said, hurrying to the table. She put both hands on the sullen twins' shoulders and bent close. "You see, Fiona was only trying to tell you the correct way to say it. And you know something? When Fiona was a little girl we did the same thing to her." She continued trying to explain the importance of good grammar.

Shoving her cards into the pile, Maggie announced she didn't want to play anymore. Lucy followed her sister's lead.

"Well, what about me?" Jack called, pretending to chase after them as they flew off in search of Elizabeth.

"And what was that all about?" Fiona asked.

Her aunt shook her head and sighed. "They're like two little wood sprites. They're absolutely devoted to one another. Lucy's the more delicate of the two. And Maggie, well, as you can see, she's a little pepperpot."

"She's a rude little thing, I'll say that for her." Fiona put the lid on the pan.

Aunt Arlene laughed. "Actually she reminds me a lot of you."

"I wasn't rude!" She spun around. "Was I?"

"You were a very forthright child." Her aunt smiled. "But no. You were never rude."

Cheers rose from the den where Uncle Charles, Rudy, Ginny, and Susan were watching a football game. There was a squeal in the hallway, now racing footsteps as the twins ran upstairs calling, "Miss Hollis! Miss Hollis, Rudy wants you to come down!"

Fiona opened the door and looked into the hallway, but Rudy wasn't there. So far they hadn't been in the same room for more than a few seconds at a time. He seemed not only ill at ease in her presence, but so subdued that on his last trip into the kitchen her aunt had felt his forehead to see if he had a temperature. He looked flushed. His cheeks were bright red. She was sure he was coming down with something, she said. No, just tired, he assured her, avoiding Fiona's stare.

Now with the potatoes mashed there was nothing else to wait for, was there? Fiona asked as she opened the oven. She began to pull out the turkey pan, but her aunt insisted she wait; it was too heavy to lift by herself. Actually, all that was left now, Aunt Arlene said with a grunt as she turned the corkscrew into a bottle of white wine, was the cook's toast. Fiona said she'd go get Susan and Ginny, who had helped with most of the preparations.

"No dear, I'd like it to be just us," her aunt said. She handed Fiona a glass and took up her own.

"To another great Thanksgiving, thanks to you, Aunt Arlene." Fiona raised her glass. "And one more perfect turkey!" It was traditional that the cook and her helpers started celebrating first.

"And to you, my dear Fiona," her aunt said, touching her glass to Fiona's. "I love you." She smiled and patted her cheek. "We can't say that enough, can we? It's as important to say it as it is to hear."

"Aunt Arlene!" Fiona was alarmed to see her aunt's eyes filling with tears. "What's wrong?"

"Nothing. Nothing's wrong," her aunt assured her. "It's just you remind me so much of your mother. The other night after I saw her locket I couldn't sleep. I kept thinking of her and remembering how close we were. And then I got up and came downstairs. Elizabeth heard me. She thought I was upset because of her. But I told her how it was my sister—that I missed my sister so much. And you know what she said? She said, 'But Mother, thank goodness you have Fiona.' It's true. And I don't think I've ever actually thought of it in quite that way, but I'm so glad I have you," she whispered, then hugged her again, this time with a desperate ferocity. "I am! I'm so glad, so very, very glad."

Fiona closed her eyes. "Thank you," she whispered.

Her aunt pulled back to look at her. "I hope you know how much you mean to us."

Fiona nodded and made herself smile.

"I mean to all of us—your cousins, me, your uncle. Especially your uncle, Fiona. I know he may not always show it, but he loves you dearly. Dearly, Fiona." Her voice broke, and she had to take a deep breath. "You have a very special place in his heart. You know that, don't you?"

"Yes," Fiona said as they took up the glasses and began to sip their wine. She did know that and knew as well how cramped a place it was from all the times she had been unable to fit into it. But today her aunt deserved only happiness, or at least the comfort of its façade.

A few minutes later Rudy hurried into the kitchen, then stopped as if surprised to find Fiona there.

"Rudy! Just the man I need," her aunt said, opening the oven door. She asked if he'd take out the turkey for her. "Give him the oven mitts," she told Fiona.

"Oven mitts," Fiona repeated, slapping them into his hand as if he were a surgeon. She kept trying to catch his eye as he lifted the turkey onto the counter. She wanted to touch the small cut on his chin where he'd nicked himself shaving. When he turned she smiled, but he looked away. As her aunt peeled back the steaming aluminum foil, he declared it the fattest bird he'd ever seen.

"Um, it is big, isn't it," Fiona said, leaning into him so she could see.

"Fiona, give me that baster, please?" her aunt said, pointing back at the stove. "And Rudy, would you mind telling Elizabeth we'll be eating in about twenty minutes?"

"That's what I came in to tell you," he said. "She wants to stay in her room. She said she feels shaky. Dizzy or something," he added wearily.

"That's ridiculous!" Fiona said, seeing her aunt's crestfallen expression. "I'll get her down," she promised, emboldened as much by the wine as by the affection that was seeping like warm oil from every pore. She loved her aunt and her cousins, loved them all, but mostly she loved Rudy, she thought with a surge of desire for this dear, awkward, ungainly man knocking over the trash now as he asked her aunt what else he could do.

"Just get her down here, you and Fiona, please," her aunt said with a deep sigh.

She followed him up the stairs. He needed a haircut. The ends of his hair curled over his collar. There were tiny moth holes in the back of his thin gray sweater. On the top step she grabbed his hand and pulled him around the corner into the bathroom. She locked the door and roped her arms around his neck. As she was about to kiss him, he turned away. "Rudy!" she protested as he reached back to remove her hands. "Rudy," she whispered. She laid her face against his chest. She could hear his heart thumping. She closed her eyes and put her arms around his waist. "You smell so good." She rubbed his hard, lean back.

"No, don't," he said, standing stiffly against her.

"Don't what?" She lifted her mouth to his.

"No!" He stepped around her and opened the door, then turned back. "Is this it? The only way you can feel anything. Is it? Is it, Fiona?" he demanded, with startling bitterness.

Nodding, she forced a smile. "I guess I can't fool you, can I, Dr. Freud?"

Aunt Arlene had placed a twin on Elizabeth's left, and one directly across from her. Rudy sat on her right with Fiona next to him. Happy to finally be near Elizabeth, the twins were telling her everything that had happened since she'd been in school. Jack stood to make the toast, his reedy voice buzz-sawing on Fiona's nerves.

Rudy's back was to her as he leaned forward listening to Jack. He finally has a family, she thought, more hurt than angry. That Elizabeth didn't really love him wasn't important, as long as the rest of them did.

There was so much to be thankful for, Jack was saying: his father's well-deserved appointment to the Superior Court bench. Elizabeth and Rudy's engagement. Ginny's baby . . .

"And Billy Leitener's got his appendix out!" Lucy suddenly remembered to tell Elizabeth, who smiled wanly and patted the child's hand.

"So now he can't go see the Christmas village!" Maggie leaned forward to add.

"Shh," Elizabeth whispered, finger to her lips.

"And we're thankful also to be sharing this wonderful day with Maggie and Lucy, our very special guests," Jack said, winking at them. He thanked his mother for another memorable holiday and for all she did for everyone throughout the year. And of course his father, whose love and devotion to his family was his finest achievement and inspiration for them all.

"Hear, hear!" Fiona said, raising her glass in her uncle's direction. She felt badly. No matter how hard Jack tried, things always seemed to fall flat because he was so stiff and formal. She sympathized with the twins squirming in their seats.

"And now in closing," Jack continued, "I'd like to take this opportunity to not only thank my beautiful wife, Susan, for all the happiness she's given me, but to share . . ."

"Can I have a roll?" Lucy asked Elizabeth, who stared resolutely up at her brother.

"Here," Fiona whispered with a flip of the roll onto the amused child's plate.

". . . some wonderful news . . ."

"Can I have one too?" Maggie hissed.

". . . with all of you."

"Sure!" Fiona said, and as she took another roll from the silver basket, felt her aunt's touch fall lightly on her wrist.

"Wait, dear," Aunt Arlene whispered, and Uncle Charles's disapproving eyes flickered the length of table.

"We're going to have a baby. Susan is pregnant! We just found out yesterday!"

They scrambled from their seats to kiss Susan and hug Jack. Susan couldn't stop smiling. Tears streamed down Aunt Arlene's cheeks. Ginny asked what she did first when she found out. Susan admitted that she had gone straight to the mall and bought a maternity outfit.

"I knew it!" Ginny cried, laughing. "Imagine if it's a girl," she told Elizabeth. "Can you just picture what that child's wardrobe will be like?"

"Yes," Elizabeth said with a faint smile.

Halfway through dinner Elizabeth sat back in her chair with her eyes half closed. The gaiety was taking its toll. Her brief energy was being drained by the twins. They not only vied with each other for her attention, but with the family as well. Rudy asked if he could get her anything. She shook her head no. She hadn't touched her dinner. The talk had returned to babies, and Uncle Charles had just issued what he called his "Grandfather's mandate." Both babies' first trips to Disney World would be with him and Aunt Arlene.

"That's not fair!" cried Ginny and Jack, though both were grinning at him, especially Jack, who had finally managed to please his father without any help from anyone, other than Susan, of course. They're all so screwed up, Fiona thought, and they don't even know it.

She asked Rudy if he'd ever been to Disney World. He hadn't. "Poor thing, then you can go too," she said, reaching under the table to pat his leg. She left her hand flat on his thigh. He moved his leg, but she did not lift her hand. She grinned at him. She could feel Ginny staring.

"Well, why don't you go there on your honeymoon then?" Ginny asked, looking from Elizabeth to Rudy.

"You should," Susan agreed. "It's amazing the number of couples who do."

Elizabeth gave a slight nod.

"I know," Rudy said. He reached down and removed Fiona's hand.

She put it back. "But Lizzie's already been there," she said, leaning into him to look at her cousin. "You should go someplace you've never been. Someplace new and exotic. And romantic. I can just see it, the two of you in tiny little bikinis laying in each other's arms in the hot sand on a deserted beach on some tropical island." She looked at Rudy and dug her fingers into his leg. "You'd probably never come back, would you? I mean, it's so cold here, and so unfriendly."

He had been staring at his plate, nodding. He glanced at her now with a pained smile.

Ginny asked if her sister remembered their last trip to Disney World. Elizabeth sat very still, head slightly bowed, as if to recall some detail, the pause just long enough to draw everyone's uneasy attention.

"Elizabeth?" Uncle Charles finally said. "Are you all right?"

Eyes closed, she nodded, though her head stayed bent. Rudy put his arm over the back of her chair and asked if she wanted to go upstairs.

"No," she said softly as the twins watched with growing concern.

Ginny suggested she go into the den and rest on the sofa for a few minutes.

"Are you still sick, Miss Hollis?" Maggie asked.

"I'm fine," Elizabeth said in a faint voice.

"Do you have a headache?" Lucy asked.

Elizabeth shook her head, unable to answer.

"I think Miss Hollis is tired," Uncle Charles said with a great flurry of cutting the rest of Lucy's turkey, though she had already announced she was finished eating. "It's hard work being a teacher, you know."

"Is Miss Hollis your favorite teacher?" Susan asked the girls.

"Yes!" Lucy cried.

"Because she's the prettiest one in the whole school," Maggie said.

"And the nicest too!" Lucy added.

"Of course she is," Aunt Arlene agreed, her fearful gaze locked on Elizabeth.

"I'm sorry," Elizabeth gasped, burying her face in her napkin.

"Elizabeth?" Aunt Arlene started to get up.

Elizabeth looked up with the bunched napkin at her chin. "I'm ruining everyone's wonderful holiday."

"No!"

"Of course you're not!"

"Maggie," Uncle Charles said quickly. "Tell Miss Hollis we've all had our share of down days, and now it's just her turn, that's all."

"We've all had our . . . ," Maggie began, then shook her head in exasperation, making everyone laugh.

Fiona rolled her eyes and poured another glass of wine. She looked around as she sipped it. They all began to talk at once, their skillful chatter meant to take the focus off Elizabeth. See? It didn't matter if she were a little quiet and depressed. They could still have a good time. Ginny and Aunt Arlene were discussing the merits of chestnuts in the stuffing. Susan and Jack were asking Rudy what a saddle block was: Susan didn't think she wanted natural childbirth.

And what would be considered natural childbirth? Uncle Charles inquired from his end of the table. The twins giggled and whispered to one another. Fiona shifted in her chair and pressed her leg against Rudy's. Uncle Charles asked Rudy's opinion of Memorial's maternity unit. Rudy said he'd been quite impressed with what he'd seen of it so far.

Fiona moved her hand higher up his thigh and was amused to see him gulp. He leaned over the table now as Uncle Charles told Ginny he didn't understand why she'd rather drive all the way into Boston to have the baby instead of just having it at Dearborn Memorial.

"What if it's seven-thirty in the morning and you're stuck in commuter traffic on Ninety-three ready to deliver at any moment?" Uncle Charles asked.

"Well then," Ginny said, "I guess I'm—"

"Screwed!" Fiona burst out, her laughter splintering through the awkward silence like glass shards. She clawed Rudy's thigh.

"Just make sure your driver's got a couple deliveries on his résumé," Rudy said. His mouth was tight with anger.

"How about you? Do you have any?" Ginny asked.

"Yah, is your O-B as good as your G-Y-N?" Fiona murmured, moving her hand again.

"You just call." Rudy's stricken gaze fixed on Ginny. "Day or night and I'll be there."

"Umm," Fiona sighed. He was becoming aroused.

Her uncle asked Rudy if he knew Archie Heglund, the newest hospital trustee.

Rudy cleared his throat. "What was the name again?" he asked, blinking.

"Archie," Fiona said, trying not to smile as she leaned closer. She touched his shoulder. "Archie Heglund," she said softly. His nearness made everything else seem small and out of focus.

"Uh, no sir. I don't think I do," Rudy said, ignoring her.

Jack spoke up quickly to say he knew Heglund. "We've met him!" he told Susan, who agreed. Yes—they'd socialized a few times, though she couldn't recall exactly where. "Oh yes," Aunt Arlene said. "He's the one whose sister married that Indian doctor. Pradish. Pranchis. Something like that, I forget."

"Pradiz," Uncle Charles said in a pained voice from the end of the table. "Dr. Pradiz."

"Yes, Pradiz," someone said.

"Pradiz," Fiona repeated, still amused by their earnest chatter that seemed to be disappearing down a deep hole right now. It was silent. The chimes in the hallway clock sounded.

"Fiona, would you help me with something out in the kitchen for a minute?" Ginny asked, rising abruptly. She stood in the doorway, waiting. "What in God's name are you doing?" she hissed the minute the door closed behind them.

Fiona stared back a little dizzily. "I have no idea what you're talking about." She steadied herself against the counter.

"Yes you do, and so does everyone else, but we're all trying to act like it's not really happening."

"Are you done?"

"Fiona, don't do this. Please, not to your own cousin. My God! Not here! Not in your own family!" Ginny said with a shudder of disgust.

"Fuck you." She turned to walk away, but Ginny held out her hand.

"You know, I used to feel badly for you. I used to think it was just your way of getting attention. But not anymore. Because you're mean, Fiona. You're mean and you're selfish. You don't give a damn about anyone else but yourself."

"Get out of my way," she hissed back.

"No, you listen to me," Ginny said, her wide, mannish face at

Fiona's. "Elizabeth's confused enough. Don't ruin this for her. Don't take advantage of her when she's like this. And don't have anything else to drink!" With that, Ginny pushed the door, smiling as she held it open for Fiona.

Fiona was trembling as she sat down. She poured herself more wine, then stared at Ginny and took a sip. Her hand shook as she set it down. She didn't even want it. Her stomach hurt. Elizabeth smiled now as the twins tried to tell the same story. Rudy was telling Aunt Arlene how to make Chinese pancakes. Each detail only seemed to enchant her more, her aunt who hated Chinese food, her toothy, horse-faced aunt, this calculating woman whose own blood came first, whose caring had always been more antidote than affection. Look at them all, so smug and safe in their pretenses. She shouldn't have come back in here. She should just get up now and go to Patrick's, even though she'd made about as big a mess of that as she had everything else. But screwed up as Patrick was, at least he cared about her, while no one here really even wanted her around. She had become an obligation, and a dreadful one at that. They never enjoyed her company or cared what she thought. They didn't know anything about her, didn't want to know, yet she knew everything about them. Silence burned in her throat with their burgeoning jocularity. "Be good," Lizzie had pleaded in her childhood notes under the door. "That's all they want, just for you to be good." Fiona was a thirty-year-old woman. Thirty years old, but at their table still a child. Ginny and Jack burst out laughing at something Susan had just said. Fiona reached across the table and picked up the slumped cranberry mold, balancing the plate in her palm. Her aunt's token serving was an uneaten blob on her dish. No one else had wanted any of the blood-red, runny mess made by a trashy slut who couldn't do anything right, much less get gelatin to set. She offered the plate to Rudy and asked if he'd like some.

"No, thank you," he said.

"I made it," she said before he could look away. "It only looks bad."

"Oh. Well. Sure," he said, taking the plate. "I'll have to try some then." He spooned out a soupy serving, then passed the plate to Elizabeth. "Fiona made it." He tasted it. "Delicious," he said, then ate the rest while Elizabeth served herself and gave a small portion first to Maggie, who said she hated soup, then to Lucy, who grimaced and shivered with disgust. The pitiful concoction went next to Uncle Charles, then down the opposite side of the table until everyone had some on their plates. Fiona looked around slowly so that each one knew he was being watched. They were all eating. "Very good . . . perfect timing . . . tasty . . . ummh," they murmured, not to her or one another, but to themselves, quietly, uneasily, so keenly moored did each one feel under her reproachful scrutiny.

When her uncle finished, he looked up into her stare. "Well!" He patted his belly. "Thanks to Fiona, I don't think I have room for one thing more," he said with a weak smile.

"And we haven't even had dessert yet," Susan said, and Jack groaned.

"Remember now, you all have to take leftovers home." Aunt Arlene began stacking the soiled dishes being passed to her.

"And we'll send a nice dinner home to Grandpa too," Uncle Charles promised the twins as he took their dishes.

"And I'll make up a plate for Patrick," Fiona said over the rattle of china. "He's all alone today. He probably didn't eat a thing."

No one said anything.

"He hasn't been feeling too good lately. As a matter of fact, he's in pretty bad shape," she said, conscious of how loud her voice seemed in the stillness.

"I'm sorry to hear that," her uncle said.

"Are you?" she said, irritated by everyone's discomfort.

"Come on, Fiona," Jack chided, shaking his head.

"What, Jack? You want me to be quiet? You want me to just sit here and listen to all of you? Why? Why can't I talk about what I want?"

"No one said you couldn't, Fiona," her uncle said with an imploring smile.

"No, you don't have to!" she said, then looked around, so stung by their cold eyes she didn't know what to say for a moment.

"Well!" her aunt said, looking anxiously around the table. "I know I say it every year, but what I'm most thankful for is that no matter our trials or tribulations we can still be together on this lovely day."

"That's beautiful, Mother. Thank you," Ginny said, and the others echoed agreement.

"Well, maybe for you all it's a lovely day," Fiona said, angry at the tremor in her voice when she felt so strong. Now Rudy's leg pressed against hers and stayed there. "But I feel like them," she said, gesturing to the twins. "You know? A waif? Like, it's a holiday, so let's be kind to the less fortunate. I mean, isn't that what this is?"

"No!" her uncle declared, his magisterial tone riveting everyone bolt upright in their chairs. "That's not what this is. This is a family. Everyone at this table. Every one of us. And most especially you."

They all stared at her, except Aunt Arlene, who had put down her knife and fork. She sat very still, hands folded in her lap, eyes closed.

"That's nice to hear, Uncle Charles, but I'll tell you the truth. I haven't felt it in a long time."

"Fiona!" Elizabeth gasped.

Ginny shook her head in disgust.

Under the table Rudy patted her leg.

"It's just that I'm sitting here listening to everyone talk. I mean, you all have each other, and the one person, the one parent I finally have, I can't say anything about. And it makes me feel like I don't count. Like nobody wants to hear it." She looked from her uncle at one end of the table to her aunt at the other. Neither would look at her.

"But it's not you, Fiona," Jack said, surprising her. "It's him, he's a difficult person."

"I know, but that's how life goes. Just because he's difficult, I mean, he's still my father. It's not like I had a lot of choice in the matter. And the thing is, it's not always easy, but we're trying to become part of each other's lives. And it hurts that none of you will accept that. You know what I mean?" She looked around again.

"Well, you make a good point," Jack conceded.

"Anyway, it's been really great. Finally being able to have that kind of a relationship, you know, where you feel so naturally close to someone," she said, hating the hollowness in her own words. She wasn't trying to convince them of anything, just inform them. "In fact I've even talked him into selling his land, believe it or not. Finally!" she said, her light little laugh of relief directed at her uncle, whose hands remained clenched on the table. "After all these years. And I told him he should take a long trip and see the world. Do you realize that in all the time he's been back—from Vietnam, that is—that he's never left Dearborn. Poor man, he's never been anywhere. Not even for a day. He's spent almost his whole life in that house."

"By his own choice, Fiona," her uncle said.

"I don't know. Some ways it seems like he's been a prisoner there all these years," she said, voice rising.

"Some people need to be home." Rudy spoke quietly, looking at her. "They don't want to be anywhere else. Home is all they care about."

"Yes, as long as they live in the real world! As long as they're not using it to hide out," she said.

Elizabeth shuddered. Tears leaked down her face. She tried to smile for the twins' sake, but her mouth only quivered. Aunt Arlene and Ginny hurried to her side. Rudy tried to put his arm around her, but she crumpled forward, sobbing into her hands. Uncle Charles shook his head, glowering at Fiona.

"Oh for godsakes, Lizzie!" she blurted, so caught up in her explanation that it took a moment to comprehend what was happening. "I didn't mean you! Will you stop? Will you please just stop? This is so pathetic! How long can you keep this up? Why don't you just say it? Say what you mean! Tell them! Go ahead! Tell them what's really wrong." She paused, conscious of Rudy staring at her. "Do you want me to, Lizzie?" she asked softly.

"Leave me alone," Elizabeth groaned.

"Fiona," Rudy pleaded, shaking his head.

"Just leave me alone. Please, please, please," Elizabeth continued groaning.

"It's you she means, Rudy. She can't even stand to have you touch her."

"Fiona!" Uncle Charles demanded. "I think you'd better go now."

"Charles!" her aunt cried, and everyone looked away.

Fiona threw down her napkin and rushed into the kitchen. She was fumbling through the closet for her coat and bag when Rudy came in and asked her not to leave.

"I have to," she said over her shoulder. She felt panicky, but strangely exhilarated. And strong. Stronger than she had ever felt before.

"No, they're upset. They don't want you to."

She spun around. "Rudy! You're just like them. You've got it all ass-end-to. The thing they *don't* want is to be upset. The thing they *do* want is for me to leave. Peace—that's all they really want. Well, they can all go to hell!"

"Calm down, Fiona. Now you just calm down." He tried to put his arm around her. "We need to talk."

"We did before, but we don't now!" She pulled away, smiling.

He put both hands on her shoulders. "We still do. You know we do," he whispered.

The door pushed open then. Uncle Charles came into the kitchen. She tried to back away, but Rudy didn't let go. Her uncle's face soured with disgust. He turned and went back into the dining room.

"There," she whispered, still smiling. "Now they can hate me with a clear conscience." She tried to push past him to the back door. "Let me go. I have to go!"

"No, Fiona, wait!"

She grabbed him. "Then come with me!"

"I can't. I can't just walk out on her, Fiona. I can't do that."

"You are! You're just like them. Peace at any price, that's all you really care about."

There were lights on inside Patrick's house. Tree branches lifted in the cold, sharp wind. A plastic grocery bag tumbled across his rutted front lawn. Soon it would be dark. A thin plume of smoke rose from the narrow chimney. She sat for a moment with the engine running, then pulled into the driveway. There had been no mention of her in Jack's Thanksgiving toast, and if she had said anything they would have all denied it. Not one of them understood. She parked the car and knocked on the door. The front curtain moved. Patrick opened the door, then walked away. She followed him into the living room, where he sat back down in front of the television. He had been watching a football game. There was an indentation of his head in the matted pillows. He'd probably been lying on the divan for days. She sat down and asked if he'd eaten yet.

"What do you care?"

"We could go somewhere and get something to eat."

The ashtray overflowed with cigarette butts and spent, twisted roaches. His scarred boots sat on the coffee table surrounded by empty beer cans and bottles.

"I don't like strangers handling my food." He put his bare feet up on the table.

"I'll cook something then," she said, uneasy now with his legs blocking her way.

"Because you're not a stranger, right? So what the hell are you then?"

"I'll go see what you've got." She started to get up.

"No." He grabbed her arm. "I know what I got. Nothing. That's what I got. Do you understand?"

She sat back down and stared at his grimy hand until he lifted it away. His fingernails were rimmed with dirt. His hair hung in greasy strands and his cheeks were black with stubble. Only his scar gleamed, tender and waxen. The front of his shirt was stained.

"I'm sorry I didn't call last night," she began slowly, not wanting to agitate him any more than he already was. "I fell asleep, and then I had to leave first thing this morning. They wanted me there early, you know, to help out and everything. And I was going to bring you a dinner," she said, conscious of his cold, narrowing eyes. "But then things got a little tense."

"Yah, and who the fuck cares!" he said with a savage kick that toppled the coffee table in an explosion of ashes and cans. The boots flew off and bottles rolled across the floor.

She jumped up. "I better go."

"No! Please stay!" he begged, peering up at her. "I'm sorry. Please." He pulled the table back up. "Please stay. It's just I've been alone too long. I'm a little off kilter here, but I'll be okay."

She eased back down.

"I almost called you there. You know how many times I drove by?

Maybe a hundred. I just kept going around and around. I got all these things to say, and now I can't remember," he said, rubbing his eyes so hard his fingers made fleshy popping sounds on the lids. "My head, I got all this shit in my head. It builds up, so when I call, you gotta pick up the phone. I can't keep it all straight."

"Well I'm here, so tell me now."

He looked at her and kept nodding. "That's the thing. I can't. I can't even tell you, so you're thinking one thing and I'm saying something else, so you don't trust me. It's so hard. And I can't help it because I have these, these feelings." He looked away quickly, staring at the television for a moment. "Shit! I'm way too messed up here, and I know I gotta get it all straight, so you'll understand, and I'm trying. I am. Believe me, I am. The thing is, I keep feeling so trapped. I gotta get outta here. I can't do this anymore."

"Do what?" She didn't dare move. She could see and hear and feel his pain. He would finally tell her about himself and her mother.

He hunched forward and stared down at the floor. He was almost panting. "I don't know," he said with such anguish his words seemed less spoken than excreted. "I don't know how to say it. I can't! Jesus Christ, I can't! I want to, but I can't! I can't! Not here. Not the way things are."

"Why? Why can't you?" she asked softly.

"Because no matter what I do here, I lose. I fucking, fucking lose!"

"I don't know what you mean," she said as he stared at her. "What do you lose?"

"You."

"No. You won't lose me. Of course you won't." She tried to smile, then bit her lip to see his poor face so twisted with misery.

"You know what I mean, don't you? You know what I'm talking about, right?" he asked so desperately that she flinched back.

"I'm not sure. Maybe I don't," she said.

"I mean, I love you! I love you so much I can't do anything! I can't think straight," he growled, his tortured face at hers. He squeezed her wrist. "I don't care about anything anymore. All I want is you. That's all I want. I don't care what happens. We won't say anything. We'll just go. They'll never find us. We'll—"

In one motion she sprang from the divan to the door, then ran down the walk with his frantic muttering close at her heels.

He grabbed her arm as she got into her car. "See! That's why! That's why we have to get away from here, away from all this shit! So you'll know! So you'll understand!" he was shouting.

She couldn't close the door, but she had finally managed to get the key into the ignition. She turned the key, then jammed her foot down on the accelerator. He jumped back as the car shot ahead. "Oh God. Oh God. Oh God," she cried as the car squealed over the lawn. He was running after her barefoot. She turned sharply onto the road, and it wasn't until his house was no longer in sight that she dared slow down enough to close her door.

Chapter 20

■

The water burned her back. She scrubbed her arms and legs with the washcloth until everything stung. Her doorbell was ringing when she stepped out of the shower. Certain it was Rudy, she groped through the steam for her robe, putting it on as she ran to the door. Now the bell rang in urgent, stabbing bursts. Patrick! Her hand jerked back from the knob. Everyone had warned her, and now it had come to this.

He was knocking. She heard Mr. Clinch's door open. "Can I help you, sir?" Mr. Clinch asked.

"I'm sorry. I didn't mean to disturb you. I'm looking for my niece."

"Uncle Charles! I was in the shower," she said, opening the door, any relief she felt blunted by his grim stare. Only anger could have brought him here on Thanksgiving night.

Mr. Clinch disappeared behind his closing door.

"Can I come in?" Uncle Charles asked, already inside and sitting down. She wanted to take his jacket, but he said he could only stay for a few minutes. Perched on the very edge of the sofa, he sat with hands clasped and elbows tight at his sides as if afraid to touch anything.

She sat in the opposite chair, clutching the lower half of her robe closed. She offered him a glass of water. She had cider. Or tea; he only drank tea at night.

"Nothing, thank you." He wet his lips and swallowed. "Fiona," he began, then sighed.

"Uncle Charles, I'm sorry. I didn't mean to ruin everyone's day. I really didn't."

"No, I'm sure you didn't."

"It's just I've been having a hard time lately with some things." She looked back at him. "With a lot of things."

"It's not just lately though, is it, Fiona? Things have been hard for you for a long, long time, haven't they?"

She nodded, even guiltier now with his tone of kindly concern.

"It hasn't been easy. I know that." He sighed. "Believe me, I do. And at times it's been all I could do to sit by and watch you in so much . . . so much turmoil." He leaned forward. "Because you're very, very dear to us, Fiona. To your aunt and me. All we ever wanted was to do the right thing, to do our very best for you."

"I know. And I always disappoint you, don't I? No matter what I do."

"I didn't say that."

"But that's why you're here, isn't it?"

"I'm here because I want to help you."

"Well that's a switch. Last I heard, I was beyond help."

"Fiona, please. This is hard enough." He closed his eyes and rubbed his temples. "All I want," he began in a low, pained voice, "is for you to be happy. That's all I've ever wanted." He looked up and she was shocked to see his eyes bright with tears. He took out a handkerchief and blew his nose.

"Oh, Uncle Charles. I'm sorry. It's this anger. I'm always taking it out on people. I mean, I know it's not your fault that my mother left and that Patrick's so screwed up. In my head I know all that. But in here," she said, fist at her chest, "it's all such a mess. Nothing makes sense. Nothing feels right. It's like I always have this feeling I'm in the wrong place at the right time or the right place at the wrong time. Do you know what I mean?" she asked, then laughed before he could reply. "What am I saying? Of course you don't," she scoffed, then seeing him wince, added, "I mean, like you and Aunt Arlene, it all comes so naturally, it's easy for you to do the right thing." She tried to laugh again. "You can't help it. You're both such good people."

"Goodness doesn't just come naturally, Fiona. Believe me, it doesn't," he said with startling intensity. "It's always a battle. Always!"

"I know, but you've got to admit, it's a whole lot easier when people think you're a good person. When they treat you that way," she added.

"That can be its own burden," he said in a harsh whisper. "A terrible burden when people think more of someone than he does of himself." He sat very still for a moment, and it saddened her to realize he meant himself. Aunt Arlene was right. He didn't know what a good man he was. She tried to tell him how much she had always admired him and how much it had meant to her the other day when he dropped everything and came when she called.

"I mean, it was like the two of us, you know. I mean, we were both in it for the same reason. Just to help poor Larry." Her voice faltered under his now blank gaze. "I mean, you didn't have to do that, but there you were—"

"Well, be that as it may," he interrupted, "my main concern now is for Elizabeth."

"Yes, and poor Lizzie, she's going through the same thing too," she said softly, trying not to be hurt. "You know, thinking she has to do what everyone expects of her whether she wants to or not. And now she's just turning it all in on herself."

He stared at her. "Then how can you do this to her? Why would you, when you know she's so vulnerable right now."

"What do you—"

"Or is that why? Because there's a weakness, so you think it's all right to just take what you want."

"No!"

"And I don't think you even care about him, because it's me, isn't it?" He stared, his face ghostly pale. "It's me you're really trying to hurt."

"I'm not trying to hurt anyone!"

"I couldn't figure it out at first. I couldn't understand what was going on. They seemed so happy, so right for each other. And then it all started falling apart. You can't do this, Fiona! It's tearing Elizabeth apart. It's destroying her, and I can't just sit back and do nothing." He rose suddenly and stood over her. "I can't let this happen. Just like I can't watch you keep throwing your life away. So at least this way," he said, pulling a folded paper from his breast pocket and handing it to her, "I can help give you another chance."

It was a check for twenty-five thousand dollars. Stunned, she kept looking at it.

"This way you can go somewhere, Fiona. Get a fresh start. Make a life for yourself. This isn't what you want, is it?" he said with a sweep of his hand. "It couldn't be. Bad enough what it's doing to Elizabeth, but it'll devastate your aunt Arlene. It will. I know it will."

"Oh, I see." She dangled the check between them with a weak laugh. "This is why you came."

"When you need more all you have to do is let me know."

"You want to know something funny? For a minute there I really thought you came here to help me." She dropped the check and it fluttered onto the table. It was all as ridiculous as it was horrible. "Jesus Christ, I must really be some pain-in-the-ass loser!" She picked it up and stared at her name in his blunt, black script.

"I'm trying to help you the very best way I can."

"Oh! Lucky me."

"And just so you'll know, Fiona, I've talked to Rudy. I've explained that as far as I'm concerned this was nothing more than an aberration brought on by any number of tensions and pressures, confusions, misunderstandings."

"Really?"

"Yes, and he agrees," he said without hesitation. "And also agrees that no one need know, most especially not Elizabeth."

She turned away. She would rather gouge out her eyes right now than cry. She got up and hurried into the bathroom. He tapped on the door and asked if she was all right. She sat on the closed toilet lid with her head in her hands.

"I'm okay," she said when he asked again.

"Everything will be all right, hon. You'll see."

She looked up, astonished. It was the soothing voice she remembered as a child when he would sit on her bed holding her hand after a nightmare. "Uncle Charles?" She opened the door. She put her arms around him and buried her face in his shoulder. "Oh, Uncle Charles, all I want is for you to love me, but everything keeps getting so messed up. I'm sorry. I'm so sorry."

"And that's why." He stiffened and held her out at arm's length. "You just need a change of pace, that's all. A fresh start." He smiled.

"You think that's what I need?"

"Yes, hon, you not only need it, but you deserve it," he said with a wink and a clubby nod.

"Look at me, Uncle Charles, look at me! I'm a mess! Everything I touch turns to shit. Going away's not going to change anything. No. It's the exact opposite. I need to stay right where I am and deal with my problems. And I'll be the first to admit I've got them, believe me, and that I do need your help. But not that." She gestured at the check. "Not paying me to get out of your life." She tried to laugh. "I need you to be patient with me. And to keep on loving me." She paused, but he didn't say anything. "That's what I really need right now." She hated her thin, groveling voice.

"It's all in the way you look at this, Fiona. You think I'm trying to get you out of my life, but I'm not. I just want to see you happy. I just want to help you. Fiona, call Lucretia Kendale. Tell her you'll go to Florida with her."

"Maybe you better go now, Uncle Charles." She felt sick to her stomach.

"Don't be upset. That's not what I—"

"I'm not," she interrupted. "I just need to be alone, that's all."

"Are you sure?" he asked, obviously relieved as he eased toward the door.

She nodded.

"Oh! And one more thing. There's no point in saying anything about this to your aunt." He went back to the table and picked up the check. "This is just between you and me." He handed it to her again, this time watching closely to make sure she truly understood. "And that way you'll feel better about it. It'll be easier for you." He smiled and patted her hand that still held the check.

As soon as the door closed, she started to tear the check in two, then stopped. Instead she dressed quickly and grabbed her car keys. She would deposit it before he changed his mind. Or she changed hers.

She had just left the ATM in the bank parking lot when she saw Todd Prescott come out of the Quik-Mart with a gallon of milk. She watched from the car. His weary, plodding gait and downcast eyes depressed her even more. "Hey, Toddie, whatcha doing?" she called, forcing a smile.

He hurried toward her, grinning. They talked through the open window for a few minutes, their breath steaming the air between them.

She said she was sorry to hear what had happened that night after he'd left her place.

"No you're not," he said, smiling. "Come on, Fee, admit it. You told Patrick to nail me, right?"

"It wasn't Patrick! He didn't—"

"Yah, he did. But a short memory's better than a long trial." He reached in and held her chin. "And besides, I didn't want to cause you any more trouble than I already have. I mean that, Fee. I really do."

Staring at him, she removed his hand. She said she hoped he was all better. Just some occasional twinges in his lower back, he said, which had turned out to be a blessing in disguise because it had gotten him out of the grunt work at the furniture store's warehouse.

"I never was much of a heavy lifter," he said.

"I know," she said, and he laughed.

He was spending time in the showrooms now. After that he'd be in the billing office a while. His father wanted him to learn the business from top to bottom.

"You're being groomed." She hugged herself against the cold.

"Yah, like the thoroughbred I am," he said as a blast of icy wind ballooned up the back of his jacket.

She made herself laugh. "Well that's good. I'm glad everything's going so well for you," she said, then shuddered with a sudden chill. Her teeth were chattering.

He hunched closer to the window and touched the side of her head. "Your hair's wet. No wonder you're shivering. You better get going." He slapped the side of the car and stepped back. He seemed tired, but the weight he'd gained made him look healthier than he had in years.

His hair was short and his eyes were clear and bright. He waved and called goodbye.

"I'll turn on the heat." She started the engine. "Come on, get in! We can talk for a few minutes."

He glanced back at the fluorescent glow, the windows patched with paper signs advertising the week's specials. He switched the jug of milk to his left hand and climbed into the car. He asked how Thanksgiving had gone. All right, she said, updating him on all her cousins, though she could see he didn't really care.

She asked him how his day had been. Stressful, he said. They'd had dinner with his parents. The problem was his mother's complete control of Sandy and the girls. His mother was the only one who could make the girls behave, so Sandy never said anything. "So I don't know. I guess it's okay. After a while it just starts getting on my nerves, that's all."

"Well," she began, her bruised and jumbled thoughts scrambling to assemble themselves. "That's because Sandy's so young. So . . . what's the word I want . . . no, not childish, not immature. But naïve! That's it. You know what I mean? She was like that with Maxine too. And with me!" She looked at him and didn't dare blink. She felt herself clinging to the side of a sheer cliff. This was it. A last, desperate chance. "It was scary sometimes. I mean, how needy she was. But then look where she came from. I mean, she's done so well when you consider all that." She gulped with complete self-disgust. It wasn't jealousy, or even that she knew life with Sandy would be a disaster for him, but her own excruciating loneliness right now.

"I don't know." He sighed and looked out the window. The milk sat between them. "Mostly it's my father. He's driving me nuts. Like today he tried. He really did. He tried to be pleasant. But then, little by little, he's right back to it, watching me like a hawk, you know, ready to pounce at the slightest thing. He just looks at me and I feel like such a loser. And Sandy doesn't get it. She says I'm just being super sensitive, that my father's only trying to help."

"See, that's what I mean. She's so young." She put her hand on his arm. "But give her time. She'll learn."

"Hey!" he said with a broad smile. "How about a quick beer. C'mon!"

Pacer's was jammed. The minute they came through the door old friends called out to them. She had forgotten how many people came home to Dearborn every year at Thanksgiving. They were still in the doorway of the bar, and it seemed they'd already been stopped to talk at least twenty-five times. Lance Bowman had just bought them a beer and was telling them about his limo rental business in Hartford. He had a fleet of six stretch limos and two super stretches. His wife, who was a former runner-up for Miss Missouri, had her Ph.D. in Renaissance art. "What about you?" Lance asked Fiona, shouting over the garbled voices and the music.

"I'm still working on mine," she shouted back, following Todd into the bar.

They quickly found themselves surrounded by more old classmates, all delighted to see them still together.

"Well, do you live together?" asked Laura Clay when Fiona said they weren't married. Laura had just bought a house in Lincoln, Nebraska, with her bushy-haired husband, Thomas, whose clerical collar and black shirt indicated some kind of religious affiliation.

"No. We just get together now and again," Fiona tried to explain. Todd pulled her close and whispered in her ear, but she couldn't hear what he said.

"You what together?" Laura leaned closer and asked with a sly smile.

"We're friends!" Fiona shouted.

"And what else?" Laura asked.

"Let's get the hell out of here," Todd said at her ear. "Bye," he called to Laura, who asked where they were going.

"West Palm Beach," Fiona called back as Todd steered her through the crowd.

"West Palm Beach?" he asked when they got outside. "What's West Palm Beach?"

They sat in the car with the engine running for heat while she told him she was moving to Florida.

"I wish I could do that, take off and start all over again."

"No you don't. Oh God." She sighed, looking back at Pacer's. "If only we'd just done what we were supposed to."

"I thought we did!"

"I'm serious, Todd. I mean, everyone in there," she said, pointing. "They've all got good jobs. They're married. They've got kids, houses, nice cars."

"We could have had all that," he said.

"Yah. If we'd wanted, right?"

"No. If they'd left us alone—our families—if they hadn't interfered, we'd probably still be together," he said, touching her cheek. He ran his fingers through her hair the way he used to, combing it back from her face.

"We were so young." She sighed, trying to keep her eyes open. She leaned her head on his arm. The gallon of milk pressed into her hip.

"But we knew what we wanted," he murmured against her mouth.

Maybe he was right, she thought as they kissed. If their teenage elopement hadn't been thwarted, they might have been forced to grow up and make something out of their lives. Maybe it had been the same for her mother and Patrick. If the war hadn't come and her aunt and uncle hadn't interfered, then they might have been able to work out their problems.

Todd sat back suddenly. "There's one thing I have to say though. Well actually there's about a thousand, but the most important thing is that I'm sorry for all the trouble I've caused you."

"You think you can get off that easy? Uh-uh," she said, bringing her mouth to his. "No. You're going to be in my debt for a long time. You owe me." They all do, she thought. Todd, Brad Glidden, George, Rudy, every goddamn one of them. From now on she'd just take what she wanted and not look back.

"When do I start paying you back?"

"Now's fine." She pulled out of the lot. As she drove, he kept adjusting the angle of the heating vent. She told him to turn it down if he was too warm.

"It's not me. It's the milk. The girls won't drink it if it's not real cold."

The car hit a bump and the frame vibrated. "Do they need it now? Is Sandy waiting for it?" She lifted her foot from the accelerator.

"No," he said, waving her ahead. "She's probably already got some." He shook his head and sighed. "She probably called my mother and they ran it right over." He chuckled. "Actually it's kind of funny. They're, like, at her beck and call. On the one hand they think she's ignorant and trashy, but then again she's like their last hope. You know what I mean?" As they came into town he slid down in the seat.

"Who are you hiding from?"

"Take your pick," he said, adding that tonight it would probably be his father. Last week Todd had bumped into an old friend so they stopped at Dunkin' Donuts for coffee. When they came out his mother was sitting in his car waiting for him.

Her skin crawled. It was like being sixteen again.

"No!" Todd said at the light when she put on the directional to turn into the Quik-Mart lot. "Keep going! They've probably got my car staked out." He slid even lower.

"Then I'll drive you to Sandy's." She turned up the hill toward the little house the Prescotts hoped would finally make a dependable man of their wild son.

"No!" He insisted he wanted to be with Fiona.

Then they should at least drop off the milk, she said, slowing down.

"No!" he shouted. "Jesus Christ, Fiona, keep going!"

"I'll just leave it on the front step."

"No! No!" he groaned, his hand over his eyes.

"But what if the kids need it?"

"Okay, that one!" He peered over the dashboard. "The blue one."

The only light in the tiny house shone from an upstairs window. She parked at the curb, grabbed the milk, and ran it onto the top step. Her hungry gaze took in the butterfly pattern of the taut lace curtain on the front-door glass, the skimpy grape ivy in the adjacent window, the two little red snow shovels and the tall one leaning beside the door. She hit the buzzer, then sprinted back to the idling car and drove away. "There. Don't you feel better now?"

"No."

The minute the door to her apartment closed he took her in his arms and kissed her. She couldn't tell if he was in a hurry or wild with desire. After a few minutes she eased away, and he tried to pull her back. "No, don't, Todd. Please. This is just one more dumb mistake we're both going to hate each other for."

"I've never hated you, Fee. Never! How could I?" he said with such stunned conviction that she tried to smile.

"Oh God," she cried, covering her face with her hands. If only he could fill that terrible emptiness, but leave the rest of her alone.

"Poor Feef. He nuzzled his face in her hair. "What can I say? What can I do? Let me make you feel better. You know I can. I know all your secret places." He ran his hands up and down her back as he kissed her neck and shoulder. "There. There, now," he crooned. "You want me, don't you? You know you do."

"But I don't," she gasped against his neck, sweet with another woman's fragrance. "I really, really don't." She wanted Rudy, but he belonged to Elizabeth, and in their goodness neither would abandon the other. They were better and stronger than she was. Better and stronger in every way.

"Then you need me, baby, that's what it is. We need each other, and right now that's okay."

"I just feel so sad," she whispered.

"Sad!" He stepped back and pulled off his shirt, then began to un-button hers. "I'll cheer you up," he whispered as he slipped off her blouse.

"How?" Oh God, she thought, just to be able to smile, to feel lighter inside.

"You'll see." He was unsnapping her waistband.

She had forgotten how sweet he could be, his touch as soft as his voice. She shivered as her skirt slid to her ankles.

"God, you're beautiful." He reached back to unfasten her bra. "I forgot how perfect you are." He dropped the bra onto their pile of clothes. She stood with her arms at her sides. He circled his finger around each breast. "Do you want me to stop?"

She shook her head. No.

He followed her into the bedroom, then stood over her talking as he removed the rest of his clothes. "I think about you all the time. I mean that. Even when I'm . . . even when I shouldn't be." He laughed as he lay next to her.

"Oh yah? What am I, the other woman in your fantasies?" she asked, and as she began to move against him she understood the immediate comfort Elizabeth must have known with George. There was no self-consciousness, nothing wrong or alarming about being with Todd again. Their bodies eased together.

"You *are* the woman." He looked down at her. "You always were," he said, lowering himself so that his smooth soft shoulders grazed hers.

"Then what happened?" She groaned, her eyes closing heavily as he rose and fell above her. She wanted to be taken someplace far, far away so that she didn't have to leave. So she could stay.

"I was a stupid ass." He almost sounded angry. His body began to pound against hers.

"And you're not anymore?" she gasped.

He didn't answer. His eyes were closed. Music was playing somewhere in the building. She could feel the deep thumping bass. His head arched back. His mouth gaped open. "Uh, uh, uh," he cried, then fell with a ragged panting whimper.

She stared at the diffusion of light on the windowshade. Beyond a distant affection she felt nothing. Nothing but complete self-disgust. She was a fool. Her days had been wasted in empty places, her energy spent on troubled people who could never love her. And to think that this may have been their greatest attraction sickened her.

She asked if he wanted a ride home now. When he didn't answer she realized he was asleep. He was snoring. She put on her robe and closed the bedroom door. In the kitchen she filled the kettle then put it on the stove for tea. There was a light tapping on her door. She turned, startled, afraid it might be Patrick, then assured herself he wouldn't risk coming here and being seen by her neighbors. It was probably Mrs. Terrill trying to locate the source of the music, which seemed even louder now. When she opened the door Rudy hurried inside. He'd been trying to call, he said, but her phone must be off the hook. He was glad she was still up. He had to see her before he went to the hospital tonight.

"But I told you not to," she whispered, trying to keep him by the door. "And I meant it."

"But I have to tell you what happened after you left."

"I don't want to hear it." She didn't need all the humiliating details.

"No, listen! I finally got Elizabeth to sit down and—"

"Shh," she said, moving to position herself in front of the strewn clothes.

"Oh. I'm sorry." He looked around the darkened room. "I woke you up, didn't I?" The softer he tried to speak the more agitated he became. His hands flew. "I'm sorry. I should have thought. You do, you look tired."

"Well I am. I'm tired. I'm too tired for anything right now." She reached for the doorknob.

He put his hand over hers. "But I might miss you in the morning. You'll be at work."

"So? What does it matter?"

"What do you mean, what does it matter? It's the most important thing I have to do right now! The most important thing I've ever had to do!"

"Shh!"

"What do you mean, shh?" He glanced at the closed bedroom door, and she froze. "It's all right," he said, smiling. "No one can hear us."

"It's late. Please," she said. "I don't feel very well. Will you please just go?"

He kissed her forehead. "Alright, but listen—Elizabeth knows. I told her. I told her everything." He tried to pull her close. "All we have to worry about now is each—" He looked stunned as she tugged back. She hit his arm and he let her go.

"Why did you do that?" She felt panicky. "What about my uncle? He said you wouldn't. He told you not to! Didn't he tell you I'm leaving?"

"No."

"Well I am! I'm going to Florida. I am. I'm leaving. I have to!"

"You're leaving? What do you mean? Why?" His chest seemed

sunken, his cheeks hollow, as if all the air were being sucked from his body.

"Because. Because I have to. I hate it here." Because another man's semen was leaking down the inside of her thighs. Because now her entire family despised her.

"What you hate is in here," he said, tapping his temple with his forefinger. "And that goes with you."

"Oh Jesus!"

"You know it's true." He reached for her hand, but she folded her arms and shrank back.

"Rudy, please go. Please! I'm really tired."

"What is it? What's wrong? Everything's going to be all right. Really!" He bent to kiss her, and she moved away. "All right." He nodded and tried to smile. "I'll talk to you tomorrow then." He opened the door, then turned quickly and came back in. He closed the door and stood looking down at her. "Look, whatever it is, I love you, Fiona," he said softly. "You know that, right? I'm so much in—" He glanced past her with a startled look as the bedroom door squealed open.

"Shit!" Todd said, standing there in his red silk bikini briefs. He stepped back and closed the door.

She shook her head. There was nothing to say, nothing at all.

"I'm sorry. I guess I misread all the signs," he said with a more discerning glance at the pooled clothing. "I didn't mean to. I'm sorry." He sighed.

"It's Todd," she said.

"Oh. Sure. Todd," he said, remembering and touching his forehead. "The butterfly bandage. The accident. The old boyfriend. The one that Patrick . . ."

She nodded.

"Looks like he's healed pretty well." He bit his bottom lip and glanced past her as if he expected Todd to return and verify this. "So is he the reason you're going to Florida?"

She shook her head.

"He's not going with you?"

"No. As a matter of fact, he's getting married too."

"I'm not getting married. You know I'm not."

"That's too bad. Husbands, those're the ones I like best."

"You think I believe that?"

"Well if you don't, you should," she said, opening the door.

"I love you, Fiona." He swallowed hard. "As pitiful as that may sound."

As soon as he was gone, Todd darted out of the bedroom. She sat on the arm of the chair, watching him dress. He stuffed his socks into his pocket and slipped his feet into his loafers, then with a muttered curse sat on the sofa and put on his socks, then his shoes.

"So I take it you're not spending the night," she said as he grabbed his jacket from the back of the chair. "Apparently no great flame has been rekindled here. Or at least, so it would appear."

"I better leave," he said with a sheepish wince.

"You don't have to."

"I gotta get back." He zipped his jacket.

"Get back where?" She wanted him to say it.

"Sandy," he said with a quick, guilty shrug. "She hates being alone, especially now."

"What do you mean, now? What's now?"

"Now that she's pregnant."

"Oh that's right. You're going to have a baby!"

"You knew that," he said warily.

"Yah!" she said with a bitter laugh and threw up her hands. "So what the hell was this all about?" she asked in an attempt at anger, indignation, censure, anything but this emptiness.

"I guess we just needed the same thing," he said, watching her.

"What?" she asked, fists clenched at her sides.

"To see if we're still as bad as we think we are."

"And are we?"

He shook his head sadly. "Tell you the truth, Fee, I think we've lost the touch."

Chapter 21

The day after Thanksgiving was the start of the Christmas shopping season and also the coffee shop's busiest day of the year. Breakfast had been crazy. There was a large coffee stain down the side of Fiona's uniform, her pockets sagged with tips, and she was exhausted. Rudy's words last night coursed through her mind, while everything about Todd seemed fuzzy and distant. But then, wasn't that how it always went the next day? What was done was done. No sense in beating herself up over what she couldn't change. Next time she'd . . . next time she'd what? Not bring him back to her apartment? Just take him in the car? No. There'd be no more next times because she was going to get the hell out of here and Dearborn as soon as she could. The hardest part would be telling Chester. She glanced up at the clock, hoping for at least a lull before the noon rush. At the moment, she only had one party, a family of eight. Good-natured and boisterous, they were on their way back to New York City after spending the holiday with their parents. One of the women had been in high school with Ginny and Jack. She remembered their younger sister, Elizabeth, but seemed confused as to who Fiona was.

"I know! I remember!" the dimple-cheeked woman said. "You're the . . . the . . ."

Slut. The bastard, Fiona was almost whispering.

". . . the cousin! The little cousin!"

Her acknowledgment was a weary nod. At the ring of the order bell she dragged into the kitchen. Chester was slicing white meat from one of the turkeys he had roasted early this morning. A huge pot of soup simmered on the stove.

"What the hell're you doing?" he demanded as she lifted the lid and took a deep breath of the fragrant steam.

"It's my turkey facial," she called back.

"You can't be doing that!" he said, gesturing her away with his knife. "Jesus Christ! One hair, that's all it takes, and the next thing you know I got the Board of Health in here trying to shut me down."

"One hair, huh?" she said, pretending to pluck a strand and dangle it over the broth. "Just give me the word, Chester, and I will set you free."

"Only if you can turn it into a pot of gold while you're at it."

"What about this?" She took the deposit slip from her pocket and showed it to him.

He whistled, then after a closer look whistled again. "What's that?"

"A payoff. It's what my family's paying to get rid of me."

He looked confused. "No, really. What's it for?"

"Really. That's what it's really for!" She stared dully at the slip. Twice this morning she'd come in here to the phone to call Rudy, but then couldn't be sure whether she'd be calling to say goodbye or to beg him to come with her. No matter how long or far she ran, she would always be trying to outdistance one person and one person only—Fiona Range. Rudy was right. What she hated most was her own weakness, her inability to see anything through to the end. And now, just when Patrick needed her most, here she was, only too ready to quit on him as well. If she left now she would end up like her mother, always running, never confronting her devils. "Twenty-five thousand." She sighed, crumpling the slip into her pocket. "I suppose I should be flattered. I mean, that's how valuable a pain in the ass they think I am."

"Hey, it's not bad work if you can get it."

She watched the wide, glinting blade cut thin, deft slices from the breast until he hit bone. "Well, for an adequate fee, you could be rid of me too!"

"You mean I been paying you every week now for how long to make my life miserable, when for the same money I could've just said, 'Go!'" He laughed.

"Exactly!"

The door swung open and Donna stuck her head through. "Fiona, your big party must want you. I keep hearing your name."

She gathered her orders and started for the door.

"Wait!" Chester hollered with a wave of the knife. "What do you mean, the money's to get rid of you? You're not gonna quit on me, are you?" he called, his face screwed up as if he might cry.

"I'll be right back." She backed into the noisy dining room balancing plates, two in her hands and one on each arm. She knew at once by the angled heads at the silent table, and the women's keen eyes, that the tale of Fiona Range had just been told in all its titillating detail. The husband in the maroon U. Mass. sweatshirt, who had been kidding her only moments ago, now asked sheepishly for more coffee. She went to the hotplate by the register where Maxine had just brewed two fresh pots. She glanced out the window as a faded blue station wagon went by. She stepped closer to see if it was Patrick, but the car had already turned the corner. She waited, staring out at the gray, sunless street. Two men hurried by in long dark coats, their conversation vapor in the air. Patrick's car should be coming by any minute now. If he stopped she would run out before he came in and caused a scene. She looked up at the clock. Two minutes passed. He had warned her himself to stay away. Uncle Charles had begged her to leave him alone, but how could she abandon Patrick now? They were so much alike; father and daughter, each fouling themselves so badly, so irreparably that they couldn't be loved. Because if they couldn't be loved, then they could never be hurt. Three minutes. It must not have been him, she decided, with a deep sigh of relief.

There was a blast of cold, damp air as the front door opened and two women entered carrying shopping bags. Maxine and Donna leaned over a booth, visiting with Scotty from the gift shop across the street, so Fiona grabbed menus and started to lead the women to a table in back. Maxine looked up and gestured to the table by the window. That's where she wanted the ladies in their glistening fur coats to sit, right up front where everyone could see them. The door began to open and close on a steady stream of customers until every seat was taken. Three parties waited by the register.

Fiona was pouring the coffee at the long table when she heard a noise in the kitchen. It was a sound of such strange urgency that she stared at the kitchen door.

"Hey!" one of the men cried, jerking back in his chair. "Look what you're doing!"

"I'm sorry," she mumbled, righting the pot as the brown puddle dripped over the saucer, streaming to the edge of the table. "I'll be right back." She hurried into the kitchen.

A man in dark clothes darted behind the pantry shelves.

"Patrick!" she gasped as he lunged from the end of the workbench. He grabbed her wrist. His fingers dug into her flesh. There was blood on her arm. She thought his nails had punctured her skin, until she saw the gash down his arm. He was bleeding. There was a knife in his other hand. The long wide blade was streaked with blood. He kept grunting the same sounds, over and over.

"What is it?" she asked, thinking he'd been hurt. "What do you want?"

His face met hers, answering not in a voice but a low, dark rendering of such pain and outrage that not a single syllable was discernible. He's speaking another language, she thought, as the knife fell so close to her foot that a cold spatter hit her ankle. All she could do was say his name as he pulled her toward the back door, yanking her arm to force each step. Her mind fixed on peculiar details, though none seemed connected. The workbench was covered with gleaned bones, dark meat and white not just mixed but bloodied. There was a turkey carcass on the floor. A tray lay against the door of the walk-in cooler. The floor was wet and slippery. Slimy, brittle shells cracked underfoot. The bowl of eggs from the workbench was upside down on the floor. There were smashed eggs everywhere. Some of the yolks were still whole and shimmering.

"Where's Chester? What did you do? Oh my God!" she cried, looking down.

He sat slumped on the floor against the oven door, his chin deep in a bib of scarlet stain with his head dangling so far forward she understood at once the horror of Patrick's deed. He shoved her out the back door, then into his car through the driver's side. Holding on to her, he climbed in and started the engine. She pleaded with him to let her go, but even as he backed out of the alley and turned on squealing tires he still gripped her wrist. The old station wagon rattled and creaked as he sped up Chestnut Street. Blood glistened on his whiskered cheek.

"What happened, Patrick? What did you do? Tell me, please tell me," she begged.

"I said I had to see you, but he kept saying, 'Get out! Get out! Just get out!' He had a knife, but I just kept going. I never said a word," he panted. "I never laid a hand on him. But he went and jumped me."

"He jumped you?" she said, trying to grasp hold of the words floating through this nightmare as randomly as all the other debris, street signs, tree trunks, and house clapboards now flashing past the window.

"He jumped me from behind and he shouldn't have done that. He never should have done that," he insisted in a high, wheezy, tear-torn voice. "I tried not to lose it. I tried not to, God damn him! I tried. I really tried, but he went and jumped me!"

"He shouldn't have jumped you," she said, watching the young woman ahead with two beagles on red leashes. The woman had long black hair. It was a day like any other. It was all so ordinary. An elderly man and woman were rolling trash barrels down their driveway. Nothing bad could possibly happen. "He shouldn't have done that," she said.

"No, I know," he agreed as he turned onto Ridge Street. He was speeding down the rutted, winding road. The entire car vibrated. He let go of her to drive with both hands on the wheel. "I just wanted to talk to you. I kept calling, but it was always busy, so finally I called him. I called Hollis, that no-good son of a bitch thinks he can run my life forever. 'Let her go,' he kept saying. 'Let her go, Patrick. I beg you.' But I told him, I told him straight out. 'No way,' I said. Not anymore. Uh-uh. From now on it's me! I'm calling the shots!" He looked at her.

"From now on I say how it's gonna be, not him! Me!" he said, thumping his breast.

"What do you mean?" she asked numbly.

"I'm gonna take care of you. I promise."

"Patrick," she said, but the car skidded on the curve, and he muttered angrily. A light snow had begun to fall. It coated the windshield.

". . . get the hell out, that's what we're gonna do," he was muttering as he peered over the wheel.

"Maybe he's all right. It probably looks worse than it is," she said and tried to close her eyes against the dreadful vision of Chester's dangling head.

"He's dead!" He glanced at her with a laugh of disbelief. "He's fucking dead! Oh Jesus Christ," he groaned, punching the side of his head. "What happened? What the hell happened? What, what, what, what, what goes on in this fucking head of mine?"

"He jumped you. We'll tell them what happened. I'll help you explain it," she said. "He shouldn't have jumped you. He had a knife and you were startled. You got scared. It was like some kind of flashback, like Vietnam. Like everything that happened there, only all over again. It's not like you went in intending to hurt anyone. I mean, you were a hero. Everyone knows that."

He looked at her and laughed. The exit was ahead. He pulled abruptly into the right lane.

"Patrick, I'm not going with you. I don't want to! Let me out, please?"

"No, you're just scared, but it's going to be all right! I promise! I love you, Fiona," he said with a smile so wide and wet she could feel it in her stomach.

"But I don't. I don't love you, Patrick. I'm sorry, I don't."

He swerved into the breakdown lane, then stopped with the motor running. He held on to her arm.

"You know I don't," she said. "Not that way, not the way you want. That's sick! Don't you understand? I feel sick to my stomach every time you say that." The car rocked as traffic whizzed by, sleeting the windows with dirty slush.

"Why? Why can't you love me?"

"You know why. Because of our relationship."

"We don't have a fucking relationship!" He pounded the wheel. "Do you understand? Do you? Do you?" he demanded, his voice so wracked with frustration and rage she was afraid to answer. To agree or argue right now could be catastrophic. And yet she sensed that her fear gave him solace and strength, that in spite of his own panic it fueled his resolve. He put his hand on the back of her neck, and she stared back at him. "If I tell you who your father is then there'll be nothing in the way. Then you can love me the way I love you." He pulled her face close, his breath hot on her eyes.

"Don't," she gasped, struggling to turn her head as he moved even closer. "Please don't."

"Don't what? Don't tell you? Why? Because you already know? You do, don't you? You know it's him." Eyes glittering, he regarded her terror with a chilling, gleeful intensity. "Your uncle Charles," he said, pressing against her, his beery breath sour on her mouth.

"No!" she cried, recoiling as her brain exploded with odd images and inexplicable phrases. "That's ridiculous," she was saying as he closed his eyes and kissed her. He clutched her hand against his chest. The front of his shirt was wet and sticky. The smell, dark and metallic, as familiar as foreign: blood, Chester's blood. Her stomach heaved and she pushed him, gagging. He reached out and she hit his arm. Muttering, he threw the car into gear and squealed into traffic, heedless of the honking horns.

"He can tell you himself. That's what we'll do then," he panted as if warning her. "I'll let him tell you."

The car rattled loudly as he drove over the metal-gridded bridge into Collerton. He turned onto Essex Street. She was shocked and relieved when she realized his destination was the courthouse. An outburst there would be mortifying, but at least she'd be safe. Chester's body had surely been discovered by now. The police were probably already at the courthouse waiting for Patrick. As he turned into the parking lot, she expected to see a line of cruisers, but there were only cars, all white with the gently falling snow. The security guard opened the door of his square hut and peered out. Recognizing Patrick, he smiled and waved them through before ducking back inside. Of course, she thought, no one knew what he had done, that he had struck with such savagery as to have nearly severed Chester's head, that the smudge on his cheek, like the stain on his shirt, was not mud or oil but blood. No one knew, no one but her.

Gripping her arm, Patrick slid over the seat after her, then steered her across the lot. Theirs were the only footprints through the fast-falling snow. She wasn't wearing a jacket over her uniform. She was shivering, but instead of cold she only felt numb. She was acutely aware of everything around her, even the most random detail, though it was all happening beyond her realm. She was her own witness. Her senses were sapping her will. Because fear's bouquet is as sharp as it is deadening, she could see, smell, hear, feel, even taste more keenly than ever before. But she was powerless.

"Here!" He nudged her down the slippery well of subground stairs that led to a wide metal door at the rear of the old brick building. He tried to turn the knob, but it was locked.

"Patrick, what's the point? Why don't we . . ."

"What's the point?" he muttered, fumbling a ring of keys from his pocket. "I'm going to show you the fucking point." He inserted one in the lock. The door creaked open into a musty dimness. Praying for someone to emerge from the shadows, she held her breath as he pushed her through the narrow, low-ceilinged basement. Surely they'd see her terror, his wild gleaming eyes. They passed the clanging furnace room, then storage rooms piled high with bulging tan and gray cardboard file boxes.

"Hey, Patrick," a redheaded man in dark blue pants and shirt called from his work cubicle. He was clamping a glued leg back onto a battered oak chair. "You're back!"

"Yah, you goddamn creep," Patrick muttered under his breath, pushing her along.

"Wait!" she tried to call back, struggling to turn. "Please . . ."

"No! No!" Patrick grunted, butting his body into hers to move her around the corner. "Don't! Don't!" he warned, leaning so hard against her that her spine dug into the cinder-block wall. "Don't make me do that. Don't make me hurt anyone. I've got a gun, and I swear I'll use it," he said, reaching behind to his waistband. "I will. You do know that, right?"

She nodded.

"So be quiet. That's all, just be quiet now, real, real quiet," he whispered as they climbed the rear stairs, their footsteps up the metal treads tolling the dull, hollow *clung, clung, clung* of a cracked bell.

At the first landing she turned toward the stairs to her uncle's office on the next floor.

"Keep going," he grunted, opening the door, then guiding her down the long, noisy corridor. People huddled in clumps of two and three, most too preoccupied to glance her way. Look at me! her brain screamed. Can't you see what's happening here? Desperate to catch someone's eye, she stared at each face, then realized how futile it was. His shirt was dark enough to camouflage the blood, and a shivering bare-armed waitress merited little notice by people whose own calamities were so near at hand.

"The next one," he said. All along the way small numbered signs jutted like metal flags above each frosted-glass door. They stopped at Courtroom 114. She recognized the clear, strong voice that rose and fell behind the closed door.

"No!" She balked, pulling back. "They're in session."

"He'll call a recess."

"No!"

"Go on in." He reached past her to open the door.

It was one of the larger courtrooms. Most of the seats were taken. The bailiff glanced over his shoulder as they entered, then gave Patrick a quick nod. They paused in back. A muscular young man in a tweed sports coat and sharply creased chinos stood before Judge Hollis with head bowed and hands folded. He looked to be in his late teens. The balding, portly lawyer at his side was Will Canty, an old friend of her uncle's. Everyone in the first row appeared to be members of the young man's family. Well-dressed and neatly groomed, they gave the Judge their somber and most respectful attention, glancing sadly now and again at their censured relative to nod or frown with one or another of the Judge's admonishments.

If her uncle had seen her enter with Patrick, he gave no indication of it. Black-robed and tall on his elevated bench, he was a striking presence with his pure white hair and robust coloring.

He couldn't possibly be her father. It was beyond the ken that he would ever allow anything in his life to spin so much out of control and come to this. No. Not him. Not that kind and decent man who had always forgiven her, no matter her sins. But he wouldn't now. Not this time. This time she had overstepped the last bounds, and now the monster she had created would devour them all. She listened intently as if her uncle's earnest eloquence might somehow pry loose this frenzied grip from her arm.

The young man had been charged with breaking and entering in the nighttime and vandalism. There was a smashed sign on a gas station roof, broken skylights, and lubricating grease poured over a computer keyboard. Her uncle asked the young man what made him think he could take or ruin what belonged to someone else.

"I don't know, Your Honor," the young man said. "I guess I just had too much to drink."

"Is that your excuse?"

"No, sir."

"I would hope not, Jared, because there is no excuse or entitlement that allows such actions. This is a society of laws, a society where order must prevail," her uncle said sternly, though she could tell he felt badly for this young man and his shamed family. If she closed her eyes he might be speaking to her.

The bailiff turned then and whispered that they had to sit down if they wanted to stay.

"We need to see the Judge," Patrick said in a low, edgy voice.

"He'll be done pretty soon," the bailiff said.

Fiona stared back with widened, pleading eyes.

"No. No, I gotta see him now. Right now," Patrick said.

Uncle Charles leaned over the bench with clasped hands, all zeal and concern focused on this errant youth. "Life will be a lot simpler for you, Jared, once you accept the hard, but, in the end, quite easy fact that there is right and there is wrong. I know it's fashionable nowadays to call everything that's off balance and in between the gray area. But it's not gray, it's just moral blindness." Her uncle slipped on his glasses, then looked up with a start. His mouth gaped. Fiona could only stare back, unblinkingly culpable and desperate.

"Come on now, Patrick," the bailiff quietly urged. He started to put his hand on Patrick's arm.

"No!" Patrick said. Heads turned. The bailiff paused, glancing between Uncle Charles and Patrick.

"Excuse me," Uncle Charles said to the young man, then looked to the back of the courtroom. "Why don't you go up to my chambers, Patrick? I'll be there shortly." He closed a file, then leaned forward to speak to the young man.

"We don't have time!" Patrick called. "She needs to see you. Now! Right now!"

Her uncle stood. The officer in the front of the courtroom had been walking slowly toward them. When he was a few feet away, the bailiff went to touch Patrick's arm again.

"Don't!" Patrick snarled.

"Patrick, please!" Fiona said.

"Get out of my fucking way!" Patrick bellowed.

"Oh my God," a woman gasped, and people cringed in their seats.

"That's all right," her uncle said, hurrying down the three steps from the bench. "Everything's all right. Nothing to worry about. We'll just need some time here. There's been a misunderstanding, that's all." His voice was low and reassuring as he moved closer. "So we'll be adjourning this session for the rest of the day, Tom," he told the shocked court officer. "It's a misunderstanding, that's all."

"Are you sure, Your Honor?" the court officer said.

Her uncle pushed open the door. "We can go up to my—"

"You come with us," Patrick ordered him. The astonished bailiff asked if this was all right, and the Judge assured him it was. He'd be right back.

Moving quickly along the busy corridor, Fiona kept pace between the two men. Her arm was wet under Patrick's hold. Sweat ran down his temples.

Still in his judicial robe, her uncle walked with the file under his arm. "Good morning . . . Hello, Jim . . . Attorney Danisch . . . Good morning," he quietly answered his colleagues' amazed stares at this outrageous breach of judicial decorum, especially by one so demanding of it.

They hurried down the rear stairs, then along the same dim passage to the back door. Any minute now she expected voices to bear down, ordering them to stop, but they were already opening the heavy metal door and climbing the snowy steps to the parking lot.

"Are you all right?" her uncle asked, his hand at her elbow.

She nodded and looked away, ashamed. The snow fell faster now, the flakes bigger and wetter as they hit her face. Patrick ordered her uncle behind the wheel, then pushed her into the backseat with him.

"Start the car!" Patrick said.

"Now, Patrick." Her uncle sighed, putting a black-robed arm over the seat and looking back. "We can talk here as well as anywhere else. There's no sense in driving when the roads are—"

"Start the car. I said, start it! Come on! Start it!" Patrick demanded.

"The roads are going to be very slippery, Patrick," her uncle said in his most reasonable tone.

"Fuck the roads! If you don't get us out of here I'll blow your fucking head off!"

"What? You mean you have a gun?" her uncle said, starting the car. He glanced in disbelief through the rearview mirror. She nodded.

"Yah, I do," Patrick said, as the bald wheels rolled crunching over the snow, past the white-shrouded security shack. Inside, the guard hunched over a newspaper.

"Where on earth did you get it, Patrick? Do you have a license?" Uncle Charles asked, as he turned the corner slowly onto Essex Street.

"Jesus Christ! Are you serious?" Patrick said with a squeal of laughter that razored up Fiona's spine. "That's good, Judge. That's really, really good!"

"You don't need a gun to talk to me, you know that," her uncle said.

"Yah, well it's not me that wants to talk, Charlie." He nudged her leg with his. "Go ahead, ask him. Ask him!"

Eyes downcast, Fiona shook her head. She was numb, nothing but dead weight in this raging current. He nudged her again, insisting she ask. "No," she whispered.

"Patrick, look, why don't—," her uncle began.

"Shut up! You just shut the fuck up!" Patrick shouted, pointing at him.

Her uncle's mouth opened and closed. His face was blood-red. He looked only at Patrick. She was mortified, not for herself but for this man who in kindness had raised her, receiving little in return but trouble and shame.

"It's me you're mad at, Patrick, so why—," her uncle started to say.

"No!" Patrick roared. "I'm not mad. I just hate your fucking guts, that's all!" He sat back, smiling as he took her hand and squeezed it.

"All right then, it's me you want to hurt, so look," Uncle Charles said, putting on the directional. "Why don't I just stop and we'll let Fiona get out, then you and I can work things out."

She kept trying to catch his eye in the mirror to shake her head no. He had no idea what had just happened to Chester. She wouldn't leave him alone with this madman.

"No, you fucking phony asshole, you!" Patrick roared, laughing. "I want her to hear it from you. That's why she's here. So you can tell her."

"I don't think Fiona feels very well, Patrick. I think she needs some rest. Why don't we drop her off? That way you and I can talk, and then we'll get her later."

Patrick doubled forward and stamped his feet with feigned hilarity. "She'll get all the rest she needs—after," he said, springing forward. He jammed his fist into the back of her uncle's neck. "After you tell her the truth. Turn there! Get up on Four ninety-five." He pointed to the exit sign ahead. Peering, her uncle leaned over the wheel. Only one wiper worked. Even at full speed it couldn't keep the windshield clear. The car shimmied as they turned onto the exit ramp, and she prayed for a breakdown.

After only a few miles they got off the highway. They seemed to be heading toward the outlying section of Dearborn where Patrick lived.

But now, after a series of quick turns ordered by Patrick, they were entering the Dearborn Industrial Park.

"In there!" Patrick said when they came to the Millstone Corporation sign. It was a large tan building of glass and stone. Patrick directed Uncle Charles through the half-filled parking lot, then around the back of the plant, past loading docks, now down a narrow paved road that provided access to two large blue Dumpsters. The road seemed to end at the woods where a reflector-studded chain was stretched between two concrete posts. Here the snow lay undisturbed and unsanded. The tires whirred and the car began to slide. "Slow down," Patrick yelled, and Uncle Charles hit the brake hard. The car spun in a half circle. Fiona watched her uncle in the mirror as Patrick shouted for him to straighten it out. He had deliberately gone too fast. He had tried to get the car stuck in the deep gully along the side of the road. Now she saw fear in his darting eyes, as if he knew exactly where they were and how this would end. When he looked back she wanted to tell him how sorry she was for this and for all the pain she had caused him, but he was staring at Patrick.

"We can talk better here now, can't we, Judge?" Patrick sighed, leaning forward.

"Patrick, let her go. Please," her uncle begged.

"Oh, we're all gonna go, but first Fiona wants to know who her father is, that's all." He shrugged. "Simple enough, huh?"

Jaw clenched and grim, her uncle turned back.

"Tell her, you hypocrite, you fucking phony!" Patrick bellowed at the back of his unmoving head. "All right then, get out." When her uncle had gotten out of the car, Patrick told him to remove one end of the chain from the post.

She watched him trudge through the swirling snow in his narrow English wing tips, his stiff white collar high above the black robe that was blowing around his knees. After the chain was lifted, he got back in and righted the car. He drove a little way past the posts, then got out, as Patrick directed, and rehung the chain across the road. Her uncle's breath seemed labored as he climbed back into the car.

"Do you feel all right, Uncle Charles?" she asked as the car inched over the snow.

"Don't call him that!" Patrick exploded with a slap on the back of her uncle's head. The car stopped and Uncle Charles started to turn around. "Keep driving, you bastard! You fucking no-good, phony bastard!" Patrick screamed until the car began to move again. Patrick told him to follow the road up into the woods.

"Where are we going?" Fiona asked Patrick. Her teeth were chattering. She was afraid of what he might do if she spoke to her uncle again.

"Tell her," Patrick said, grinning.

"We won't get far," her uncle warned, inching along the old logging road that from here on in was narrow and unpaved, and now with drifting snow, treacherous.

"We'll just go as far as we can then. Hell, I mean, isn't that what we've been doing all this time anyway?" he said.

"Why, Patrick?" Uncle Charles suddenly cried in a pained voice. "What good will it do?"

"A lot. Because I love Fiona, but, you see, we got this . . . complication. She thinks I'm her father. No matter what I say, she won't believe me, so I want you to tell her the truth so we can be together, so we can go someplace and get away from here."

Too ashamed to look at her uncle, she averted her eyes.

"I already told her," Patrick continued. "But now you have to tell her. So go ahead, tell her! Tell her!" he said with a swipe at the back of her uncle's head, a gesture almost infantile in its feebleness, but for the hatred twisting his scarred face.

He stopped the car and shifted into park. They were surrounded by whiteness. Tree branches sagged under the heavy wet snow. Her uncle looked back, glaring. "And then what, Patrick? What else?" he asked, his voice trembling with outrage and disdain.

This seemed to calm Patrick. He smiled and fell silent for a moment. "That's all," he finally answered. "That's all I want."

"And what happens to Fiona then?" her uncle asked.

"She's coming with me. I'm going to take care of her." She felt her insides sink as Patrick put his arm around her shoulder and pulled her close. "So tell her. Tell her you're not her uncle. That you're her father. Tell her, Charlie. Come on. That's all I want. That's all you have to say."

Afraid to cross Patrick and unable to look at her uncle, Fiona sat with her head bent.

"I'm not asking for any of the shitty details," Patrick said. "All I want is—"

"Is that true, Fiona?" her uncle asked in that all-too-familiar tone of incredulity and disgust. "Do you love him?"

"Tell her!" Patrick demanded before she could answer. "Tell her! Tell her!"

"You forced her here, didn't you? Just like you forced me. It's not the truth we're here for, is it? Because you don't really want that, do you, Patrick? Think about it. How could you? How could you possibly? No. This is my punishment, isn't it? To watch you hurt Fiona. To watch you defile her. Well it's not going to happen. I won't let you. Not her. Not here. No! You'll have to kill me first!" He threw the car into reverse. He couldn't turn, so he was trying to back down the way they'd come. Patrick roared at him to stop. The wheels spun and the car fishtailed, then slid sideways off the road down into the gully, coming to rest against a thicket of snow-bent branches. Uncle Charles continued to shift frantically from drive to reverse, trying to get traction, but the treadless tires only spun and spun and spun with a high, sickening whine.

"Get out!" Patrick said, clambering from the tilted car. He reached back for Fiona, her resistance futile as he dragged her out by her ankle and wrist. Coins jingled and rolled down her leg, making holes in the snow. "Now you!" he ordered her uncle, who followed quickly when he saw her outside.

Her teeth chattered as she hugged her bare arms against the snow. Patrick paced back and forth, his frantic demand that Hollis admit paternity sounding childish and hysterical here on this abandoned road in the middle of a snowstorm.

"Have you thought this through, Patrick? To its logical conclusion? To the end?" her uncle asked.

"Yes!" he said, suddenly embracing Fiona so tightly that she could only bow her head. "Of course I have. We both have."

"No! No!" she cried, trying to push him away. She jammed her elbow into his side and ran to her uncle. "I'm sorry. I'm so sorry." She tried to tell him that she had never wanted anything like this to happen. "I should have listened. I know that n—"

Patrick grabbed for her. Turning, she backhanded his face with such force that he staggered sideways and caught himself on the car. His face was so tight with rage and anguish as he came toward her that his eyes seemed to bulge out of his head.

"Leave me alone!" she screamed, terrified by his seething torment. "I'm not going with you. Do you hear me? I don't want you near me. Don't touch me! I hate you! I hate you!" she cried as he seized her arm.

"Get your hands off her!" her uncle demanded, pulling at him, and with that, Patrick swung and hit him in the belly. Her uncle doubled over, then sank to his knees, bracing himself with his hands in the snow.

"Bastard. No-good bastard," Patrick muttered and kicked him in the side with a sickening thud, continuing to kick with each outburst. "She was just a kid, like me. That's all she was. Just a kid and you fucked her. You had everything, you bastard. You had a wife and kids, but you didn't care, did you, you bastard. You had to take away the one thing I had, the only girl I ever had. I loved her, and you ruined it! You ruined her! You ruined everything. You took away my whole life, you sniveling bastard, you . . ."

Her uncle gasped as he struggled to stand. He looked up and his eyes rolled. He needed help, but she couldn't move, didn't dare because everything had become blurred and distant. There is a sound snow makes as it falls through trees. Unnoticed, the sound is soft, barely a whisper, until it is listened to, and then one hears each flake after flake against every branch, needle, and leaf, and the falling whiteness becomes a rush that grows to such a steady, deafening roar that there is no boundary, no definition left between earth and sky.

"I loved her," Patrick was shouting. "No matter what happened to me, I knew she was there waiting. And then when I came home, everything was different. I couldn't believe it. She'd bleached her hair. She was gonna have a baby any minute. It tore me apart, but I went with her when she had it. He didn't, the bastard, but I did! I did! Because I loved her!" he insisted, staring. "She was the only girl I ever loved. Until you."

Helpless, Fiona shook her head. There was nothing to say. Not a word, not a single word existed for this moment, for such a revelation. The pulsing stillness pressed against her breastbone. What irresistible madness had brought them here? Whose sin? He kept saying her name. Fiona. Fiona. Fiona. She backed away.

"I'll take care of you. I will. I swear, I always will," he whispered. His icy hand gripped her arm.

No. No. No. No, she answered each lure, but he was already leading her to the woods. He would show her. She would know. She would finally know. She would know everything.

"Don't go, Fiona!" Charles Hollis pleaded, holding his side as he struggled to stand up. "Don't go with him!"

His hobbled footsteps followed, scrambling to keep pace, crunching the crisp leaves under the new snow. The line of spindly pines on the high ridge signaled their destination. Her wet uniform stuck to her back. Staggering close behind, Hollis panted with exertion and pain. Here, the overgrown road steepened, narrowing to the width of a path. She followed Patrick as he climbed the ridge with so little effort that he was suddenly at the top waiting. Halfway up, her foot exposed a streak of ice and she slipped back down on all fours. Hollis made it to her side as she was getting up.

"He doesn't know what he's doing," he said.

"I know," she said.

"Listen to me!" he gasped, holding his chest. "He's crazy! He's out of his mind!"

She nodded. "He killed Chester."

"No. Oh my God, no," he groaned, looking wildly around. "The quarry. You can't go up there. Come on. Run. We can get back down . . ."

"He'll just come after us," she said, amazed he would think they could get away.

"I'm waiting! Get up here!" Patrick bellowed, starting toward them. "Don't make me come all the way back down there!"

"If we hurry . . . ," Hollis started to say as she began the slippery ascent again, grabbing branches and saplings to hoist herself along. Patrick stopped, waiting until she reached him. She followed him to the ridge, then a hundred yards farther until they were looking down into the quarry, its black stillness barely marred by the pelting snow. This was the highest point, the drop from here at least sixty feet. The sheer granite walls below had only a few jagged ledges wide enough for any accumulation of snow.

"She's down there," Patrick said so calmly she merely glanced at him.

Hollis's panting grunts grew louder as he approached them.

"In her car," Patrick continued. "In the trunk. I put her in the trunk, after. I didn't know what else to do." He closed his eyes and shook his head.

"Why?"

"It wasn't the baby. That wasn't it. She was supposed to put it up for adoption. They wanted her to, him and Arlene, but then she changed her mind. She wouldn't. She refused, and they were so mad. 'Alright,' I said, 'let's get married then.' I told her it was all right. I could handle it. I'd take care of her. But she said no, she couldn't. She said they'd given her money to go away. They wanted her to move someplace else so people wouldn't know she'd had her sister's husband's baby. Ten thousand dollars. It's all down there with her in a blue shoebox. She brought it in to show me. I begged her not to go. She had to, she said. She got up and said she was going to go pick up the baby. I told her I'd go with her then. It didn't matter to me as long as we were together. She started to cry and she kept saying no, I couldn't, and I kept telling her yes, yes, yes, I could. 'I have to,' I said. And then she said she didn't love me anymore. She said it was him she loved. Her brother-in-law. Her own sister's husband. That's why she couldn't stay, and that's why she couldn't give her baby away, and that's why she had to be honest and tell me she didn't love me.

"'I don't care,' I said. 'I love you,' I kept trying to tell her, but she wouldn't listen. That's all I wanted, for her to listen, but she kept trying to get away. My hands were on her neck, and then she was dead. So I put her in the car and drove it up here and pushed it over. It went down fast. And then it was over. Everything. The whole rest of my life. It was just over."

Fiona was backing away, but he hadn't yet noticed.

"Fiona," Hollis said.

"She's down there," she told him numbly. She pointed to the quarry, but he looked only at her. "She's in the trunk of her car," she said.

He stared, blank-faced and unmoving, his shock and loss, she realized, surely greater than hers, for having known Natalie. And, if it was true, for having loved her. All color had drained from his cheeks, paling his flesh to the whiteness of his hair, of the snow that fell heavier now, and faster, coming at them slantwise, almost horizontal with the gusting wind. He was trembling, his beautiful blue eyes now dulled to gray, like clouding ice. "I'm sorry," he choked. "I'm so sorry."

She nodded.

"So what do we do now?" Patrick said, facing them, arms folded, his back to the quarry.

"Let's go back down," she said.

"I'm talking to you, Judge!" Patrick said sharply. "What are we supposed to do now?"

"I don't know," Hollis said wearily as he continued to shake his head.

He is. He's in shock, she thought, watching the realization of Natalie's death overtake and empty him.

"Well, we can't keep pretending, can we? Can we?" Patrick shouted, his voice breaking when he got no answer.

Hollis shook his head.

"You should've let me tell them when I wanted to. But then I'd've never gotten to know Fiona." Patrick looked at her. "I even thought about trying to be who you wanted, but then I'd see you and it'd be her all over again. You sound just like her. You got that same scratchy kind of laugh. You even walk like her." He touched her cheek with the back of his hand while Hollis looked on. "I love you." He held her chin, forcing her to look at him. His eyes closed as he kissed her.

Even holding her breath, she could smell Chester's blood. It seemed to come from his mouth.

"Hold me," he whispered and put his arms around her. "Please hold me. Just for a minute. Please, Fiona. Fiona," he pleaded as she stood rigidly against him. Then, remembering the gun, she raised her hand to the small of his back and drew it slowly across his waist. If there had been a gun it wasn't there now. She pulled away.

"You're freezing," he said. "Here." He took off his flannel shirt and slipped it over her shoulders.

Chester's blood was damp on her breast. "We better go back down now," she said, expecting him to lunge at her.

He nodded.

"Are you coming?" She was afraid to turn her back on him.

He didn't answer.

"The snow's getting really bad. You can't stay up here." She stepped away.

He turned and walked to the rim of the quarry, standing so close the toes of his boots stuck over the edge.

"Patrick," she said, so afraid of startling him she could barely utter the words. "Please. Don't. Don't do that. We'll help you. My . . . the Judge and I, we will, we'll help you." She looked entreatingly at Hollis. "Tell him. Tell him you'll help him. Please!" she begged as Patrick's body curled, tensing forward so that he almost seemed to be teetering. "Say something!" she begged, shaking Hollis's arm. "Please! Please!" She shook her head in disbelief. "What's wrong with you? How can you just stand there?"

Patrick turned then with dazzling wet eyes. He almost seemed to be smiling. "Tell her. Tell her, Charlie. Tell her what you told me. Because it's the same thing, isn't it?" He looked at Fiona now. "She was down there two years and I couldn't take it anymore. I was going out of my mind, so I went to his office and told him they could stop looking for her. I told him everything, where she was and what I did. I said how I couldn't live with it anymore, knowing what I did, knowing she was down there. 'I don't care what happens,' I said, 'I just gotta get it all straight.' And he said, 'But now, Patrick, what's the point?' That's what you said, right, Charlie? That's it exactly, right? 'What's the point of going to the cops?' you said. 'Nothing's going to change,' you said. 'Nothing'll be different. Natalie'll still be dead. It'll just ruin everything for everybody.' That's what you said, right?"

"I said I'd help you, and I tried," Hollis said quietly.

"But you didn't try hard enough, Charlie!" he bellowed, pointing down at him. "And now look. Everything's ruined! Every fucking thing for everybody! And it's all your fault! Not mine! You're the one! It started with you!"

"What do you want, Patrick? Tell me what you want."

As Fiona backed away, each step brought her closer to the terrible reality of his deed. All those years. He had known all those years. Day after day, keeping at arm's length not the troublesome bastard niece but the vile product of his deadly sin. He had denied her not only parents, but sisters and a brother as well.

"I want you to keep trying to help me, Charlie. C'mere. C'mere and help me some more. Come on," Patrick urged with sad quizzical wonder as if, even now, he were marveling at the breadth of his own impotence when measured against a stronger man's desperate frailty. "Help me! Help me! Help me!" he cried.

She turned and ran down the snowy hill. The same anchoring saplings and branches now stung her face and arms as she thrashed past them. "My God, my God, my God," she was panting when she got to the car, snow-covered and tipped into the culvert. Arms folded, she stood waiting. A few minutes passed—days, weeks, years—before a dark figure emerged from the curtain of snow, making his way down the hill.

"Fiona, it's all right," he gasped, hand at his chest. "Everything's going to be all right."

"Where's Patrick?" She looked past him. "Is he coming? He is, isn't he? Isn't he?"

"Fiona, listen to me. There was no stopping him. I tried, but he was out of his mind. He just kept raving. He wouldn't listen to me."

"What happened?"

"I tried to stop him."

"What do you mean?"

"He jumped."

"You pushed him, didn't you? He wanted you to, and you did, didn't you?"

"No!"

"You're such a liar. He said you knew. All this time you knew she was down there."

"Fiona, listen—"

"All those years, and you never said anything."

"He was crazy, Fiona," he insisted, his face so close there was no snow or trees, only the blue vastness of those eyes. "I tried to help. I always did, but he hated me."

"Of course he did! It was your secret balancing his."

"My secret? My God, Fiona! You don't believe anything he said, do you? He was out of his mind. He just killed a man!"

"But he was telling the truth. I know he was."

"No!"

"He told me the truth, but you can't. You're a liar. You've always been a liar. Every day, everything that happened, every moment between us, it was all a lie!"

"Fiona, listen. I need your help. Please. We can do this. Please! I beg you," he groaned.

"We can do what? Keep on living this lie?" Her hair stood on end. "What will you do when I tell the truth? Will you call me a liar?"

"Fiona, listen to me. I'll always take care of you. I promise."

"Always?" She couldn't help smiling. "The way you took care of Patrick?"

"Please, Fiona, it's not just me. Think of your aunt Arlene."

"Did she know?" she asked, pointing toward the quarry. "Well did she?"

"No, not about that."

"No, she knew. Oh, maybe she never knew for sure, because she never wanted to, but in her way she knew. She had to. She knew my mother was dead."

"No! No, I swear she didn't. How can you say that? She's been so good to you."

"Really? Then what the hell was she thinking every time I called you uncle? Was she thinking of me and how apart, how different I always felt from everyone?"

He closed his eyes and seemed to shudder. "This will destroy her. Do you understand? It'll be the end of everything."

"It already is."

"No! No, don't you see? No one has to know but us. Please, Fiona. I've tried to be a good man. I've tried. My God, you know I have. I never shirked my responsibility. I did the right thing. I raised you and took care of you."

"Isn't that wonderful! You raised me!"

"I was good to you. I was!" His voice broke.

She stared at him. He actually believed it. "But Uncle Charles, don't you see? It was all bullshit, just bullshit. That's all it ever was."

"But not anymore. We'll get through this. I promise. We will!" He tried to hug her, but she pushed him away.

"We will?"

"Yes, as long as we're honest with each other."

"No. As long as I'm your screwup niece, right? Crazy Fiona, always trying to tear the wonderful Hollis family apart? The slut? Oh, she's just like her mother, isn't she? And poor Judge Hollis. He's such a good man, such a goddamn good man, you son of a bitch, you." She hit his chest. "You're my father. My father! Tell me you're my father! Tell me!"

He shook his head.

"Why can't you say it? Why?"

His mouth opened and closed. "It was the worst thing I've ever done," he finally gasped.

"But it was me who's paid the price all these years. Not you. Me!"

He covered his face with his hands. His shoulders quaked, but he made no sound at all. There was nothing she could do, nothing she felt like doing. Nothing but watch him grow smaller and weak. His spine curved, bending him so far forward that for the rest of his days he could not see the sky, just the ground, and only that shadowed portion nearest him.

The world would know that he was her father. Patrick's body would be located the following spring. Though it would take a few days more, the old rusted car would be dredged up in a creaking disgorgement of mud as the enormous crane swung it onto dry ground. And just as Patrick had said, there in its trunk would be the remains of a young woman with raggedy bleached hair, a once blue shoebox, and thousands of dollars in cash. But all the rest would be their secret, a bond forever inextricable as it is with flesh and blood.

Chapter 22

He has been with her mother, so when his eyes open on Fiona's picture he is startled, then angry to find himself awake again, still here, trapped among the living. This is his hell, this long, helpless wait for the end. The hallway floorboards creak and his breath catches. He watches the door with the same trepidation and need he felt for the child he couldn't risk loving. It is only the wind. Soon another winter will be hard upon them, and here he sits propped against pillows. Dust grows on the wheelchair in the corner. There is nowhere he wants to go. He does not miss the court. Travel is difficult and he is easily confused. Green Mountains, Rocky Mountains, what's the difference? He has seen more than his share of mountains, oceans, grand houses, gardens, and museums. His universe is now this cluttered room that used to be the den. On cold, wet days the unused fireplace gives off an acrid stench. There is a constant grayness to the light. His grandchildren fidget in his wretched presence. He watches television, mostly the news, but he knows it's bullshit, all bullshit. The nurse reads the paper to him every morning. His mind wanders and he dozes fitfully, dreaming of his children. Their forgiveness is painful. He squirms when they insist on his virtue. He knows the sterile portrait it was, how skilled his careful rendering of morality and grace, instead of real goodness with its raw, awkward beauty born of struggle and pain. Fiona watches, silent because she knows. She knew long before she sat beside him in teary anger and triumph, staring at each sibling, when he said, "I am Fiona's father."

The police got to the house first that day, so the minute he and Fiona came through the door Arlene knew. But then, she has always known more than needed be told. Everything is different between them. There is no need for pretense. Duty and her inexhaustible kindness sustain him now. Love had been her journey and destination, but since Natalie it has all been aftermath, a silent struggle to maintain this delicate mechanism that neither dares probe too deeply. With that fatal error in judgment his good life ended, and deceit began, the first lie to his wife being that he had never stopped loving her, the second being that he had never loved her sister, had never found, sought, invented opportunities to be alone with her, the next being that it had been purely physical, a brief affair that began with her loneliness and her pursuit of him when Patrick went away. In truth it had begun years before, when she was fourteen and already a woman whose wild beauty and impulsive energy made a weak man's tired wife seem even plainer. In the end when he would not leave Arlene, Natalie told her sister everything.

The last lie is safe with Fiona. She will never destroy her aunt with the revelation that for all those years he knew Natalie lay curled in the trunk, that he knew and did nothing, until that moment on the ledge with Patrick's swaying plea—*Come on, help me, Charlie. This is your chance. Your last chance. Help me one more time*—when he finally did. He stepped forward and held out his arm because the good a man does, like the sorrow in his heart, has to count for something—if not honor, then for some shred of redemption, he was begging Patrick, but the words were as futile against the wind as the falling snow.

Arlene opens the door. His body stiffens with indignation. The nurse is here. She will bathe him and change the bag, the bullshit, all the bullshit. Arlene ignores his squirming. She must be so tired of it all. He certainly is. The nurse says she ran into Elizabeth and George downtown last night at the Merchants' Bazaar. Their little boys are such gentlemen. Arlene smiles. She leans down and repeats it to make sure he's heard.

He wishes he could be as proud as she is, as good and as grateful, but how can he when it's all bullshit. It's all been such bullshit.

"Charles," Arlene scolds. "Mrs. Cooper doesn't need to hear that kind of language."

"Sorry," his loathsome tongue finally manages to say.

"I know you are." Arlene sighs, wiping the corner of his mouth with a tissue.

Speaking over his head, the nurse asks when Fiona's due.

"Fiona?" he struggles to ask, but they continue talking. "Coming?"

"No, Charles. The baby. Mrs. Cooper asked when Fiona and Rudy's baby's due."

He tries to hear the rest. His brain throbs with the effort, then his eyes close heavily in the glow of Natalie's trusting young face.